Oh Dara!
If memories remain a lustrous sea shell
washed upon the shore of times inner eye
then pressed to ear discover
not one ocean but two
singing together a melancholy refrain
of wave on wave of sorrow

Oh Dara! Oh Dara!
All prayers are but a veil upon death's dark door.
But how mourn the loss of a living bridge
between two oceans of faith and wisdom

Oh you noble gentle invader
You were
You are
A broken bridge
between us and a golden dream

Oh unkempt forces of dark resentments
Oh crimson line on golden throat
Oh unkept tryst with unmet aspiration

A golden bird sings your requiem
No more poems for you, Oh Dara
The heart can cup but so much sorrow
Oh Dara! Oh Dara!

— Amit Dahiya Badshah

'*Ocean of Cobras*' is about a gap in Indian history. A lot has been written about the great emperors Akbar, Jahangir, Shah Jahan, Aurangzeb but the battle of succession between the sons of Shah Jahan was actually one of the turning points in Indian history'

— DNA

Ocean of Cobras took me back in time. The description of the battle scenes are riveting, transporting you into the heart of the battlefield, feeling you are holding Alamgir, Emperor Babur's sword. Murad Ali Baig's description of hunting with the Bhil tribals, life in the zenana, intrigues of the Imperial Durbar, the treasuries, are enthralling.

— Bob Rupani, author of *'India's 100 Best Destination's, The Royal Udaipur RR GLK 21'*

'*Ocean of Cobras*' is a heady cocktail of adventure, romance, betrayal, battles of the mind and sword and much more. Well researched, it gives insights into court life, marriage ceremonies, tribal customs etc., and, most important, it is a jolly good read.

— Roswitha Joshi,
author of '*Life on the Rocks*' and '*India Dreams*'

"Absolutely fascinating. The style is hypnotic and urges the reader on to the next page"

— Nazima Aziz

OCEAN OF COBRAS

The epic battle for the soul of India between
Dara Shikoh and Aurangzeb

Murad Ali Baig

tara
India Research Press
Flat. 6, Khan Market, New Delhi - 110 003
Ph.: 24694610; Fax : 24618637
www.indiaresearchpress.com
contact@indiaresearchpress.com;

2015

OCEAN OF COBRAS
Murad Ali Baig

1 0 9 8 7 6 5 4 3 2
Second impression

ISBN 13 : 978-81-8386-128-1
ISBN 10 : 81-8386-128-8

Printed for Tara-India Research Press at *Manipal Technologies Limited.*

Contents

A LONG LOST MANUSCRIPT

Dusk was just reddening the sky as a section of ten soldiers under captain Alistair McDonald gathered in the courtyard of the Sawan Pavilion inside Delhi's Red Fort after most of the Indian workmen had departed. It was 1863 but no soldiers could ever forget the carnage and excitement of the Great Mutiny six years earlier. McDonald, a sapper of the Bengal Engineers, had been in the small squad under lieutenant Duncan Home that had laid mines under the Kashmeri Gate, which had enabled British troops to breach the outer walls of the city of Delhi in September 1857. Home died in the valiant effort and had been awarded a posthumous Victoria Cross. A musket ball had wounded McDonald, crippling his shoulder but in recognition of his gallantry, he was retained in the army, even though he was fit only for light duties.

He had now been given the task of supervising the demolition of a large number of lesser palaces, *hamams* and other buildings in the centre of the Red Fort, where a regiment of British troops were to be billeted in a new set of barracks. They had already demolished the Rang Mahal, Hira Mahal, the *zenana hamam* and several other buildings. The demolition was not difficult as the team of about a hundred Indian workmen would first pry loose the red sandstone and marble slabs on the walls with hammers and chisels and then smash up the stone and brick masonry behind them with crow bars and pickaxes. The stone slabs were carefully stacked nearby to be reused for the construction of a big new regimental barrack that was to be built in the middle of the fort.

McDonald's British officers and soldiers had to, however, keep a vigilant eye. It had been discovered that some of the Mughal nobles and other ranking officers who had lived in the rooms of the palaces had made several hidden cavities behind the stone slabs where they secreted some of their jewels, coins, documents and other valuables. The workers had to be carefully watched to prevent them from stealing any of the items that they might find. Sometimes bundles of papers would also be found though they were mostly business accounts, property deeds, inheritances and letters or poems written in Persian. These papers were mostly quite worthless but were taken to McDonald to be checked, before being sent to the troops billeted in nearby buildings as kindling for their cooking fires. Major Gillispie, McDonald's superior, had ordered that all Mughal orders bearing the imperial seal, paintings and other important or seditious documents had to be sent to his office near the Kashmeri Gate to be scrutinized.

Every hour or so there would be a shout as something new was discovered. On a table near his chair was a small collection of silver and gold coins as well as a few necklaces, rings and two rusty daggers with jeweled scabbards. A pile of old Persian papers lay on the floor in the corner to be moved to the regimental kitchens. McDonald had, however, quietly pocketed a small ring with a dark red stone. It would not be missed and would make a nice present for his dusky bibi Rehana who lived with him in his rooms above a shop in Chandni Chowk facing the main gate of the fort. He looked forward to the evening when he would drink a cup of fiery aniseed Arrak brought by Rehana's little brother Salim, followed by supper and a night with Rehana.

He was about to get up and leave when he saw a corporal Murray walking briskly towards him, followed by an Indian worker carrying a small wooden box that had been found under the steps to the second floor. The box was locked but the brass hasp easily came away from the rotting wood to reveal something wrapped in a length of faded red silk. Both soldiers were very disappointed when Murray cut the strings of the cloth to reveal nothing except several bundles of old papers that were put on the floor next to all the others.

McDonald was about to leave when he saw a few words written crudely in French letters standing out from among the Persian text, on this top bundle. He paused to look at the papers again and decided to keep the folios aside to study them the next day. Like all the British officers who lived in India, he was fluent in a number of European languages and also knew how to read and write in Persian that continued to be the official language for communication with the natives. When he tried to read the first folio the following day, he found that the language was too full of Persian metaphors and poetic exaggerations for his taste. He, however, realized that it seemed to be a document that might interest Major Gillispie to whom the bundle of papers was soon dispatched and much later, translated into English under his supervision.

Do not burn these folios!

Do not destroy these papers!

They are very valuable!

I am writing these words boldly in Persian, Hindustani, Turki and French so that whoever finds these folios will pause to look at them and preserve the only true record of the great Mughal battle of succession.

I do not know when this manuscript will be found but I beg you to believe me that these folios contain the only complete and absolutely truthful record of the court of Shah Jahan, the most magnificent of the Mughal emperors, especially during the fierce battles of succession between his four sons.

These five great battles- at Dharmat, Samugarh, Bahadurpur, Khajua, and Deorai were to almost destroy the great empire, resulting needlessly in the death of over two lakh of the empires finest young men with many more seriously injured. These battles were much more than just a struggle for the richest kingdom in the world. They were also a struggle between the followers of orthodox Islam, the religions of the Hindus and the liberal ideas of Sufi saints seeking the unity of all religions.

It is a tale of great courage, cowardice, intrigues, romance, depravity, cruelty, triumphs and tragedy where the power and prestige of the Mughal empire was pitted against the cunning, tenacity and determination of prince Aurangzeb.

A tale such as this has never before been penned.

You may now know the real story

Prince Dara Shikoh with wise men in a garden, 1640
by Bichitr

Source: Imperial Mughal Painting, by Stuart Cary Welch (New York: George Braziller, 1978), p. 111

Durbar of Prince Aurangzeb, 1658
By Bichitr

Source: Imperial Mughal Painting, by Stuart Cary Welch (New York: George Braziller, 1978), p. 112.

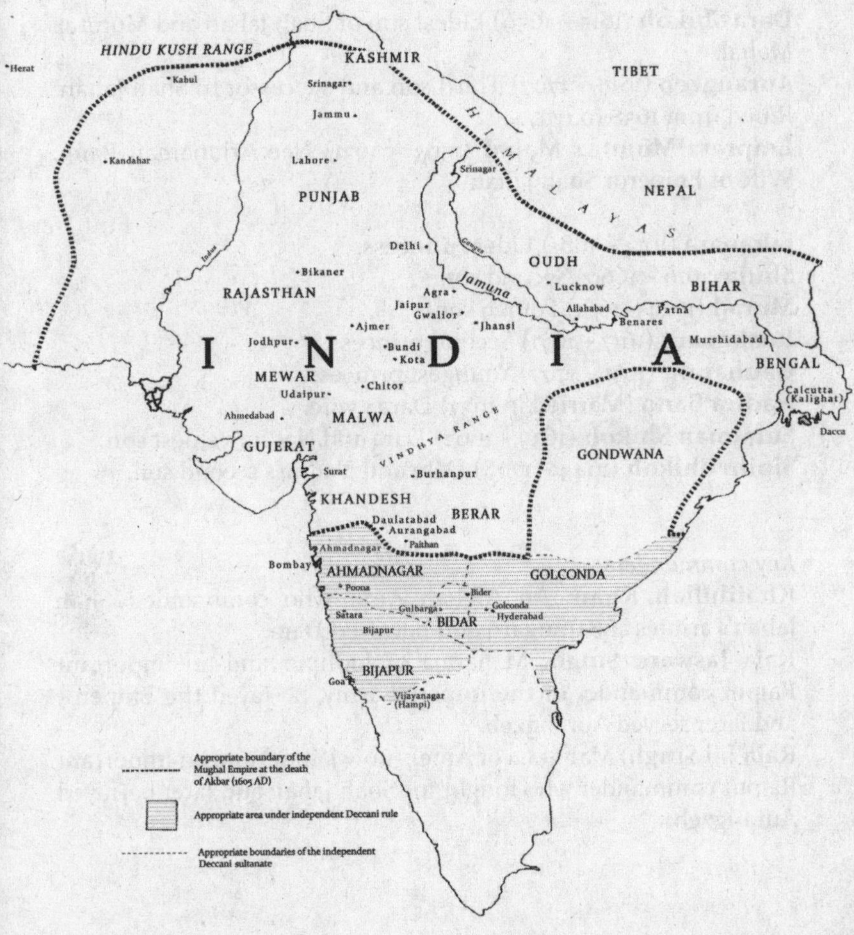

(Map modified from original as per requirements of the narrative)
Source: African Elites in India by Habshi Amarat (Mapin Publishing Gp Pty Ltd, 2006). p. 32

Main Characters

Mubarak Ali. A eunuch in the royal harem and narrator.
Shah Jahan (1592 – 1666) The 5th Mughal Emperor, born prince Khurram. Ruled from 1628 to 1658. Died a prisoner.
Dara Shikoh (1615 – 1659) Eldest son of Shah Jahan and Mumtaz Mahal.
Aurangzeb (1618 – 1707) Third son and successor to Shah Jahan. Ruled from 1658 to 1707.
Empress Mumtaz Mahal (1593 – 1631) Nee Arjunaman Bano. Wife of Emperor Shah Jahan

Jahanara (1614 – 1681) Eldest princess.
Shuja (1616 – 1660) Second son.
Murad (1624 – 1661) Fourth son.
Roshanara (1617 – 1671) Second princess.
Gauharara (1631 – 1707) Youngest princess.
Nadira Bano (Married in 1633) Dara's wife.
Sulaiman Shikoh (1635 – 1662) Dara and Nadira's eldest son.
Sipihr Shikoh (1644 – 1708) Dara and Nadira's second son.

Key commanders:
Khalilullah Khan. An Afghan Amir who commanded Shah Jahan's armies at Samugarh and betrayed Dara.
Raja Jaswant Singh. Maharaja of Jodhpur and an important Rajput commander of the Imperial army, betrayed the Emperor and later served Aurangzeb.
Raja Jai Singh. Maharaja of Amer (now Jaipur) and an important Rajput commander who fought for Shah Jahan and later betrayed Aurangzeb.

The Great Mughals
1526 -1707

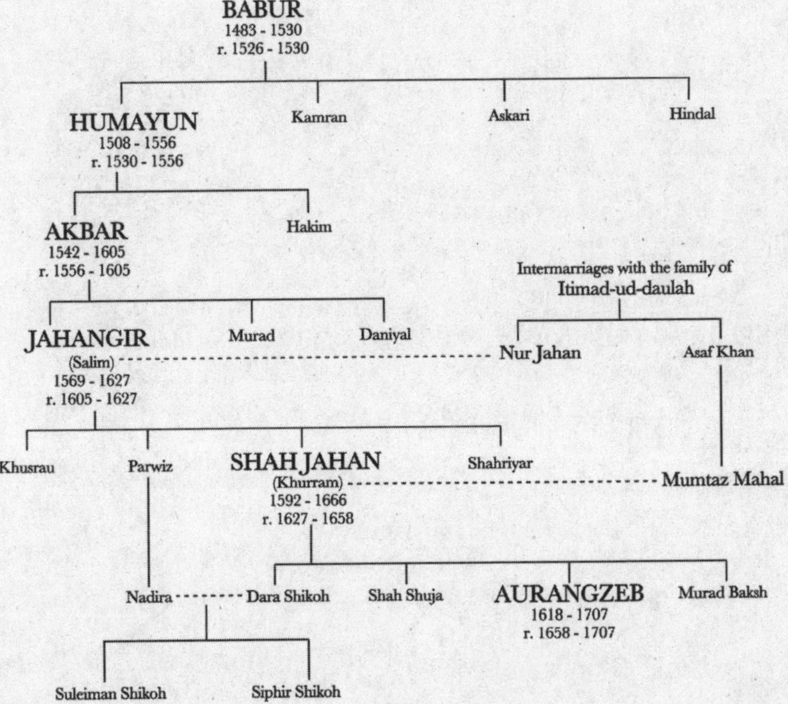

CHAPTER 1

Triumph and Tragedy

A tiger looks magnificent when it strides proudly through the sun dappled shadows of the forest but it is the insect on his skin that best knows about the cuts, bites and sores that also afflict it. The courtiers, nobles and scribes may be able to describe the magnificence of the great Mughal Empire that they admire from a distance, but only a humble slave of the court can describe all that lies hidden below the surface of this majestic world.

A tiger can instil more terror in the hearts of a beholder than any other animal but people often forget that the tiger was once just a playful cub innocently chasing the leaves blown by the wind. Those who remember Aurangzeb today visualize a stern, austere visage and a face that seldom smiled, and will find it difficult to imagine that he too, was once a small boy capable of the innocent pranks of childhood.

Everyone had laughed uproariously when young prince Aurangzeb caught a small frog in the courtyard of the palace in the Agra fort and slipped it down the back of his sister Roshanara's dress. Her hysterical screams rang through halls of the *zenana* (harem) and had all the slaves rushing towards the little princess, fearing that something terrible might have happened. The Emperor too, was roused from his afternoon siesta and was very angry at being disturbed. Aurangzeb stood sniggering behind a pillar as his sister jumped around furiously, trying to get the slimy creature out of her clothing but he was soon silenced when summoned before his father.

He stood crestfallen before the flow of the Emperor's angry words but his little face bravely tried to hide his feelings of hurt and confusion. He just could not understand why his father was so curt with him; it had, after all, been an innocent act of childhood mischief. He would have never been so severe with any of his other children.The Emperor's barely disguised dislike and distrust towards Aurangzeb left the boy feeling deeply pained. His earliest memories were of a caring mother but a father who, though always courteous, had never demonstrated any of the love that he lavished on his other children.

Aurangzeb in his naïve, childlike ways, wondered, as he had many times before, what he had done to deserve such treatment? How was it that the Emperor was kind and loving to his brothers and sisters, yet so cold and aloof with him? There had always seemed to be a certain distance between them, as if on purpose; an invisible wall built around the Emperor that almost forbade the young prince to get closer. To add to this sense of injustice was his father's open and undisguised love for his eldest brother Dara Shikoh, who it appeared, would be forgiven for any lapse or mistake on his part.

A glow of bitter jealousy and anger burned in his heart as he respectfully endured his fathers' angry words. Dara stood beside the emperor with a smug satisfied grin on his face. As

Aurangzeb watched him, his calculating mind considered how he would have to get even some day. Though his sober face betrayed nothing, no posture of outward politeness could hide the emotions that coursed swiftly beneath the surface.

I, Mubarak Ali, had been a nine-year old eunuch when I first entered the service of the royal family. I had also been surprised at the emperor's cool disdain towards Aurangzeb, which was the only discordant note in this otherwise happy family that I was to serve for forty years. As the princes grew older, the discord continued to grow with the result that, for the sake of harmony, the emperor would, on a number of occasions find some reason to send Aurangzeb away from the court. A royal figurehead was often needed to lead a Mughal army against a rebellious vassal prince but this prestige was not enough to quench the fire burning in his heart. Aurangzeb was not a fool and he realized that he was being banished from a family in which he craved the easy love and affection that his brothers and sisters so enjoyed. Rejection, as I later discovered, was a terrible feeling. Everyone experiences anger, jealousy or greed at some point in their lives, but these emotions quickly pass. A sense of rejection, however, leaves a lasting bitterness and no rejection can be as painful as one that is perceived to be without justification.

Aurangzeb was eleven when I first knew him. His pale countenance and hard black eyes would seldom wear any smile or show any marks of friendliness. In his formative years of being sent away on several military campaigns, he was to channel these feeling of bitterness and rejection into warfare and the study of religion. The love and comforts that his siblings enjoyed within the walls of the palace were ones he never received. As a result, he matured fairly early and quickly learned the skills of war and administration but never lived the life of princely luxury. Rather, he found solace within the traditional doctrines of Islam, the pages of the Quran and the teachings of devout Muslim scholars.

Although all the children of the family had the same education, Aurangzeb's personal ineterst in the traditions of the Islamic faith led his belief to be widely different than his siblings. On one of his earlier campaigns in the Deccan, Aurangzeb met a passionate Sunni scholar called Syed Amin who warned the young prince against the Shia traditions of powerful Persian *Umraos* and convinced him that the philosophies of the Sufis, with their worship at the tombs of saints, would bring good Muslims closer to the religion of the idolatrous Hindus. Realizing the stark contrast between his unfair treatment within the family and the attentiveness, care and power of Syed Amin's teachings, Aurangzeb was easily influenced by the scholar.

In later years, his traditional views of religion were to set him apart from his siblings, especially Dara, who eagerly sought the similairities between all the religious faiths of Hindustan. The two brothers would never see eye to eye- Dara whom Aurangzeb saw as the royal favourite, a pampered prince indulging in philosophy and art; and Aurangzeb, whom Dara considered a religiously orthodox fanatic with a narrow view of world. The petty squabbles of their childhoods were to magnify over the years with the sour memories of the many things said or done. But paradoxically, despite their chronic differences, their destinies seemed to be inextricably bound together and were to drive them, along with the empire, to the very brink of disaster. Their fortunes were so tightly intertwined that humiliating or defeating the other was to become a driving force in both their lives. Though, they always observed the elaborate courtesies and polite manners of the Mughal court, their somber faces masked the fiery passions coursing just below the surface.

As a slave in the Mughal court, through my interactions with many different kinds of people, I was to learn about the mysteries of human nature and relationships. But I was never able to fully comprehend the schism between the two princes. I knew them to be good men in their own ways, both of whom I served and greatly admired but was unable to fathom how their thoughts, words and actions seemed to always be in a state of intractable conflict.

Some people claimed that it was their stars that were crossed. They told me that Dara, born on March 20, was influenced by the sign of Aries, ruled by fire, while Aurangzeb was born on November 3, in the sign of Scorpio, ruled by water. Fire and water being mortal enemies can never mix; fire cannot burn water but water can quench fire. Aries, the ram, will recklessly venture to the highest mountains but Scorpio the scorpion, lurking in the shadows, can inflict a deadly sting to anyone who dares to disturb it.

When Dara and Aurangzeb were together with the family, there was always a current of tension in the air. My Hindu friends told me that such a conflict must have been due to mortal enmities in their earlier incarnations and that they were powerless to change their karma or the decrees of their fates. Not even an emperor can make his children love each other and the intense fires of suspicion and hatred between Aurangzeb and Dara were to gradually infect all the others in the palace as well.

Jahanara, the beautiful princess, the eldest child of the royal family, was six years older than Aurangzeb, followed in close succession by his brothers Dara and Shuja. His sister Roshanara was just a year older than him, while his brother Murad was six years younger. His baby sister Gauharara had been born long after when his mother, Arjumand Bano Begum, died in childbirth. She had borne fourteen children in her nineteen-year marriage to the devoted emperor Shah Jahan. Aurangzeb remembered her well as the only person who had loved him without reservation. Her death had been a terrible sorrow to him but he learned long ago how to hide his feelings and mourned in silence and prayer. Jahanara was to become Dara's closest friend while Roshanara, jealous of her elder sister, was to become Aurangzeb's closest ally. Even the amiable Shuja, young prince Murad and Gauharara the youngest princess, were to be drawn into the whirlwind of conflict over the years.

Shah Jahan was a very loving father who tried to keep a close family, as he firmly believed that the bloody battles of succession among all his ancestors were because the rival princes were usually the sons of different queens. He believed that the children bourne by the same father and mother, without the goading of rival queens and their factions, could sustain a continuing love for each other. He naively thought that by naming Dara as his successor and giving his other sons important responsibilities in rich but distant governorships there would be an easy succession. He had little idea that the angels of destiny were to mock his dream and let loose an ocean of blood far more devastating than the struggles for succession of any other ruler at any time in the history of the world.

As a child prince Dara had a wicked sense of mischief that was to often cause him many unnecessary problems. He loved teasing everyone around him and took special pleasure in mocking those who were too serious, pompous or opinionated. We rolled with laughter as he imitated the strutting stride of our commander Mahabat Khan, who constantly twirled his thick moustaches; or mimicked our austere tutor Abdul Latif Saharanpuri and even the graceful swaying walk of his sister Jahanara. When he curled up on a bed pretending to be asleep with a happy smile on his face, we could immediately visualize his brother Shuja. His best imitation, however, was of Aurangzeb's unsmiling visage as he put on his prayer cap and solemnly sat on his prayer mat.

One day Dara smeared a little honey inside Aurangzeb's embroidered cap so that it attracted an army of tiny ants. Later, when Aurangzeb put it on his head, he leapt about in a frenzy, to everyone's amusement, trying to get rid of them. Aurangzeb was furious for several days and his black eyes looked menacingly at Dara, who he rightly believed was responsible. He could hardly forget that a similar prank, played by him on his sister Roshnara, a year earlier had earned him the wrath of the emperor but had now attracted no reprimand for Dara. The anger, envy and bitterness brooding in Aurangzeb's heart against his elder brother ~~only~~ magnified as they grew older, ultimately dominating his life. For Dara too, the mere presence of Aurangzeb was enough to make him surly or mischievous as he had utter disdain for his unyielding seriousness, and in later years, religious orthodoxy.

Through their lives, Dara openly despised Aurangzeb's rigid views and could not tolerate his pious sermons about all the wickedness he claimed was being practiced in the court. He could barely contain his laughter when Aurangzeb, one day, suddenly got up and left the room without permission when Shah Jahan ordered a *hookah* and a glass of wine. Dara mischievously asked, "I wonder what would happen *Padishah Hazoor* if you ordered Aurangzeb to drink a glass of wine? I wonder if he would obey you, our emperor, or the *Mullas* that teach him?" Shah Jahan was not amused and Dara's words faded out in a long embarassed silence.

But despite of his sour relationship with his younger brother, Dara grew into a charming and sensitive prince. However, he was so involved with the adventures of the mind that he had little time or serious interest in matters of state, which were imperative for all the noblemen of the empire. He could therefore, at times, be needlessly brusque with the generals and court officials who did not feel that their importance was sufficiently appreciated. Flattered by the many people seeking his blessings, he was not sensitive of the need to keep a constant hand on the pulse of important supporters among the many rival factions of the empire. Nor did he fully appreciate the need to nurture the loyalties of fickle nobles and generals with the lubricant of continual appreciation, gifts and flattery. He quickly lost interest in things that he considered trivial and many mistook his sudden and sometimes curt disinterest as marks of arrogance and pride. Being far too forgiving, Dara also failed to understand that fear was often the foundation of respect. Kings and princes needed to cultivate an aura of fear and he was usually too reluctant to punish those who needed to be chastised. I, was to later observe that, in this regard, Aurangzeb knew better and that even his own children were aware of the terrible price the smallest act of disobedience could bring.

You may want to know about my own history, of my competence as the writer of these folios and of how I am able to so truthfully tell the complete story of this mortal struggle. I had been born into a noble family as my father Firdoz Ali had come to the court of Emperor Jahangir from Herat in Persia. As an able horseman and leader of men, he quickly rose to earn the rank of an Amir, commanding two thousand horsemen. He distinguished himself during Jahangir's capture of the hill fort perched on a high cliff above the Ban Ganga River at Kangra.

My beloved mother was the daughter of a French count who had served in India and died of wounds in Bengal. My father had rescued her from a slave market when he was sent with a small Mughal army to chase out the Portuguese, who were trying to set up a trading post on the Hoogly without the emperor's firman. She was born in Hindustan and had become as much a native of our land as any locally born lady. Her infectious laughter and her light brown eyes would fill our hearts with warmth. She spoke fluent Persian and Hindustani but with such a charming accent that everyone would be immediately entranced. She knew enough of her native language to teach us a few words. I did not know it at the time but this slightly foreign pedigree, that set me apart from all the other people at the court, was to one day become an asset.

My father, however, made the mistake of supporting the abortive rebellion of Shah Jahan's eldest half brother Khusrao against his father, Jahangir and was killed during the melee of the contest. As with all Mughal *Umraos* (nobles), his estate was immediately confiscated and his family was reduced to instant ruin. I was but a child of nine and was taken along with my beautiful mother and family members into the household of a brutal Afghan Azim Khan who had me rudely castrated and sold in the market as a common slave. My mother, unable to bear the sorrow, died soon after. After the leisure of gracious living with my loving family, it was a terrible shock to be so brutally humiliated.

But the angel of good fortune did not wholly desert me and I was lucky, when one of the emperor's agents looking for a comely slave for the imperial *zenana*, saw me and bought me to serve the family of the emperor. I was fair and tall for my age and had a confident but courteous manner. With a ready smile, a friendly disposition, a diplomatic tongue and a willingness to always help others, I quickly made friends with all the members of the court.

My good looks, breeding and charm helped to make me a great favourite with all the royal princes and princesses. As I was very discreet, I was to become privy to many of their deepest secrets. I found it fascinating to observe the preparations of the queens and concubines for their nuptial encounters and the machinations by which so many pampered women, disappointed with such few opportunities for love, would find ingenious ways to indulge their sensuality. Few know as I do, the lengths to which women can go to assuage the intensity of their desires.

The chroniclers of the courts could only write what their patrons wanted them to record but none of them were as close as I had been to all the players or as immediate a witness to the grandeur, the intrigues and the wickedness that were also a part of the courtly scene. I was often seated just behind the royal princes and could hear not only the words spoken by the nobles but also the cynical whispers of the secrets being exchanged.

I was to personally watch the royal princes evolve during this mortal contest for the Mughal throne. Dara grew from a philosopher and painter into a resolute military commander. Shuja matured from an indolent noble into a surprisingly able general. Aurangzeb, who was the most experienced soldier, displayed unflagging energy and a willingness to suffer any privation to achieve his objectives. Even the handsome young prince Murad demonstrated courageous valour. Despite the luxuries of the decadent court they had retained their fierce Timurid pride and were all brave and resolute soldiers on the battlefield. Unlike any of the other eunuchs, I had also been a soldier and fought for prince Aurangzeb at Jhansi and Aurangabad and for prince Dara at the battle of Samugarh and commanded part of his army at the final battle at Deorai. I can, therefore, write every detail about all the great battles and skirmishes of the era as no courtly scribe can possibly describe.

What do the courtly chroniclers know about the heat, dust, sickness and fatigue that kill more soldiers in any campaign than the swords of their enemies?

What do they know about the stench of a battlefield where the nostrils are assailed by the revolting smell of gunpowder, the stink of rotting bodies, the foul odour of shit released by the dead and the sour sweat of abject terror?

Concerned only with the elegance of their flowery Persian prose, how can these scribes possibly imagine the choking clouds of dust and smoke or the agonized screams of the grievously wounded men and animals that haunt the dreams of every soldier?

What royal scribe can know, let alone describe how loyal troops can turn into robbers in a trice, scrambling to loot the baggage trains of even their own masters? How can they imagine the cruel lust for plunder that fills the eyes of the looters as they eagerly rush to every battlefield like packs of ravaging hyenas blind to the agony of the wounded, from whose fingers they callously rip off jewlery and even gouge out the gold and silver from their teeth?

What do they know about how soldiers lustfully seek out the women of their foes? All soldiers hanker for the loving arms of wives and lovers they leave behind so it is often the sound of screaming women that assails the ears as soon as the thunder of gunfire and the clash of swords dies away.

Moreover, how can any courtly scribe possibly understand, without having seen and experienced it, how quickly proud warriors can betray their sworn allegiances for the sake of power, position and the insidious temptations of wealth.

I have been witness to many a great moments of joy, wonder, triumph and tragedy while in service of the royal family. One of my most treasured memories is the awe that had gripped the imperial court when Dara confounded both the *mullahs* and Brahmins by propounding the astonishing thought that a great shining golden river of common faith ran through both Islam and the many faiths of the Hindus. The *maulvis* had muttered their disapproval when he had started to add Sanskrit to his knowledge of Persian, Turki and Arabic languages but were aghast when he began listening to groups of learned Brahmin scholars and began quoting some of their heretical thoughts. They were not too disturbed when he released the first Persian translations of the Upanishads and the Bhagavad-Gita, that had earlier been hidden in the secret libraries of a few Brahmin priests. But they were appalled when the erudite prince had the audacity to declare that this heretic philosophy was none other than the `*Sirr i-Akbar*' or the great secret, which he suggested, was none other than the `*Kitab-al-Muknum*' or the hidden book mentioned in the fifty-sixth chapter of the holy Quran itself.

Dara had believed that Allah, known by many different names to the different people of the world, loved all his creations and had over the centuries sent thousands of his messages and messengers to all the people of the world to enlighten them and lead them to *jannat* (heaven). He believed that it was the bigoted priests who could not see beyond what had been taught to them, refusing to accept that Allah was a loving and merciful god for all of mankind.

Aurangzeb condemned all such thoughts as dangerous heresies. He was deeply influenced by a passionate Sunni scholar, Syed Amin when he had been a young prince leading an army into the Deccan, who had instructed him on some of the fundamental tenets of Islam. During his frequent visits to the Deccan, Amin had warned Aurangzeb against the Shia traditions of the powerful Persian *Umraos* and convinced him that the philosophies of the Sufis, with their worship at the tombs of saints, would bring good Muslims to believe in the religion of the idolatrous Hindus.

Dara believed that Allah was the god of all people but for Aurangzeb, Allah was a Muslim God. Dara wanted to bring all people into the loving bosom of a merciful and benevolent Allah but Aurangzeb believed that the Mughals had a moral duty to convert all the people of Hindustan into Muslims.

How was anyone to know that this conflict between the simple and lofty ideas of Dara and the inflexible orthodoxy of Aurangzeb was to inflame the minds of so many people?

Who could have guessed that Aurangzeb would have Dara's scholarly endeavour branded as a heresy and use it as a moral weapon to alienate many of his Muslim supporters?

How were we to know that such a loving idea could lead to so much bloodshed and sorrow?

What could have warned us that this conflict was part of the struggle for the Mughal throne and would cost more lives than any battle of succession in history?

How were we to know that this battle for succession would also be a battle for the very soul of India; that this would be a battle between Dara's belief in the essential unity of all religions and Aurangzeb's conviction that the straight path of Islam was the only way to human salvation?

A cobra is the most venomous and beautiful serpent to be found in Hindustan and cobras were to play a strange part in the dramatic events about to occur. I vividly recall the shock and wonder at a durbar just before the unveiling of the Taj Mahal when a messenger suddenly arrived breathless, with an urgent message from prince Shuja, who was our *subedar* (governor) of Bengal. A scroll was hastily taken out of a sealed golden cylinder and read out to the emperor. It reported that at about an hour after sunrise lakhs (100,000's) and lakhs of cobras had suddenly appeared from the east of his capital at Rajmahal like a huge river, some four *Kos* (10 miles) wide and that these serpents had kept moving like the undulating waves of an ocean until nearly sunset. In the middle of the flood was a snake of great size carrying on its wide spread hood a small white serpent. In alarm the local people had climbed trees, barred their doors and climbed onto the roofs of their houses but no harm had come to anyone.[1]

No one in the court was able to understand the significance of the strange event and the emperor looking bemused had softly asked, "How astonishing! What can be the meaning of this awesome occurrence? Something so strange must surely be a terrible omen! We must find out what it means!"

He summoned his astrologers and star gazers who hastily gathered in the court. They muttered among themselves and hesitantly gave a number of conflicting opinions. One cautiously suggested that it was a sign that a great tragedy was about to occur, while another suggested that this event meant that all the wickedness of the empire was taking its departure. A third astrologer said that the Hindus considered cobras to be the guardians of wealth and it was a sign that great wealth was about to come to the empire. I heard a courtier sitting behind me whisper that it might just as well mean that the wealth of the empire was about to go away.

From among them, a Hindu astrologer called Diwani Das stood up and very solemnly said, "*Padishah Hazoor,* I believe that it is a definite omen that great evil will overwhelm our great empire unless we can search out and destroy that small white snake that leads this ocean of cobras."

---

1 A full account of this amazing event is recorded in the 'Storia do Mogor' written by the Venetian gunner Nicclao Manucci who had served with Dara Shikoh and the Imperial armies during the War of Succession. The story of the flood of Cobras is related on page 218 of volume II of 'Storia Do Mogol' that relates many anecdotes of a very complete history of Shah Jahan and his sons.

The emperor said nothing but suddenly grew pale and looked very troubled as if he had remembered something he did not wish to share with us. It took several years before we understood this strange warning that *Azrael*- the winged angel of death- had given us of the terrible events that were destined to soon devastate the empire. It took even longer for me to learn about the identity of that white cobra that would be responsible for the disaster that this strange omen had foretold.

The emperor sometimes called Aurangzeb a white snake, causing Princess Jahanara to, one day, remonstrate with her father saying that such a hurtful epithet was needlessly humiliating. Shah Jahan had looked down, apologised and had whispered to her that many years earlier when he had been fleeing through the Deccan as a young rebel against his father Jahangir, he had met a *faqir* who had warned him to beware of a third son who, he said, would have the pale skin of camphor and piercing black eyes of a cobra. Jahanara had sharply retorted that an emperor should not heed the words of a wandering soothsayer and never spoke of it again. Though she had dismissed it at the time, Jahanara now began to understand why he had always been so short and suspicious of Aurangzeb. However, many years were to pass before any of us were to learn her secret.

These tears that cleanse the heart of hatred

...are purer than laughter and sweeter than mockery.

Love that is cleansed by tears will remain

eternally pure and beautiful.

CHAPTER 2

An Empire on Horseback

Cries of excitement rang through the camp as the big hunting party cantered out from our huge tented city an hour before sunrise. I, now aged eleven, was riding just behind the princes waiting for the emperor to join us and take his position at the centre of the line of hunters. Dara led the way, followed by Shuja and little Murad who was jumping about in his saddle with excitement. Jahanara and Roshanara rode along with the empress seated in the screened howdas of elephants that took their positions just behind us. Only Aurangzeb, who had been sent away a month earlier to lead a small army to chastise the vassal ruler of Berar in the Deccan, was not with us. It was early spring and the weather was cool and clear. The forests were lush and thick after good winter rains and game was abundant.

A wide ring of nearly a thousand horsemen had gone out the previous evening and were now herding the wild animals through the thick jungle into the nets, spears and muskets of the soldiers waiting at the lower end of the valley. We were positioned in two extended lines when the sun came up. Armed with lances and swords, we sat on our restless horses with several soldiers armed with muskets and bows positioned between us. A second similar row of hunters was positioned about three hundred paces behind us to kill any animals that were able to slip past our line. This distance between the lines was to ensure that musket balls and arrows from one line would not reach those in the other. We waited, breathlessly, as the rising sound of drums and the shrill voices of the distant beaters began to slowly come closer. I was sitting on a small grey horse next to prince Murad and could see prince Shuja and Dara further down the long line.

There is something terrifying about tigers that can fill an entire jungle with an atmosphere of menace. It is bigger than a lion and is a solitary hunter that lurks in the shadows to attack in sudden fury. No animal can match it for its ferocious anger. We had heard many terrifying stories about their cunning and the power of their long teeth and claws but this was the first time we were to actually face them in the wild. To our excited minds the approaching beaters seemed to be moving forward so slowly that we felt they would never reach us. Our hearts beat furiously as panic stricken game began to race past us, making our horses twitch, shiver and roll their eyes with fear. The first to break out were an assortment of wild birds, we ducked our heads in fright as a number of jungle fowl exploded out of the bushes just over our heads in noisy flurries of feathers. Then came some small animals like hares and foxes. We had all been ordered to not fire our muskets until bigger game came closer. The only gunfire we could hear was the occasional shots from the soldiers in the approaching line of beaters who fired at any animal that tried to cut back through their line.

Our horses became so infected by growing excitement that they pawed the ground and tossed their heads in agitation. I heard a loud whinnying to my right and saw a large brown horse suddenly rear up, throw off its rider and bolt backwards through the bushes. A minute later we heard the loud crack of a musket as a panic stricken soldier in the second row shot at it thinking that some big animal was crashing through the jungle in his direction. The wounded horse screamed in pain making all the other horses even more jittery.

The first muskets in our line began firing as small barking deer tried to rush past us jinking through the bushes and rough ground. Some of the soldiers had gun bearers with loaded second muskets but many preferred to use their short Mongol bows which could rapidly fire a number of arrows one after another. Small groups of wild boar followed the deer. We had been warned to be careful as their sharp upward curving tusks could tear out even the belly of a horse. They were followed by big chital spotted deer, huge nilgai with small horns, tall sambhar deer with spreading antlers and a rhinoceros that crashed through our line. Our pounding hearts almost stopped as we fleetingly saw a few leopards slinking towards us, furtively looking for gaps in our line as they tried to rush past.

In the distance we heard the growl of a lion, followed by the roar of disturbed tigers that were the most dreaded but prized of all shikar animals. Suddenly, a tigress rushed out of the bushes very close to the sixteen year old Dara who without a moment's hesitation, spurred his horse forward and lowered his spear to strike the angry beast. As it was coming directly at him, the lance slid over the top of its skull and stuck in the back of its neck. Dara's lance kept the furious animal at a short distance until the tiger reared up to snap it in two. The enraged animal would have surely pounced upon Dara if prince Shuja had not bravely cantered up behind it and thrust his spear through its side. The stricken tigress let out a blood curdling roar but was quickly dispatched by several soldiers who rushed up and fired their muskets. Though Murad was just six, he too had managed to ride close behind us on his small pony and was screaming with excitement.

An hour later the sweaty horsemen dismounted from their horses and the entire camp rushed forward to admire the trophies. Apart from some thirty-four gazelles, there were eleven big deer including a large sambhar stag with huge antlers. There were also three tigers, a leopard and a lion. There were twelve fat wild boars and a number of plump pheasants and jungle fowl. The rhinoceros had broken past our lines but the *sikaris* produced another prize of a huge python that was nearly ten paces long and as thick as the leg of a man.

Emperor Shah Jahan, who had been in the centre of the first row, now rode up. At the age of forty-three he looked every inch the dashing monarch in his scarlet and yellow cloak. He had just killed a tiger with his long muzzle-loading match lock musket and then expertly shot three leaping gazelles one after another, with his Mongol bow.

Our triumph was, however, rudely shattered when the emperor dismounted and strode up, his face livid with anger. He was furious that the princes had been exposed to so much danger. Shouting angrily, he threatened the attendants who cowered before his furious rage as he screamed at them, "How dare you neglect your responsibilities and allow the young princes to try to kill an animal as dangerous as a tiger!" Turning red in the face he roared, "I would have had you whipped and then thrown into a prison filled with poisonous snakes if any harm had come to them. In fact, I will have you whipped even now for your carelessness! Call the master of the hunt and the head of the household here to me immediately"

The *shikaris (*hunters), attendants and other servants all prostrated themselves flat on the ground and were sweating in fear of the severe punishment they knew they were about to receive. I don't know what possessed me but I could not bear the idea of such injustice to my new companions.

To everyone's surprise I suddenly stood up, respectfully walked towards the emperor and bowing low said, "*Padishah Hazoor*, your servants have spared no effort to protect the royal princes but the princes had been so insistent that they could not restrain then. This man, Abdus Razzaq has been injured while he was trying to hold back Dara's horse. *Hazoor*, you may recall that as a young prince you yourself used to hunt dangerous animals. *Padishah Hazoor*, I humbly submit that you should be proud of your sons for the riding skills and hunting abilities they have so bravely demonstrated today."

There was a long moment of stunned silence and even the emperor looked surprised. His flushed angry face, however, softened and he summoned me to come towards him with a gesture of his hand and gravely said, "Well, here is a young slave who seems to have the courage to stand up for his companions but what about all of you? Will any of you stand up to defend this young eunuch for daring to defy the command of the emperor?"

There was yet another long silence until we heard the sweet voice of princess Jahanara from behind the screen of her palanquin saying, "Abbajan *hazoor*, he is only a poor firangee (foreigner) who does not understand our customs. He had done his duty and bravely defended his companions. You, Abbajan *hazoor*, who are so renowned for justice, should not punish a brave boy."

The emperor's face softened and he turned towards his beloved daughter and said, "This young slave is indeed very fortunate that a royal princess should speak up for him." He then turned towards the people standing or prostrated before him and said "Enough of this nonsense! Now get up and get back to your duties so that we can all enjoy a feast of these fine animals." I was trembling as I slowly walked back to my station but noticed that, despite their sober faces many of my new friends seemed to smile or nod at me in approval.

Early the next morning the feast was soon forgotten when the camp was disturbed by the sound of excited shouting as the *shikaris* appeared with a huge captured tiger that was angrily trying to tear at the bars of a cage that was far too small for it. The master of the hunt excitedly related the tale of its capture. The *shikaris* had spread out a large pot of liquid molasses on the forest floor and covered the sticky mess with leaves and then tied a goat in the middle of it. When the tiger killed the bleating goat, it discovered the molasses sticking to its paws and in the fastidious way of all felines, immediately sat down to lick itself clean. But to its consternation, it found itself covered with even more of the sticky mess on its legs and back and went into an absolute frenzy as it tried to lick itself. By dawn the poor beast was utterly exhausted and was roaring in piteous anguish. The *shikaris* were then able to approach it and easily throw a heavy net over the unfortunate animal. Oh, how we laughed! The whole camp was hugely amused and the *shikaris* got a few well earned pieces of gold. The poor bewildered tiger seemed to sense the hilarity of the camp and looked quite sad and dejected.

At our evening meal the next day, the emperor told us that the royal *shikar* was not just for the thrill of the hunt but was also a way of impressing the local chiefs. “When I was a small boy my grandfather Akbar got word from his spies that the Amir of Mahendergarh was about to revolt. Akbar was not a man to hesitate and without a moment’s delay mustered a small army of ten thousand troopers and covered the fifty kos to Mahendergarh in two days and proceeded to enjoy a leisurely *shikar*. The rebellious chief immediately realized that it would be foolhardy to attempt to defy such a quick and decisive emperor. Mustering even a small army so quickly for a hunt was warning enough to any rebel. He was very soon bowing before Akbar, professing his loyalty and paying the long overdue tribute. He also presented him with four pairs of beautiful black horses fitted with jewelled and gilded bridles and saddles.”

He smiled and added “An emperor has to be quick and decisive or else subjects will be encouraged to rebel.”

I soon learned that the Mughals, behind the outer veneer of being a cultured and even decadent people, continued to follow many nomadic customs of their Mongol ancestors. From early childhood, every able bodied nobleman had to ride a horse, wield a sword, draw the powerful Mongol bow and fire the long *juzail* muzzle loading musket. They also continued to lead much of their lives in a nomadic fashion in tented camps.

The imperial camp was a huge tented city that could control the empire, while continuously on the move from Afghanistan to Bengal or southwards towards the Deccan. Thus, the Mughals spent as much time in these tented cities as in their beautiful city palaces. There were actually two sets of identical tented cities with similar furniture and fittings for over five hundred tents. One set would be folded up every morning and moved about 8 *Kos* (16 Miles) each day, while the occupants of the earlier camp would leisurely ride one day's march to a previously prepared camp (about 4 *Kos* away) to occupy an identical city awaiting them. Teams of imperial horses were also maintained at *sarais* on the royal roads at about 4 *Kos* distances where the inn keepers had to provide food and shelter for other travellers. Relays of these horses kept here, would convey urgent messages as much as a hundred *Kos* in a single day and keep the emperor informed of even the smallest whispers of dissent or scandal and enable him to be in constant control of his widely scattered governors in the provinces.

The Mughal armies were no longer the light and nimble horsemen of their Mongol forebears. Our grand procession through the land would be preceded by a mounted band with long trumpets and kettledrums followed by 300 camels loaded with silver and gold. Then came the emperor's establishment with hawks and cheetahs, eighty camels, thirty elephants and twenty carts with the official records. They were followed by a hundred camels carrying water for the royal kitchen. Fifty camels and a hundred carts followed carrying the Emperor's wardrobe and jewels as well as presents for successful commanders. The cavalry battalions came next, followed by the elephants of the emperor's establishment. The artillery with a train of cannons on their heavy four-wheeled gun carriages pulled by teams of female elephants and bullocks followed and behind them came the heavily laden carts of the shopkeepers and servants. Last of all came a rearguard of the infantry.

The great imperial caravan was on its way to the fortress of Burhanpur that commanded the southern approaches of the empire. From here, Mughal armies tried to keep the perennially rebellious Shahi vassal kingdoms of Ahmednagar, Berar, Bidar, Golgonda and Bijapur obedient and diligent in paying their annual tributes. The royal route travelled down the wide Chambal River past Gwalior and was now moving towards the kingdoms of Ranthanbhor, Bundi, Kota and Jhalawar. We would, however, take a short diversion to go to the sacred city of Ajmer.

The camp was never allowed to move until *Amir Shirazi*, the chief astrologer, declared that the time was auspicious. He would take readings from his complicated astrolabe, a mass of books, tables and maps of the skies and would sometimes, even study the cracks of the burnt shoulder blades of sheep and gazelles before making his solemn pronouncements. Every morning he would ask the emperor about his dreams and make him breathe on a bowl of water before making him drink it as a benediction. The emperor would sometimes be impatient until his vizier found that the astrologer's pronouncements could be hurried by the passing of a coin or two. At times of battle or major ventures his advice was always taken very seriously.

Plunder from wars had been the main source of Mughal imperial income during the empire's early years until *karz*, or land revenue, replaced plunder as the main source of the empire's wealth. But the spoils of conquest continued to sustain the Mughal armies, making it necessary to constantly expand and seek new avenues of plunder. When the Mughals began to wallow in luxury, their great empire lost its purpose of existence.

The *Mir Bakshi,* or Quartermaster controlled each tented city assisted by the *Mir Saman,* or Master of Materials. They would collect as many sheep, goats, cattle and grain as was possible from the surrounding villages to meet our huge requirements for fresh food. Big teams would fan out to collect fodder for the horses and cattle. The drinking water for the royal household was pure Ganges water carried in huge silver vessels but water for the camp's normal drinking and washing had to be collected in big water skins and copper pots from every surrounding river and stream by a thousand camels.

The emperor and his entourage lived in the big crimson central tent, in the ancient tradition of the Mongols. Public meetings were held in front of it under a big awning that was protected from possible hostile arrows or musket balls by a *'Lal Purdah'* or a thick crimson curtain. Crimson had been the colour of Timur and had now become the royal colour of the Mughal emperors as well.

A big cluster of tents pitched just behind the Emperor's tent were of the royal *zenana,* surrounded by a tall folding screen of interlinked wooden panels that could only be entered through two well guarded sets of doors. This was where his beloved wife, Arjumand Bano begum and her family also lived, commanded by the chief eunuch Isa Beg. Mumtaz, though large with her fourteenth pregnancy, was well accustomed to all the hardships of long journeys with the loving companionship of the emperor. She was serenely beautiful with the fair skin of her proud Persian ancestry and eyes the colour of dark green velvet. She wore long ringlets of shining black hair that cascaded down her back. She was usually carried in a large screened palanquin swinging gently on the shoulders of six sturdy bearers but she sometimes, rode in a screened howdah behind the emperor on his huge elephant. Most of the ladies of the *zenana* would be carried in simpler palanquins though some of the younger ladies preferred to ride horses, wearing long veils of fine muslin to hide their faces. Some of the older ladies and a few that were sick would lie in long wicker baskets slung on either side of big camels. The serving women of the *zenana* travelled in big gaily coloured covered bullock carts drawn by huge humped white bullocks with long horns.

Dara, forever consumed with curiosity, wanted to know everything about the people of the camp and would send me out to inform him of every detail as if I were his eyes and ears. It was no hardship for me as I was equally curious and loved to wander through the camp.

I had observed that the tents were carefully laid out in large squares with those of the generals, vizier, the *bakshi*, the *mullah*, the astrologers and other important courtiers close to the emperor's tent. The tents of the dancers, jugglers, wrestlers, courtesans and entertainers were located a little further away, along with the neat tents of the senior Mughal and Rajput officers. Further back, were the less orderly rows of tents for the common soldiers, tradesmen, jewellers, perfumers, horse chandlers, armourers, bankers, bakers, barbers, confectioners, blacksmiths and suppliers of all the goods and services that the big city needed.

After leaving the incense scented tents of the imperial family, my nostrils were assaulted by the strong scents of the camp. The aroma of food being cooked at a number of camp fires all over the encampment, was mixed with the pungent smell of wood fires and the sweetish scent of cow and horse dung cakes that were used as fuel. The stink of fresh dung at the huge paddock for the horses and cattle was overwhelmed by the nauseous stench that came from the long screened ditches where the camp would all go to defecate.

I soon discovered that the camp also contained numerous places for drinking and music and a few bordellos to meet the baser needs of the soldiers who were so long separated from their families. I was shocked when one of the servants from a bordello sidled up to me and offered me a handsome reward if I would join them. I angrily hit him with my wooden stave and told him, "You should know that I am a slave of the imperial court. I will report you if you pester me again and your dirty business will be banished from the camp". He dismissed my threat with derisive laughter as I walked away.

The most interesting part of the huge camp was the thatched huts of the colourful gypsy *banjaras* who transported our supplies on their big bullock carts. The sturdy *banjara* women worked side by side with their men and boldly showed their faces. They wore thick brightly coloured skirts that would swing as they walked and covered their arms with many rings of ivory and silver given to them by their men folk to honour their services over the years. Their loud and colourful abuses could shame the crudest soldier. I had to stop going to their camp after some time when some of the women discovered that I was a eunuch and began to tease me mercilessly.

One day a saucy dark skinned girl with huge bright eyes and a wide colourful skirt deliberately bumped into me and began to grope under my tunic. Before I had time to react, she deftly undid the string of my pyjamas and then called out loudly, "Come quickly! Come quickly! Come quickly!

Come and help me look for 'the little man' this poor boy has lost!" Groping in my groin she cried out in mock anxiety, "it is not under his clothes. Where has it gone? Where can it have disappeared?" Some of her friends joined her in groping me, as I desperately tried to pull my clothes up and clumsily run away. My hasty departure was followed by loud hoots of laughter.

It may have been a trivial incident but it upset me deeply. With my head lowered, I quietly entered the royal tent and leaned against a pole in a dark corner. Tears welled up in my eyes as I lamented my unfortunate destiny. As there seemed to be no one around I began to speak softly to myself about my terrible misfortune. Between sobs I muttered, "Praise be to Allah but lord... what evil have I done to deserve such a cursed fate. Oh! How I wish I could be a man; a complete man without this mutilated body that makes me such an object of mockery and contempt."

A soft sound made me turn with a start. I saw that princess Jahanara had quietly walked into the tent and was standing behind me, having heard my bitter words. She slowly reached up and wiped the tears coursing down my cheeks with a corner of her muslin *peshwaz* and said, "You must not let the unkind words of foolish people upset you. Good fortune often hides within the bosom of what we think are great misfortunes. Had you been a complete man, you would never have been allowed to serve us in the *zenana* and we would never have known such a kind and courteous friend. Do not be upset...for Allah alone knows what joys and sorrows are intended for each of us in this life and in the life hereafter." I was deeply touched by her tender concern but had to go out and be alone for a while.

After the the young princes returned from the royal hunt, they retired to the harem where their attendants had already prepared baths and laid out fresh clothes. Later, all the womenfolk crowded around to hear about their exploits. Jahanara, the tall and beautiful seventeen - year old elder princess had her mother's dark green, almond - shaped eyes and tall lissom body. She smiled and encouraged her brothers to relate their adventures turn by turn. Even the six year old Murad Baksh drew gentle laughter as he excitedly tried to relate all that he had done and of how he had bravely attacked one of the slain tigers with his wooden sword.

Dara the sixteen - year old eldest prince was, as always, the centre of attention. His handsome and easy going fourteen - year old brother Shuja rested indolently on silk cushions, while the fifteen year old princess Roshanara, always conscious of her slightly misshapen mouth that drooped down a little on the left side, said nothing but intently listened to all that was being related. She was neither tall nor pretty, had a tendency to giggle nervously and was very much in the shadow of Jahanara. Her quick intelligence could, however, be very amusing but she was at a difficult age and tended to quarrel with her siblings. She suddenly sat up and said, "Aurangzeb has just sent me a letter saying that he has left Burhanpur and is on his way to fight against the apostate Shia ruler of Berar and..."

Interrupting her rather abruptly, Dara said, "Our dear brother Aurangzeb always enjoys playing at soldiers! He has missed a wonderful *shikar* and seems to be drifting further and further away from his family with every passing day. I wonder how we can get him to take an interest in something other than war and religion."

Those that were present nodded in agreement but Roshnara looked at her eldest brother with a scowl on her face. Only Jahanara seemed to understand that though Aurangzeb was indeed drifting away from his family, the real reason for his absence from the *shikar* was the seemingly unending conflict between him and Dara.

Later that evening, a banquet was laid out in the Emperor's tent and the entire family was invited to eat with him. At meal times everyone ate in silence unless specifically asked a question by the emperor who leaned back on a jewelled *divan* with a huge red *gaotakia* (bolster) and pulled deep puffs of white smoke from an ornate golden hookah. Smoke from incense sticks and sensors swung around the chamber filled the air. These were not just to sweeten the air but were also to keep the tents free of mosquitoes, flies, bugs, spiders and other insects that infested the country. Musicians played softly on a variety of instruments like the small Persian harp and a stringed *sarangi*, accompanied by Indian instruments like the *sitar*, castanets, flute and *tablas*.

The royal family all sat on the floor on rich carpets as the delicacies were served on large silver trays by the slaves. They were filled with heaps of steaming rice cooked with meat and saffron. I was assigned to go to each diner with a long necked brass vessel containing a cool sherbet made from cherries. As I made my way, I tripped on the edge of a carpet and fell, spilling some of the sherbet and involuntarily cried out, "*Merde, alors!*", a most indiscreet French profanity.

Jahanara looked up quickly and asked, "What did you say?"

Feeling very embarrassed I replied, "I am very sorry. It is just a *firangee* expression I had learned from my mother".

Jahanara asked what it meant to which I sheepishly said, "Oh! It's nothing much, it is just an expression".

Jahanara clapped her hands and repeated *'Merd, alors'* several times and I was later mortified to learn that the other princes and princesses began to use this vulgar expression on several most inappropriate occasions. I was unable to tell them that *'Merde'* was a very dirty word and prayed that no one who knew the French language would ever overhear them and expose me to punishment.

In the privacy of the *zenana* the women were allowed to show their faces without a veil. Princess Jahanara was truly a most beautiful woman with her long dark hair falling to her shoulders in a cascade of little ringlets. My heart lurched just looking at her serene beauty. Even more than her beautiful features was the twinkle in her laughing eyes and her cheerful and gracious nature. Although, I was just eleven I imagined that she was looking at me with affection and interest.

One day she asked me, "tell us more about yourself, Mubarak. Tell us something about your *firangee* mother and her family."

Feeling very embarrassed I lowered my head and remained silent but she was a princess and princesses can at times be insistent so she spoke again more loudly, "How is it that you, who can speak so bravely to the emperor, can barely open your mouth to speak to us?"

Feeling very self conscious I modestly stood up and rather stiffly said, "My mother's father was a French count named Jean Baptiste Boileau who served in the court of the French King Louis but he had to flee his country after killing a count when challenged by him to a duel."

"Count? Count? What is this count?" demanded Jahanara.

I hesitantly replied. "A count is a nobleman like one of our *Mansabdars,* who has the command of an important city."

"And dooel, what is this dooel you are speaking about?"

"A duel is a fight to the death with swords or pistols when two noblemen need to directly settle a matter of personal honour. I was told that one of the great ladies of the court had fallen in love with my handsome father and when it became known, her angry husband felt obliged to redeem his honour. According to the French custom he challenged my father to a duel where the two noblemen, each armed with a pistol, would walk away from each other for ten paces and then turn and try to kill their opponent with just one bullet. My grandfather's bullet was true and his opponent later died from the wound. The family of the dead nobleman was, however, very powerful and my father had to flee the shores of France and seek service in foreign lands. He first served in Turkey and then fought for the French in south India from where he went to the small French colony in Bengal."

Jahanara shrugged, "This dooel seems to be a very strange custom. In our land if a husband had been wronged he would have first severely punished his wife and then taken a party of his followers to kill the man who had besmirched his honour."

Though the episode may have been quite trivial I found that the other members of the *zenana,* who had been listening intently, began to treat me with greater respect than before. Noble blood, even if it was foreign blood, in the veins of a slave seemed to have value in the Mughal court.

As I had been appointed to care for the young prince Murad, I was required to accompany him throughout the day. So along with the children of the royal household, I too woke to the call for the first *namaz* (prayers), which was an hour before dawn and bathed, dressed and had a light meal. It was then time for study. Our teacher was the tall, severe looking white-bearded *mullah* Abdul Latif Sahanpuri, who made us all learn the Quran by heart in the alien language of Arabic. It was not however too difficult as the language was poetic and would often be followed by wonderful stories about the life of the prophet and the many heroes of Islam.

Though Abdul Latif was a gentle teacher he was very strict about our writing and made us all very proficient in Arabic calligraphy. Little Murad would frequently get a sharp rap on the head as he tended to fall asleep. One morning as he jerked away he spilled his inkpot on to my clothes. Before I could hold my tongue I loudly cried out "*Zut*".

Jahanara looked up laughing and again asked, "Zoot, Zoot"... Is this some other *firangee* word that you just uttered?"

I nodded sheepishly and said that it was just an exclamation that meant nothing but was surprised that it too was soon being used by all the family.

The two hours of our lessons would be followed by a break for food and refreshments, after which the princes eagerly rushed out for a session of training at arms while the princesses attended to stitching and cooking. The princes were most fascinated by the weapons. Our *talwars* were cavalry swords, long enough to slash at the enemy horsemen as well as the infantry on the ground but not so long or heavy as to make them unwieldy in hand-to-hand combat. They were curved so that the blade, following an arc with the soldier's arm as radius, could easily curve through the body of an enemy from a galloping horse without having to tear open a large wound.

All the soldiers wore round steel helmets with a spike and tassel on top and a nose protector and linked chain mail to protect the neck. They also carried small round shields of steel or rhinoceros or boiled buffalo hide. The heavy cavalry wore a steel breast plate over a thick woollen vest with overlapping steel plates to protect the back, arms, shoulders and legs. The light cavalry on their smaller ponies mostly wore leather body protection with metal plates and carried thick leather shields. Some of the cavaliers carried long lances with colourful pennants and punching daggers called *katars*[2] or *jamdhars*. This was a uniquely Mughal weapon.

The most difficult weapon to master was the famous Mongol bow[3] because it was very hard and needed great strength to pull back. Archers had to also learn to fire them

---

2 The katar had a thick sharply pointed two sided blade with a grip held crosswise to allow it to be punched hard to penetrate enemy breastplates in close combat.

3 The unique recurved Mongol bow was made from several layers of well seasoned hard wood and bone glued and bound together with sinew and took almost a year to make. The thinner ends curved away from the bowman so that the bow string first pulled the ends inwards before bending the harder centre. A short bow could thus be pulled back very far to send a deadly arrow a distance of over two hundred paces. The bow was only about three feet long and could be conveniently carried in a leather holster on a horsemen's side.

rapidly on horseback. As using the bow required both arms, great horsemanship was also needed to control the horse only with the knees.

Every day we had several hours of practice in swordsmanship and mastery of bows and muskets as well as instruction about cannons and the manufacture of rockets and gunpowder. The princes were not allowed to wield real swords as no one was allowed to shed royal Mughal blood. We, therefore, learnt many of the tricks and tactics of attack and defence with wooden replicas that were of about the same length and weight. I was usually the practice partner for young Murad and we had smaller wooden swords but as I was quite tall I sometimes, practiced with the other princes as well. One afternoon, one of our young officers picked up Murad's wooden sword and gave it to me and asked me to attack him. I charged in furiously, only to get my sword easily deflected and received a hard whack on my back that had me sprawling in the dust, much to everyone's amusement. Angry, I attacked once more to again find myself flat on my back. I attacked a third time, pretending to attack even more furiously than before, but checked myself at the last minute to slip my sword under my opponent's outstretched arm and aim my point at his chest. He was surprised but had the good grace to applaud and teach me a few other tricks of swordsmanship.

There were wrestling matches almost every day on a soft patch of freshly dug earth. We would eagerly watch some of the strongest or nimblest Turki, Afghan and Rajput wrestlers but were most impressed by a small wiry Chinaman who, with a quick twist of his body, could usually throw down much bigger opponents. As he did not have many friends, I went up to him one day and praised his skill. He gave me a broad smile and said he would be happy to teach me some of his tricks. He showed me how the strength and momentum of an opponent could be turned against themselves by pulling them in the direction of their own movement and then pivoting their rushing mass off the hips to send them flying. When I tried to rush at him he caught my arms and lowered his body before quickly straightening up to send me flying through the air. After a few days I began to understand the secrets to his success I did not know it at the time but the lesson was to stand me in good stead many years later. Over the weeks, we became quite good friends and I was fascinated to learn that eunuchs were very highly prized as commanders in the Chinese empire and many were important generals of both land and sea. The Chinese kings trusted eunuchs because as they had no families they had no desire to have their own dynasties and would give undivided loyalty and devotion to their masters.

Two hours before the evening *namaz* were devoted to horsemanship at the paddock outside the main camp. As the cavalry was the main arm of Mughal warfare, all the princes had to learn to be good riders and become proficient in wielding the long curved *talwars* and long lances while at full gallop. They had to also master the art of quickly lifting up the short Mongol bow from a holster at their left sides to fire at least six deadly arrows into a straw target while at full gallop. Princess Jahanara sometimes accompanied her brothers and insisted on firing the muskets and surprised us all by very accurately shooting the heavy weapon at a distant target.

Some of this training was in the company of regular soldiers on their manoeuvres and the princes had to learn how to ride in formation and respond to all the battlefield commands. The Mughal and Rajput officers and generals took great interest in the military education of the young princes. The Mughals still followed the system begun by the legendary Genghis Khan, who believed that no man could control more men than the ten fingers of his hands, thus the smallest Mughal unit was a section of ten men who had to be absolutely obedient to their leader - so if the leader swung his tasselled Yak tail lance to the left everyone turned left or if it pointed ahead it showed the direction of the charge. Ten units of ten made a company of a hundred and the units could execute very quick changes of direction to confuse an enemy. Ten groups of a hundred made a battalion of a thousand commanded by a '*hazari*'. The head of two to five thousand horsemen was called an *Amir.* Most of the great *Umraos* had commands of five thousand but royal princes were sometimes given honorary ranks of eight thousand or more.

The sons of Adam may wield the most magnificent weapons

but the birds and the trees will not be impressed

nor the rivers or oceans around them.

Chapter 3

The Passing of a Queen

After the lush forests along the Chambal River, our great caravan passed the great fortress of Ranthambhor and arrived in the dusty plains of Rajputana. Ranthambhor was our first introduction to the magestic forts and palaces of our valiant Rajput vassal rulers. A few days later, a feeling of excitement gripped the entire caravan as it approached the holy city of Ajmer Sharif that held a special place in every Mughal heart. A hundred years earlier, Emperor Akbar had walked barefooted from Agra to Ajmer to seek the blessings of the Sufi saints for a long sought after son. And though Ajmer was a place of spiritual importance, it was also one of great beauty. The lovely gardens and mosques around the big Anasagar Lake that was further surrounded by a wide ring of rocky hills, was a most pleasing sight.

Our storytellers told us that Dara had been born at Ajmer near the smaller Sagartal Lake sixteen years earlier on 20th March which marked Nauroz or the spring equinox. Astrologers had declared that they had never seen such an auspicious alignment of the planets and had confidently predicted a brilliant future for the little baby. They had said that though he was ruled by the Zodiacal sign of Aries, Taurus was ascending in the east making him a great religious luminary. With Jupiter, lord of all the planets in his ninth house, he was destined to become a great monarch some day. One of the eunuchs leaned over and whispered to me that another astrologer had however told him that Saturn commanded his tenth house, which could lead to confusion and lack of authority. He cautiously added that as the birth was on the cusp between Zodiacal signs of Aries and Taurus it could also lead to indecisiveness.

We made our way to the tomb of the revered Sufi saint. The mace bearers cleared the entrance of beggars and supplicants as Shah Jahan scattered a handful of coins for them. We were respectfully greeted by the bearded caretakers. To show his reverence, the emperor placed a huge green brocade cloth with gold edging and a large heap of rose petals on the tomb of the saint. Following the others, I entered the inner sanctum of the *dargah* (tomb)and slowly closed my eyes to pray. My mind became calm and aware of the power of many thousands of prayers rippling like an invisible electric storm all around the tomb.

I opened my eyes and studied the sacred mausoleum of Khwaja Moinuddin Chisti whose divine spirit, or *wali*, was believed to be so pure that it had the power to intercede with Allah and his prophet Muhammad on behalf of all the oppressed or suffering. He was called the *Garib Khwaja* or the saint who cared for the poor. After covering the grave with the rich cloth, we sat down in the adjoining hall to listen to the *kawwals* who sang ecstatic songs to the sound of drums and wind instruments. A tall Sufi in a brown robe entered and rotated slowly with his hands raised to the heavens. He was followed by two more dancers wearing white clothes with long wide skirts that would rotate outwards almost stiffly from the spinning force of the movement. They rotated faster and faster with one arm raised to the sky and other pointing to the ground as they beseeched Allah to let the ocean of his divine love pour from heaven through them to bless everyone on earth. We sat mesmerized by this dance of the whirling *dervishes* and the insistent rising notes of the drummers and musicians.

As we rose to leave Roshanara turned to one of the caretakers and anxiously enquired, "Our brother Aurangzeb must have come here last month to pay his obeisances to the Khwaja when he was on his way to the Deccan?"

The bearded caretaker looked embarrassed and rather reluctantly replied, "Yes... young prince Aurangzeb did indeed come here but he refused to pray at the *dargah*. He said that prayers should only be offered to the almighty Allah and that it was not proper to pray at the tomb of any mortal man, regardless of how highly he may be esteemed."

Dara looked up with a smirk on his face and said, "Beloved sister, you should know by now that our dear brother has a very narrow view about our religion and does not believe that revered saints have the power to intercede with Allah."

As we left Ajmer, resuming our journey to Burhanpur, we passed many groups of villagers who prostrated themselves before the emperor. I was surprised to see the shabby clothes of the people and the sorry state of their habitations. Many abjectly poor subjects nearly killed themselves in their desperate scramble to collect the small silver coins thrown from the golden *howdah* of the emperor's elephant.

I was later told that almost all the wealth of the empire was in the hands of a few thousand noble families who would compete with each other in flaunting their wealth and generosity, while most of the other inhabitants lived in poverty in shabby city houses or thatched mud huts close to their meagre fields. What amazed me was that most of these women would always wear some silver or even gold jewellery on their persons. The poor people were always very particular to keep themselves and the insides of their habitations scrupulously clean but their dwellings were often surrounded by vile smelling untidy piles of filth.

There was no occasion for another hunt on our renewed journey as the forests were now dry after a prolonged drought, leaving the people of the villages in a pitiable state of starvation. With averted eyes and scented cloths covering our noses, our cavalcade rushed past areas where the stench of rotting bodies hung in the air. Our hearts went out to the nearly naked children with distended bellies that came out to meet us with their hands outstretched in the hope of getting some food. The emperor ordered the royal cooks to make huge cauldrons of a nutritious *khichdi*, a mixture of rice, lentils, condiments, and spices cooked in rich meat gravy that we distributed as our caravan progressed.

On our journey south we stopped briefly at the palaces of the Rajput chiefs of Bundi, Kotah and Jhalawar where we were warmly greeted. Our procession of elephants, camels and horses was led into a wide field through the cheering crowds by imperial mace bearers wearing bright red and green turbans. We were entertained at great receptions, especially at the beautiful palace on top of a hill at Bundi. We marvelled at the charming balconies, ornamentation of every window and door and admired the skill of their craftsmen and painters. During the ceremonies the vassal rulers offered many beautiful gifts including a most magnificent gilded saddle encrusted with jewels and a matching set of beautifully crafted swords and shields.

The Emperor responded to the grand welcome by having our huge 'Mass of Clouds' canopy erected on a plain, near a deep step well below the hill. Everyone was astonished at how quickly the huge white tented structure, with numerous cloth arches and scarlet and gold edgings, was erected. The emperor had a grand banquet for the rajah and other men folk while the empress had her own reception, to which the wives of the Rajput chiefs were invited. They modestly kept their heads covered by thin brightly coloured veils but whispered in hushed voices that they had never witnessed anything so splendid or grand.

Jahanara ordered me to stay close behind her as one of the Rajput princesses introduced the Mughal royal ladies to the leading women of this important Rajput kingdom. She found some of their jewellery very interesting but could not enquire about them as the slightest interest on her part would have made the Rajput ladies, immediately, take off the ornaments to offer them as gifts. She was especially fascinated by a particular jewel with many gems that would be secured to the hair and made to fall to one side of the forehead, in a small cascade of glittering stones and asked me to find out where it was made. I was able to discretely speak to an elderly Rajput lady and express my admiration for such fine jewels. She boastfully told me that this clever piece called a *jhumar* was made by a wonderful craftsman who lived just below the palace. I was able to locate him the next day and commission some beautiful pieces that made Jahanara very happy when they were later brought to her.

Though I had seen and spoken to many of our Rajput *rajahs* at the durbars in Delhi, this was the first time that I was able to meet and understand something about these Hindu families who had become our loyal allies. The clan of the Hadas, who ruled the huge territory between Ranthambhor, Bundi and Jhalawar had been opposed to our empire until Akbar was able to win them over by diplomacy, making them one of the most important fighting clans in the Mughal armies.

I befriended Brijendra Singh, one of the young Rajput princes, who took me around the palaces to show me how they lived. I was terrified when we were angrily accosted by an old white-haired woman near the ladies chambers, until Brijendra told her that I was a slave and also a eunuch. She then softened and proudly showed me some of the colourful clothes and intricate jewellery worn by Rajputs. Brijender also showed me some of their weapons and armour, explaining to me about the proud Rajput traditions and chivalry.

He showed me portraits of their heroes painted on the walls of a long gallery, narrating the glorious tales of battle, victory and death. I was quite shocked when he showed me a painting of a Jauhar ceremony in which a number of Rajput women threw themselves into pits of fire rather than face the horror of capture and slavery. "Many of the queens and other women also practice *sati*, climbing onto the funeral pyres of their husbands so that they can go with them into the next life", he said, "There is a *sati* ceremony to be performed this evening; would you like to come and watch?" I hastily told him that I had many duties in the evenings and politely declined.

A few days later as our imperial caravan neared the ancient city of Ujjain, our Rajput commanders implored the Emperor to stop for a day to enable the Hindu officers and soldiers to visit the very ancient Shiv temple of the town. Although the emperor was not happy to encourage such non-Islamic customs, he recognized the need to keep the Hindus in his service happy and gave his consent.

Dara was however curious to know about this sacred Hindu place and the religious customs of the people. As it was impossible for him to join the officers, he ordered me to go with them and give him a report about the pilgrimage and the rites at the temple. I happily joined the small cavalcade that left the camp at dawn the next day. The Hindu officers and soldiers left behind their uniforms and dressed in the simple white clothes of common pilgrims, walked the four Kos journey to the tall Mahakaleshwar temple on the banks of the Shipra River. I was surprised by the number of women that had been living in our camp until they came out on this procession. They all wore colourful clothes with pretty bangles and anklets that made a delightful tinkling sound as they walked. There was great happiness on the faces as they sang in high pitched voices.

It was the first time that I had ever been into a Hindu temple and I was amazed to see the fervour with which the thousands of devotees folded their hands, bowing and praying before a very ancient idol of a god called Shiv. In some of the surrounding temples were large idols of the Elephant God Ganesh and the Monkey God Hanuman. To the continuous sounds of bells and chanting, the devotees bathed in the sacred river. They then went into the inner sanctum of the temple to give small offerings of flowers and food after which the priests blessed them and anointed their foreheads with a crimson tilak.

When we returned to our camp the next evening Dara questioned me very closely wanting to know every detail of the rituals and customs. The other princes and princesses joined us and seemed surprised when I told them what my Hindu guide had said about the devotees were not actually praying to the stone idols themselves but to the powerful spirits they believed resided within them.

The royal procession, next crossed the big Narmada River surrounded by a range of rocky hills to enter the basin of the river. Our destination was Burhanpur which commanded the royal route to the Deccan. There were other routes to the south through the lands further east but these were far too thickly forested and inhabited by wild Gond tribes. They were also too infested with tigers and other dangerous animals to be safe for travel.

As we were descending the hills before Burhanpur, our Empress went into her fourteenth labour[4]. The *dais* (midwives) attending to her were very troubled when she said she heard the cry of her unborn baby inside her stomach, as they considered this a bad omen. She was in labour for two agonizing days and must have had a premonition that her end was near because she suddenly summoned Shah Jahan to her side and asked him to make for her a tomb such as the world had never seen before. She then called her children to her side and made them take a solemn oath that they would stay united and loyal

4 The thirty-eight year old Arjumand died on 17 June 1631 after a labour of thirty hours leaving behind Shah Jahan aged 42, Jahanara 17, Dara 16, Shuja 15, Roshanara 14, Aurangzeb 13, Murad 7 and the baby Gauharara.

to their father and ensure the eternal glory of their great Timurid name. Only Aurangzeb, who had earlier been sent on a campaign to the Deccan, was not there to give his pledge.

After a very difficult labour a baby girl was born. But the bleeding would not cease and the golden soul of our empress Arjumand rose from this vale of tears to soar through the pearly gates of paradise. The emperor was completely devastated with sorrow; his beard turned white almost overnight. The wails and lamentation in the *zenana* would have moved a heart of stone.

One of the court poets penned some beautiful lines:

'She brought from the groin of her exalted king
fourteen royal issues into the world
of these, seven now adorn paradise
while the remaining seven are the candles of the land.
When she embellished the world with these children
she waned like a moon after fourteen.
When she brought out the last single pearl
She emptied her body like an oyster'.

Her body was ceremonially washed with camphor water and then anointed, draped in a shroud and buried in a small tomb at the Zainabad Garden on the south bank of the River Tapti, opposite the imposing fort. This was to be a temporary crypt to await her final interment in the magnificent Taj Mahal that Shah Jahan said he would build to immortalize her memory at her beloved city of Agra.

For no fault on her part, the poor little princess Gauharara bore the blame for her mother's death throughout her very long life. When the midwives tried to pull her reluctant little body from her mother's womb, they may have pressed too hard on her skull with the result that her face became unnaturally small and slender with huge haunting eyes. The word *gauhar* means pearl in Arabic and like a pearl, she was to grow into a pale and strangely luminous young woman. She would often wear white clothes that made her appear even more like some other-worldly creature. She would silently glide, run or skip barefoot through the *zenana* like a wistful but friendly ghost.

As she grew older she quietly listened to everyone but very seldom opened her mouth to speak. She was to become especially fond of the easy going Shuja but seemed to also have a liking towards me. She often sat beside me, softly singing some tuneless song and whispering strange words that I always found difficult to understand. In the beginning, I thought that she was a little strange in the head but I was to later discover that her whispered warnings would always be prophetic. No one paid any attention to her words that seemed to be in curious riddles but as I began to take note of them I was warned of many strange events before they happened.

After the death of the empress, the gracious Jahanara became *'Padishah Begum'* or mistress of the royal household. Her just and loving nature enabled her to enjoy the love and devotion of all her brothers and sisters except for the bitter Roshanara, who was always secretly envious.

The Emperor now sent orders for Aurangzeb to return immediately from the Deccan campaign he had been sent to lead and was very angry that he took so long to return. When he eventually arrived to console his father ten days later, he was very severely chastised. But he smarted even more when Roshanara whispered to him that Dara had fuelled the emperor's anger by mocking his heartlessness every day.

The emperor's dislike for this third son was to steadily develop into deep suspicion that we discovered had been mainly caused by an incident that occurred many years earlier, when Shah Jahan had been the fugitive rebel prince Khurram, being pursued through the Deccan by a small imperial army. Mumtaz begum, who was again pregnant, had a sudden craving for apples[5] that were impossible to find in the Deccan but being a devoted husband Khurram had dutifully set out to search for them. As if by a miracle he soon came upon a *fakir* who held a red apple in each of his hands. He offered them to him saying, "Take these apples and fill your nostrils with their scent. As long as you can smell the fragrance of these fruits on your hands you will be safe from danger. But beware if the scent goes... you will then be in danger of betrayal by your third son who has the white colour of camphor and the piercing black eyes of a cobra". He told Jahanara the whole story many years later, who told no one but me and I in turn, later related it to Dara.

Aurangzeb had proved himself time and again to be a brave, loyal, disciplined, energetic and capable leader of men. People long remembered his steadfastness in moments of crisis. Who could forget how he, as a young prince had stood unflinching with just a sword in his hand when an infuriated elephant, knocked down his horse

5 The episode of the apples is in Waldamer Hansen's 'The Peacock Throne' quoting from Niccolo Manucci' 'Storia Do Mogor' (vol 1, p. 173)

and angrily bore down upon him? The angry beast had first been distracted by Shuja and general Jai Singh who had immediately rushed forward with their spears. Shuja, without hesitation was at his brother's side, while Dara, riding on the far side of the warring elephants, could not have come to his aid. Fortunately, the angry animal turned back to the unfinished battle, sparing the princes' lives. But Aurangzeb's calm fearlessness in the face of grave personal danger was never forgotten. It was something he was to often demonstrate in future years as well.

Shah Jahan had warmly embraced him immediately after the incident but scolded him for his rashness. Aurangzeb had then bowed graciously and scathingly replied, "If the fight had ended fatally for me it would have been no matter for shame. Death drops the curtain even for emperors.... the shame lay in what my brothers did."[6].

I had been witness to the entire event and upon hearing this comment, felt it to be gravely unjustified. Of his two brothers, Shuja who was nearer, came immediately to his aid whereas Dara, stranded on the far side, could not. Aurangzeb spoke in the heat of the moment; the near death experience influencing his words. Though his proclaimation condemned both his brothers, it appeared as though it was directed only at Dara, making it seem that his eldest brother chose conciously not to help him. Their strained relationship since childhood had led Aurangzeb to continually be suspicious of Dara's actions and intentions.

When prince Dara was born it had been predicted that he would go down in history as one of the greatest rulers of all time. Four years later, Aurangzeb was born on the 3rd

6 Sir Jadunath Sarkar cites Hamiduddin in his 'History of Aurangzeb' (p43)

of November at the insignificant town of Dohad in Gujarat during a terrifying hailstorm. An ominous new star, shaped like a porcupine, had appeared in the skies followed by a comet with a long tail. The court astrologers had been very troubled by these strange portents but could not agree on what they foretold. They had noted that the young prince would be strongly ruled by Saturn and the moon, and that these would make him austere, cold blooded and cruel. They said that the influence of Mars, the god of war, would also be destined to make him a soldier of great determination and ruthless authority.

The beautiful box that the parents have made

for the safety of their wealth

can easily become a dark prison

for the souls of their heirs.

CHAPTER 4

Lore of the Jungle

The emperor was so devastated by Mumtaz begum's tragic death that he would walk about in slow circles, as if in a daze and was unable to attend to the matters of state. We had to spend many months at Burhanpur while he tried to recover from his grief. I was beginnng to grow very restless in the sombre quietness of the mourning court so, I asked Dara one day for permission to spend a few days in the jungle with the *shikaris* with whom I had become quite friendly. As with my recent visit to the Hindu temple at Ujjain I think Dara granted me permission because he wanted me to go to places where he would not be allowed; so that I could tell him all about them.

I did not realize it at the time but I was soon to be introduced to a world completely different that I had ever experienced before. The jungles were a mysterious and dangerous world inhabited by tigers, snakes, scorpions and many other wild creatures. We were also told since childhood, many legends of ghosts and evil witches lurking in the shadows of every tree; waiting to pounce upon unwary travellers and steal their souls. I was to however, discover that the forest was actually a beautiful world where people could live safely with just the protection of nature. Though we considered the forests around us to be dark and mysterious, I had seen that our *shikaris* walked with almost careless confidence into the forests and was curious to know more about their strange world.

I spoke to Bhumiya, the leader of our *shikaris* and asked him to take me with them into the thick forests near the Tapti River for a few days. He was a short, dark and wiry tribal of the Bhil clan with an ever cheerful smile. He had a natural politeness but was never servile like most of our cringing servants and slaves. I once questioned him about why he always stood so proudly and never bowed to superior officers. He simply answered, "Only animals bend forward because they have spines that lie flat. I am a Man and a Man must stand upright. We bow to no one except the Great Spirit that has made us and all the many creatures in the world around us."

He made me leave behind all my fine clothes, except for a coarse light brown shirt and pyjama and told me not to apply any rose water or perfume as the scent would immediately betray my presence to the animals of the jungle. He wanted me to walk barefoot like them but my feet were too soft so they made me some soft leather sandals with a back support and taught me how to run silently through the forest like them, in an effortless sliding lope, hardly lifting the feet from the ground. It was difficult in the beginning but I managed to keep up with him and his team of twelve *shikaris* as they fanned out to see what game the jungle contained. As I entered the forest I wondered, how they dared to travel into the thick jungle alone when there were so many dangerous creatures lurking everywhere.

Bhumiya said that no one should ever be afraid of the jungle and needed to learn to regard the forest as a friend who can feed, shelter and protect you. He explained that all the animals that we feared were busy with their own lives and would never try to hurt anyone unless, they were provoked. They also feared humans and could sometimes attack out of this fear. He warned me to never look a tiger directly in the eye as that eye contact could itself be a provocation. I was also told that I should never make quick or jerky movements but always move gracefully. If I were to ever be confronted by a dangerous animal I should lower my head submissively and slowly walk away backwards to show that I was respecting it.

There were always many interesting things that happened every day in the forest. One morning, we came to a large meadow where a herd of about fifteen wild elephants were peacefully grazing under the watchful eyes of two old matriarchs who ensured that the calves did not stray away from safety of the herd. The *shikaris* explained that elephants can never be completely tamed and retain a wild streak even after many years of domestication. But, even adult wild elephants could be quite easily domesticated and trained once they became familiar with humans. He said that they were very intelligent and could become deeply devoted to their handlers, if they were treated well but could be very vengeful if, treated with cruelty.

One day, we stopped in our tracks as a huge cobra, more than six paces long, suddenly rushed out of a bush as if to attack us. Bhumyia crouched down and slowly lifted his open left hand above the wide hood of the serpent that was raised almost to the height of his hips. Singing a soothing song he began to rotate his left hand in front of the snake's eyes that began to follow its movement with its tongue flickering as it sought out the scents of its adversary. When the serpent seemed to have calmed down, Bhumiya suddenly moved his right hand to firmly grip the snake just behind its head so that it could not turn and bite him. Its tail now began lashing about and wrapped itself around Bhumiya's body. He did not seem worried but began to stroke its head with his free left hand until it began to relax and loosen its coils. After some time, he lowered the cobra to the ground and slowly released his grip on its neck. The beady black eyes of the serpent turned to look at us balefully one last time and then slithered off into the bushes.

I was very tired after the first few days but was soon able to run almost as lightly and quietly as the Bhils. We mostly ate the meat of small animals and birds that they shot with their little bows and arrows and these were cooked with some wild vegetables, roots, mushrooms, leaves and herbs collected from the jungle. We slept on the ground on soft beds of leaves collected from the forest. They showed me some trees and plants with broad leaves that could be used for shelter when it rained.

The Bhils were masters at imitating the calls of birds and animals, enabling them to communicate with each other without betraying their presence. Their cries of peacocks, pheasants, magpies, crows, lapwings, eagles and other birds as well as the cries of a small Kakar, barking deer, or *chital* were also signals telling the others where the game was moving and where they should position themselves. Bhumiya explained that a hunter should always note the wind direction because when the wind blew towards the game they would be able to smell our presence and hear the smallest sounds we made. He tried to show me how to track the game but I soon realised that it would take me many months to learn their skills.

After a few days, I began to lose my fear and feel comfortable in the forest. They had four lean dogs with long legs and deep chests. They seldom barked but were very useful in guiding the *shikaris* and were only fed on scraps of meat and bones from the kills. Bhumiya said that the dogs had to stay hungry to be good hunters. They were allowed to chase rabbits, rats and small game but were so well trained that they would only give chase when given permission.

They also showed me how to catch the little fish in the streams we came across. We made little dams with stones and small nets with pieces of cloth as well as small baskets woven out of reeds, growing along the shore. When the water in a shallow dam was beaten hard with a heavy stick, some of the little fish would be so stunned that they would float to the surface and could be picked up by hand. I also learned an important but rather unpleasant task of cleaning out the bowels of the fish, animals and birds that we killed.

I was getting a bit confused as we were constantly running along twisting tracks in and out of the curving paths and gullies and asked Bhumiya how they were not getting hopelessly lost. He said nothing, but stopped me when we got to the top of a small rise and showed me how to look at distant objects like a hill on the far side of the river to get an idea of where we were. I also learned to look at the line of the shadows of the sun. In the morning, it pointed towards the west, while at noon it pointed to the south and to the east in the evenings. At night, he showed me how to find *Dhruva*, the star that was constant in the northern sky, as well as some other stars that could help us keep our direction on dark nights when the stars were brightest.

I was to discover that there were also a few people who lived in the forest. One day, we encountered a bearded ascetic who wandered unarmed through the forest as if completely oblivious of all the dangers that it contained. He would sit motionless for hours softly singing some strange songs. When Bhumiya reverentially went up to him and asked if he was in need anything, he smiled gently and said that he wanted nothing as the forest gave him all. There were enough wild fruits, roots and plants to feed him as well as numerous herbs that provided all the medicines that any man could require. He said that all the animals and birds were his friends. Out of curiosity I asked him, "But what about tigers and leopards? What about a hungry animal?"

He smiled and told me that no animal would harm a familiar friend and said, "Every week there is a tigress that comes here and sits with me and listens to my songs. Last month it came here with two small cubs and she even allowed me to stroke them."

On another occasion, we were suddenly disturbed by the sound of a musket shot. As we cautiously approached through the bushes we saw that a small group of seven, armed men were skinning a deer. Bhumiya told me that they were a gang of robbers who lived by preying on unprotected travellers. He said that they were mostly fugitives who had escaped from prison or former soldiers who, because of age or injury, were no longer fit to serve in the armies of the emperor or any *rajah*. Bhumiya contemptuously said that they had no respect for life or the lore of the jungle. I learned that there were several such roving bands of wandering criminals who would unhesitatingly loot and molest any unwary traveller.

One evening, we entered a small tribal village just as dusk was approaching. Bhumiya whispered to me that this was a village of a very primitive, dark - skinned tribe of small people who never ventured out of the forests. Though they spoke in a different tongue, Bhumiya said he could understand what they were saying. We were cautiously welcomed into village of about forty people who were busy preparing for a full moon festival. A group of four drummers first began to strike their little drums dancing as they snaked around the central courtyard between a rough circle of round huts made out of thorns and branches of trees.

They first walked slowly, in rhythmic dancing steps and were joined by other men and women who were all naked except for small pieces of cloth or bark that covered their loins. The bare breasted women then formed a circle and danced towards one side, while the men formed a wider circle around them and danced in the opposite direction. The drummers changed their rhythm and the dancers stopped and began dancing with each other in pairs. A little later they stopped to drink some intoxicating liquid from a large gourd that a small boy was offering them. When the dance resumed, the rhythm gradually got faster and faster till the eyes of the dancers were rolling in joyous delight as some of the dancing pairs slipped off laughing into the darkness.

Suddenly, the drums were silent and a small, very thin and incredibly ugly old woman with rotting yellow teeth rushed into the centre of the clearing with a terrifying shriek. She ran through the circles of dancers waving her outstretched arms as if she were some kind of crazed bird of prey and came to a halt before a large stone slab on which she fell flat with her arms and legs twitching violently. Bhumiya whispered to me that as the rains had been late they were going to offer a big sacrifice to their gods asking for rain to feed the forests that also fed them all. He said that if the sacrifice of a goat or a dog did not satisfy the gods they would have to offer a bigger sacrifice. Perhaps even a human sacrifice.

A poor sacrificial dog was now gently pulled onto the rock and all the villagers came to stroke it and making loving sounds. An old man now slowly pulled its head backwards and opened its mouth to make it swallow some of the intoxicating brew. A little later the old woman cautiously approached the sleeping dog holding a huge stone with sharp serrations along its edge with which she killed it with one stroke. She then collected all the blood in a wooden bowl and reverentially began to spread a little of the blood on to the foreheads of all the villagers and also sprinkle some on the ground along to perimeter of the village. She then dropped a few small pieces of meat on top of another big rock. Bhumiya whispered to me, "That is to feed the crows who will come in the morning. The tribals believe that crows are the souls of their ancestors and that it is a good omen if they take the sacrificial meat."

The old woman now returned after daubing blood around the village and suddenly turned on me and pulled me with surprising strength towards the wide sacrificial stone. I was quite terrified and the thought that I might be made an object of sacrifice made me quake with fear. She suddenly let out a loud shriek followed by hideous laughter and said something to the villagers. Suddenly, I found my arms and legs held and my clothes roughly removed. I twisted furiously as I desperately tried to hide my emasculation. When my clothes were stripped away they all stopped and looked in wonder and then they all burst out rolling about in loud laughter.

They then let me go and I hurriedly put on my clothes

again. The old crone approached me again and stroked my face with great gentleness. She looked deeply into my eyes and reverentially daubed some blood on my forehead. She also made me drink some of the intoxicating brew that gradually made me feel very light headed and calm. My senses slowly relaxed and let me hear many soft jungle sounds. I began to see a huge river of fireflies that looked like little fairies floating through the air and saw streams of many strange colours swirling all around me. I also imagined that I could see the ghostly faces of my father and mother as well as many other people I had nearly forgotten. After some time, I saw a very blurred image of Dara's head with a benign smile on his face flying through the air and then a very aged face of Aurangzeb weeping alone on a very small golden throne. I was to recall these strange visions many times in later years but it was a long time before I was able to understand what the vision had meant.

Bhumiya came to me after a while and told me what the old crone had been cackling on about. Looking deep into my eyes she had said that when they saw me they thought that they had found a perfectly formed and unblemished young man who would have made a perfect sacrifice to make their angry gods happy and felt great sorrow that I had been deprived of all the joys of manhood. Her hard hands had stroked my face with surprising gentleness and she said that I had a pure soul and would always float gently above many violent events that I was destined to witness. She said that I was going to see terrible death and destruction; would hear the deafening thunder of battle and suffer many horrible hardships but that my soul would be untouched by them all. She had then looked deep into my eyes again and said that I would only suffer great pain from a deep attachment to a beautiful woman who I would never be able to possess.

When we left the village to resume our journey an old man followed us to the edge of their clearing and began to nail some thorns on to the trees that we had passed. Bhumiya explained that these were to hold up a sacred web of spirit power that, like a huge invisible spider's web, would keep the village safe from tigers, snakes, scorpions and other dangers that the evil spirits might send.

We became good friends over the days together and Bhumiya told me to try to understand, love and respect the spirits of the forest and the spirits that he said lived in every rock, tree and river. He said that they believed that these *jivas* (spirits) were the real owners of the forest. He told me that we should respect these *Bhumi Devtas* (earth deities) *Jal Devtas* (water spirits) and many other spirits. He explained to me that as human beings we were intruding into the kingdom of these spirits and must always seek their blessings if we were to be safe from danger and be successful in our *shikar*. That was why we should always place little offerings of flowers and food near big trees or rocks before entering any new part of the forest. He added, that we should also sing some songs to please them. He said that when one learned to feel the power of these spirits one could feel their protection and walk fearlessly.

He showed me several small shrines of the forest gods in the base of big trees or next to large rocks as well a few for the malevolent ones that he said also inhabited the jungle. He said that the *Churail*, or witches with their feet pointing backwards, were the spirits of women who had been so badly scorned that they refused to pass into the underworld, where all souls go, but chose to stay behind to seek revenge. Some were so angry that they would inflict serious harm on people unless they gave blood sacrifices of chickens, goats, cattle and even human beings. He said that there were also a number of mischievous spirits that were the *jivas* of small abandoned children. He explained that before children became old enough to remember they had no fear of anything; small children had an amazing ability to laugh and play even when suffering the most terrible hunger and hardship; and if they died these little lost souls loved to skip and dance through the shadows of the jungle and play mischievous pranks upon unsuspecting people.

I asked him to tell me about the great gods like Allah or Shiv or Vishnu that the people of the cities worshipped. Bhumiya paused and then slowly said, "People create gods to suit their own situations. As people now mostly lived in big cities under the rule of a great king who has conquered many smaller kings, people also began to believe that there must also be a great god who rules over all the other smaller gods." He said that people in villages still worship their local gods. For forest people the spirits of the forest were most important.

One day, we came to a very tall rock near a stream that was flowing towards the Tapti River. Bhumiya placed a few flowers before it and prostrated himself on the ground. I followed his example and lay on the ground for some time. I could initially hear only the soft sounds of the forest but was gradually filled with such a deep sense of peace that I completely lost track of time till I felt Bhumiya's hand on my shoulder, "Baba the Great Spirit surrounds every living thing with its soft radiance to make it strong and secure. I think you could become a good *shikari* one day as you will quickly learn how to speak to the Great Spirit and be able to get his blessings to protect you on your own long journey."

When I returned to the imperial camp ten days later, my friends rushed up to warn me that prince Dara was very angry with me for having been away for so long. Instead of avoiding him, I immediately went to him before he had time to build up any feeling of anger. I presented him with the claws of a bear that we had killed and his curiosity quickly overcame his anger. Later, while I was relating my experiences — except for the time when I had been stripped naked to be sacrificed — to him and the other princes and princesses we were joined by our learned tutor Abdul Latif Saharanpuri. He asked me to continue and did not interrupt my narrative but sat quietly listening intently to my account. When I had finished I hesitatingly asked him about what the *shikaris* had told me of the forest shrines and the many *jivas* inhabiting the jungle and of my experience of serene tranquillity.

He looked very thoughtful and said that I had indeed been fortunate to have had such a wonderful spiritual experience. He told me not to be troubled but that I should rejoice. He added "it was said in the holy Quran that the world around us is filled with many *farishta*, angels, *djinns* and other silent messengers that inhabit the universe of Allah. They are guardians that walk before and behind his every creation so that He may know all that they do and all that is in their minds. When we pray we should think of these guardians that are all around us and in our times of trouble, pray that they may always be there to bring us the protection of Allah".

Most of my companions, contemptuously, thought that I had just wandered off to enjoy myself. Dara later questioned me very closely and admitted that he envied my adventure as none of the royal princes would ever have been permitted to go into the jungle. The experience was to stay in my mind for many months and gave me a deep understanding of the faith of tribal people. I also learned that these poor people of the forests who we considered to be dirty unlettered fools had knowledge of many things that we city dwellers had long forgotten.

In nature everything is alive and all things are free

The glory that Man reveres is but a shallow dream

that any storm can instantly sweep away

Chapter 5

First Blood

The affairs of the Mughal Empire had been neglected for nearly two years as Shah Jahan continued to mourn the passing of Arjumand Bano. The rebellious Rajah Jhaujhar Singh Bundela of Orchha, having sensed the emperor's despair, seized the opportunity to usurp the throne of Orchha as well as capture the old Gond capital of Chauragarh. Reports were coming in that he was also encouraging some of the nearby *rajahs*. These were serious affronts to Mughal authority that could not go unchallenged.

Then, when an appeal from Debi Singh, the son of the late *rajah* of Orchha, was submitted for help to reconquer Orchha it provided a perfect justification for imperial intervention. The emperor immediately ordered a punitive expedition under the overall command of the emperor's uncle the redoubtable Shaista Khan. Debi Singh was offered the Orchha *gaddi* and led a small independent army commanded by one of his kinsmen. To lead the force, an imperial leader with royal Timurid blood flowing in his veins was necessary in order to establish Mughal authority.

As prince Dara had gone to Lahore and Shuja was in Benares, the emperor had to suppress his personal reservations and Aurangzeb was again given nominal overall command.

Aurangzeb was delighted with this responsibility as he had been smarting at the Emperor's cynical rebukes and was burning with ambition to prove his mettle as a soldier. Seeing his face glow with pride and displaying one of his rare smiles, I took the opportunity to approach the prince and requested him to take me as part of in his entourage as a personal attendant. I knew all the intricacies of court life but also wanted to learn all I could about an army at war. Though the ever observant Aurangzeb knew of my friendship to Dara, I had been very careful to maintain good relations with all the princes and princesses.

I was now just thirteen but was tall and muscular for my age and looked about sixteen. Aurangzeb, who also looked older than his fifteen years, examined me steadily with his penetrating black eyes and said, "You will find army life very hard. I do not know if you will be able to face the hardships of soldiering after having wallowed for so long in the luxuries of the *zenana*?"

I bowed and courteously said, "*Shahzade hazoor*, I am very confident that I will be able to endure hardships of war as well as anyone; and I am willing and eager... very eager... to experience war and learn the skills necessary not only for every Mughal prince but also for those who serve and sometimes, even council them. If fortune favours my destiny I might even follow the example of other famous eunuchs like Malik Kafur, who had risen from common slaves to become a great general in the service of their masters. I beg you to please allow me to accompany you on this enterprise."

Aurangzeb, looked up from the papers he was studying and absent mindedly said that it was not customary for a eunuch of the *zenana* to venture outside the palace but he did need someone he could trust to look after his treasure and his personal possessions. He, however, warned me that it would be very hard work. I replied by saying I would be deeply honoured to serve him in any capacity and assured him of my loyalty and devotion.

Although, Aurangzeb was supposed to stay in the background and remain a figurehead commander, no Mughal general could oppose his single minded determination. He quickly made it clear that he wanted to take active command of a part of the campaign. So without waiting for his full cavalry units to assemble, he led a small army, without elephants to slow them down, out of the great fort of Gwalior towards the small fort of Jhansi; while the two main Mughal armies approached Jhaujar's seat at Orchha that was only some eight Kos east of Jhansi.

The fortress of Jhansi[7] was a small but well designed fort, about forty kos south of Gwalior. It had a well fortified gate to the east and a moat below the tall battlements on the north, east and southern sides that made approach very difficult. There was however a huge steep sloping rock surface on the western side that had no moat to protect it and the fortifications above it were not very high. The eastern gates were protected by high buttresses and towers from where the defenders could easily pick off the attacking infantry with their cannon and muskets. A long firewall

7 The Jhansi fort was not very old and had been part of the Orchha kingdom. It was sacked in September 1635 by armies led by Aurangzeb. It was to gain great fame two centuries later as the base of Lakshmibai, the Rani of Jhansi, who was killed near Gwalior while fighting the British in June 1858. The British then took possession of the fort and posted a garrison there.

running along the inner wall of the battlements enabled the defenders to easily move along it to shoot down at the attacking soldiers, push away their ladders, or pour flaming oil, stinking offal or big stones on them.

Aurangzeb surprised everyone by displaying an unexpected gift for quick movement that would take his enemies by surprise. Though, he never moved until he had obtained accurate information about an enemy's resources, disposition and intentions. He obtained these from Mughal official as well as his own personal spies. The ruler at Jhansi, a vassal to Orchha, had been counting on the usual leisurely arrival of a huge Mughal force with a cumbersome baggage train. However, Aurangzeb moved and lived like a common soldier, sleeping on the ground on a rough cotton mat, eating simple food and drinking the same water as his soldiers. The defenders at Jhansi were thus surprised when a small force of some five thousand soldiers was upon them before their spies at Agra and Gwalior had time to send them a warning.

Aurangzeb quickly set up conspicuous artillery positions facing the main east gate with a few guns facing the long southern battlements. His first move was to use his new Persian long range brass cannons to bring down the flag of Jhansi state. The rectangular flag was shaped in two diagonals, one of saffron and the other white, fluttering over the citadel above the main fort. A Portuguese gunner, Miguel Dais, a known marksman, either by skill of sheer luck, brought down the banner and part of the citadel wall with his second shot. The Mughal soldiers cheered lustily at this devastating strike.

The attackers then began a cannonade on the well defended east gate to give the impression that these were preludes to a full fledged assault at this point. The infantry and cavalry stayed within sight with the purpose of drawing the defenders and leaving the western part of the battlement undermanned. Aurangzeb's engineers also pretended to examine the ramparts as if looking for places to cut tunnels for setting off gunpowder charges under the battlements.

The defenders fired back occasionally but their outdated cannons were too small to have any impact. Cannon and musket fire continued through the night with occasional shots into the town to wear out and exhaust the garrison, while Aurangzeb quietly mustered most of his infantry behind a grass covered embankment protecting the western wall.

At a half ghari, or twelve minutes, after the dawn *namaz*, Aurangzeb ordered the assault by a small infantry battalion. It was still dark when six columns of soldiers carrying long bamboo ladders ran silently towards the battlements, crossed the shallow ditch and started climbing the long rocky slope below the western wall. The drowsy defenders did not see them till it was too late to raise an alarm and could only muster a sleepy company of soldiers to stop two of the attacking columns. The attackers easily killed the defenders and ran along the firewall, on the inner side of the battlements, and moved to the semi circular southern wall to cut down the defenders as they tried to climb up from inside the fort. Soon, there were enough Mughal soldiers gathered on the firewall to command the battlements and mount an attack on the inner citadel itself.

The surprised defenders were running about and screaming helplessly, in a state of utter panic and confusion, while the *rajah* discovered that he was now trapped in his own citadel on the top of the hill without enough time to organise a *jauhar*, or fire pit, for the immolation of his womenfolk. Rajputs preferred death to dishonour and they were not only preparing to die but wanted their womenfolk cast into a sacred fire rather than become slaves. Although, I knew that loot and plunder were the normal conditions of war it was a great shock to witness the savage rape and pillage that came after. The screams of the women and children in the citadel were soon joined by those of the wives and children of the shopkeepers, craftsmen, jewellers and their women who knew that they would not be able to preserve either their property or their modesty from the ravening attackers.

While I was most thrilled by the experience of war, I had not been prepared for the carnage following the victory that court writers are so careful to omit from their glorified accounts lest it should offend the sensitivities of courtly readers. My ears were first assaulted by the agonized screams of the wounded and pitiful shrieks of the captured and then my nostrils assailed by the rotten egg smell of burnt gunpowder and the stench released from the sphincters of the newly killed. The small courtyard in front of the citadel was a sea of blood from the many broken bodies and it became difficult to see through the acrid black smoke and dust that burned the eyes.

As soon as there was a heap of bodies our soldiers would post a few of their comrades to keep guard while the rest pounced upon the dead and wounded and searched their clothes, cummerbunds, turbans and even their shoes for anything of value. A small pile of coins, jewels, rings, weapons and other trinkets was soon collected by a *risaldar* (troop commander) and was to be later divided up among the soldiers.

A small band of screaming Rajput defenders suddenly

sallied out of the citadel wearing bright orange turbans but without armour to signal their suicidal determination to die rather than become prisoners. For high born Rajputs, capture meant disgrace and an unacceptable loss of caste that was worse than death itself. Their blazing inflamed eyes betrayed the consumption of the intoxicating *bhang* (marijuana) and opium as they wildly rushed at the attackers. Though they suffered grievous wounds, the *bhang* seemed to make them impervious to pain or fatigue, hacking away till they were all cut to the ground. One frenzied soldier, furiously attacked me and I just managed to deflect his sword with my shield and thrust the point of my sword through his throat. He fell to his knees, spurting blood from his mouth with a horrible gargling sound. Though my stomach was churning with excitement, I had no time for gloating or remorse and quickly followed a section of our troops up the steps of the citadel.

The army was now able to attack the main gate of the fort from the inside to let the other troopers enter. The cavalry that had, up till now, played no part in the battle, clattered into the inner courtyard waving the square red and gold imperial banners on their lances. The sounds of clashing steel were now being drowned by the cries of the wounded and the screams of those being looted or raped. Only Aurangzeb's elite force were allowed into the citadel where, they not only captured a bevy of beautiful women but also a great collection of treasures worth more than a Crore (ten million) rupees.

I was horrified by the brutal treatment of the women, who were repeatedly violated by the savaging soldiers without regard even to their age. I was filled by sudden rage when I saw a young girl of about fifteen being dragged away by her thickly plaited hair and on a sudden impulse, rushed in to hit the soldier holding her on his head with the hilt of my sword. He furiously turned on me but I shouted loudly and told him that she was to be taken to the royal *zenana* and he should leave her alone.

He angrily stared at me but relented after seeing the point of my bloodied sword near his throat. He went off in pursuit of some other unfortunate victim, while I dragged the screaming girl by the plait of her long hair into a small adjoining room and closed the wooden door and locked it with an iron chain hanging from the low frame. I, then turned to the terrified girl and softly said, "Do not fear. I will do you no harm."

I saw the dead body of a Rajput defender lying on the floor and commanded her to help me strip it of its clothes. He wore a gold ring and I found some jewels and coins in the lining of his cummerbund and inside his turban. I kept most of them, as even eunuchs need money for their personal needs but gave three silver coins to the surprised girl, telling her that wherever she was going she would need some money.

I then turned my back and told the girl to take off her clothes and put on the discarded clothes of the dead soldier. She whimpered in apprehension but began to do what I had demanded. She suddenly cried out as she saw blood on the soldier's yellow jama from the musket ball that had killed him. I angrily told her that if she wanted to save her life and virtue she should forget about her modesty and quickly wear them. She cowered in terror when I next approached her with my sword and proceeded to cut off her long plait of hair. Though my sword was very sharp, the hair was not easy to cut but I gruffly told her, "Your long hair will betray that you are not a man. Your life is more valuable than long tresses that will soon grow again."

When she had changed I helped her retie the yellow turban on her little head, while she steadily looked up into my eyes with apprehension. When she was dressed, her frightened face looked quite incongruous in the oversized soldiers clothing. I then went to a smoking brazier in the corner and took out a handful of ash and rubbed it on her cheeks. She backed off in horror but I smiled gently, and told her that even in a soldier's clothes her pretty face would get her into trouble, so I must try to make it look as dirty and inconspicuous as possible. She looked deeply into my eyes and suddenly fell to her knees and placing her head on my feet, begged me to not leave her as her family was dead and she had nowhere to go. I lifted her up tenderly and so dearly wished that I were man enough to keep her with me but then told her that it was impossible for her to come with me as I was only a slave with the emperor's *zenana*.

As the sounds of fighting and looting subsided, I cautiously opened the door and saw that there was no one around. We slipped out of the building and walked quickly to the western battlement from where it was a short climb down to the rocky slope below — aided by one of the ladders the attackers had left on the wall. Upon walking some distance, we found two wounded Rajput defenders cowering among the trees below the fort. Leaving the girl with them I looked around and soon saw a few rider-less horses cropping the grass. Slowly approaching them, I held out my hand with a clump of grass and gently took them by their reins. The two Rajput soldiers mounted the horses with the girl sitting behind one of them. I made her sit astride like any other soldier and told them to go north towards the small Rajput kingdom of Datia just some fourteen *Kos* away, giving them a few silver coins each for food, fodder or other needs.

My emotions were in a state of turmoil. I now began to feel the enormity of having killed a human being and was for the first time overwhelmed by the emotional storm that a woman can inflame. I had been used to a close proximity with women but these relations were those of duty and could never have had any passion or personal involvement. I had been dependant on others all my life and now for the first time, had been faced with a young girl who was in need of my protection. Her wistful little face was to haunt me many times in the years to come. I was to often wonder if I would ever see her again.

After the noise and dust had settled, Aurangzeb and a group of his officers walked among the wounded. He led a special prayer of thanksgiving, the *Namaz e Shukrana*, in the main courtyard attended by most of the Muslim officers and men. The chief *hakim* then administered a large dose of opium to the severely wounded to ease their pain or to speed their passage to the celestial world. They also carried red hot iron rods in charcoal braziers to cauterize severe bleeding from severed veins or arteries. To everyone's surprise Aurangzeb also had the wounded enemy soldiers rounded up and ensured that they also got the little black opium balls and other medical treatment. He later addressed the captured enemy soldiers and praised their bravery but regretted that their *rajah* had abandoned the Mughal cause. He said that their bravery and loyalty had been proven and those who chose to serve the Mughal Empire would be welcomed and well rewarded.

The Mughals and their Rajput allies only suffered sixty five dead and two hundred wounded as compared to four hundred opposing Rajput dead and nine hundred wounded. In the annals of the Mughal Empire it may have been a small victory but it was one in which speed and surprise had won the day. From start to finish the conquest of Jhansi had taken just two days and the victory greatly alarmed Jhaujhar Singh who had been relaxing in his beautiful Orchha palace in the forested valley of the Betwa River.

A few days later a Mughal force under the nominal command of Debi Singh stormed a hillock overlooking the river with its beautiful palaces, cenotaphs and temples adorning both banks. These included a palace especially built by Bir Singh Bundela for Jahangir. But to underline the punishment for Bir Singh's rebel successor Jhaujhar Singh, Aurangzeb ordered the lofty temple to be demolished. Debi Singh unfortunately proved to be a weak ruler and facing opposition from several Bundela chiefs was unable to control the area and later retired to Chanderi allowing Orchha to come under Mughal control.

Jhaujhar Singh, having insufficient time to organise a *jauhar* of his womenfolk tried to kill his wives and daughters with his own sword and those who survived were taken to the Mughal harems. These included two beautiful young princesses who were sent to the imperial *zenana*. One was tall and more handsome than beautiful with the skin the colour of old honey and the other was small and so fair that, one could see the tiny veins under her almost translucent skin. Jahanara was to later take them under her charge and call them Amber and Pearl.

After the victory, the soldiers collected outside the Orchha fort in the early evening to celebrate their triumph. After a hearty meal, Aurangzeb had all the treasures, trophies and captured weapons displayed. He then ordered his *bakshi* to distribute half the booty among the soldiers. They were piled in a number of heaps and the commanders of each company distributed them among their men. One fourth of the loot was to go to the emperor and one tenth was the share for himself and the rest was for his officers and their men. He said that he wanted nothing for himself but asked the *bakshi* to keep his share in the *toshakhana*(treasurestore) so that he could use it to buy some of the latest lightweight brass cannons made by the *firangees*. The troops rejoiced and praised the young prince to their compatriots. This praise was quite genuine for Aurangzeb had fought, rode and worked as hard as any common soldier.

Rajah Jhaujhar Singh fled southwards into the thick tiger infested forests with a small band of followers towards his new base at Chauragarh, near the Narmada River, where he thought the Mughals would not be able to follow him. But Aurangzeb was not one to let his quarry escape so easily. He summoned the leaders of some of the wild Gond tribesmen of the region and offered them a handsome reward and employment in the Imperial service if they could bring him *rajah* Jhaujhar's head. Jhaujhar and his Bundela Rajputs were no match for these forest dwelling tribals and Aurangzeb had his trophy six days later, when they lifted up his fly speckled head from a basket laid at his feet. So bribery and cunning had succeeded where force of arms might have failed.

Young prince Aurangzeb gained much more than just the severed head of an enemy. His Muslim soldiers had all noted his leadership, military acumen, discipline, piety and ability to gain his objectives. His Hindu soldiers saw that he was resolute and fair. He had shown a natural aptitude for command, a sense of strategic insight, a determination to gain his objectives by any means available and a willingness to undergo the hardships of a common soldier. The word quickly spread in the Mughal and enemy camps that here was a shrewd, determined and resourceful Mughal prince who was destined to go far.

A few weeks later, Shah Jahan was to follow his son's example and order the demolition of Bir Singh Bundela's other great temple at Mathura and construct a large mosque at the site, to signal the triumph of Mughal temporal and spiritual power. Shah Jahan had been troubled by the growing following of a new Hindu deity called Krishna who, according to legend, had once been a prince living as a cowherd at a place near Mathura called Brindavan. So he felt that a big mosque in the area would also serve as a timely reminder to the people of the power of Allah and the temporal might of the Mughal emperors who upheld his exalted name.

I was at the Imperial durbar soon after and heard a petition from some of the *mullahs*. Their white bearded leader bowed and said that after a century of peace and prosperity under the just Mughal rule, many Hindus were beginning to rise above their former modest stations as farmers, traders and artisans. He said that they now had some new deities called Krishna and Ram that were rapidly gaining popularity as the Brahmin priests seemed to have the ability to produce new gods and goddesses for the gullible and superstitious Hindus with remarkable facility.

They told me that a Brahmin poet called Tulsidas, who had recently lived at the town of Awadh (that had earlier been called Saketa on the River Ghaghara, some hundred *Kos* east of the capital) had written a long lyrical poem in praise of a hero of ancient Hindu myth called Ram whose worship had suddenly caught on like a summer fire to affect almost every Hindu household. Many Hindus began to call this town Ayodhya. I was also told that the Brahmins had initially been horrified that the long poem had been written in Braj, the local Awadhi language, and not the sacred Sanskrit but when it became so popular they were quite happy to accept it. The petitioners complained that noisy annual festivals over several days enacting scenes from this legend of Ram would go on till late into the night in almost every Hindu locality.

When I asked one of our Hindu slaves about these new deities he explained that the old Hindu gods like Shiv and Vishnu, though they were deeply revered, were not depicted in such a human a form as these new deities called Krishna and Ram. When I told prince Dara about it he ordered me to visit a festival and tell him about it. I, therefore, quietly slipped out of the court one evening and visited a local *Ramlila Mela* where the epic story of the old legend was being re-enacted by actors over a number of evenings.I found the drama and festivities were very entertaining and noticed the great joy it gave to the participants and their audiences who all seemed to be mesmerised by the heroic story and its message of honour and righteousness.

How can brothers embrace each other on a battlefield
... still smoking with the stench of gunpowder?
How can a minstrel compose a beautiful song
... under stars clouded by gun smoke and
the sounds of terror.

CHAPTER 6

The Moulding of Mughal Princes

After two months of soldiering in Bundelkhand, I was very happy to return to the capital and resume my former duties at the palace. I was conscious that I had grown taller and matured during the past year and noticed that many of the ladies and female slaves of the court began to look at me with much greater interest.

The spirits and vitality of our emperor Shah Jahan had also revived after chastising the Bundela rebels and he was pleased with the reports about young Aurangzeb's role in the quick victory. He proudly honoured the prince in full court with a long embroidered brocade *saropa* (robe), a valuable sword, costly jewels and an increase in his *mansab* (rank of command). The gold edged robe was emerald green (the colour of Farghana) and adopted by the Mughals for all displays concerning people of the imperial family. Aurangzeb, with great modesty insisted that the honours should be shared with Shaista Khan and Debi Singh, whom he praised. He showed a wise prudence by doing this to allay the jealousies that always swirled around the court.

Dara was the only one who did not seem happy about the honours and praise being heaped on his younger brother. I was sitting just behind him at the ceremony when he slowly turned to me and mockingly whispered, "What an empty spectacle all these military ceremonies are. As if there is nothing more important than shedding oceans of blood and then heaping high honours, robes and treasures on the butchers? What a waste of our empire's gold! What a waste of valuable lives! Brother Aurangzeb has, however, distinguished himself on the battlefield so, I must also seek a military adventure to show that I can do even better."

I began to understand that despite his many wonderful qualities Dara had become so used to always being the centre of attention that he resented Aurangzeb being praised. Though he was very friendly with his easy going brother Shuja and very indulgent with young Murad, he was always wary of the sly, ambitious and energetic Aurangzeb who, in turn, displayed a barely concealed contempt for his eldest brother.

On the following day, Dara approached the emperor and after bowing respectfully said, "*Abbajan Hazoor*, like all of us I am very proud of my brother Aurangzeb who has so distinguished himself in our recent campaigns at Jhansi and Orchha. I, too, seek an opportunity to prove myself on the battlefield. Though peace now prevails over most of your great empire, there is a troublesome problem on our very doorstep that needs to be removed. There are several bands of river pirates who plunder and pillage the many boats carrying goods, pilgrims and passengers on the river Jumna that flows past these very walls. The boatmen between Dilli and Patna down the river are in constant fear of their lives. I seek your permission to take out a force to subdue them."

The emperor turned to his vizier and after discussing the proposal for a few minutes said, "These river pirates are indeed a very troublesome problem. Make a detailed submission of how you propose to eliminate them and if it is practical and does not put you into great personal danger, we shall most certainly consider it."

Dara summoned a meeting of his officers the next day and invited a group of boatmen from Agra to meet and explain their problem. Their leader explained to Dara, "*Shahzadeh Hazoor*, travel on the river has become very dangerous as these armed pirates, fearlessly, attack our barges that are being poled up and down the river usually at dawn or early dusk — when it is still dark. They loot our possessions and kidnap our passengers. They seek ransoms for the men and ravish the women. Only last month, the daughter of a very respected *Mullah* was kidnapped and even this holy man had to pay a huge ransom to get her home unharmed. We have to hire expensive soldiers to guard our boats and protect ourselves. We try to move in groups but the pirates are becoming bolder all the time".

Mughal soldiers were mostly horsemen and unfamiliar with rivers so, Dara invited Abdul Rasool, a handsome young man from among the boatmen, to collect a small force of a hundred armed soldiers who would be willing to fight the pirates. It took a month to assemble and train this force as well as build a small fleet of small fast boats. I was also able to find a European soldier who helped us make a new kind of oar like those used in Europe that enabled the boats to move much faster. These boats carrying armed soldiers as well as a few small *Zamburak* cannons began to patrol the river near Agra. The piracy immediately diminished but mainly because the pirates, aware of the river patrols, stopped their raids.

A month later, Dara summoned us and said, "Our patrols have undoubtedly had a salutary effect but we have not removed the problem entirely. We need to capture or kill some of the leaders of these pirate gangs or else the problem will constantly recur. We should now pretend to slacken our vigilance to encourage the pirates to resume their vile trade and then surprise them with a trap." He then dismissed the others but secretly summoned Abdul Rasool and said to him, "I am also going to pretend that you have betrayed me and will have you dismissed and disgraced. But fear not! No harm will come to you and you will be well rewarded if you succeed in this mission, I am entrusting to you. When your disgrace becomes known you will have no difficulty being accepted by one of the leaders of the pirate gangs and gain their confidence — so that we can know where they operate from, who their members are and when they plan their next raid."

Two months later, just before winter was approaching we got news that the leader of a large gang operating from near Mathura, just up the river from Agra, was planning to loot a large flotilla of some twelve barges, bringing a valuable cargo of goods up the river from Allahabad. We made sure that the flotilla looked an easy target with the boats carelessly scattered about with few armed guards. In the middle of the flotilla were two barges filled with well armed soldiers who were out of sight, hidden below large sheets of thick cloth. On the night before, the flotilla reached Mathura. I was deputed to take six of our fast boats up the river from it, while another six boats were to follow some distance behind the fleet.

It was very pleasant being rowed up the river under a starry sky with the soothing sound of water lapping against the sides of the boat and we passed Mathura just before daybreak. As the light strengthened we watched geese, ducks and other birds on the river's edge.

When we were about two *Kos* upriver of Mathura, we hid our boats in a cove behind a screen of tall rushes and waited through the heat of the day. Just as it was getting dark we heard the sound of muskets being fired and knew that the pirates were attacking the flotilla. We immediately leapt into our boats and rowed down the river to join the attack against the pirates. The pirates had been surprised by our soldiers who suddenly sprang up out of the two central barges to send volleys of deadly gunshot into the ten attacking boats. A few boats capsized and many pirates jumped into the water trying to swim for the shore. Our boats now approached and shot many of the pirates who were trying to escape. Three of their boats now turned down the river in an attempt to escape only to find themselves trapped by other boats that were rowing upstream.

Two of the pirate boats in desperation turned and attacked the barge where Dara was commanding the operation. They had emptied their muskets and were now shooting arrows that killed some of the men poling the barge. They closed in and three thin dark pirates leapt onto the barge wielding their swords. Dara with a few soldiers immediately attacked them, jumping over a gap in the planking to expertly deflect a sword blow. He then twisted his sword arm to almost sever the arm of the leading pirate. The rest lost heart and dived into the river where they were easily picked off. The brief exchange had been a small but significant victory.

On the next day we had the bodies of the dead and injured pirates laid out on the wide steps of the Mathura *ghat*(river steps) where Dara addressed a large crowd of locals, "Praise be to Allah who has blessed us with a victory against these wicked pirates. Let this be a lesson to all those who dare to disturb the peace and harmony of our great kingdom. We Mughals may be a nation of horsemen but all should know that we have the power and will to seek out and destroy those who commit cruelty and injustice regardless, of whether it is on land or water. I know that there are many other pirate gangs but they are now warned that we will not allow our people to be terrorized and will seek and destroy them wherever they may try to hide."

The crowd sent up loud cries of approval and cried, "Praise to Allah... Praise to the Mughal Empire... Praise to Dara our brave Mughal prince. Praise be to Dara. *Allah ho Akbar. Allah Ho Akbar*!"

Dara now retired to a nearby tent set up for him to rest where he later met Abdul Rasool who was secreted into his presence, dressed in the shabby clothes of a poor mendicant. He bowed and Dara gave him a small bag of gold coins, thanking him for his valuable service. Abdul Rasool said that the main gang of a pirate called Jalua had been completely destroyed and that all the other pirates were now too terrified to try to resume their vile trade. As Adbul Rasool's life would now not be safe in Agra, Dara requested for him to travel to a Mughal *mansab* in Punjab with his recommendation so he may be employed there.

Word of our victory with several exaggerated accounts about prince Dara's personal bravery soon spread throughout the empire. In a short span of a few days, people began to regard him as not just a pampered Mughal prince but also as a brave and resourceful leader of men.

The emperor wanted a full report of the engagement and then complimented Dara for his cleverness and courage but gently admonished him saying, "It is good to be brave but foolish to be foolhardy. A prince does not need to expose himself to so much danger."

Then to my great surprise he summoned me and said, "Mubarak Ali, we are informed that though you are a slave in the *zenana* you have done good service to both the princes, Aurangzeb and Dara. In recognition, I present you with this ceremonial dagger with which you may continue to protect the royal family". I was quite overwhelmed to receive the jewelled *katar*, a uniquely Mughal punching dagger, in a crimson velvet sheath, along with the high honour that the present implied.

As I was withdrawing Shuja smiled and said to me, "Let me add my commendation. As you have so ably served both Dara and Aurangzeb, you must serve me next." I hastily muttered some words indicating my willingness and stammered my thanks for his generous thought. I now began to understand that this most unexpected honor was to raise my status above that of all the other slaves in the *zenana*.

The bold actions by Aurangzeb and Dara however made Shah Jahan realize that if his elder sons were capable of such military victories, he now had three adult princes bursting with energy and ambition, each capable of posing a danger to him personally. He understood that they had to be given substantial responsibilities to occupy their turbulent energies. He could hardly forget that he had himself rebelled against his father Jahangir who too had also once rebelled against his father Akbar. Though he was deeply devoted to his family he was too much of a realist not to know that the ties of blood would turn to water when inflamed by ambitions for the rich Mughal crown.

It was thus in the year 1044 Hijri (1635 AD), that Shah Jahan decided that the nineteen year old Dara was to be given command of the coveted northern approaches of Afghanistan and Punjab with their capitals at Lahore and Kabul. But as Shah Jahan could not bear his favourite son leaving his side, Dara was seldom allowed to go to his *subbah* alone. He usually went there only when his father visited Lahore or Kashmir.

The eastern approaches with the rich province of Bengal, was awarded to the seventeen - year old prince Shuja, despite his growing weakness for wine, opium, music, women and other luxuries. He was to govern this rich but hot and humid region for many years. The fifteen year old Aurangzeb was given command of the southern approaches, where he had to cope with the chronically rebellious vassal rulers of Ahmadnagar, Berar, Golconda, Bidar and Bijapur. The rulers of these nominal fiefdoms were also of the Shia sect that the emperor hated. The emperor always had a nagging concern about the possibility of their uniting with the Shia Shah of Persia to surround the Mughal Empire. Prince Murad, who was just eight, would have to wait several years before being given command of the western approaches of Gujarat with the rich and bustling new port of Surat.

At the Agra court a meticulous daily routine was followed by all the nobles, whenever the emperor was at the capital. I often stood behind the princes when our emperor would begin his day soon after the dawn namaz. He would go the *jharoka-i-darshan*, the carved balcony of the Agra fort overlooking the sands of the Jumna River to be publicly seen by his subjects. The assembled people would joyously shout, "*Padishah Salamat... Padishah Salamat...!*" (salute the emperor). If the emperor failed to appear at the daily *jharoka* it was thought to be a sign that he was sick and could lead to disturbances and insurrections.

Any citizen could approach the emperor by pulling on a velvet covered cord that rang a row of little bells. They would then be given permission to address the emperor on any matter. The Vizier would take notes of all complaints and the emperor would immediately give relief or order an investigation. Some of the subjects would simply give long speeches in praise of the emperor and the great Mughals hoping to gain a few coins or an opportunity for advancement. They all knew well that clever flattery was always appreciated.

Shah Jahan was a large man who looked every inch an emperor in his striped silk pyjamas and flared gold brocade jamas; covered by a light muslin *peshwaz* with a beautiful jewelled dagger hanging from his waist. Huge jewels shone from a white egret feathered broach rising from a huge round emerald set in a dazzling gold band with huge rubies and emeralds circling his elaborately tied striped turban. Strings of huge pearls and a fortune of precious jewels on his person proclaimed him to be the richest and most magnificent monarch of the world.

The next imperial function after the morning meal, was usually at the *Diwan-i-Am* or hall of public audience where he would sit for two hours on his crimson brocade covered *takht* in a raised pillared balcony. Thirty-six military and civilian officers would stand in rows below his marble platform to assist in answering the petitions proffered by a crowd of people who stood on the far side of a low stone railing. Some of the princes sat in a small balcony while the ladies of the *zenana* were allowed to see and hear the proceedings through stone screens behind the throne. Large carpets, pulled by ropes that went through the wall, slowly swung above the durbar hall to gently stir the air. Fan bearers on either side of the throne also used peacock feathers or white horse hair whisks to drive away the flies.

When the emperor entered, everyone stood and bowed until the *alkabi* (herald)announced the *alkab*(proclamation) calling everyone to attention until the emperor was seated. The *gurzedar* then struck a golden *gurz* on the floor with a loud clang so that the proceedings could begin. The courtiers or petitioners were expected to perform the *konish*, which meant to bow low with the palm of the right hand pressed to the forehead to symbolise that petitioner's were symbolically placing his head in the hand of humility. This was followed by touching the eyes and heart.

The *Mir Tozak,* or master of ceremonies, would then loudly announce the names of all those who were to be honoured or punished in the open court. One day, after disposing of a few cases he called the name of our general Mahabat Khan who had just returned from a successful campaign to chastise some of the troublesome chiefs near Attock on the Indus River. The emperor placed a red robe of honour on his shoulders along with a string of jewels and announced an increase in his *mansab*.

After this, a minor Afghan chief, Malik Jivan, from Dadhar a small fort near Kandahar, was brought in chains before the emperor and charged with betraying his Mughal commander, leading to the loss of a fort on the Indus. He could not defend his conduct and was therefore condemned to having his head crushed under the foot of an elephant. The *Mir Tozak* then asked if anyone wished to speak in defense of the prisoner. To everyone's surprise prince Dara rose and after performing the *konish* said, "Respected *Padishah hazoor,* I have known this rebellious Afghan to have also been a bold and brave soldier who has cleared much of Punjab of a band of vile brigands. It is common knowledge that his Mughal commander Naeem Sayyid unfairly humiliated him over some trivial matter. He undoubtedly deserves very severe punishment but I submit that his life should be spared. I submit that he should be deprived of his rank and privileges but offered an opportunity to redeem his honor."

The emperor paused, conferred with his *diwan*, and then declared, "Malik Jivan, you are indeed very fortunate that a royal prince should speak in your favour. Even though betrayal is a very grave offence we have decided to spare your life and command that you should join Qasim Khan who is commanding our forces fighting against the Portuguese in Bengal. If we hear that you have been brave and loyal, your former position and estates will be restored to you."

With tears in his eyes, the *malik* prostrated himself before the throne and then bowed before prince Dara before slowly withdrawing.

Many noblemen and some common citizens now made their submissions turn by turn for justice or for imperial generosity in elegant language as everyone tried to outdo each other in the old game of flattery and sycophancy. An old lady broke down in tears and said, "*Padishah Hazoor*, my son's estate was confiscated on his death in your service and I now have no means to feed my seven children. My husband died while working loyally in your service and I want to give my three sons a good education so that they too can loyally serve you."

The emperor turned to one of the court clerks and told him to ensure that she got a monthly stipend of twenty Rupees to sustain her family. The old lady again bowed low and tearfully said, "*Padishah Hazoor* I had earlier been given a stipend of thirty Rupees but it has suddenly been stopped." The Emperor now looked angry and asked the *Mir Bakshi* to personally look into the matter and ensure that the earlier stipend was not being stolen by one of the venal officials.

On special days like a coronation, *Nauroz*, the birth of a prince or when the emperor visited one of his major regional capitals like Lahore or Allahabad there would usually be the grand ceremony of '*Tuladan*' that had originally been a Hindu ceremony of weighing a ruler against valuables. The emperor or a royal prince would sit on a square brocade cushion on the large iron pan of a huge weighing scale, while the other pan was filled with costly valuables that were later distributed among the people. The ceremony attracted thousands of spectators and caused great joy whenever the ceremony was held.

Though the Mughals continued to follow some Mongol and Turki traditions they also readily incorporated many other customs that pleased them. Although *Nauroz*, or the ceremonies of the Persian New Year, marking the spring equinox, was an old Persian custom, they overlooked their own Sunni tradition and the eighteen day celebrations with feasting, music and dance was eagerly followed throughout the empire. In fact, every religious custom and holiday was enjoyed regardless of whether it was Muslim or Hindu. *Dusshera, Divali* and *Holi* were also eagerly enjoyed. The influence of the numerous Hindu wives in the harems also resulted in many Hindu prayers and blessings being publicly uttered by Brahmin priests before any journey, military campaign or other great undertaking.

Early one morning, Shah Jahan summoned Dara to go with him to inspect the royal treasury in a huge basement below the fort, and I was commanded to accompany them. We went in through two small but very strong iron doors with a number of locks. Some of the inner chambers and lockers could only be opened with keys in the emperor's own possession. We soon entered a huge hall, lit only by flickering torches hanging on the walls. Our eyes were dazzled by the huge collection of precious jewellery that made the mythical treasures of Allauddin's cave seem puny.

There were two gold and three silver thrones, a big golden chariot that had been dismantled and folded into smaller sections, a hundred silver chairs and more than one hundred thousand silver plates and vessels. The treasurer showed us a number of large basins that he said contained six hundred *maunds* (twenty thousand kilograms) of gold, twenty maunds of pearls and fifteen maunds of emeralds and rubies. Long necklaces of gold, pearls and precious stones hung from special racks and there were also several tubs of cut and uncut diamonds with the great Kohinoor, the queen of all diamonds, shining in a special glass casket. In addition to that, there were over a thousand gilded saddles studded with gems and thousands of swords and daggers with precious stones embedded into their hilts and scabbards. Each sword was given a special name and different swords were offered every day for the emperor to wear. Babur's famous sword *Alamgir* with a white jade handle in the shape of an eagle was displayed in a special case. Scattered here and there were numerous wooden chests containing little leather bags full of gold and silver coins to make them convenient for distribution.

I soon learned that apart from Agra there were large royal treasuries at Lahore and Dilli and smaller ones at Ahmadabad, Allahabad, Rajmahal, Surat, Patna and Aurangabad. The loyalty of the keepers of these treasures was ensured by making their families live, almost as hostages, in a carefully guarded colony close to the fort. The *Mir Bakshi* and the emperor himself used to conduct regular inspections to check that there was no pilferage because these royal treasures were an important engine for the Mughal war machine.

One day, after a *Tuladan* ceremony on the occasion of *Nauroz,* the emperor removed his royal turban, which had a great round ruby and two wide strings of seed pearls, and gravely placed it on Dara's head who was asked to sit on a smaller gold throne next to the great Imperial throne. Such honor, symbolizing his clear intention to make Dara his successor, however caused an immediate stir among the nobles as well as jealousy among the other princes who were present.

I was sitting behind the imperial family in the screened balcony behind the throne when I overheard Roshanara viciously whisper to one of her personal slaves, "Look at how besotted the old fool is over Dara. He is completely blind to how Dara consorts with all these Brahmin unbelievers and is deaf to anyone who even suggests that he is becoming a heretic. He has become so proud that he has no interest in the affairs of empire. Everyone knows that Shuja and Murad are lazy and drunken buffoons and that only Aurangzeb will be capable of holding the empire together after our father. But the emperor is always scornful and suspicious of everything Aurangzeb does and Dara loses no opportunity to mock him".

Jahanara had also overheard her and turned to say "Beloved sister, do not say such bitter words. You know that our father is wise and just and knows best what is good for the empire." Feeling rebuked, Roshanara looked hard at her but with eyes that seemed to be on the brink of tears.

From time to time the imperial court had interesting guests from the white nations of Europe. There was Augustine de Bordeaux, the jeweller from France who helped the emperor with the design of the Peacock Throne, as well as a Venetian jeweller, Geronimo Verroneo. There was a constant string of Englishmen like William Norris who were presistently trying to secure firmans for trade in Surat and other ports, as well as a few Dutch travellers. We also met Jean Baptiste Tavernier, a very talented French jeweller and the French doctor Francoise Bernier. There was also the Italian artillery officer, Niccolao Manucci, who had become fluent in our languages and was to later become a good friend of prince Dara and be with him through most of his battles. There was Father Buzeo the Portuguese priest who was a very fine person except that he was forever trying to convert people to his faith with its thousands of gaudily painted idols of saints. There was also a meddlesome Portuguese friar called Sabastian Manrique.

I was very embarrassed one day when Jahanara summoned me to speak to a French visitor in his own language. I pleaded with her saying that I had only learned a few words as a child and had now forgotten the language. As she was watching from behind a stone screen I had to summon my courage to approach him saying, "*Bon Jour Monsieur Jean Claude, comment allez-vous? J'espere que tout va bien*" It was a very simple basic greeting asking him how he was but he seemed surprised and responded in Persian with a broad smile saying that I had spoken with quite a good French accent. Jahanara, who was watching from behind a screen, seemed delighted with the silly game but I was very glad that she did not demand any more such embarrassing demonstrations.

Jahanara seemed to take a special delight in teasing me and though I was very often embarrassed I did not mind. In fact, her jesting was so utterly charming that I would seek every opportunity to be close to her so that I could watch her beautiful face, her laughing eyes, her graceful movements and the joyous sound of her clear ringing laughter. She would also speak to even the humblest slave with unfailing courtesy and kindness. All the court loved her and I found her to be utterly bewitching.

Wrestling matches were held every Wednesday and were very popular with many nobles and citizens of the city who collected on the sands between the fort and the river and would wager large sums on their champions. The two reigning champions were a huge wide - shouldered Turk and a tall dark - skinned soldier from the Deccan. One evening the dark Deccani drew a huge round of applause when he threw the Turk out of the lime marked ring after a long and closely fought encounter. He bowed below the royal balcony and the emperor threw down a small bag of gold coins. He then smiled and looking up said that he would wager his bag of gold against any champion in the Emperor's entourage who could stay in the ring with him for more than three minutes. This remark caused an immediate buzz of noisy excitement among all the courtiers that was interrupted by the shrill giggling voice of Roshanara who said, "Why not have our own champion Mubarak Ali challenge this Deccani hero? I will add ten gold mohrs to the wager"

I was absolutely dumbfounded and tried to hide my embarrassment until the emperor summoned me with a gesture of his hand and said... "We think this is a splendid idea. Mubarak Ali has become quite a big fellow and has been training with our soldiers. Let the people know that the members of the court are not all effete and soft. I will raise the wager by a hundred gold mohrs."

I now had no choice and, feeling very self conscious, was escorted to the long silken rope ladder with thick wooden slats that lowered me to the sands below the sandstone wall. I was then taken into a small makeshift tent where attendants removed my clothes and tied a stout blue cloth *langot*, or a coarse cloth, around my hips and loins and covered the rest of my body with oil. The langot was intended to hide the loins and allow the wrestlers to grip each other's otherwise slippery naked bodies. Although I was actually quaking with fear I decided that I must face the ordeal with outward calm and dignity.

The slim Deccani, who was taller than me, bowed and smiled as I approached him and I bowed in reply. When he put his arms on my shoulders I immediately knew that he was a man of great strength. I pretended to resist and then allowed him to pull me clumsily towards him but I then moved suddenly and was able to slip out of his grip. There was a little applause but it was be short lived as the Deccani was no longer smiling. This time I did not wait for him to pull me towards him but rushed in first to grab him by the knees but he was too quick and easily moved away. He then got a firm grip on my langot and pulled me down onto the sand where he lay on my chest steadily pressing my back flat to the ground. I did not resist too much and allowed him to wrestle me almost flat but just as he almost pinned my back on the ground for victory I arched my neck backwards and rolled and twisted quickly to slip out of his grip once again. The Deccani, now quite angry and wanting to put an end to the farce rushed at me in all seriousness. I luckily remembered the trick taught to me many years earlier by the little Chinese wrestler near Ranthambhor and quickly moved forward to meet his rush with a lowered hip that allowed me to pivot his momentum to send him flying out of the circle.

There was huge applause all around. Many of the bystanders, who had wagered on my very unlikely victory, had won large sums and came rushing towards me to share their winnings and gave me handfuls of silver and gold coins. I bowed to the emperor and to the Deccani and slowly climbed back up the long ladder. I, then humbly approached princess Roshanara and placing my little heap of winnings at her feet said, "*Shahzadeh Khanum* (lady princess) I must thank you for giving me this brief moment of glory. These winnings are only because of your blessings."

I could see that she was very unhappy. Far from humiliating me as I knew she had clearly intended to do she had instead been the instrument of my getting unexpected honour. Her avaricious eyes showed that she was torn between accepting the pile of coins lying at her feet and graciously allowing me to keep them. But with everyone's eyes on her she had very little choice. So with rather bad grace she crudely dismissed me saying, "You have won them... take them away."

The younger noblemen would sometimes play the old Mongol game of *Chaugan* where two opposing teams of four to eight riders would try to hit a hollow wooden ball of a very hard wood with long sticks. The wood did not burn easily and a glowing ember placed inside it made it glow in the dark through a number of small holes. The ball had to be hit between flares planted on poles in the ground defended by horsemen of the other team. It was an exciting game and a great test of horsemanship in which Dara excelled, Aurangzeb was quite capable but the easy going Shuja would often be unseated. In Kandahar, I was to later witness a similar game played by our soldiers using the carcass of a small goat that they would try to wrestle away from whoever had caught it. Chaugan was a brutal game needing great strength, tenacity, ruthlessness and excellent riding skills.

One of prince Dara's proudest moments as a father happened many years later when his tall and handsome son Sulaiman Shikoh, then sixteen years old, had scored by hitting the ball three times through the goal posts. He was so handsome, with narrow hips and broad shoulders, that a flutter would stir among the ladies of the *zenana* who would stop whatever they were doing and rush to the balcony to watch him play. The usually benign smile on his mother's face would vanish and she would look pale and anxious while watching the game because everyone knew that the players could sometimes suffer serious injuries. We were all overjoyed when his team won and came to receive rewards of jewelled daggers from the emperor.

Sulaiman had an easy smile, a confident manner and an amazing way with horses and seemed to make them move much faster than any of the other horseman. We all marvelled at how nimbly he swerved through the opposing horsemen and how surely he seemed to command the field. With his engaging charm he was, everyone agreed, destined to have a brilliant future. He took soldiering very seriously and had been given command of three thousand horsemen who he thoroughly trained under a European officer. He gave them a new distinctive livery of bright green Jamas with red silk sashes that made them very conspicuous. He led the training himself and made them more than just good horsemen. They were to become a thoroughly disciplined and loyal unit that could execute the most complicated field manoeuvres.

I went with the emperor and Dara one day to a wide barren field south of Agra and marvelled at their intricate manoeuvres. With just the waving of his banner he could make a galloping mass of horsemen approach in a line, spread out into a square, a diamond and many other formations. It was almost like watching a shoal of fish moving effortlessly in a lake. And, as he trained with them he gained their love and devotion.

Dara, who had been looking on smiling proudly, suddenly spurred his horse forward and patted Sulaiman on the shoulder and said, "What a magnificent spectacle! Your boys will make a very fine battalion but they need more than just good horsemanship and swordsmanship. How many of your soldiers can use the bow at full gallop? Let me show you something. He cantered back to one of his own soldiers and took his bow and quiver of arrows. He then wheeled around and galloped towards a tall dry tree into which he quickly fired six arrows one after another of which four hit the target.

Everyone cheered at this skilful demonstration and Dara, though breathing very heavily said, "My son, I am not as young or as fit as your troopers, or all six of my arrows would have hit that tree. When you can get a company of your troopers to use our famous Mongol bow like this, their barrage of six hundred arrows will be more devastating to an enemy line than a squadron of your horsemen. The muskets of enemy defenders can stop a cavalry charge but they will fall like sheaves of wheat when hit by at close range by so many arrows. Your horsemen can then easily ride through the gap in their devastated ranks to ensure certain victory. "

We journey along twisting paths hewn by fate

and even our best intentions and determination

cannot change its course

Chapter 7

A Life of Leisure and Luxury

For the next few years I was almost, continuously at the court in Agra. As the princes grew older my responsibilities increased as did my involvement in the many events in their changing lives. I also continued to live in the *zenana*, becoming a friend and confidant to most of the princesses. The royal princesses were never allowed the company of a man because the great emperor Akbar had decreed that no Mughal princesses should marry to ensure that no son-in-law outside the royal Timurid bloodline could ever make a claim to the Mughal throne. I suspect that the law has also been established because no proud Mughal emperor wanted to have to lower his head to another man as would have been necessary if he had a son in law.

It took a few years for the emperor to fully recover from his bereavement and he was persuaded by Houri Jan, the mistress of the harem, to bestow his favours on a number of beautiful girls especially collected for the *zenana* from all over the empire. The Emperor lived in his own private chambers where even the princes or princesses were seldom allowed except by invitation. The only other occupants were his personal bodyguards of big Tartar amazons whose sweet feminine tongues were in sharp contrast to their muscular torsos. They were deeply loyal to the emperor and would fight to the death to protect him.

Many beautiful young ladies were now specially prepared for the honour of enjoying the bed of the emperor with sixteen stages of beautification. Extra body hair was first gently removed by rubbing with a specially oiled porous stone. The limbs were then massaged with herbal oils to stimulate the sensations and to make the skin as smooth as silk. A little concentrated saffron water mixed with henna was usually applied to their breasts to make the natural colour of the nipples even more alluring. After washing, perfuming and decorating the hair on their heads and having baths in warm milk with several perfumed lotions they were ready to be presented to the emperor.

Houri Jan in her youth had been a celebrated courtesan. She taught her innocent and often incredulous charges all the ways about how to best please a man, to find out where they were sensitive or ticklish, to know how to gently breathe soft words into their ears, to know where they should touch and kiss the face or body and how to speak honeyed words in soft melodious whispers. She made them understand that the act of love was to be played as if the bodies were musical instruments to be stroked with changing rhythms of fast or slow, violent or gentle to give infinite variety and keep a man enthralled.

One evening the emperor asked for the exquisite little Pearl, niece of Rajah Jhaujhar Singh who was only sixteen and quite overwhelmed with fear and shyness. She had long and lustrous hair that instead of coiling it on top of her head, were gathered up by a silver coloured silken sash behind her head and allowed to cascade down below her tiny waist. Her small breasts were accentuated by a long string of pearls hanging from her slender neck and could be seen through the fine muslin of her dress. Amber, her tall and handsome cousin, stroked her arms and tried to encourage her.

After some time Houri Jan came in from the emperor's chamber and announced that the time had come. She kissed Pearl on the forehead and put a small pinch of some white powder under her tongue that she said would make her feel calm and serene. But I was amazed that, when the time came for her to enter the emperor's chamber, how bravely she overcame her natural modesty and gathered up the resolve to uphold the honour of her womanhood.

Although I had been deprived of my manhood, I had not lost my sexual sensitivity and, have to confess, took an almost morbid interest in all these preparations. As the sensual proceedings slowly unfolded the residual vestiges of my male organs would stir and feel almost painfully pleasurable. I noticed that the ministrations, that needed several hours of stroking and counselling, was stimulating not only to the girl being prepared for the emperor but affected all the other women in the *zenana* as well. Not surprisingly many of the attendants would secretly hold hands or caress and fondle each other in unseen nooks of the *zenana* as soon as the first shadows of darkness began to creep in.

I had also noticed that unlike men, who usually keep their innermost secrets very carefully guarded, women seemed to be surprisingly willing to share their deepest personal secrets with careless abandon even to casual acquaintances among the women. As a eunuch, I was not considered a man and was therefore privy to many such confidences. I also noticed that women were far more practical than men when it came to accepting personal setbacks, or even very deep humiliations.

Though women could be extremely fussy and contrary, they would quite realistically accept difficult situations and seemed to be surprisingly willing to surrender their bodies to ugly or unsavoury men provided they were rich or influential. Actually, the women had very little choice as they were never free to do what they wanted except with the consent of their menfolk. They knew that a woman, regardless of her beauty, intelligence, wit or wisdom was powerless without a protector and would therefore accept almost any patron provided he had the wealth or power to protect them.

But of one thing they were not tolerant. They found it difficult, nay impossible, to accept any slight to their personal pride especially if the shame was to the knowledge of the other women in society. Though they were always very possessive about money, jewels and valuables, they would rather lose a fortune than lose face. As they grew older many women were therefore quite content if their men took other wives or concubines provided their own superiority and status in the household was clearly declared. It was a happy household where the lesser wives and concubines showed deference and respect to the senior wife. Over the years, I discovered that women were strange creatures indeed. When they were young, slim and innocent they would cling to their men like a tender vine to a big protective tree. But when they grew older and stronger they would often, like a vine, suck out all the vitality of their protectors and leave a sad and shrivelled old trunk.

But despite their elaborate preparations the ladies

were often disappointed because the men were very often too preoccupied with affairs of state, or even worse, too intoxicated with an excess of wine or opium to have any interest in them. Our emperor, however, very rarely indulged in intoxicants though he sometimes enjoyed the fine golden wines from Shiraz or the sweet red plum wines from China and smoked a few small balls of special opium. Dara also drank with great moderation; Shuja drank and smoked opium to excess as did the impetuous Murad Baksh when he grew older; Aurangzeb alone would not allow a drop of any intoxicant to pass his thin unsmiling lips.

I learned that most men seemed to have very little sensitivity except for in the small area of their manhood and would usually satisfy themselves in a hasty burst of activity without understanding all the many thousand parts of the human body that could so enhance the wonder of physical union. Being a eunuch I saw the matter differently and I was constantly surprised at how male and female organs, that were such small parts of human bodies, could so hugely inflame human passions as to cause mindless bloodshed, brutal murder, bloody wars and utter insanity among both men and women. I had little inkling that I was soon to witness how lust could even cost an emperor his throne.

With the departure of Dara, Shuja and Aurangzeb to their own households the *zenana* had become too full of feminine quarrels, gossip and intrigues for my liking and I would seek every opportunity to go to the palace of my prince but for a most unexpected development. The massaging of the legs, arms and bodies of the women in the *zenana* could only be done by women as men, even the eunuchs, were not allowed to touch the bodies of any lady. But the fingers of women are not as strong as those of a man and the services of a few eunuchs were secretly used for massaging any lady who had a painful sprain, backache or chronic pain. I was therefore often quietly secreted into the chambers of some of the ladies after dark though I suspect that my handsome face and muscular physique might have been an added attraction.

Roshanara once tried to get me to massage her but I was frankly revolted by her fat sweaty form and pale white skin and always found some excuse for refusing even though, I knew from her hard eyes that she felt scorned and would one day make me pay heavily for the rebuff.

One afternoon princess Jahanara, while holding a glass of sherbet in her hand, slipped in some water dropped by a careless slave and hurt her back and elbow though, with the blessings of Allah, no bone was broken. I, immediately rushed in to assist moving her to her little chamber and hurried out to secure some herbal oil that would help reduce the soreness. But she continued to be in pain and whispered to me to come to her as soon as it was dark. But it took time before the *zenana* retired for the night as there were many women and slaves milling around that evening preparing a new concubine for the emperor.

Later that night when I entered her chamber I found Jahanara lying very still under a large sheet of fine muslin suspended from the roof to keep away the mosquitoes. She graced me with a faint smile and said that her twisted left ankle was very painful. My hands trembled when they touched her cool smooth skin that was the colour of pale sandalwood. I lifted her slender perfectly shaped foot and she moaned softly when I rubbed the ankle and massaged the blood upwards to take the pain up the veins of her calf. She shivered when my fingers traced the curve of her pretty foot and she moved faintly signalling her appreciation. Then she suddenly caught my hands and pulled my hands to massage her undamaged right leg as well. After a few minutes I moved to her side to massage her bruised elbow and forearm. We now both became aware that something quite magical was beginning to stir inside us that neither of us seemed capable of stopping. Then she again caught my hands when I was about to stand up and go. She was trembling as she held my face with both hands and slowly pulled it down to press it against her own. We lay together for several minutes breathing heavily and were filled with feelings of a most desperate yearning.

Jahanara was a very beautiful woman with the soft, dark green almond shaped eyes of her blessed mother, a perfectly sculpted nose with just the faintest trace of a Timurid curve above her full lips. I was now barely able to control myself as I softly brushed my lips over her forehead, her ears, her eyes, under her chin and lips until, in a near frenzy of hunger, our lips found each other and we seemed to cling together in a seemingly endless eternity. Her beautiful eyes were open and I felt as if I was being drawn into the dark depths of their dilated pupils. Jahanara trembled again and slowly put my face between her breasts where the soft satin of her gown parted to reveal soft gently swelling mounds. The raisins crowning them stiffened as my tongue circled them slowly before closing gently around them. A small beam of moonlight entering through a small window allowed my eyes to participate in this feast for all the senses. Then the soft down on her shapely arms seemed to stiffen in a surge of sensual passion.

She tensed as my lips and tongue slowly traced the outlines of the little pit of Venus on her gently curving stomach and she let out a small involuntary scream when my tongue traced a downward path till it found the mounds of her womanhood. I could hardly control myself and the remaining vestiges of my lost manhood began to ache with a strange but incredibly pleasurable pain. We lay together breathing heavily as we savoured the intoxicating scents of our panting bodies until we saw the early morning light beginning to enter the *zenana* and heard the sounds of the court slowly coming to life. I rose with a start, quickly gathered up my things, looked about furtively and slipped out.

What could have been more pathetic than a eunuch in love? I was aflame with frustrated desire that seemed to consume every thought and stimulate every pore of my body. I walked aimlessly in such a daze that I became very forgetful and earned a few well deserved rebukes for being negligent with my duties. There was an aching hollow space that seemed to fill my entire chest and I felt totally helpless and powerless. I had no interest in food or any of the luxuries around me. I had read about men in love but had never dreamed that I might myself one day become a victim of a deadly arrow from the bow of Anais, the ancient Persian goddess of love.

Loving, stroking or even touching a royal princess was quite unthinkable in the Mughal court and would have attracted very severe punishment, banishment from the harem or even execution so I could not even think of seeking advice or comfort by talking to any confidant. I could not forget that one of the concubines in Emperor Jahangir's court who had been caught with a lover had been buried up to her armpits in the hot sun and finally killed under the foot of an elephant. To be caught being intimate with a princess of the royal blood would have attracted the most severe punishment and also brought great shame to my princess.

For the next few days Jahanara and I were unable to look at each other and guiltily avoided each other's eyes but we were acutely conscious of each other's presence every moment of the day. But such a strong thirst could not remain unquenched and I would look for every opportunity to quietly slip into her chamber whenever it was possible. A fire had now been kindled and I found that I was even becoming jealous of the time that my princess spent in the inner sanctum with the emperor whose devotion to his beloved daughter was open and unashamed.

There used to be great excitement when the *durzees* (court tailors) would visit the *zenana* usually in the late afternoons. One day they brought some pyjamas made of a very fine new silk from China. With a yelp of joy Roshanara rushed up and eagerly grabbed one in a bright pink colour while Jahanara picked up one in a pale shade of green. When she put it on and walked about to see how it fitted it showed every curve of her form so seductively that my mouth became dry with hunger and longing. Much later that night I marveled at how the contours of her body felt as my hands slowly glided over the soft shimmering fabric. The excitement and intimacy between us made me shiver involuntarily.

Our secret encounters continued for several months but we had to be very careful as the *zenana* was often too busy at nightfall for me to be able to enter Jahanara's chamber. Our trysts were nearly exposed one night when I picked up a pigeon's feather and asked Jahanara to close her eyes and lie very still. She began to giggle and squirm deliciously when I used the feather to tickle her behind the ear and along the sides of her lips and eyes. Emboldened by her eager response I moved the feather down the side of her neck and over her breasts where the little raisins stiffened with pleasure. Gently pulling aside her clothes I continued to use the feather to explore her entire body. She almost cried out when I tickled the soles of her feet and was getting increasingly aroused as I moved up to stimulate her back. But she cried out involuntary when I began to tease the mounts of her womanhood.

Her cry was loud enough to attract the attention of some of the other slaves who we could hear rushing up to enquire if there was anything amiss. I hastily hid behind a small closet and lay as still as my heavy breathing would allow. Jahanara rose, collected her scattered clothes and unbolted the door to assure the anxious slaves that she had only had a bad dream and that all was well.

The adult princes had their own chambers in the palace but as they grew older began to live at their own havelis. Dara lived in a large estate on the side of the Jumna River not far from the fort. The other princes seldom stayed at the capital except for when they were summoned by the emperor for special ceremonies or events. The emperor would sometimes visit the palaces of his sons if there were a banquet, a birthday, a new baby, a wedding or some other special occasion.

One day Dara invited our emperor to his beautiful newly constructed haveli for a feast. He also went personally to all the princes and princesses to request them to attend. Except for Aurangzeb they all readily accepted but Aurangzeb scowled and asked, "Why this extravagance *bhai jaan*? We all make or refurbish new palaces. What need is there for a lavish banquet to boast that you possess so many beautiful things? But thank you, I will definitely attend unless I am summoned on some duty."

Dara ignored the sarcasm in his voice and mildly said, "I am very glad because I have a special present for all the guests and something for you that I am sure you will appreciate.", hoping he could convince his younger brother to attend this grand feast.

There was great excitement among the emperor's family who had never been there before. Rich purple carpets with silken cushions, and silver and gold embroidery covered the floor of a large and cool underground hall beside the river and there were special large mirrors imported from Aleppo[8], to decorate the walls with the result that the hall seemed to be of infinite size. I was very amused to see how both the ladies and the men kept glancing up to discreetly admire their own images or to stare at some of the others who did not know that they were being watched.

Huge five tiered golden vessels offered a profusion of delicious dishes while ambergris, eaglewood, sandalwood and other kinds of fragrant wood burned slowly in silver braziers to perfume the air, while a large silver trough with the necks of seven serpents sprinkled scented rose water. Several ladies from the emperor's *zenana* accompanied him and what a sight it was with the faces of the most beautiful ladies of the realm visible in this hall without their purdahs. I doubt that the world had ever seen so many beautiful and magnificently attired women ever before. Some of the younger princesses brought a large silver bowl and a golden vessel to help the emperor to wash his hands. The guests also washed their hands the same way with the slaves helping them. The water would be very carefully poured

---

8 Sir Jadunath Sarkar cites a manuscript by Hamiduddin in his History of Aurangzeb (p79)

from a golden urn with a curved snout. A silver sieve would be held under the hands so that the water fell softly into the shallow silver pan below. A very soft *mul mul safi* (small muslin towel) would then be offered to dry the hands. At the end of the meal this routine was repeated.

After a deafening sound of cymbals, drums and trumpets, the feast would begin as slaves richly attired in bright silk pyjamas of different colours and coats of fine white muslin brought forth a long procession of dishes laden with the choicest foods in the empire. The guests, turn by turn, sampled small helpings of the many delicious offerings for nearly four hours. The slaves also went to all the guests offering small cups of the finest wines. At the end the guests were presented a new specially concocted frozen sherbet made from the pulp of apricots and plums chilled with crushed ice, brought down from the mountains of the north.

The feast was not just a feast for the palate but for the eyes as well and a number of sinuous dancing girls with tiny bells tinkling on their dainty ankles and bracelets on their arms came turn by turn laden with some of the finest jewels from the imperial *toshakhana* to dazzle all of us. An offering of *paan* generally signalled the end of a meal. *Paan*, also called *beeda*, would be offered in a gold or silver *tabak* or tray. Sculpted silver and a few gold *peekdaans* (spittoons) would be placed near the diners for them to spit the chewed *paan* into.

Prince Aurangzeb, like all the other princes, had arrived but he refused to enter the hall and sat down conspicuously on the stairs near the entrance where he partly blocked the entry of the other guests. He later offered a ridiculous explanation that he had been suspicious that with just one entrance door to the hall Dara could have easily made all his guests prisoners.

He was later persuaded to enter but refused to eat anything and then, on the plea that he had to say his prayers, suddenly stood up and left the gathering without royal permission. Shah Jahan became so angry at this rude behaviour that he barred him from the court for seven months. It was the gracious princess Jahanara who later remonstrated with the emperor and restored the disgraced prince to the emperor's favour but he was again sent away from Delhi to a distant command.

I then heard a whispered remark from the little princess Gauharara who had quietly entered and was sitting next to me... *"Nazar! Nazar! Nazar*! The evil eye will every time haunt the one who now seems to be the most fortunate. The envy in every eye and the envy in the hearts of all the spirits that are witnessing this event can turn this golden glory into dross. No one can be called fortunate until after death closes the gate. All good fortune is but a passing fancy. A mirage! A beautiful shimmering mirage!"

Shah Jahan kept the huge territory around the capital under his direct authority in the hope that his sons would be so occupied in distant regions as to pose little threat to each other and also too distant from each other to unite against him. But as events were to later reveal even the best laid plans of mortal men become as worthless as specks of sand in a desert when *kismet* so wills it.

Life moves us bodily from one place to another

...but it is fate that determines all our destinations.

Chapter 8

The Courting of Nadira

Inscrutable indeed are the ways of destiny. Who could have known that from the loins of a once penniless Persian nobleman called Ghiyas Beg there should issue three of the most beautiful and powerful ladies to grace the Mughal Empire. He had first appeared in the court of Jahangir as a penniless nobleman but his charm, culture, intelligence and elegant words helped him rise quickly until he become the Khan-e-Khanam or the Prime Minister, the most powerful of all the noblemen of the realm. He was later titled Itmad-ud-Daulah that meant 'pillar of the empire'. His daughter, the beautiful but scheming Noorjahan, was to become Jahangir's twentieth but favourite wife. Later his equally beautiful granddaughter Arjumand Bano begum became Shah Jahan's chief wife and came to be known as Mumtaz Mahal. A generation later, it was her niece who was to captivate prince Dara.

All these women combined exceptional beauty with high intelligence, wit and the ability to cheerfully suffer the tribulations of long rough travel and make huge personal sacrifices for their royal consorts. They also had the rare gift of being able to make their husbands laugh, which, I discovered, was the best way to a man's heart. Ghias Beg's wife Asmat begum had endured great hardships while coming from Persia to Hindustan and may have taught her children and grandchildren to do the same and become such perfect companions to their husbands that they would look at no other woman when they were there. Mumtaz had also suffered terrible privations for five years while the future emperor was a rebel fugitive. Despite great hardships while being chased all over Hindustan she had not only endured the hard travel and rough food but had delivered four children.

The ladies of the *zenana* waited eagerly for Holi one of the many Hindu festivals celebrated by the Mughals from the time of Akbar. It was a joyous festival celebrating the advent of spring, where coloured water and coloured powder were thrown in a frenzy of gay abandon followed by feasting with music, dancing and the drinking of cool beverages — liberally laced with small doses of the intoxicating bhang. While the ladies delicately sprayed each other with coloured water the men would be rougher. They would scoop up coloured water with leather mugs from large cauldrons and splash everyone. On Holi, everyone from nobles to common citizens set aside all their protocols and mixed without regard to status or religion. They also abandoned all responsibility and spent the day in happy revelry. It was, therefore, of little surprise that an unusually large crop of babies would follow towards the end of the year.

While Holi marked the advent of spring on dates according to the lunar calendar, the nobles of the court also enthusiastically followed another spring festival that was set according to the solar calendar. This began from the time of

Humayun and was the Persian festival of Nauroz marking the spring equinox. The eighteen day festivities included a small three day mock bazaar set up just after dark with many bright lights. It was held inside a big courtyard of the palace called the Mina Bazaar where the ladies of the court and the wives of the leading courtiers would set up little stalls, as if they were common shopkeepers, out to entice the patronage of the emperor, princes and other great Muslim nobles. The charming sellers without purdah would set out their wares and haggle like fishwives while simultaneously flirting outrageously. The buyers, pretending to bargain, were quite easily persuaded to part with huge sums for their tawdry trinkets.

This bazaar was also an occasion when many pretty young ladies from all the noble families were allowed to venture out of the jealously guarded privacy of their own *zenanas* to be seen by the other nobles of the realm. Not surprisingly, many encounters would result in betrothals and marriages. The eye of the emperor would, however, sometimes fall upon the wives or daughters of some of the noblemen and there were many who were quite willing to gratify the emperor in the hope that their husbands or fathers might gain high imperial position, valuable gifts or other honours.

The graceful Jahanara had set up a small table where she displayed some very cleverly crafted glass animals and birds secured from the Portuguese at Surat. Princess Roshanarahad a basket of colourful glass bangles that she had secured from the Deccan. Her slightly twisted face looked unhappy as very few courtiers would stop to enquire about the goods that she was offering for sale. Even the baby princess Gauharara was enjoying herself as visitors bought some of the little cloth dolls she was selling.

Some of the wives and daughters of the leading Umraos also had little stalls including one displaying a number of very colourful velvet Turkish slippers called barbushes set up by the beautiful red headed wife of Khalilullah Khan, one of the empire's leading Afghan generals. The emperor seemed quite captivated by her and while passing, I heard her saucily hint that she quite willing to be squirreled into the *zenana* later that night.

This flirtatious scene was then quite unexpectedly disrupted when the normally very quiet little Gauharara suddenly knocked over her table of and began screaming, ... "No! No! No! ... Bad! Bad! Bad! ... Abbajan go! Abbajan go! ... Abbajan go from here! ... Go from this woman!"

Everyone was very surprised at the vehemence of this little girl and could not understand why she was so upset. The emperor however laughed it off, picked her up and kissed her before handing the weeping child to her maid.

The flirtatious lady was to become quite a regular visitor to the emperor's chambers but none of us ever suspected that this casual affair would one day shake our very destinies. It was much later that we learned the affair had caused great anger and jealousy to her husband. Though this important Mughal general was a fierce warrior on the battlefield, he quailed before his wife's fiery temper and became an object of widespread mockery, when word got out that she had roundly beaten him with her pretty barbouches when he reproached her for her infidelity. This seed of petty jealousy was the main contributor to the most devastating betrayal and catastrophe.

It was during the excitement of this festive occasion that Dara Shikoh first set eyes on Nadira Bano, his late mother's niece as well as the daughter of Shah Jahan's dead, elder, half, brother Parvez. Nadira had inherited her aunt's graceful beauty and serene temperament. She was not as tall as Arjumand Begum and her greenish eyes were of a lighter shade, illuminated with streaks of gold and brown. When he saw her, Dara seemed to lose interest in all the other beauties in the hall and spent an inordinately long time haggling dreamily with just this one flower seller. Everyone laughed when he later emerged triumphantly carrying a gigantic bundle of roses.

Dara married her two years later and was to remain her devoted companion for twenty five years. Like all Mughal princes he was expected to have a number of wives and concubines but after Nadira entered his life he just did not seem interested in other women. During the later part of his life however, the prince grew arrogant and began to stray, finding solace in the arms of concubines and dancing girls, but it was only his one true love that was to stand by his side to the very end, never once faltering in her devotion. Nadira was so deeply devoted to his happiness that she was to herself introduce a few beautiful concubines into her *zenana* to please her beloved husband when she was indisposed or in an advanced state of pregnancy.

Two years later, there was great excitement at the court when the preparations for the grand wedding began at the mansion of Nadira's late father. Dara, who was almost consumed with impatience, sent me to her house constantly bearing some gift or other to declare his undying devotion.

Just before it was time for Nadira to observe *maaiyu* (a ritual period of seclusion before the marriage ceremony) all her male relatives came to see her before she retreated into a quiet corner of her *zenana*. During these days no male member of the household, not even her own male relatives, were allowed to see her until it was time for her to bid goodbye to her family after the *nikah* ceremony. Nadira was escorted by the ladies to a large, beautifully adorned, hall that was to be her retreat during this period of *maaiyu*. She was divested of all her beautiful jewellery and was made to change into simple soft lightly coloured garments

She now had to lie on a large finely carved bed, with solid silver legs over which was stretched a richly embroidered *palangposh* (bed cover) with motifs of flowers, fruits, leaves and birds. Two large velvet *masnads* (bolsters) and several small intricately decorated cushions were then placed on the bed. Nadira was then led to this bed which she was not to leave until her wedding day except to bathe or relieve herself. She was not allowed to do anything on her own and had to submit herself completely to a group of ladies entrusted with the task of making her look as beautiful as the full moon on the day of her wedding.

A long stream of merchants eagerly awaited their turn to present the finest wares of the world for approval and purchase by the family of the bride. As their entry into the *zenana* was strictly forbidden they would display their precious items on large silver platters brought out by the household servants who then placed them before the royal ladies for their selection. Apart from the bride all the other ladies were keenly interested as they all also wanted to look their best on the great day. A mood of gaiety pervaded the *zenana*; there was much light hearted bantering including some mild bawdy chatter with the undulating beat of the *dholak* (drum) sounding in the background.

I stood at a short distance, thoroughly enjoying the happy scene. The richly attired and bejewelled women all sat together, teasing each other and joyfully expressing their appreciation of the rich offerings being presented one after another. They were constantly passing on some bauble or silky stuff for the perusal of another or leaning over each other to have a closer look. Minstrels in a hidden alcove sang old songs praising the delicate beauty of the bride and the masculine good looks of the groom

What a dilemma for the ladies! It was so difficult to choose from all the rich fabrics. The warm red browns and bright green *'tie and dye'* fabrics that Nadira's great grandmother and grandmother had worn, or the *phulkaris* of the north-the exotic colourful embroidery of Kutch and Kathiawar with small fragments of mirror stitched into the fabric like paillettes that her grandfather Akbar had brought to the court and made popular among the nobility. There were gold brocades from Benares, Chinese silks and satins brought from the port of Surat with patterns bearing romantic names in praise of the moon, stars, sunshine, nightingale's eyes, or a peacock's neck. The *Mul Mul* (muslins) from Macchlipatnam, a port city of the Deccan and from Dacca in Bengal that was so light and fine that a full thirty yard length of it could be put inside a coconut shell.

Jahanara had for some time been holding a delicate piece of *sansani* fabric, sometimes against the light and sometimes against herself to see how the pleats fell. Roshanara, who till now had been sitting aloof showing neither pleasure or appreciation, suddenly nudged one of her small group of

personal attendants and said in a loud whisper, "...and why is my beloved elder sister so besotted with that flimsy piece of *sansani*? Is she planning to spread some sensation herself? Are we perchance going to celebrate her wedding sometime soon?"

One of her giggling cronies now mischievously asked, "But pray, who will be the lucky man?"

Everyone looked down in an uncomfortable silence pregnant with malicious curiosity.

"...Who knows? Perhaps it will be Mubarak... Who else!" cried Roshanara shrieking in high pitched laughter.

Her gaze shifted from Jahanara to me with ill disguised scorn but everyone could see the vicious pleasure she was getting from embarrassing her sister and humiliating me. One of her friends hooted with raucous laughter along with a few embarrassed giggles from some of the women, though most of them looked down and delicately put their hands to their mouths.

Emboldened by the response Roshanara loudly continued, "But no! how can that be? There will also have to be the *dawat-e-walima* (consummation ceremony) as well! How can that be?"

Giggling loudly her sycophantic friend again took up the sordid theme "Yes! How can the marriage to be consummated if the groom is a eunuch?"

This was followed by loud shrieks of laughter and Jahanara flushed red in great distress though she was too dignified to stoop to an angry or sarcastic retort. I was now sweating and absolutely mortified to suddenly be the centre of all this bawdy attention. But questions angrily churned in my mind.

Why was Roshanara using me to insult Jahanara?

What did she know of our secret attachment to each other?

We had been so discreet in the sharing of our love but had anyone observed us?

Could anyone have guessed our affection from our unguarded glances at each other?

I was torn between raging anger at this wicked woman and deep anguish for my beloved princess who was being so viciously humiliated. But I was helpless. I could say nothing. As a poor court eunuch, I had to know my place. I had to swallow my pride and suppress the vicious retorts that welled up to the tip of my tongue.

Under the pretext of going out to fetch some *paan* and *sherbet* I retreated to the farthest corner of the hall and then quietly slipped away. I staggered to a small balcony overlooking the river and sat there seething with anger for a very long time. The emotions I had so desperately tried to hold back now turned to tears of frustration and flowed unchecked down my cheeks as a dull ache gripped my heart. I may have been just a slave and a eunuch but I was still a man and would never forgive this malicious princess. One day, I swore to myself, I would have my vengeance.

Evening was setting in and the ripples on the river flashed red and gold like reflections of a flickering fire on a burnished copper shield. A cool breeze began to blow from the river and birds flew homeward to their nests. Cattle lowed mournfully as they were being herded home. Little lights came on, one by one, in the homes all along the far shore. There seemed to be, I thought, some purpose to everything except for my own miserable existence.

I, suddenly heard my name being softly called and turned to see Jahanara standing before me, looking at me full in the face. I marvelled at the delicacy of her beauty. The soft light from the early stars seemed to impart a dream like quality to her lovely face. My heart lurched and I stood up and said with more force than I intended, "Do not let your sister's poisonous tongue upset you. Remember the Persian proverb... *she has swallowed so many serpents that she has herself become a viper*. Too many people love and respect you and her malicious words will soon be forgotten if, we can pretend that they do not affect us."

She studied me and slowly came closer and put her arms around my neck. We stood there feeling the warmth of our bodies and marvelling how their contours seemed to so perfectly fit into each other. But I noticed something in those eyes that I had not seen before. She spoke softly, "I wish with all my heart that Roshanara's cruel taunt might have been true and that we were not so sadly cursed ... you with your manhood torn out of you and me a prisoner of the command of my great grandfather."

"Yes", I whispered "How I wish we could just quietly go away somewhere and be together without all these prying eyes following us."

She held me closely, "I know that we will always be in each other's thoughts and who knows, perhaps we may someday be able to get away from all the intrigues of the court. Perhaps we may be able to live quietly in a beautiful forest near a river or lake. Would it not be wonderful?"

I felt her smiling; her optimism gave me strength as I embraced her tighter.

Dara and Nadira, what a marriage it was!

In the end, I was told, it cost three million rupees though half of it was borne by Nadira's wealthy family. The four royal princes rode together with their entourage and made a grand entrance at the Diwan-i-Am from Dara's palace on the Jumna. It was celebrated with the biggest display of fireworks the empire had ever seen. The emperor gave Dara a string of huge pearls and a robe of pearly white shimmering brocade and placed his crown on Dara's head as Jahangir had earlier done for Shah Jahan on the day of his own marriage. Everyone cheered except for Aurangzeb whose pale countenance looked as indifferent as always.

The groom and all the male family members with him first performed the *hennabandi*, a Hindu ritual that had now become a Mughal custom. The men thrust their hands, palms up, through a sheer cloth screen so that the ladies sitting on the opposite side could decorate them with a mixture of henna and turmeric. Dara accompanied by Shuja, Murad and Aurangzeb followed the emperor on horses as the groom's family made their way to Nadira's home.

The *nikah* ceremony took place at an auspicious time carefully set by our astrologers for just after midnight. The emperor and Nadira's uncle, representing her late father, sat solemnly as the Maulvi in black robes conducted the ceremony. The bride and groom sat some distance from each other in separate enclosures. The *Nikahnama*, or the legally binding contract in which the *Meher*, or marriage gifts, specifically detailed was separately signed by the groom and the bride.

Everyone congratulated each other after the ceremony was over. Dara bowed before the emperor who reached out and embraced his most beloved son. Her mother assured Nadira of the great love and care that she'd get in her new home as she warmly embraced her. Dara was now led into Nadira's inner quarters where women of all ages awaited him. First the older women relatives blessed the young couple. As the elders withdrew, the younger women eagerly rushed in and began to tease the bride and groom. Outside, the guests presented their lavish gifts that included many jewels, fine clothes, horses and elephants. A grand wedding banquet was presented to the thousands of guests and the entire riverfront was aflame with bursting fireworks. It was a truly unforgettable event in which everyone celebrated. The festivities continued late into the night till the first rays of the sun were seen and then, the proceedings of the ceremony of *Rukhsat*, or the sending away of the bride, began.

Dara, who had been resting in the *Mardana*, or men's portion, was now led back to Nadira and seated beside her. A light meal was served to them. The women fed small delicacies to Dara who very graciously tried to please them all by accepting small portions of every offering. Nadira wept quietly and despite insistent cajoling ate almost nothing. Several curious rites were performed by the women to ward off the evil eye -- whole red chilies were waved around their heads and flung over burning coals; they would every now and then circle their heads with their closed palms and then knead their knuckles on their heads - all this to the accompaniment of blessings.

Sad songs of *bidai,* or departure, were sung by the women without any musical instruments. Nadira was then gently led out of her father's home. A copy of the holy

Koran was held over her head and a sequined red cloth stretched over it as she was guided into the *doli* or bridal palanquin. Overcome by emotion she was now sobbing uncontrollably.

I accompanied the procession to Dara's palace where the bride was greeted by the women of his family, who again held a Quran and red cloth above the head of their new daughter-in-law. Joyous songs were sung, blessing the newlyweds and sweets were distributed. Nadira was seated and the ladies of her new home lifted the veil modestly covering her face, and uttered exclaimations of joy at her beauty and gave her their gifts. Nadira's family now offered the customary *nazzar* or tribute in the form of several small presents. She then offered the most exquisite gifts her uncle had provided for Dara's sisters and other royal ladies of her new home.

A number of other small ceremonies continued till it was dark and Nadira was escorted to the bridal chamber, which was fragrant with flowers. Small rituals were followed by laughter and teasing. Gold dust was applied to Nadira's eyelids and lips and a sweet smelling *ittar*, or rose perfume, was rubbed with a cotton swab on the pulse spots of her face, neck and wrists. She was then made to sit on a bed of flowers with her feet folded to one side and her palms resting on her knees.

Words of advice and encouragement came from all directions.

"Say *salaam* when he lifts the veil", one suggested. "Don't refuse him any wish", advised another. "Don't forget to offer the milk and the *paan*", someone else added.

An older woman, placing her hand affectionately around the bride's shoulder whispered some advice into her ear and then quietly said, "You very well know that any marriage is *mukammal*... or valid only when the wife's womb bears fruit. You have to ensure that this happens at the very earliest." "Of course it will be so," said another lady, "the bride and groom are in love with each other and our beloved emperor will surely have a grandson within a year."

Amid peals of happy laughter all the women except one female attendant now withdrew, leaving the bride alone in her chamber. Tired and happy, most of the occupants of the *zenana* then retired to their own rooms. In a corner the singing, however, continued.

Dara now appeared with a single attendant, who also withdrew as the prince neared the bridal chamber. But there was to be no rest for me. Before retreating I brought out the small bundle tucked away in my pocket and Dara, taking it from my hands, turned around and disappeared into the bridal chamber. He would now lift Nadira's veil and offer the most exquisitely worked necklace studded with priceless gems. It was his first personal gift as a husband to his new bride.

"O Allah", I prayed in my heart, "grant them bliss and many beautiful children ".

Just before it was light, the next morning, the groom went back to his own chamber. Though Dara did not call me, I was immediately awakened by the laughter and giggles coming from the bridal chamber. Several young ladies and Nadira's personal maids were now there and another beauty ritual began.

Some of the older women of the *zenana* followed and the senior most lady discretely took Nadira aside and anxiously asked whether the marriage had been consummated.

Nadira's shy nod of affirmation was greeted with loud cries of happiness. In the evening, there was the *Dawat –e-Walima* or the banquet for the celebration of the consummation of marriage where the ladies feasted in the ladies *zenana* while the men celebrated in the *Mardana*, or men's quarter. On the fourth day, the bride, along with some women of her new family, visited her parental home where they were treated to another lavish banquet before returning to her new home.

Marriage is the golden ring

... it begins with a glance and ends in eternity

CHAPTER 9

Deccan Diversion

Shortly after the accession of our emperor, his former adversary Malik Amber, a clever Abyssinian who had governed Bijapur, died and the Deccan was again thrown into turmoil. The rich lands south of the Narmada River had been conquered several times but the Mughals could not establish a stable rule over the five Shahi rulers of Berar, Ahmadnagar, Golconda, Bidar and Bijapur. These Mughal vassals had become wealthy and powerful and would shamelessly throw off their pledged loyalties, whenever they felt Mughal power seemed weak or ineffectual.

When numerous ploys had failed to settle the states of the Deccan, Shah Jahan decided to personally lead a huge Mughal army to the south. After a quick series of skirmishes and diplomatic manoeuvres, several treaties were made with the rulers one after another and he gained huge indemnities for the empire. The emperor returned triumphantly leaving Aurangzeb as his viceroy at the town of Khirki that was later renamed Aurangabad. Little did Aurangzeb know that he would be destined to spend most of his life here and later be buried here as well.

Shah Jahan knew that he had to be prudent concerning the possible ambitions of his sons but it was becoming clear that he felt threatened only by Aurangzeb. Although Aurangzeb was aware that I was closest to his eldest brother, I had always been very careful to maintain good relations with him. I was also very curious to see how he had matured since the time when I, as a young slave, had served him at Jhansi and Orchha.

One morning, when he had been summoned to the court I visited him, gifting him a beautiful small book based on stories from the Holy Quran. He thanked me coolly, when I congratulated him on being given such an important command. I, then hesitantly asked if he would be generous enough to allow me to join his entourage once again. He looked at me steadily for a few seconds and then said, "So after many soft years in the service at the *zenana* you wish to do some hard campaigning once again, do you?"

I replied with great deference that even though I might be just a poor eunuch, I was man enough to ride a horse, wield a sword and bear the hardships of a soldier. I also reminded him of how diligently I had served him earlier. He looked at me steadily with his hard black eyes, in which light seldom shone, and said, "Yes, I remember that you had served me honestly and diligently in Jhansi and Orchha. You work hard and have never betrayed me. I will think about it. Come and see me tomorrow."

I was aware of Aurangzeb's ruthless reputation and knew what it would have meant to be on his wrong side. I was beginning to sense that the rising ambitions of all the young princes would one day lead to conflict and therefore wanted to know more about the waging of war so that I might also be useful on the battlefield one day.

This time, too, I was made responsible for his treasure. Our advance party with a battalion of a thousand horsemen made a fast journey in double stages to Aurangabad, arriving in just three weeks. I quickly discovered that the Deccan was very different from the gentle terrain of the north with undulating plains covered by thorny trees growing mostly on dry red rocky soil. There were some fertile areas of black earth surrounded by a large number of very strange hills that rose abruptly from the plains in very steep slopes to great height with flat mountain tops. These hills were natural fortresses from where a defender could easily see and shoot down any attacker who dared to climb the escarpments. It was not suitable for Mughal cavalry except for the rather narrow plains between the hills.

While the climate of the region could be quite pleasant in winter, it suffered from unbelievably heavy rainfall in the monsoon months that turned dry water courses into raging torrents of dirty red water. There could be unremitting heavy rain for days on end that would wear down the nerves of soldiers stuck inside their leaking tents. This rain made the hard soil turn into sticky red clay that clung to the feet and discoloured the clothes while numerous insects and snakes would suddenly appear. To add to our misery, the soldiers and their horses would be attacked by disgusting blood sucking leaches and would suffer from numerous sores and sicknesses. The long summers, however, were very dry and hot and there could be severe famines if the rains failed in any year.

It was fortunate for us that the enemies of imperial forces from the vassal Shahi states also preferred to fight as we did on the open plains where cavalry could work effectively. But we were being increasingly harassed by small bands of hardy Maratha bandits who would fall upon any unprotected baggage train and then vanish with their plunder into the hills. They were very difficult to pursue because they knew the steep mountains and the paths that went through them. The few Maratha infantrymen in our ranks were very tough though often loud and quarrelsome. Many were to later become competent cavalrymen as well. We did not know it at this time but with the training in arms that the Marathas received in our service and in the Golkonda and Bijapur armies, they would later become formidable enemies who were eventually destined to shake the Mughal Empire to the core.

The attacks of these Maratha raiders were very troublesome. They would ambush the trading caravans passing through Aurangabad, laden with goods travelling from the east coast towns towards ports on the west coast. The caravan masters would beg us for protection against the depredations of these savage *dacoits*. One day Aurangzeb was outraged when it was reported that these brigands even had the temerity to attack and loot a peaceful town, under our protection, on the banks of a river flowing from the high ghats (hill slopes) to the west. One of our commanders Shabat Khan now came forward and bowing low said that he knew the area and asked permission to mount a punitive raid on the stronghold of these savage bandits.

Aurangzeb reluctantly gave me permission to join Shabat's retaliatory raid. Shabat was a wiry officer with a short beard and the fierce yellowish eyes of a tiger but he possessed a clever and resourceful mind. He gathered together a team of officers and explained that as the bandits had spies in every town we needed to move with great speed and stealth. We, immediately, set out to a small town on a tributary of the east flowing Godavari River and waited for a caravan belonging to a rich caravan master to arrive. We persuaded him to bring his caravan of about twenty carts into a large walled courtyard and empty all his goods into a few big huts that were locked up safely. Under cover of darkness some five hundred horsemen and troopers now arrived. At dawn when the caravan left, each covered cart carried about ten fully armed soldiers. I travelled with this caravan that was, as usual, accompanied by a small guard of about ten armed *paidas*, or bare legged foot soldiers, and an equal number of horsemen.

Two hours before dawn while it was still dark, Shabat led the rest of his group of some three hundred horsemen and first went southwards to deceive anyone who might have been watching his movements. He then turned westwards up another valley parallel to the valley where our bullock carts were to leisurely travel. By the time the sun had come up they had reached a small pass connecting the two valleys and the soldiers dismounted and hid in a thick forest above the plain to rest and wait for events to unfold.

About an hour after sunrise, we heard distant whistles and saw some mirrors flashing on the escarpments above us and knew that the bandits were watching the movement of our caravan and signalling to each other. I was sitting in the leading cart and saw fields of bajri, a tall millet seed, growing on the roughly ploughed fields of black soil. The small villages around us had shabby huts made of stones and thatch surrounded by walls of thick thorns to keep out tigers, leopards and even a few lions that would otherwise prey on their skinny cattle and goats.

The caravan route on the left bank of a little river, now went through a narrow defile that we knew would be the perfect place for an ambush. Sure enough, we were not disappointed. Suddenly about a hundred bandits astride short wiry horses rushed out of a small ravine on our left, followed by an equal number of screaming armed *paidas*. Our caravan guards now turned and ran back towards the carts to encourage the bandits to follow them. When they were about twenty paces away our soldiers pulled back the thick cloths covering of the carts and opened a withering fusillade of musket shots and arrows at close range. Scores of bandits fell off their little ponies and lay dead or dying in front of us in a screaming mass of tangled bodies.

Our soldiers then climbed down from the carts and crawled under them from where they were safe to continue firing. One group of bandits managed to survive the fusillade and again spurred their horses towards our carts. I, along with the other soldiers, hastily climbed out from under the carts to fight them off with all our strength. The charges of our muskets were now spent so we had to rely on our swords and lances.

One of the bare legged Marathas protected only by a thick cotton coat and a cloth turban tightly wrapped around his head, rushed at me. I turned as if to flee but continued the turn to face the surprised attacker and slashed his right shoulder with my sword. He cried out in pain but continued to attack and we exchanged several sword strokes till he began to weaken and I was able to thrust my sword through his stomach. I had no time to gloat as the fighting was furious all around me. One of my companions had been injured by a tall Maratha who was advancing to kill him so I slashed at his legs making him fall down. It took us several minutes before we were able to subdue the rest of the attackers. The other bandits tried to retreat and return our fire from behind a screen of big rocks but they soon became a dense confused mass as more Marathas, unaware of the carnage in front of them, continued to pour down the little valley behind them.

Shabat and his horsemen had in the meantime, quietly cantered down the hill and now charged at them from the rear. Caught in a pincer, the bandits were helpless, though many of them scattered and tried to cross the muddy river or scramble up the rocky cliffs around us. But Shabat was not satisfied with this victory. More than fifty bandits were dead and more than twice that number were injured. After ruthlessly slaughtering most of the wounded bandits and sending back the prisoners in our carts he cruelly tortured them to tell us where their hideout was located. Without waiting to give the enemy any time to regroup, he immediately turned our troop of horsemen west to seek out their village some four Kos away on a plateau above the little river.

Because of the rough and rocky ground it took us over two hours to reach this habitation of a dozen stone houses and about a hundred thatched huts. The little plateau was surrounded by steep cliffs so the poor inhabitants, who had only just learned of their defeat, had nowhere to flee to. The Mughals, despite having a sneaking respect for their fighting skills, hated the Marathas who they considered to be uncouth and loud. So they mercilessly killed every man and raped almost all the women. This rape was not for pleasure but as a humiliating punishment that the women and their families would never forget. Shabat Khan insisted that the Maratha women should not be killed as he wanted them to live to tell their people of what terrible fate lay in store for those who dared to challenge the Mughal might.

We found quite a large hoard of gold, silver, jewels and

other treasures in one of the stone houses as well as ten excellent short muskets that the bandits must have looted from the Portuguese. We also released about twenty women made prisoners by the Marathas including two high born ladies for who they had been demanding large ransoms.

We returned to Aurangabad in triumph where Aurangzeb raised Shabat Khan's rank to two thousand horse and announced that the Marathas had received a lesson they would never forget. But, unfortunately, this was a lesson that would have to be repeated again and again. Ten days later we were deeply shocked to learn that one of the Marathas had sneaked into Shabat Khan's tent at night and slit his throat. A month later their bandits had the audacity to loot and mercilessly plunder one of our towns just five *Kos* from Aurangabad.

I now remembered what a Buddhist scholar had told Dara in Kashmir that hatred could never be conquered by hatred but only by love. But who among these strutting warriors would listen to such pacifist sentiments.

When I got back to Agra after an absence of six months, I observed that the emperor was getting very worried about his sons. Even though Aurangzeb had been a dutiful commander, the emperor never seemed able to trust him and his military successes appeared to make him even more anxious. He was also getting increasingly troubled by reports that Aurangzeb was not remitting the full indemnities extracted from the *shahi* princes in their treaties and suspected that his third son was keeping back some of it to possibly build up a personal war chest.

Because of the constant friction between Dara and Aurangzeb, the Emperor continued his practice of sending the younger prince to distant commands while Dara was always kept by his father's side. I later realized that this was to result in Aurangzeb gaining very useful administrative and battle experience while Dara led an increasingly pampered life in Agra. Thus, paradoxically the emperor weakened his favourite son while making his third son an angry but experienced military commander.

The tension between the princes kept growing. One day, the emperor flew into a towering rage over a most trivial matter when Aurangzeb was tardy with sending him some especially tasty mangoes from a particular tree growing at Burhanpur. By the time they arrived at the court they were over ripe and inedible. Then the emperor's anger exploded a few months later when Aurangzeb did not immediately abandon his other responsibilities and rush back to Agra when princess Jahanara suffered very severe burn injuries on her lower body after her dress accidentally caught fire.

I too, was only able to return with Aurangzeb and only then learned all about the terrible tragedy. The ladies of the *zenana* used to wear a long muslin *Peshwaz* and the princess had accidentally walked too close to an oil lamp placed on the ground. When the delicate fabric flared up, three of her maids rushed to try and smother the flames and they too suffered severe burns before enough water could be fetched to smother the blaze. Two of the maids later died and our princess was in the most acute agony. Everyone loved Jahanara and was deeply distressed but none more than this poor slave who seemed to feel every twinge of her pain.

The emperor, who was deeply devoted to his family, was so distraught when his most beloved child was in such acute suffering for nearly three months that he couldn't concentrate on the affairs of the state. Her condition became so critical that after all the Muslim *hakims* and Hindu *vaids* seemed to have failed; a tall red faced English doctor called Gabriel Boughton was summoned from Surat to her side. He had to be covered from head to toe with a huge thick cloth before being permitted to enter the *zenana* and examine Jahanara. He scoffed at the medications that were being administered by our *hakims* and applied his own salve that began to take affect after a few days.

We got regular reports about Bengal where the indolent prince Shuja ruled his *subbah* efficiently enough for him to have been retained at his post for eighteen years. He ruled quite well even though he was reputed to spend whole days and nights drinking, singing and cavorting with dancers. Though Bengal was a rich *subedari*, it was so uncomfortably hot, humid and so infested with reptiles and insects that it was considered a punishment post.

Early in his rule, the emperor faced a challenge from the arrogant Portuguese, who ruled the seas from China to Africa with their big well armed sailing ships. They were exceeding all bounds by harassing the people, committing cruel acts of piracy from their port on the Hoogly River and ruining the trade from our own port at Satgaon further upstream. Their habit of kidnapping young children and forcing them to follow their religion could not also be allowed to go without chastisement.

Qasim Khan, the Mughal governor at Satgaon, laid siege to the town by blocking the wide river with a number of boats chained together to block reinforcements coming up from the sea. He then secretly laid explosives in a tunnel under the battlements and then pretended to prepare for an attack. As the Portuguese defenders collected to defend the gate a huge mine was set off killing hundreds. The cowardly men quickly abandoned the fort and broke through the barrage of boats with a flaming raft leaving about four thousand women and children to their fate. Qasim Khan ordered the prisoners to be marched to Agra in a pitiful procession that took eleven months. All their plaintive prayers to their idols of the Virgin Mary and many other saints proved futile and hundreds perished on the terrible journey. The men were given the option of death or converting to Islam while the women and children were sold into slavery. Jahanara took one pretty freckled girl to serve her and later got her suitably married to a nobleman.

Gujarat was another important province but Prince Murad Baksh was too young to rule it when his brothers were appointed as governors in the north, east and south. Surat was the most important Mughal port. Twelve years later, the twenty eight year old Murad, now a tall, brave, handsome but foolhardy youngest prince, was given the *subadari* over this important territory. He ruled this area without any great achievements to distinguish his languid rule.

Surat was a rich and bustling port and due to Gujarat being a peaceful area, the port city had few fortifications. Some of the Arab *dhows* were large enough to be able to carry over two hundred sailors and passengers. They arrived from the west with the summer monsoon winds and brought in Abyssinian slaves, ivory and mahogany from Africa and the best horses for the Mughal armies from Arabia. They used to also take back large shiploads of ordinary stones and bricks that were scarce in the desert regions of Arabia, along with more valuable cargos of grain, salt peter, textiles and spices with the winter monsoon winds that blew from the southeast.

The Portuguese, however, interfered with all this trade, levied irksome duties and disturbed the annual pilgrimages to *Makkah*. These arrogant, pompous people were the least liked among the *firangis* because they almost always broke their promises and would insultingly claim they held no sanctity to any pledge or sacred oath made to a heathen. The British, French and Dutch, however, were always true to their pledged words and were therefore allowed firmans to set up several trading establishments. Their factories were large warehouses where they had high walls protected by their own soldiers armed with excellent muskets. Surat was a bustling town that boasted of the finest food of the world.

Murad encouraged the traders to prosper with little hindrance as long as they paid reasonable taxes. His army was kept battle ready and he organized an annual show of strength to serve notice to the increasingly aggressive Marathas and keep their ambitions in check. He lived in great luxury and enjoyed the favors of ladies of every nation when he was not too intoxicated. He was a genial and lovable master who was greatly liked by his officers and men.

Many are those who turn their backs to the sun

and see naught except the long shadows of their ambitions.

CHAPTER 10

Quest for Religious Unity

During the reign of Shah Jahan, Hindustan was under Mughal rule and was therefore a Muslim country. Though the Hindus greatly outnumbered the Muslims, they were mostly farmers, artisans and merchants. They and the Jains, Buddhists, Christians and others were freely allowed to follow their own religions and customs, as long as they did not disturb public order. Prince Dara hated any kind of discord and was deeply troubled that the orthodox religious leaders of all the faiths could become so vehement about the absolute perfection of their own beliefs; and so obstinately intolerant about the beliefs of others. Although brought up as an orthodox Sunni, he had been greatly influenced by the Sufi saints who had been honoured by his great grandfather Akbar. Like Akbar, Dara also wanted to try to build a bridge of harmony between all religious beliefs.

One day, Dara came back from the court in a state of great excitement as the emperor had decided to go to Lahore and had asked Dara to go with him. The visit would also be an opportunity to meet the revered Sufi saint Mian Mir. Before we left I was summoned by Jahanara who said to me, "You are very fortunate to be going to Lahore while we have to while away our time in this heat. We all deeply revere Mian Mir and I want you to please take this little copy of my humble poems to him and ask him to bless it for me." Our fingers grazed as I slowly took the book from her and I felt an almost electric sensation at the mere touch of her hands.

We travelled for three weeks on the royal road from Agra to Lahore, a city we called the gateway to Hind that was the most frequented of all the Mughal routes. It carried a huge volume of trade between India and Persia, Balkh, Badakshan and the more distant lands of Turkey, Arabia, Europe and China. For the convenience of the many travellers, our emperors had planted rows of tall banyan, peepul, jamun and other leafy trees on both sides of the wide road to provide shade even in the hottest months of the summer. Along the route there were also fortified caravanserais at every four Kos, or a full day's march, with police *chawkies*, or posts, with armed soldiers to keep the travellers safe. These large *sarais* had a huge central compound where carts, bullocks and horses could be parked or tethered. There were a number of rooms along the rectangular outer walls for travellers who could sleep in comfort. There was also a large covered hall for the elephants though camels were always kept outside because of their bad odour.

Nadira Banu begum had not been able to conceive again after bearing their first child, a beautiful girl called Jani, causing Dara to fall into deep depression. When Dara met the revered divine Main Mir at Lahore he was so electrified with a spiritual ecstasy when they embraced, that he fell down in a swoon. Later, he said that he heard the voice of silence as the prophet had once related, "like the sound of silvery bells and the beating of a distant drum." Dara's health miraculously recovered and Nadira became pregnant again and prince Sulaiman Shikoh was born to great rejoicing throughout the empire.

The Quadri order of Sufis, founded by Abdul Qader Jhalani from Gilan in Persia, condemned the narrow dogmatic Muslim faith of the orthodox Mullahs with its excessive attachment to the perishable and material world. Mian Mir did not even encourage the wearing of the Sufi cloak because it could attract attention and material gifts from devotees. He returned all gifts that were offered to him with a blessing and disdained all things worldly. It was said that while in the contemplation of Allah he could pass an entire night with just two lungfuls of breath.

The Quadris believed that the strict observance of religious rites and pious rituals could not alone lead to God but could instead stifle the relationship between the individual and The Eternal. They advocated a faith free from fear and built on love, trust, harmony and an absolute surrender to God. Mian Mir believed that Allah was a loving and a merciful father who forgives all his creations. Such was the power of Mian Mir's luminous humanity that even the gurus of the turbulent Sikh faith came to him seeking his guidance and made him lay the foundation stone of Harmandir Sahib, their sacred Golden Temple, when it was being built at Amritsar.

Dara invited the savants of all philosophies to participate in the discourses held at many places that he visited. Leading orthodox Sunnis as well as Shias, Sufis, Zoroastrians, Christians, Buddhists, Jains and Brahmin philosophers were all invited. One of the many visitors to these discourses, who Dara later came to greatly admire, was a strange naked Armenian Jew from Persia called Sarmad, who had first embraced Islam before joining one of the numerous Hindu sects. He wrote the most beautiful poetry ridiculing the orthodoxy of all religions and possessed a quick and often irreverent wit. Sarmad became so strongly attracted to Dara that he was to follow him through all his triumphs and tribulations right up to the last days of his life.

As Kashmir was only an eighteen day march from Lahore, Dara looked forward to visiting this beloved area of his *subbah,* since Kashmir had always been a favourite destination for all the Mughal emperors. Dara was, as always, utterly captivated by its beautiful limpid lakes surrounded by wooded hills, overlooked by high pine-clad hills with snow covered peaks in the distance. As it was summer we all enjoyed going out onto the lake in the slim low *shikara* boats. It was truly a paradise with clear blue skies and a climate that was almost perfect. We would often gather above the huge Dal lake overlooking the beautiful Chashmashashi (royal springs) gardens, built by Shah Jahan. We would meet at the ruins of an old Buddhist monastery that Dara named Pari Mahal or palace of the celestial fairies[9].

On clear days it was wonderful to see the huge expanse of clear water stretching out below with the Hari Parbat hill in the distance that had a little fort built by Akbar. Workers quickly cleared away the shrubs that had grown among the ruins but Dara told them to preserve the old Buddhist structure. Even as it was being rebuilt, we would sit together on one of the big terraces descending towards the lake and have philosophical debates in an atmosphere of enchanting beauty. At dusk little lamps would be lit in hundreds of little

9 This beautiful old structure still stands and was later a centre for astrological studies before it was turned into an observatory. Today it is a popular tourist spot overlooking the entire valley.

alcoves in the walls. I was told that in earlier times little statues of the Buddha had been placed in them. When the little flickering oil lamps in these alcoves were lit the effect was truly magical.

Dara was not impressed by some of the *fakirs* and *sadhus* who made a great virtue out of ritual penances, instead of spreading spiritual love in which he believed. One emaciated bearded *sadhu* who had been standing on one leg for many years came forward hopping on his one leg. He was mouthing quotations from his scriptures and was reluctant to engage in any discussion. The lower part of his slightly bent leg was so swollen and black with the accumulation of blood that he had kept a young boy to continuously massage it.

Sarmad observed him for some time and then mischievously asked, "Tell me learned sage what spiritual merit can be gained by this painful posture that you have so long been suffering?"

The *sadhu* arrogantly answered, "You will not understand that it is the intensity of the pain that helps me focus my mind on the great cosmic spirit."

"If it is pain that leads you to this ecstasy of divine union, then pray tell us why are you allowing this young boy to lessen the pain by massaging your leg?", Sarmad asked.

"How can you understand that the longer one savours the pain the greater becomes the pleasure of cosmic ecstasy?" said the *sadhu*, evading the question.

Sarmad continued, "I confess I do not understand you. How can suffering bring any man closer to God. What I do understand is the importance of alleviating pain and suffering from the lives of everyone." He then looked up to the sky and recited, "The mullah says that Ahmad (The

Prophet) went to the heavens Sarmad says that the heavens were always inside Ahmad."

I can find no spiritual merit in penances, sacrifices or rituals. What merit can there be in wearing clothes such as the prophets are said to have worn? If any prophet had a beard or wore loose robes how can imitating these objects benefit any believer or have any spiritual merit? Followers should respect the teachings of the wise but not their habits or their material possessions...The priests of every faith try to frighten their devotees to conform to their doctrines with the threat of the fires of hell but, I say, that there is no fire in hell. I say that the fiercest fires are inside the hearts of sinners who leave this world filled with burning anger, hatred, jealousy, unrequited greed, pride and lust."

He again turned to the sadhu and said, "May I also ask what is spiritual about the things that people eat? Wise sadhu, tell me if you will eat this delicious piece of mutton Kebab?"

The sadhu angrily replied, "Never! It has been cruelly taken with the life of a poor animal. It will pollute the purity of my body and weigh down my karma to bind me to another terrible cycle of mortality."

Sarmad replied, "What you say about cruelty, wise one, is very true but is there anything you can eat that does not require its cruel death? Should I refuse to eat an apple, if I can hear the apple cry when it is violated by my teeth? Just because most of us cannot see, hear or feel the pain of a plant does not mean that they do not suffer and cry out as much as any other living thing... Why should people listen to priests, who know nothing except their own scriptures? Please try to explain to me how the meat of a pig or of a cow can possibly pollute their souls?...are they not also the beautiful creations of Allah?

Pilgrimages and fasts may be pious austerities and good for the bodies but how can they quicken the spiritual journey of any man? Alms given to the poor, sick or needy may help their suffering but how can any spiritual merit be gained by donors who turn healthy people into grovelling beggars? Sacrifices, donations, rituals, penances, fasts and pilgrimages fatten the Mullahs, Padres, Pundits, Monks, Rabbis and the priests of all religions who will, therefore, go to almost any limit to keep their followers as their slaves on the authority of scriptures that they themselves have created."

Sarmad began to warm to his theme, "By persuading their credulous followers to believe that they possess magical powers to intercede with God, his prophets or his angels these very same priests, hungry for the offerings of their followers, make exaggerated claims of having the power of miraculously produce sons, save the sick and dying, produce good harvests, curse enemies, or gain victories or great treasures or boons. Can a single priest show me proof that they can assure a place in heaven or a better incarnation? May I also ask, who wrote the scriptures of all the religions? Do you know that not one of them were the words of God or even the words of the prophets. They were... every single one of them... the words attributed to them by mortal scribes many years, even centuries, after their deaths."

He went on, "How many of our learned Maulvis can even tell you who wrote the holy Quran?" He looked around the group who looked bewildered and asked, "Do you think it was The Prophet Muhammad?" When some of the audience nodded he vehemently added, "How could it be The Prophet? Do you not recall the very first words of the holy book where The Prophet says... '*I cannot read*?' If he could not read how could he possibly write the Quran?"

Seeing the perplexed look on every face he went on, "All of you will say that you believe in the 'Last Judgment' but may I again ask how can there be a 'Last Judgment' without a 'First Judgment'? Can any of you tell me of this 'First judgment'?"

Dara also met the great mystic Mullah Shah as well as many other scholars of different religions. Mullah Shah, was tall and and had the most beautiful face with radiant blue eyes that sparkled like sunlight through a spring of clear water. He was a scholar of the Sharia who now joined the debate and said "The holy Quran only began to be compiled about six years after the prophet's death when the first Khalif, Abu Bakr, commanded one of Muhammad's companions, to collect all the sayings of the prophet and put it into writing. The Quran was finally compiled some twenty years later and all the other accounts were gathered up and burned."

He then explained, "But the Suras of the Quran, although they were a great inspiration to the faithful, did not answer all the questions of a changing society so, two hundred years later, several scholars travelled through the Muslim world to seek guidance from the life of the prophet and collected them in book called the *Hadith*. The holy books of the Jews, Christians, Hindus, Buddhists, Jains and other faiths were all similarly written by mortal men many years after the death of their prophets. All of them kept on evolving over time as new scholars added new thoughts. I believe that no religion has the right to claim that their way is the only way."

One morning, as our little group was proceeding from our camp near the beautiful little lake of Harwan, we saw a small group of horses and palanquins on the narrow road ahead of us. It was led by a nobleman on a fine horse followed by palanquins for his ladies and about ten soldiers and servants. As they were turning around a bend we saw a young horseman recklessly riding in our direction. He was going so fast that the group had to hastily get off the road and the bearers tripped and dropped the palanquin. A young woman who had been sitting inside was thrown onto the path. The nobleman turned around and was furious when he saw that the girl had been publicly revealed without her veil. He screamed at her for being a shameless whore and drew his sword and rushed up as if he meant to kill her.

We fortunately caught up with them and Dara loudly declared his presence. The nobleman immediately dismounted and respectfully bowed before him saying, "This wretched woman has shamed me and my family and will have to be banished from my home." Dara asked, "But why should she be punished for no fault on her part? She was not responsible for being thrown out of her palanquin by that reckless horseman. Come with us to *Pari Mahal* and we can calmly discuss what needs to be done."

When we had all assembled on one of the terraces above the lake Dara asked Mullah Shah, "Please tell me revered scholar why do the Muslim women go completely veiled. Is this a requirement of the *Sharia*?"

Mulah Shah gravely replied, "Nowhere in the holy Quran does it say that women are required to wear a veil. It merely states that they should cover their chests except in presence of their husbands and slave girls."

Dara continued, "Then why do our women have to be kept in such close seclusion and are forced to wear the veil?"

Mullah Shah replied, "Why should this be strange? Modest women in so many societies... even the Hindu village girls cover their faces when in the presence of strangers. I believe that this practice of covering of the entire female form actually began, when parents wanted to hide their pretty daughters from the eyes of lecherous men who might try to abduct them. Now many Muslims and even our Rajput Umraos think that they must hide their women from the eyes of the public and are following this custom. It is, however, a purely social custom and not a religious requirement of the holy Quran."

Shabir one of our young companions leaned over and whispered to me, "But these old scholars do not know how alluring a veil can also be. Just consider how fascinating are the kohl darkened eyes of a woman peeking out from behind her veil. Can the eyes of any other girl ever look as beautiful? Have you ever thought of how eagerly you look at their dainty feet or pretty hands when they peek out from under a long burkah?"

Dara now turned to the troubled nobleman and said, "You have heard this learned scholar explain that the veil is a purely social custom. We have been witness to the entire incident and have seen that this young girl was blameless in revealing her face. The fault was entirely that of the reckless horseman who we will find and chastise. Your honour as well as her virtue remains unsullied. Please give me your solemn word that you will not punish her for this purely accidental incident."

I had been sitting in a small secluded tent with a few women in our group trying to console the unfortunate girl who was brought in weeping to sit with us. With tears flowing she hesitantly blurted out, “Sorrow! Sorrow! Oh how fickle is the hand of fate! My master Abdul Nadim is a very cruel man. He will not spare me. I will either be killed or sold to a brothel.”

When I related the conversation to Dara he thought for a few moments and then ordered the local governor to be called for. The matter was discussed and the officer assured Dara that he would easily solve the problem as Abdul Nadim was not an officer of great character and would be only too happy to release the poor girl for a handful of gold coins. She was later taken into Dara’s household and became a member of his *zenana*.

A few days later, Sarmad came to prince Dara in a state of great excitement and said that he had just made a great discovery he wanted to show us immediately. Our entire party quickly mounted the horses and rode some, four *Kos* to the other side of the beautiful smaller Nagin Lake, not far from the *Hari Parbat* fort. On a valley below it, were the ruins of a small but very old tomb[10] looked after by a few Muslim caretakers. Sarmad proudly declared that this tomb, called *Rauza Bal*[11], was the actual tomb of the prophet

---

10 The tomb of Jesus at Rosabal can be visited today and is just as Mubarak has described it. There is also a tomb believed to be of his mother Mary at Mari Asthan near the ceasefire line close to the town of Murree in Pakistan.

11 Jesus was a very important prophet of Islam and is mentioned twenty times in the Quran but Muhammad did not believe the Christian versions of the Crucifixion. It says in the Quran... ”they said (in boast)... We killed Jesus the son of Mary, the Messenger of Allah, but they killed him not, nor crucified him, but so it was made to appear to them, and those who differ therein are full of doubts, with no (certain) knowledge, but only conjecture to follow, for of a surety they killed him not. Nay, Allah raised him up unto Himself; and Allah is Exalted in Power and Wise.” Quran Sura4:157-158

Yaz Asaf, that was another name for *Issa* (Jesus), a prophet greatly revered by all Christians and Muslims.

One of the bearded caretakers told us that the prophet *Issa* had not actually died during the Crucifixion and had been given opium or other drugs in a cloth soaked in vinegar when he was hanging on the cross to render him unconscious. This may have temporarily stopped his breathing which led the Roman soldiers to believe he was dead and allow his followers to remove the body. Dara bowed deeply in prayer before the huge tombstone and immediately, ordered a proper tomb be made above the crypt of *Issa*.

Can any scripture save a man from the fangs of a tiger?

But there are some who use sacred robes to

steal from the credulous.

Chapter 11

A Mission for a Princess

I loved the buzz of soft sounds in the harem which was a bustling hub of constant intrigue and idle gossip. It was my duty to fetch and carry clothes, jewels, refreshments, messages and other things for a huge bevy of royal ladies who had little to do except, endlessly beautify themselves for the rare opportunities of enjoying the bed of the emperor or one of the princes. The *zenana* was also home to a number of older women of the previous emperor including ageing concubines, aunts and a veritable army of slaves to attend to them. With so little to occupy their energies, the women were constantly gossiping and keenly interested in the latest fabrics, clothes, slippers, jewellery, cosmetics and other baubles as they idled away their time eating, playing chess, pachesi or cards.

Almost all of them wore thumb rings with tiny mirrors and would spend many hours idly admiring themselves. These were inspired from the thumb rings worn by soldiers to protect their left hands from the whipping force of their bow strings but had become cunning devices enabling women to secretly spy on each other while pretending to be bored or disinterested. I also took great interest in the new designs of jewels like *jhumkas*, or long ear rings, studded with several precious stones like *polki*, uncut diamonds, rubies, emeralds and pearls. On their constantly massaged arms they wore a variety of *kadas*, wrist or arm bracelets, made of gold or silver studded with many precious stones. *Satdhara* and *panchdhara* or necklaces of seven or five long strings of fine gold, small pearls or other jewels were sometimes draped around the necks to highlight the shapely curves of their bosoms that were otherwise discreetly shielded by fine silks or muslins.

Some women in the *zenana* were very talented dancers. After the treaty with Bijapur in the deep south, a beautiful, dark skinned, dancer with a slim sinuous figure dressed in a wrapped skirt of rich brocade would often enthrall the audience. Most of the ladies wore Persian style clothes that had a loose pyjama tapered at the lower ends to show the shapely curve of their legs. Above the pyjama was a long colourful tunic made of costly silks or brocades and over this they wore a fine *peshwaz*, or a diaphanous length of fine Mal Mal (muslin), that was as transparent and delicate as a spider's web. In summer they often wore long loose cotton gowns in the style of their Abyssinian slaves. Soft velvet or silk slippers in numerous colours and materials covered their dainty feet.

While I took a polite interest in all these female fripperies, it was food that most interested me. It was also a subject of interest for the ladies, who showed great excitement when some new delicacy was introduced to the harem by the royal *khansamas* (cooks). *Shikaris* would often bring in venison and ducks from the forests or from nearby lakes as well as small local partridges that were greatly enjoyed. Some of our meat dishes were cooked with apples, plums, watermelons and apricots that the Mughals had brought with them from central Asia.

In my spare time I would sometimes slip in to the huge kitchens on the lower floor of the palace and watch the cooks prepare the meals. Each of the hundred cooks was the master of one dish but had to assist the others as well. Iqbal the chief *khansama*, who was used to my presence in the kitchen, often described to me the dish being prepared that night. He told me one day that potatoes, which had suddenly become so popular in our food, had only recently been brought to Hindustan by the Portuguese from a newly discovered land beyond the western seas. Another time, he asked me to taste a small red vegetable that was so hot I began to hiccough and sweat immediately. This pungent red and sometimes green vegetable had also been brought to Surat by the Portuguese along with another sweet red fruit called tomato and a strange cereal with rows of pearly yellow teeth on a thick inedible core.

He beckoned me closer one day while stirring a large pot of gravy and gestured for me to smell the concotion. The aroma was so delicious yet foreign- a blend of most exotic spices that tickled the taste buds. When I asked him the ingredients, he listed new spices like nutmeg, cloves and cinnamon, which had also been brought to our land by the Portuguese. After meals, we would usually enjoy hot beverages made from the leaves of a plant called chai imported from China and a more aromatic coffee brought from Arabia. Accompanying tea and coffee were desserts and sweetmeats. Iqbal told me that at about the time of Timur, the Chinese emperor had expressed his dislike for the brown color of jaggery extracted from sugarcane juice. Some Chinese had found a method to make it white. So our empire began importing this white sugar called 'chini' from China at very high cost, which was soon widely used to sweeten our foods and desserts.

I, like all the male eunuchs, was not allowed into the ladies *hamam*, which was another important room in the *zenana* where the women bathed together. The outer room was lined with wide marble slabs where they sat and bathed using warm water poured from basins or long necked vessels by the women slaves. After this the ladies, clad in thin cotton gowns, would enter a set of three chambers. One was filled with steam created by wood fires burning below in a big brass vessel. The second had taps of warm water and the third had cold water.

The emperor had a small *hamam* in his personal *gusul khana*. There were also a number of smaller *hamams* in the homes of the noblemen as well as many large public ones in most of the cities. Some were located near the mosques or near the main city gates to serve weary travellers numbering to a total of eight thousand *hamams* in Agra alone.

As men were mostly concerned with matters of the court they disdained any kind of commerce. They also considered it very unbecoming to even bargain with a tradesman and would usually just proffer a bag of coins from which the shopkeepers could pick out their dues. As a consequence, many of the senior women, with their own considerable personal wealth, began to interest themselves with trade and business ventures.

The husbands of the royal ladies dared not covet their

personal wealth that was guaranteed to them by the Quran as part of their marriage contracts[12]. They also had a close network of friends and relations in all the noble families and if word got out that any man was trying to get his hands on his wife's wealth, it would have been a terrible blot on his reputation. They considered their wealth as theirs alone. Thus they had the means to do vigorous business and traded in many goods. Princess Jahanara was even given the entire income from the rich port of Surat. From all this trade, a constant stream of interesting jewellery, fabrics, fruits, novelties, exotic animals and birds from distant lands were obtained and proudly displayed to the great excitement of the usually bored *zenana*.

Since the women were always in *purdah* they had to depend on agents to handle their businesses. Many agents, though outwardly humble and subservient, became rich and arrogant with the wealth they were able to siphon off. As it was very difficult for patrons to check on their transactions, the agents knew that as long as they showed reasonable profits they had very little to worry about. They also worked in a wide network of trust where the pledged word was sacred and a broken promise would spell ruin for many future generations.

One day, Jahanara urgently summoned me to her chamber where I found her looking very troubled. She believed that her agent in Surat was falsifying the accounts of her businesses and wanted me to go there to check. Giving me a small pouch of gold coins, she asked me to rush to Surat with a letter under her seal.

---

12 Sura 4:20 If you wish to marry another wife, in place of your present wife, and you had given any of them a great deal, you shall not take back anything you had given her. Would you take it fraudulently, maliciously, and sinfully? How could you take it back, after you have been intimate with each other, and they had taken from you a solemn pledge?

It took me three weeks on a pair of fast horses to get to the great port. It was here that I saw the breathtaking expanse of the ocean for the first time. I first spent several days walking along the wharfs where a confusing assortment of ships from many nations was moored on the south side of the wide Tapti River before it entered the ocean. I found the constant stench of fish and rotting garbage near the shore quite nauseating. I spent some time talking to traders to find out who were the main shippers and traders, to learn about their reputations and the names of the clients they served.

One day, I was thrilled to go out to sea on a big Arab *dhow.* This was a large ship with sharp pointed bows and triangular sails that was testing out a new set of cotton sails. The Arabs, who owned most of the ships, had little wood in their own country and got their ships built in Hindustan or Abyssinia. The workmen in Hind were more skilled and the teak from the forests near Surat were of better length and lightness for ship building. The Arabs, however, did not have a taste for the hardships and dangers of sailing on stormy seas and so most of the ships had either Indian or Abyssinian crews. The dark Abyssinian sailors, known as *Siddis*, lived in their own colonies and some were to later capture a few ships to begin a lucrative trade of piracy.

During my time there, I also visited a few taverns where they mostly served cheap, intoxicating, beverages made of fermented millets or juice tapped from coconut or date palm trees, stronger Arrak spirit was made from jaggery flavored with anise seed as well as several expensive wines. There were also small pipes and *hookahs* for smoking *bhang* or opium. I found that these intoxicants loosened the tongues and made the taverns very good places to get the information I needed.

While leaving a tavern one day, I noticed that there were several men waiting outside a room next to a small mosque. Out of curiosity I asked one of the men what they were waiting for. He looked me up and down and smiling slyly said that he was waiting his turn for the *Qazi,* or magistrate, to perform a *Muta* wedding or a temporary wedding with a beautiful girl he had found in the adjoining brothel. His eyes shone in ecstatic joy as he said, "you will not find more beautiful girls than can be found here in Surat. Here comes merchandise from every nation of the world as well as the choicest young girls from Venice, Frankistan, Morocco, Egypt, Turkey, Ethiopia, Abyssinia, Arabia, Turkey, Circassia, Georgia, Serendip, Siam, China and the Spice islands. You must go there and allow some of them to entertain you with such dance and music as will drive you mad with desire. "

Out of curiosity I entered the hall and saw that a number of men were sitting against thick bolsters all around several big rooms and the girls would enter one by one and sinuously walk around the room to the sound of musicians and singing girls. If one of the dancing girls pleased a guest, he would shower her with a few small silver coins. There was a girl from Turkey who was able to sway her stomach and hips so seductively that the men were literally salivating with desire.

As soon as a man saw a girl of his liking, he would raise his hand with a large silver coin in it. The girl would take it and usher the customer into a small room nearby where she would remove her *peshwaz* and outer clothes so that he could see her face and be fully satisfied with his choice. Some of the girls were quite bold and would flirt outrageously with any man that took her fancy. If a man wanted more intimate time with a girl, he would put another silver coin in her hand and an attendant would take him to the adjoining house of the *Qazi* who would take yet another coin to perform the ceremony as well as two more for the girl, who would then lead the customer back to the house of joy. The client would next be offered refreshments and food and could spend the night in a small room. If the customer wanted a girl exclusively for a week he had to give a gold coin."

Smiling with happiness my new friend went on, "Where in the world can an honest god fearing man get himself a personal *zenana* with so many beautiful young women? Where in the world can he have such a magnificent harem without the cost and bother of having to care for the girls? Where in the world can a respected man share the joys of a *zenana* with other like minded male friends with whom he can drink, laugh and share his experiences without the irritating jabber of women? Where in the world can a man find himself a houseful of ladies without having to listen to endless quarrels and complaints? It is paradise my friend... pure paradise!"

I was sitting quietly when a tall girl with a fair European looking face suddenly reached down and pulled me to my feet with surprising strength. Smiling saucily she said, "What a beautiful young man you are. Will you not allow me the privilege of teaching you the seventy seven secrets of Egyptian love?" In a state of panic I stuttered some excuse and fled the room to the huge amusement of all the onlookers.

I was to however soon discover that apart from these palaces of pleasure, the ports were also dangerous places where thieves and rogues lurked in every corner. I realized this when I was accosted by three rough dock workers who assumed, from my elegant clothes, that I was a good target for robbery. They did not know of my strength or my military experience so I let them come close by pretending to cower in fear until they were near enough for me to knock them down with a piece of a broken oar lying on the ground. I then caught their leader by his collar and put my jewelled dagger to his throat. I did not want to hurt him as that could have led them to seek revenge for any injury I could inflict so I let him go with a warning. The dark and bushy eyed leader now smiled and said to me in a strangely accented Hindustani, "You are a very fine fighter brother...we need someone like you in our gang. My name is Ibrahim and I hail from distant Morocco far across a sea from Europe. Come with us and I will show you something about our trade."

As I was interested in seeing new things I went with them to a long wharf where cargoes were being unloaded and lifted on to big bullock carts to be taken to their destinations. As it was just before dusk and the guards had not arrived for the night shift, they quickly tried to steal a few items from some of the parcels. They stopped excitedly at a large container that they said contained vessels of wine from Persia. Ibrahim lifted the box and dropped one corner quite hard on the ground and immediately lifted it at an angle so that its contents of the broken cask spilled out into an earthen bowl held ready to catch the spill. We all enjoyed some very tasty wine and Ibrahim explained, "We only take a little from each cargo so that it looks like a real accident and the owners do not think it necessary to complain to the authorities."

A little later we came near a high sided European ship with very tall masts and several small brass cannons showing from small square windows along its sides. Some of its cargo was on the wharf guarded by an unarmed, young, white - skinned boy. Ibrahim's friends winked as we casually walked close to the guard clearly with the intention of catching him but he surprised them instead. He stepped aside very quickly and punched one of his assailants very hard with his hand balled up in a hard fist. I had never before seen such an effective and quick way of knocking down an adversary. So, after my new friends ran away, I smiled at the boy and asked him to show me how he had used his hands. He smiled slowly and hit me so hard in my stomach that I was completely winded. He then proudly showed me how to hit the face and other sensitive parts of the body with the knuckles.

Most of the shipping in Surat was in the hands of the community of *Bohras* who, I was told, had originally come from Egypt and controlled the trade from the Persian Gulf while the trade with Africa and Arabia was mostly controlled by the *Khoja* Arabs who had come from Aden. Sometimes, a few strange tall ships from China with a number of short masts with bamboo stiffened square sails, bringing very fine wine, silks and porcelain, also visited the port.

After I had somewhat acquainted myself with the business of the port I presented myself with Jahanara's letter to her agent Dawood Shah who airily told me that Jahanara's shipload of horses from Arabia had not yet arrived. I listened to his fanciful stories and excuses of this and her other businesses under his control before saying, "But Dawood *Sahib,* I think you must be misinformed because your ship called Hawa sailed into Surat three days ago."

Dawood turned pale and commanded a servant to go and get him the ledger of records. He studied them for a minute and said, "You are very well informed young man but five of the twenty horses on it died on the voyage."

I softly replied, "Dawood *miyan*, let us not play games. I know that all the twenty four horses arrived in good health including four black stallions of the finest *Najdi* Arabian breed and I know exactly where they are stabled. You know what will happen to you if I were to report all that I know of this business to *Shahzadeh Khanum*. But I also know that you are a wise businessman, so please give our mistress a proper account of the business that she has entrusted to you and I will not say a word."

Dawood looked at me steadily for a few moments and then smiled cautiously. He then reached down and opened a drawer of a little wooden cabinet in front of the brocade cushioned mat he was sitting cross legged upon and took out a small leather bag. He opened its string and poured out a small heap of shining gold coins on the ground before me. He said, "Mubarak *sahib*, your mistress is indeed fortunate to have found such a fine, intelligent and diligent servant as you. Please accept these paltry coins as a small token of my regard for you and as a bond of our personal friendship... a mere *nazrana* to cement a long friendship."

I casually picked up ten coins from the pile and said, "Dawood *Miyan* I will only take a few of these to defray the expenses that I have actually incurred on this mission from Agra, so that this journey to make your acquaintance is not a burden to my mistress."

"And there is one other important matter"... I added "Although the elder princess is your biggest client I understand that you are also serving her younger sister. I should not share with you the secrets of the court but you are a wise man and you may know that the younger sister is jealous of her elder sister. My mistress would be very distressed if she were to know that her business is being deliberately betrayed. A man cannot hold two melons in one hand or serve two hostile masters. He may be cut in two like a piece of paper between the blades of a scissor. So I would sincerely recommend, that you only serve one. You know full well who can give you the most business and that my princess is always very just."

I went on, "There is also another business that I have been entrusted with for which I need your advice. Like the Emperor Jahangir's mother, Guljar Mariam Zamani, the royal princess wishes to commission a large ship with the main purpose of taking pious pilgrims in safety and comfort for the pilgrimage to *Makka*. As this pilgrimage will only need about six weeks before and after the pilgrimage week of *Dhu-al-Hajjah* it must be a very big vessel that can carry many passengers with a proper place for the safe seclusion of the women."

Dawood's eyes shone with excitement as he said, "My cousin Sulaiman has a big shipyard right here in Surat and will be able to build the most magnificent ship that has ever sailed these seas. Such a ship, capable of carrying some three hundred passengers, will also enable our patroness to most economically trade in very large cargoes to all the ports of the world in the remaining months of the year. As our ships are constantly harassed by the Portuguese, we will design it to carry some cannons and armed soldiers to ensure that it is never troubled by the firangis or by the Abyssinian pirates that sometimes rob our vessels and harass the passengers."

A few weeks later I gave Jahanara a full and honest report from Dawood of her numerous businesses and she was delighted that her commerce was again on a sound footing.

I did not tell her all that had transpired but I was very happy to have helped my princess once again.

Many are those who speak like the roar of the ocean

...though their lives are shallow and stagnant

Many are those who try to

lift their heads to the mountain tops

...though their spirits remain in the obscurity of the valleys.

Chapter 12

Mingling of the Oceans

Like his great grandfather Akbar, Dara enjoyed stimulating spiritual discussions at his palace, overlooking the Jumna River. After his return from Kashmir he found much more time for debate with the savants of all religions. One of his courtiers had made a lasting impression on Dara when he said, "Who will remember the kings and nobles who made magnificent palaces and tombs? But who can ever forget the luminous ideas of the great poets and philosophers?" I began to understand that Dara was being increasingly driven by an ambition to be remembered as a great philosopher just as his father would be remembered as a great builder.

Dara was increasingly consumed by an ardent desire to emulate his great grandfather Akbar's policy of religious tolerance that he believed was essential for a lasting peace in the turbulent empire. But while his great grandfather just dabbled in religious ideas, Dara wanted to go deep into every philosophy. He often quoted the words of Abul Fazl, Akbar's close friend and biographer, who had been regarded the most erudite scholar of his time:

"O God, in every temple I see people that seek Thee.
In every language I hear people that praise Thee.
If it be the mosque, people murmur the holy prayer.
if it be the Christian Church, I ring the bell for love of Thee.
Sometimes I frequent the Christian cloister
and sometimes the mosque,
But it is thou that I seek from temple to temple "

Dara's own writings on Sufism were most prolific and included biographies of Sufi saints and a treatise on Sufi doctrines. But unlike anyone else, he studied Sanskrit after being given the city of Benares and began to learn about Hindu philosophies. As his understanding grew, he slowly began to believe that Allah could not have denied the knowledge of his luminous greatness to any of the people of the world and that his many messages and messengers only needed to be found and revealed for the people of all faiths. Even though the messages had often become obscured by the huge confusion of language and the interpretations of the religious scholars and priests.

At one of his meetings Sarmad said, "Being a good Muslim does not mean just following the rules and rituals of Islam. If a man says his namaz five times a day but has his mind fixed on the objects of his greed or lust how can he ever be a good Muslim? If someone goes on a pilgrimage to *Makkah* but is always thinking of his buried treasure, his children, his mistresses, his house, his enemies or his business he never actually leaves his home and the pilgrimage is just an empty sham. The Prophet has told us that Allah is a loving and merciful god so a good Muslim must have love for all god's creations."

One of the speakers recited a couplet by the Sufi poet Waris Shah:

"I am tired of reading the Vedas and Qurans
My forehead is worn out by
constant prostrations at the mosque
But the Lord is neither in Hindu shrines nor in Makkah
Whoever finds him will find him in the
light of God's radiant beauty."

Dara laughed, joining in and added his own composition...

"Here is the secret of unity, O friend, understand it.
Nowhere exists anything but God
All that you see or know other than Him
Verily is separate in name, but in essence, is one with God
Paradise is where no Mullah exists
And the noise of his discussions and debate is not heard."

Dara's friend Pandit Kavindracharya Saraswati somberly added, "All that you say is not very different to the sayings of the ancient sages of our religion. In Ved Vyasa's epic story the Mahabharata, Krishna was never portrayed as having greater power than that of any mortal man. In fact, this Hindu hero, who is now being revered as the deity, had actually mocked the sacred Vedas of the Hindus by saying...

'beguilingly flowery is the speech uttered by the foolish
who adhere to the doctrines of the Vedas
and claim that naught else has verity'."

Abu Peeran, a Sunni scholar, was looking very surly but was listening very intently. On hearing the criticism of the Mullahs he flushed red and jumped to his feet with passion but managed to courteously ask, "*Shahzadeh hazoor,* how can you allow our religion and sacred traditions to be so mocked by these Sufis, Shias, Hindus and other heretics? Such *shirk* (heresy) is the certain path to the fire. The true path has been very clearly defined by the holy Prophet and many other pious clerics over the centuries. All these people here are only trying to misguide you. Look at these Sufis. They are nothing but tomb worshippers who try to fool people into believing that the spirits of dead *Pirs* can miraculously rise up, to intercede on their behalf with the Prophet or with Allah himself to grant them the boons they seek. Sufis claim to disdain all things material but by entreating these *Pirs* they are actually asking for material boons for themselves. The Prophet has said that a worshipper must directly address their prayers to Allah."

Encouraged by everyone's rapt attention he went on, "Sufi ideas and practices are very similar to those of the Hindus, who believe that their deities can intercede on their behalf with God to grant them material boons. These are not spiritual practices but blatant superstitions. Tomb worship is no better than idol worship that was expressly forbidden in the Quran. The Sufi *fakirs* are not different to Hindu *sadhus* who seduce their audiences with *jadoo* (magic), like producing ash out of the air such as can be done by any street magician. And you can also witness how violently they dance and how loudly they sing to mesmerize the minds of ignorant believers. These Sufi ideas sully the sublime purity of Islam."

There was a long embarrassed silence and then Mullah Shah gently responded, "Abu Mia, you are very right to remind us about the essential truths enshrined in our holy Quran but the Quran and the Hadis, also speaks of a bountiful and merciful god. So we must not lose sight of this idea of a great loving god, who is concerned about the happiness of all his creations. Our holy Prophet never encouraged the hatred that seems to so inflame so many of our clerics. Our Prophet never wanted hatred, anger and violence that cause so much suffering... and did not our Prophet also say... "those who restrain anger and pardon men Allah loves?"

Clearing his throat he added, "The Prophet gave perhaps the most severe condemnation of the tyranny of all priestly orders when he said... 'O ye who believe! Lo many of the (Jewish) Rabbis and the (Christian) Monks who devour the wealth of mankind wantonly, and debar (men) from the way of God. They who hoard up gold and silver and spend it not in the way of God, unto them give tidings of a painful doom.'

"Abu Mian, I know that you are stating the position that is held by many Islamic jurists and is taught to young students in the madrassas, but no one can say with certainty that their beliefs alone represent the true path. I believe that hatred is the sure path to hell just as love and mercy will show the certain path to heaven."

One winter afternoon, while the group was sitting at a small pavilion of the Aram Bagh on the opposite bank of the Jumna, there was a sudden stir of excitement when one of the slaves rushed in to announce that prince Aurangzeb had arrived and wished to listen to the discussions. Dara immediately rose and went to embrace him and made him sit beside him on a low cushioned *takht*. The younger prince sat for over two hours and listened attentively to a heated discourse between Sunni and Sufi scholars. His mere presence silenced many who would normally have applauded some of the telling points. One listener, however, summoned up the courage to ask Aurangzeb what his thoughts were.

Aurangzeb paused for a few moments and then said, "I think that all this discussion is a futile waste of time and energy. Everything that a man needs to know can be found in the holy Quran and Hadis. Encouraging people to foolishly think otherwise is only inviting dissent and trouble in our peaceful kingdom. What use is there in these discussions? Look at all of you assembled here. Your energies would be so much more profitably spent in studying our holy books, giving alms to the poor, teaching the ignorant or building the materials of war on which our great empire depends."

He then got up abruptly and left the assembly with a small group of his attendants scurrying behind him.

After a long silence one of the guests asked, "and prince Dara, do you agree with the religious views of your brother?

Dara paused and then replied, "Who can possibly deny the sanctity of our holy scriptures but most people only know selected portions that the Mullah's choose to teach them. The Prophet had always advocated moderation and urged his followers to reason with dissenters.The priests of all religions want to instil fear in the hearts of people to make them spend all their time in prayer. They do not want people to enjoy life with music, art or joyous festivities, except for the festivals of their own religions. Where in the holy Quran has The Prophet Mohammad said that these are forbidden and that believers should not drink spirits or smoke bhang or opium? He had only said that people should not be intoxicated. It is a sentiment that every wise person will warmly endorse."[13]

Now bringing the conversation to a close, he said, "We have had a most interesting discussion today but let me conclude by asking all of you… how many of you believe in a merciful and benevolent god as I do, and how many of you think we must only be guided by the words of bigoted priests?"

There was then a murmur of voices until one of the listeners stood up and said, "*Shazadeh Hazoor,* no wise person can disagree with all that you say but unfortunately, there are many who listen to bigoted priests that promise them peace in the next world or threaten them with the fires of hell. Everyone needs to understand that we need peace in this world as well as in the next and there will only be peace when people begin to understand that the beliefs of others need not offend Allah. We are a nation with many people and many beliefs and it is only through understanding and tolerance that there can be lasting peace between them".

Prince Dara smiled at the reply, conveying his agreement with the scholar.

I clearly recall the excitement on every occasion when some of the long buried treasures of Hindu philosophy or literature was discovered and presented to Dara's scholars. Many great Hindu texts like the Vedas, Upanishads,

13 Quran, Sura 5:90 -91 says " O you who believe! Intoxicants and gambling,… are an abomination of Satan's handiwork… Satan wants only to excite enmity and hatred between you with intoxicants and gambling and hinder you from the remembrance of Allah and from the prayer."

Bhagavad Gita and even the Mahabharata had long been buried in the secret troves of Brahmin priests scattered all over the country. These and many other works like Patanjali's Yoga Sutras were not known even to the most educated of Hindus. Dara's scholars and scribes not only translated them into the court language of Persian but also edited, copied and printed them so that these fountains of ancient Hindu wisdom would become known to all.

Pandit Kavindracharya even took Dara to Benares to meet other Hindu scholars and understand the basic message of the Upanishads. He said:

"The Upanishads tells us that the mind is divine but unfortunately, the mind that we use is the physical mind, which cannot help us in our journey because it has unconsciously accepted three non divine companions of fear, doubt and jealousy that confuse it. These three sentiments attack the mind and make it helpless. When our minds are weakened by fear, doubt, jealousy then ego enters them and destroys spirituality. We have to go beyond the domain of the physical mind. The seeking intellect believes in philosophy. The fearful heart needs religious rituals to calm it.The human mind is like a monkey swinging from fear to fear."

He went on, "There are two approaches. One is through the mind, the other is through the heart. The approach through the mind is not secure because fear, doubt and jealousy distort our thinking. But the approach through the heart is always sure. There are also powerful physical barriers like *kama* (lust), *krodha* (anger), *lobha* (greed), *moha* (attachment). When people are free from them they are free of all these evils and are able to enter the state of *Moksha (liberation)*."

A few weeks later Pandit Kavindracharya brought to Dara another long lost document called the *Bhagavat Gita* that had been lying among the scrolls of some Brahmins of the Brighu order. He said that it had originally been part of a discourse by a legendary hero called Krishna in the great Hindu legend of the Mahabharata. The text, that was now translated by Dara into Persian for the first time, contained some very profound thoughts.

He read out a few pages from it...

"Desire and attachment is the basis of all sorrow so the sincere performing of one's karma makes one detached and free. God resides in every heart but because many of us think we are no more than our bodies we become trapped by the desires and attachments of our bodies. The Gita says that God is the source of all energy and that mortal humans are mere lamps burning with a spark of that divine energy."

Dara turned to one of the Sunni scholars and asked, "Do you find anything in this philosophy that conflicts with what has been taught by our holy prophet? It clearly speaks of the need for absolute surrender to God with the same passion as we Muslims seek absolute surrender to Allah."

Dara then asked Kavindracharya, "But please tell me how can Hindus with such elevating philosophies continue the base practice of worshipping stone idols?"

Kavindracharya paused before replying, "*Shazadeh hazoor* most Hindus believe that their deities are different manifestations of *Prabhu*, the great cosmic spirit. The gods like of Vishnu, Shiv, Ram or Krishna and their consorts Lakshmi, Parvati, Radha, Sita and many others have been endowed with many benign human attributes that make them easy for worshippers to identify and respond to. These and many lesser deities, that they can see and touch, are much easier to worship with flowers and offerings. Most of our Hindu worshippers are poor people who know very little about their ancient philosophies. Like poor people everywhere they live precarious lives with hunger, sickness and fear constantly tormenting them so they try to seek god's protection with prayers, penances, pilgrimages and other acts of piety that they hope will please their gods and gain their protection."

"*Shahzedeh Hazoor,* all Hindus have to be grateful to you making our own great treasures of philosophy known to the world. The fabulous wealth of India was hidden from the western world until Alexander showed them the door through which so many conquerors were to follow in the centuries that followed. You have now opened a door to reveal to us the wonders of our own nearly forgotten ancient philosophies."

Dara, in his quest to seek a unifying philosophy underlying all religions, now demonstrated the originality of his own intellect by personally writing a most remarkable book that he called *Majma-ul-Bahrain* meaning `The Mingling of the Oceans' in which he attempted to seek the common links between the philosophies of the holy Quran and the Brahma Shastras of the Hindus.

He first compared the elements listed in Islam and Hinduism. Rather like the Islamic *Arsh-i-Azan,* (great throne) of wind, fire, water and dust, the Hindu texts speak of '*Panch Bhut*' of sky, wind, brilliance, water and earth. He went on to add that *Jibrail* (Gabriel), the presiding angel of Islamic creation was similar to the Hindu *Brahma* (the creator) while *Mikhail,* the angel of existence, was similar to the Hindu *Vishnu* (the preserver) and *Israfil* (the angel of destruction) was like *Shiv* (the destroyer). Later, he pointed out that water was the element of both *Jibrail* and *Brahma*, Fire was the element associated with both *Mikhail* and *Vishnu* while air was the sacred element of both *Israfil* and *Shiv*.

It was an idea that no Hindu or Muslim had ever thought of before and everyone solemnly nodded.

I, however, thought that his greatest work was the *Sirr-i-Akbar* or `the great secret' where he showed the similarity between the monotheistic core of the Upanishads that underlay the religions of the Hindus with the unqualified monotheism of Islam. He wanted Muslims to understand that Hindus and Hindu religions actually had many common links with the spiritual core of Islam.

Word about Dara's great work began to spread and many Hindus were first curious and later deeply gratified to learn about the many nearly forgotten treasures of their own ancient culture. I was however troubled because I learned that these reports seemed to disturb the orthodox Muslims who held Hindus in contempt and firmly believed in the superiority of their own culture and religion.

I was sitting quietly in the *zenana* one day when I suddenly sensed the presence of the fifteen year old Gauharara who was standing quietly beside me. For a while she stood in silence and then her huge luminous eyes looked deeply into mine as she slowly said, "Mubarak *Mia* my brother Dara lives in a world of thoughts and dreams. How many will understand the truth that seems to so obsess him? Your truth is not my truth and my truth may seem a lie to my sister and her truth may seem a mischief to someone else. Those who are lost in thought are also lost to ordinary people. How many of our soldiers have time for dreams? Tell me how many? Dreamers and doers... Dreamers and doers... Many are the dreamers but where are the doers? Can dreamers be doers?"

Without waiting for a response, she smiled sweetly and glided away like a pale celestial wraith, leaving me puzzled about what her words had meant.

With over a century of stable Mughal rule, many Hindu subjects were beginning to rise above their traditional positions. Apart from the respected Rajput clans, many Hindus now held high positions in the administration. They were also contributing to music, painting and clerical services. Some Muslims were therefore, beginning to resent the steady rise in their position and power. There were also some ambitious younger Hindus who dared to flaunt their wealth and assert themselves socially to the annoyance of the established Muslim families.

The new knowledge discovered by Dara's scholars should have built a great bridge of understanding if only the orthodox Muslims and narrow minded Hindus would have permitted it. But for the most part both the Hindus and Mussalmans preferred to be guided by their priests and would not raise their eyes above their deeply rooted prejudices.

Although, Dara had always been true to the words of The Prophet, the Quran and the concepts of Allah, he was openly contemptuous about some of the externals of Islam.

Aurangzeb and other narrow minded puritans began to mutter amongst themselves that he was working for the devil himself. Some even made the ridiculous statement that he was trying to make Hindustan a Hindu country.

The flower and its fragrance are one

...but the blind can only smell fragrance.

Those who close their noses can see the colors

...but are blind to its magical beauty.

Chapter 13

King of the World

The emperor Shah Jahan was indeed king of the world. After success in his every endeavour, the emperor wanted to truly live up to his name with magnificent achievements and creations. Ever since the passing of his beloved Mumtaz the Emperor had been obsessed by his dream of making a tomb for her such as had never been made for any woman before. It was a giant project that took nearly twenty years to complete.

He had repeated discussions with the best architects and designers of the land until, a vision began to slowly form in his mind. The emperor had chosen a large garden, about one Kos, down the river from the Red Fort just after a bend of the River Jumna. This property had belonged to rajah Jai Singh of Amer. Although, he was a very important Mughal general he had no choice but to accede to the emperor's wishes. Shah Jahan, in return, gave him four large havelis with their revenues which were barely adequate compensation.

The rising structure was so huge that it was soon visible from almost every part of the city. As it began to take shape, the emperor became obsessed by all the many details of the project. He would carefully study all the drawings and personally make changes or corrections. Dara told me "the monument was designed to be a magical synthesis of many things that the emperor had observed in Mughal and Rajput architecture. He wanted the huge garden to be like the vision of heaven as described in the holy Quran. It has been laid out in the classic 'char bagh,' or four garden, layout with four rectangular sections separated by stone channels oriented from north to south and east to west in which water flowed from level to level".

I went with Dara and the emperor one day to see how the huge project was progressing and nearly choked on the fine white marble dust that filled the air, blocked our nostrils and made our eyes water. We were also quite deafened by the noise of hundreds of workmen hammering out the stone blocks and small intricate carvings. We soon realized that it was a huge building soaring to the skies but had been so flawelessly proportioned that it looked smaller than it actually was. It was built in perfect harmony with the great dome standing on a large square platform with its corners shaved away to make it an eight sided base in the sacred tradition of the holy Quran that has eight main chapters. There were four smaller marble chattris (canopies) in the Rajput style next to the great dome like clasps, holding a great jewel. There were also four minarets at the corners. It was only when I stood close to it that I began to appreciate the sheer size of the great structure.

The most famous architects from Persia, Baghdad and Turkey had been commissioned but the emperor personally designed almost every detail himself. Ustad Ahmad Lahauri from Persia was in charge of the workers who sometimes, numbered up to twenty thousand and laboured for seventeen years to complete their masterpiece. The emperor had studied portraits of the tombs of Samarkand but had also been greatly influenced by the white beauty of the white marble Jag Mandir lake palace of Udaipur, where he had been given refuge when he was a fugitive prince. The fine inlay of dark stone flowers and calligraphy on the pristine white marble was inspired by the exquisite tomb of empress Mumtaz's grandfather Itmad-ud-Daulah that shone in the evening sun just across the Jumna.

No cost or effort was spared. He secured the finest white Makrana marble which was cut and transported on huge carts drawn by teams of up to twenty buffaloes or bullocks. A huge ramp that was about a Kos long was needed to drag these huge blocks on big wooden rollers up to the great height of the dome. But the walls and dome were not made completely of marble as the inner structure was mostly made of bricks and later covered by a fine facing of beautiful curved marble slabs. In his quest for perfection, the emperor even had the tiny gaps between these tiles filled with a fine marble paste to make the joints between the blocks almost invisible.

He also secured several tons of the finest jade and amber from China, coral from Arabia, garnets from Balkh, lapis lazuli and amethyst from Afghanistan and Persia. Jasper, carnelian and other semi precious stones were to be inlaid to embellish the white marble and the delicate *jali* of the many windows and arches. In accordance with the injunctions of the Quran, there were no representations of any men or animals but a profusion of exotic plants. Lilies, in purple lapis lazuli, carnations and pomegranates in pink carnelian, lotuses, poppies, lilacs and every plant in Allah's creation were to forever be immortalized on its walls.

The most amazing architectural innovation was the design of the dome itself. It was so big that Shah Jahan made a smaller inner dome above the vault of the mausoleum. Subtle Hindu motifs like the lotus and the Rajput chattris blended with Islamic elements from the golden spire on the dome, as well as to the many smaller structures. The colour of mourning now followed the Hindu tradition of white instead of blue and black as in early Mughal times.

Many important verses from the holy Quran were inlaid in black and yellow stone calligraphy; perfectly etched on the virginal white of the edifice. The tomb was so cunningly designed that it was not allowed to be absolutely perfect because it was not wise to tempt the wrath of providence where absolute perfection could only be the handiwork of Allah. One of the half columns on the side of the building was therefore deliberately made to be different to the others.

I shall never forget the gasp of awe that erupted from every mouth when the great tomb was first unveiled in all its glory. Sounds of cheering even reached our ears from the city. The huge shimmering white dome emerged like a nymph rising from the foaming waters of the ocean when the huge sheath of red silk surrounding it was slowly lowered to the ground. The huge ring of supporting brickwork at the lower levels was more difficult to remove until the emperor suddenly got the idea to allow the people of Agra to take away the bricks for their own use. Thousands of delighted towns people rushed to the site and rapidly removed them.

We later entered its inner sanctum where the mortal remains of the empress Mumtaz Mahal lay interred. The pristine white dome soared upwards and echoed the smallest sound. There was a ring of pure white marble at the base of the dome. Then the walls rose in a huge unblemished curve of some shining white material that was a new lime plaster, especially made out of marble dust, sugar and the whites of eggs and then polished to a dazzling finish.

The only dissenting voices were the mutterings from some orthodox Mullahs who disapproved of all tombs claiming that these violated the injunctions of the Quran by encouraging excessive devotion to a mortal human being. Not surprisingly Aurangzeb, who was with us on this great occasion, said nothing and looked disapprovingly at all the ostentation.

The Taj Mahal[14] was unveiled in the year 1063 of our calendar (1653 AD). As all the princes had come from their *mansabs* to Agra to attend this great occasion, Jahanara decided to invite all of them to a special banquet so that all the brothers and sisters could renew their old friendships. She made me help her with the arrangements and ordered me to invite them on her behalf and give them presents. All the princes except Aurangzeb readily accepted until I told him that in deference to his wishes she had decided to not serve any wine.

Two days later, she along with Roshanara and Gauharara and the ladies of their court fondly greeted the princes as they entered the *zenana* after so many years with garlands of marigolds and jasmine. Everyone then sat on a beautiful silk carpet on silken cushions and there was an almost immediate sound of animated chatter as they spoke amiably of many

---

14 Details regarding the construction and unveiling of the Taj Mahal are available from the writings of Mundy, (p212), Manrique vol II, Qanungo, mainly relying on Inayat Khan's Shah Jahan nama.

things that letters can never convey. They exchanged news about their children, wives, health and many other matters as well as recalling happy events from their childhoods.

Jahanara was still very beautiful, slim and graceful at the age of thirty eight. Her maid now approached and presented her brothers with beautiful satin long coats made for them in the Chinese style — with discreetly embossed figures of dragons, willows, flowers and birds — as gifts from all the three sisters. Dara immediately got up, embraced her and retired to a small chamber where he put it on. The shimmering dark blue coat looked very impressive and we all applauded. The thirty six year old Shuja, who was now getting quite fat, followed his example and soon reappeared in a beautiful coat of a pale golden colour. The thirty five year Aurangzeb looked embarrassed but thanked her for a dark green coat that he said he appreciated but would keep for some great occasion as he preferred to only wear a normal soldier's tunic. The tall twenty nine year old Murad, however, very happily put his on and looked quite dashing in a maroon coloured coat.

The princes then presented their gifts. Dara gave all the princes and princesses lengths of beautiful, gold - coloured brocade that the camel caravans had brought to Lahore from Europe.

Shuja gave Jahanara a dazzling ruby brought from Burmah, a land to the east of his mansab. He gave Roshanara a large emerald from the island of Serandip and a pale blue sapphire from Burmah to Gauharara. He also gave his brothers several equally beautiful stones.

Aurangzeb now got up and said that as his *mansab* was the only place in the world that produced diamonds, he would give them all stones that he had personally selected.

He first gave Jahanara a huge diamond, the size of a small walnut that he said had been cleverly cut in the European fashion to prevent any light escaping from inside it. We were amazed at the dazzling glow that it seemed to emit. He then went to his brothers and sisters one by one and gave them each beautiful stones in small silken pouches. As he approached Dara the silk pouch slipped from his fingers and he had to stoop down to pick it up from his feet. He did not want to be seen bending before his brother and his flushed face clearly displayed that he felt this to be a very unpleasant duty that he had to perform.

Later, as we all sat down to enjoy a great feast Jahanara remarked, "I have been seeing the Taj Mahal under construction for so many years but was quite astounded to see the complete building two days ago. I cannot believe that a more magnificent building has ever been made."

Shuja endorsed her opinion saying, "Never before! Never before! I was speaking to one of the architects from Turkey who said that it even surpassed the Hagia Sophia in Istanbul that everyone knows is the most magnificent building of the western world. He told me that he has seen many beautiful buildings including the great mosque at Samarkand but that the Taj far surpassed them all. It is the most beautiful building made by man to be found anywhere in the world. I have commissioned some portraits of it and will get my court poets to further immortalise it in poetry."

A number of delicious dishes were placed before all the brothers and sisters on individual gold plates and everyone ate in silence. When a cool *sharbat* was served at the end of the meal they all resumed their talk. Dara told them that his handsome son Sulaiman had the makings of a great soldier while Shuja said that he had never seen any woman who could surpass the beauty of his second daughter Gulrukh. Murad animatedly spoke of the wonderful shikar in his *mansab* where they would chase wild asses over the open plains and kill lions with spears on horsebacks. Aurangzeb listened to everyone with a small smile on his face but said nothing.

As everyone was leaving Gauharara stood next to me and softly said, "How wonderful it is for all the family to be together but how much more wonderful it would be if their inner thoughts could be as happy as the smiles they show on their faces."

Shah Jahan now ruled the richest empire in the world and had already proved himself to be a daring soldier as well as a connoisseur of culture but he wanted more; he wanted to be immortalized. He confided to Dara that he craved to leave a lasting legacy to establish the greatness of the Mughal Empire. After building the most magnificent tomb in the world also wanted to build a magnificent new capital that would outshine the once great capitals of Egypt, Babylon, Turkey, Persia, China or Europe. He had always got whatever he had desired and had a strong inner belief that he enjoyed the mandate of Allah to obtain anything he wanted.

He also found that over the years Agra had become filthy. It had become too crowded, noisy, dirty and malodorous for the emperor's fine aesthetic tastes. Court historians pointed out that the same thing had happened earlier, when the old capital of Dilli became overcrowded forcing the Lodi Sultans to move from Dilli to the unspoiled environs of Agra further down the Jumna.

He had often berated his town administrators for their failure to keep Agra clean and quiet and they had dutifully promised to try harder but humbly submitted that it was no easy task. The problem was that there were never enough carriers of night soil to dispose of the daily defecation of the ever expanding population. Despite the threats of severe punishments, they would dump their unsanitary loads as soon as they were out of the sight of their supervisors. Additionally, many thousands of poor people were constantly flooding into the city.

When the emperor was at his capital all his noblemen with their huge entourages would crowd into the city turning it into a confused mass of elephants, horses, camels, coaches and palanquins. The bazaars would echo with shrill cries of merchants offering their wares that would be interrupted by the strident voices of the food vendors, jugglers, snake charmers, street dancers, fortune tellers and peddlers of medicines. Thieves and pick pockets would have a field day while there were hundreds of beggars cringing for alms in every corner.

The *kotwals* commanding the police, found it very difficult to manage the seething mass of humanity. The noblemen had to use stout bearers with tall maces to open a path for them to move through the teeming throng. A golden mace signified a person of the royal blood and a silver mace the presence of a noble *amir*. Others carried tall poles from which their colourful flags would flutter.

I had noticed that most of the tradesmen lived in miserable mud and brick hovels above their tiny shops while street vendors selling tandoori bread, saffron scented rice, dals, curds, spices, sweetmeats and a wide assortment of kababs occupied every vacant spot on the roads. In some of the buildings there were also taverns that provided wines, sherbets, opium and bhang to their customers with music and dance. A number of brothels catering to rich and poor customers also flourished in almost every quarter.

One day, while walking through the confusion I saw that a woman wearing a long green skirt with a green shawl over her head was intently staring at me. Her face and eyes looked familiar but I could not remember her until she, to my astonishment, suddenly bent down and put her head on my feet crying. "I have waited for so many years to thank you for saving my life when I was just a young girl. It is because of your kindness that I have been able to come from Jhansi to Agra where I now, have a fine family with three children." She then rummaged among her belongings and pulled out three gold coins and said, "You gave me three silver coins when you saved me. I beg you please accept these coins as tokens of my eternal gratitude."

I now, remembered the young girl who I had so often thought about and felt a warm glow of happiness to know that she had survived her ordeal. I could not, however, accept her offer and gently told her, "I too am very happy to know that you are well but I cannot possibly accept the coins that you are so generously offering. Please give one to each of your children from me with my blessings. My little silver coin has grown into your gold coin. Perhaps our good wishes will together bestow growing good fortune on your children."

While Agra had become very populous and disgusting, Dilli, lacking the patronage of the imperial court, had become smaller and cleaner. With this in mind the emperor decided to build a grand new city a short distance from the old capital of Dilli. It was to be perfectly planned to immortalize his name. In this endeavour, *kismet* was to accede to the emperor's wishes and the magnificent city of Shahjahanabad was to come into being.

Work on this great project commenced six years after work on the Taj Mahal but because it was of a much simpler and less detailed, the huge fort took only nine years to complete. It was built on an open plain, north of the old Tughlaq and Lodi capitals and was a huge octagonal red sand stone structure of a *Kos* in circumference, surrounded by a wide ring of outer battlements. North of the fort was the little island fort of Salimgarh, that was to become the royal prison and was connected to the Red Fort by an arched stone bridge.

Like the Agra fort, it had a royal balcony on the east over a sandy river bank where elephant fights, military parades and other entertainments could be staged. The elephant fights were always the most spectacular. Two huge champions each carrying two *mahouts* and an array of colourful flags would be brought into a ring. This oval ring had a high mud wall to stop the fighting beasts straying into the spectators who were thronged just outside the arena. The two elephants were let in from entrances on opposite sides that were immediately closed with bags of sand. Their rear legs would be tied by stout chains attached to two other big elephants and they would only be let loose on a signal from the emperor. A third big elephant would be kept in readiness to intervene in case either of the elephants got out of control while a group of about twenty other trained elephants sat on the sand beyond the ring ready to be summoned if the enraged bulls became too violent to be separated.

Although life in Dilli was quieter and more pleasant, the emperor was to only enjoy the pleasures of the new capital for nine years before the bitter wars between his sons put an end to his reign and he was made a prisoner in Agra for the last eight years of his life. After building the Red Fort, Shah Jahan began construction of the huge but much less ostentatious Jama Masjid, just a short distance from the fort, that was intended to be the largest mosque in the world.

The emperor was not only a gifted architect but he also designed the most beautiful jewellery. He therefore decided to craft the greatest jewelled creation of all time in the form of the magnificent Peacock Throne[15] (*Takht-i-Taus*). He began planning a very large throne and canopy standing higher than the height of two men and wider than a man's arms fully outstretched and almost as deep. It was to take seven years to complete and was graven with 56 maunds (2,100 Kilos) of richly enamelled gold and encrusted with diamonds, rubies, emeralds and sapphires and then topped with a canopy of pearls supported by twelve solid gold pillars. These pillars had vine like wreaths made of the most precious stones. On top of each pillar were two peacocks with long raised tails made of emeralds, rubies and diamonds. It was designed to resemble the fabled throne of Solomon with the jewelled peacocks as guardians to the gates of paradise who could consume the snakes of the devil.

He was also a great patron of painting and Prince Dara was a great painter himself. Dara's main studio was at Aram Bagh on the east bank of the Jumna that had been the first

15 The Peacock Throne was captured by Nadir Shah of Persia when he looted Delhi in 1739 but, as it was far too big and heavy to transport, it had to be broken into smaller sections. There is a so-called Peacock Throne in the Tehran museum but it is a pale shadow of the original.

Mughal garden of Agra. When Humayun returned after his exile in Persia he had brought back two famous painters Sayyid Ali and Abdus Samad from Tabriz who started the school of Mughal miniature paintings. The Persians had been influenced by Chinese paintings and almost always painted portraits in a flat side profile with clouds, horses, mountains, trees, flowers and other features in a formal style. But the old themes were soon adapted to Indian settings and to commemorate historic or mythological events. New oil paintings arriving from Europe, including portraits of the English King and Queen, had also come during the time of Jahangir but our painters scoffed at the new techniques.

Dara had, in his collection, several wonderful pictures depicting nature in addition to some with battle, hunting and romantic scenes. He also had a fine collection of his own paintings[16]. He would often ask me to stand behind and assist him while he was painting. If I had any time to spare, I would try to imitate what I had observed. Using the small bits of charcoal and paper that had been cast aside and was quite pleasantly surprised at the results of my efforts. While some paintings were on parchment, cloth or wood, some were miniatures that were painted on ivory and bone. The drawing was first sketched in outline, usually in the colour red, then improved upon with lamp black. Over this, was applied a thin preparatory coat of paint. The outline was then carefully retraced and details and colours were slowly filled in. The artists would sit on the floor with a bolster below one knee and the painting then executed on the board supported by the other raised knee. The strokes of the squirrel hair brushes were so fine that they were sometimes almost invisible to the naked eye.

---

16 A folio of sixty eight paintings actually done by Dara Shikoh called the Dara Shikoh Album can be seen in the British Library London.

Our Emperor did not have a good portrait of his beloved late empress to keep beside him and was dissatisfied with the ones that had been made earlier. He ordered Haridas, the chief court painter to produce one. As none of the artists were ever allowed to actually set eyes on the ladies of the *zenana* who were jealously kept from public view; a few courtesans who most resembled the lady to be immortalized would be dressed up, to pose and the picture would be presented to the emperor for his approval. After several failed attempts, to produce a suitable likeness of his empress the emperor directed Dara, who in turn asked me to convey to Hari Das the features that the Emperor wanted.

Hari Das asked me, "You had been close to Her Majesty so tell me what you think needs to be altered." After several abortive attempts to correct his efforts I hesitantly picked up a piece of charcoal and paper and quickly sketched out a profile of our late queen from memory. He looked sceptical at first but then nodded and smiled and setting aside his earlier work picked up my rough outline and began to carefully fill in the details and the colours. We were both overjoyed when the emperor later expressed his happiness at the final painting.

Some of the orthodox artists disapproved of the growing influence of Rajput art in which a heavy necklace would often be placed between the ample breasts of maidens to highlight the curves of their breasts or hips. Long tresses of hair were seductively draped over a shoulder or to reach the knees after highlighting a distinct curve over the hips. Sometimes, the clothes would be shown to be so diaphanous that they would suggestively hint at the tone of the skin below.

The orthodox Muslim clerics disapprovingly said that only Allah can create life and that it was sinful to try to imitate the creations of Allah. In a discussion a month earlier, they had refused to answer when Dara reminded them of some famous Islamic portraits like those of The Prophet Mohammad riding Burak, a winged horse with the face of a beautiful woman, on his way to Jerusalem for the 'Meraj' or his nocturnal journey to the heavens. Dara also pointed out that the great emperor Akbar had commissioned more than one hundred huge pictures to illustrate the famous Hamzanama collection. These narrated the legendary exploits of Amir Hamza, the uncle of The Prophet in a series of romantic adventures, threatening events, narrow escapes, and violent acts.

One day, one of our leading artists, Hunar, almost had a heart attack when he saw that prince Aurangzeb had quietly entered the studio and was standing just behind him. Aurangzeb's informants must have told him about this painting studio so he studied a few before turning disapprovingly towards Dara who had followed him in and after the most perfunctory of greetings, said, "Bhai Jaan, how can you allow paintings that provoke such sinful thoughts... such filth... to be produced in this studio under your own patronage?"

Without waiting for any reply he stormed out with his small train of followers scuttling behind him.

As the sixty- three year old emperor was getting older, he became aware of his flagging virility and began to indulge in sex with an almost obsessive insistence. So the royal *hakims* were very hard pressed to find new potions to stimulate his diminishing potency. The procurers for the *zenana* offered huge sums to acquire the most beautiful new concubines from all over the world. From fair skinned beauties from Georgia or Circassia to a slant - eyed seductresses from China and the dark sultry women from the Deccan or even Abyssinia.

We all stared in wonder, one day, when a tall and very slender, jet black, girl with a small pretty face from Abyssinia was presented to the *zenana*. At our request she unashamedly discarded her long robe to reveal such a beautifully shaped body that it could have been a black marble statue made by one of the great European masters. Her arms and legs seemed unnaturally long and her small breasts stood out firmly above her tiny stomach, large buttocks and ample hips. Her rich dark skin, covered by very fine hair, was almost silky to the touch. The old emperor seemed to be very taken with her and asked for her several times.

He also became quite enchanted by two beautiful twin girls who not only seemed to be in a state constant of laughter but would join in together to try to please the emperor with one massaging and stimulating him while he was enjoying the favors of the other. So insistent became the demands of our ageing emperor that some malicious tongues even suggested that he was committing incest with my beloved princess. It was true that they were very deeply attached to each other and that she spent considerable time in the emperor's private quarters. Although, I knew that this malicious street gossip was untrue I would still be seized with furious anger and an acute feeling of helpless jealousy whenever someone even suggested such a possibility.

Malicious gossip swirled all around us. It was once even rumored that Jahanara had a romance with an Afghan officer called Najabat Khan. I was present at a parade and heard her innocently remark that he looked a handsome officer. But wicked tongues soon began to invent the most ingenious tales even though there had been absolutely no possibility of them meeting, let alone having a romantic affair. The speculation however died soon after when this dashing officer led a battalion of troops against the rebellious hill rajah of Srinagar on the upper reaches of the Ganges River. The attack to this mountain kingdom was ill timed and the troops were caught in a blinding snow storm. The survivors were easily taken prisoner and the *rani* ordered that their noses should be cut off to deter any other attacks on their little kingdom. She was soon called '*nakh katane wali rani*' or the rani who cuts off noses. Najabat returned in disgrace but was to continue in the army and later became quite an important officer. His disfigured nose, that he covered with a leather cover, was to however make him an object of mockery.

We had no inkling that our emperor's increasingly insatiable hunger for sex was to soon plunge our great empire into an inferno of bloodshed and sorrow.

Later, while I was quietly reading in the *zenana*, I became aware that someone was sitting next to me. That day little Gauharara told me one of her riddles that seemed to predict that these glorious times would be destined to end in disaster. We said nothing for a while till she started humming a tuneless song. After some time she looked dreamily into the distance and softly said, "Remember that the flower always blooms before it withers and dies and it blooms brightest before it dies. The brighter the bloom the sadder the death. Look at all the flowers all around us. Look at all the pretty petals lying at our feet. Red and yellow tulips will cover the fields for as far as the eyes can see. Red and yellow tulips! Red and yellow tulips!"

I looked at her but was completely unable to understand her words.

Revere beauty and become aware of the perfection of
God in every leaf, tree, flower, cloud or stream
and you will see that man's
godliness is often an empty sham

CHAPTER 14

The Afghan Misadventure

After a glorious rule of twenty years Shah Jahan began to dream of achieving even greater glory to impress the entire Muslim world. From early childhood, he had been enthused by the heroic accounts of his great great grandfather Babur. Emboldened by many of his own triumphs in Hindustan, he felt that he was ready to follow in Babur's footsteps into Central Asia. He wanted to reclaim the ancient Mughal territories of Balkh and Badakshan with the legendary cities of Kashgar and Samarkand as their capitals. He longed to be remembered not only as a great emperor or builder but also as a great conqueror, like Alexander.

On a sudden impulse he decided to give the twenty-one year old tall, handsome but hollow-headed prince Murad his first real battlefield command. He was given a large army of fifty thousand soldiers to invade and conquer Balkh, north of the Mughal territories of Kabul. After the lush forested plains and hills of Hindustan, the bleak, bare, stony and nearly treeless lands of Balkh were a rude shock for the officers and soldiers alike. While the Mughals easily gained territory, they could not engage or conquer the numerous scattered bands of hardy Uzbek tribesmen who made irritatingly elusive targets; constantly harassing their flanks and then vanishing into the dusty distance on their nimble ponies.

An emissary was sent to Amir Khan, the leader of the Uzbeks, asking why they were such cowards as to run from the field and shirk combat. Amir Khan sent a contemptuous reply that infuriated Murad, saying, "As we have no cities worth defending, do you think we would be so foolish as to risk our lives and our horses? If you persist in your folly of coming deeper into my territory I have only to wait for our ally *'General Winter'* who will soon arrive to fight our battles for us and you will surely be annihilated."

Murad recognized that there was some merit to the message as the long dreaded winter was approaching. The sparse grass on the meadows was rapidly turning brown with the morning frost and the horses were starving. Impetuous as always, Murad abruptly abandoned the expedition and returned to Kabul without even making an attempt to march towards Samarkand. The emperor was furious especially since, Murad had completely deserted his army and returned without royal permission. The emperor was also aware that this precipitate withdrawal would be regarded as a defeat and make the Mughals lose the respect of all the other Muslim monarchs.

Murad was immediately stripped of rank and forbidden to appear in court. His elder brother Aurangzeb was urgently recalled from the Deccan and sent to take command of the stranded army. He was only able to arrive there the following spring but soon found that campaigning in Badakshan was to prove very difficult especially as the barren plains provided so little to feed the soldiers, horses and pack animals. Aurangzeb's reputation however gained a boost when, in the midst of a battle, he spread out his prayer carpet and calmly performed his evening *namaz* to the astonishment of friends and foes alike. But his piety did not help and he too had to retreat before the onset of the next winter. Some ten thousand soldiers and their horses were uselessly lost without any aggression by the enemy.

It was the first great setback of Shah Jahan's reign but worse was to follow. Kandahar, the doorway to Persia, located some two hundred *Kos* south of Kabul, had long been a bone of bitter contention between the Mughals and the Persian *shahs*. It had been seized by Akbar but Shah Abbas had recaptured it from Jahangir and fifteen years later the Persian Governor, Ali Mardan Khan had been persuaded to hand it back and he went on to become an important Mughal general. After eleven years, Shah Abbas again recaptured it. It was a distant and desolate region with little wealth or treasures to justify the huge expense of a Mughal conquest.

But as Shah Jahan had always got whatever he coveted, he could not accept these setbacks and was determined to add a victory in the west to his many triumphs. Aurangzeb took the huge force that was languishing at Kabul to Kandahar even though it did not have the big guns or siege equipment needed to conquer this mud fort sitting on the top of a forbidding spur of almost vertical granite. The few Mughal assaults were easily picked off by the defenders and Aurangzeb could find no guile or stratagem to gain his objective.

The infuriated Shah Jahan recalled Aurangzeb in disgrace and posted him to the insignificant town of Multan.

Aurangzeb realized that this dreary posting on the banks of the Indus would be a serious setback for his career and reputation. It would also offer him very few opportunities of strengthening his position for the contest for succession that he knew must happen soon. As Shah Jahan kept ignoring his many requests for more important responsibilities, he swallowed his pride and wrote to Dara asking him to intercede on his behalf. When Dara approached his father with the matter, Shah Jahan looked very surprised and cynically asked, "Are you acting on behalf of that venomous white snake? I have noted your request but just remember that you may one day have to suffer from its poison." He nevertheless relented and sent Aurangzeb back to again take command of the Deccan.

Prince Dara was now given the task of capturing Kandahar[17]. Despite having very little battle experience he proudly decided to take to the field and the indulgent emperor gave him an even bigger army of seventy thousand men. He also provided a set of new and much bigger cannons manned by teams of European gunners. I was present at the grand durbar announcing his appointment but I could barely believe my ears when I heard Dara foolishly boast to a few noblemen that he would be victorious within a week and would personally drag that dog Shah Abbas to the feet of the emperor. I managed to get myself included in this grand expedition and was witness to a battle like no other in the annals of our great empire.

Dara was so impatient to prove himself in the theatre of warfare that he did not even wait for his reputed generals

---

17 The details of Dara's campaign at Kandahar, including descriptions of all the praying mullas and faquirs, is detailed in Waldemer Hansen's book The Peacock Throne and K.R. Qanungo's book on Dara Shikoh quoting from Rashid Khan.

like Jai Singh of Amer or Karan Singh of Bikaner to assemble their armies. He spoke of harnessing the power of cosmic energy as his secret weapon. He seemed to have forgotten his peaceful spiritual beliefs and was surrendering to the advice of numerous frauds who claimed miraculous metaphysical powers. By the time the army was nearing Multan, we had a virtual swarm of astrologers, magicians, sages, Hindu *sadhus*, Muslim *fakirs* and Sufi saints accompanying us. Every charlatan and trickster for thousands of miles around rushed towards Multan for a heaven sent opportunity to gain royal favours.

One holy man claimed that he commanded forty genies that could secretly kill any enemy. Another *Yogi* arrived with forty disciples whose combined prayer, he said, could make anything happen. Two mystics with their heads buried under colourful patched robes would make loud pronouncements every few hours. Another claimed to possess a wonderful flying machine without wings or feathers from which they could bombard the Persian defenders with musket balls, arrows or filth.

Our Mughal officers were clearly getting very disgusted by the strange going on, while the Rajputs were just amused. Rajah Jai Singh implored Dara to use their new cannon to begin war in the conventional way. Unfortunately, our Rajput cavalry was quite useless in assaulting such a steep fortress. The European and Muslim gunners with the help of bullocks and common infantrymen managed to pull some of the heavy guns mounted on their big wooden carriages on to a hill facing the fortress but their shots supported by big rockets were quite ineffectual.

Shah Abbas then added fuel to the fires of Mughal disappointment by sending a message complimenting the prince for providing such a splendid display of fireworks. After six months of desultory fighting the professional soldiers had become utterly disillusioned and surly. When a desperate charge of the gate was finally ordered, the superior Persian artillery commanding the heights above the forty steps cut them to pieces, followed by a charge by their soldiers who opened the huge main gates and sallied out to complete the havoc.

Dara now seemed to waken, as if from a dream, and decided to seriously consult his generals. He summoned Jai Singh and severely chastised him for the half hearted performance of his soldiers. Jai Singh, with rather surly deference, replied, "The emperor will be angry with us for our failure. But fear not, we will fight resolutely to restore our fallen honor."

Dara, after conferring with his officers, decided that the Mughals should immediately renew their attack while the Persians were still gloating. He felt that the Persians would be over confident and might open their gates again to scatter another evidently careless infantry attack. During that very night a number of small guns were secreted just below the gates and covered with cloth, mud and rocks. A thousand valiant infantrymen then charged up the steep incline at first light before the Persian batteries had time to be properly loaded and primed. Mughal engineers shielded by the distraction of the attack quietly ran up the slope and planted explosives under the huge gates.

The Persian response, though delayed, was quite effective and the batteries on the towers beside the gate began to accurately fire down at the attackers. The Mughals now pretended to waver and, as on the previous day, retreated in disarray and the Persians once again sallied out of the gate to chase the stragglers with jeering cries. This time however, the engineers exploded the mines laid out the night before to leave the huge gates hanging open and the entrance of the fort undefended. Three thousand horsemen supported by five thousand infantry soldiers who were quietly waiting hidden from the sight, under the bulging cliffs below the walls of the fort then surged forward and furious hand to hand combat followed. But it was very difficult to sustain an attack on such a steep and slippery incline, especially as the Persians had the advantage of the commanding heights. Thus, the assault had to be abandoned after a few hours.

But we were at least able to show our valour by killing hundreds of Persian soldiers and capturing two of their new cannons from near the gate along with a few other war trophies including a beautiful sword with a gold inscription chased into the brilliant steel blade that we thought would please the emperor. A little honor was certainly restored but there was to be no victory. I, however, got the satisfaction of seeing Dara regain the respect of his soldiers especially when the last of that motley collection of *yogis, fakirs,* savants and charlatans were sent away. It was a sad and final Mughal effort to capture Kandahar. Many thousands of lives and a huge fortune was, needlessly, wasted over three years on these futile efforts that ended all further Mughal ambitions to conquer these forbidding and worthless lands.

As he grew older Dara, unfortunately, began to become increasingly arrogant, imperious and impatient. He quite unnecessarily lost the goodwill of some of his own followers. The loyal *Rajah* Jai Singh may have lacked a tall military bearing but he was needlessly humiliated when Dara jokingly said that he looked like a musician. Though musicians were essential to the court as were the dancing and singing girls, they were not held in high esteem.

Dara was to also become totally infatuated with a common dancing girl called Ranadil. This tall and fair girl from Punjab was of striking beauty and her name meant clear heart. Though Dara could have easily kept her as a common concubine he embarrassed the emperor by insisting on taking his permission to marry her. He also took another fair skinned wife who was named Udaipuri Begum who had originally come from Georgia north of Turkey. I knew that Nadira Begum was very unhappy to have these new members in her *zenana* but she could not defy Mughal customs and had the good grace to make the ladies feel welcome.

When Aurangzeb returned to his Deccan kingdom it had been racked by famines, Maratha depredations and neglected administration during his years of absence; many fields had been abandoned by the cultivators and subsequently turned into jungles. A large imperial force also needed to be maintained to keep the vassal rulers of Golconda and Bijapur in check. So instead of providing revenue, the armies in the Deccan were becoming a heavy drain on the imperial treasury and a source of constant friction with the emperor. Aurangzeb had to provide some revenue for the ever hungry Mughal treasury so he sought added revenue through conquests. With the threat of war he quickly secured sizeable tributes from some of the smaller *rajahs* of Gondwana and north Konkan and he then turned upon the very rich and well administered province of Golconda that was so rich in diamonds.

Ibrahim Qutab Shah, the fourth ruler of the dynasty of the kingdom of Golconda had retreated to his nearly impregnable fortress and sent Mir Jamla as his emissary to parley with the prince. Mir Jamla, a wily Persian, former oil trader, who by his nimble intelligence and military ability had risen to be prime minister of Golconda, persuaded his master to allow him to negotiate with Aurangzeb. He was short and stocky with an ugly bulbous nose but bright eyes that shone with mercurial intelligence. He arrived at the Mughal prince's camp with a small but richly clad retinue. When he was admitted into Aurangzeb's presence he presented him with a small tray of the most dazzling diamonds and said, "*Shahzadeh Hazoor*, ours is but a poor kingdom but we have been blessed with the only diamond mine in the world. My master presents you with these little baubles as a *nazrana*, a small personal tribute, from one noble prince to another. It is just a small token to sweeten our discussions on matters of much greater importance."

Aurangzeb immediately recognized that Mir Jamla was highly intelligent, resourceful and determined and could be a very useful potential ally and took him aside for long whispered negotiations. After a long siege the Shahi ruler agreed to pay a large indemnity and also agreed to a matrimonial alliance between his daughter and Aurangzeb's dashing eldest son Muhammad Sultan.

The rich province of Bijapur west of Golconda was Aurangzeb's next target. With the death of the ruler, Mohammad Adil Shah, there arose disorder in the territory and Aurangzeb proclaimed that the Mughals must invade Bijapur as the chosen successor was not the real son of Adil Shah. Shah Jahan approved of the plan and Bijapur was besieged and conquered after a huge explosion under the battlements, laid open the defences. A gigantic booty in cash, valuables and armaments was seized.

Aurangzeb sensed that the vassal kingdoms of both Golconda and Bijapur were now so weak that they were ripe for complete annexation into the Mughal Empire, instead of remaining as vassal states that could declare their freedom at any time. He believed that Shah Jahan would be very pleased with these conquests after the disappointments in Balkh and Kandahar. The Bijapur rulers, however, knew of Dara's opposition to Aurangzeb's ambitions and appealed to him with costly presents and a request that he should intercede with the emperor to halt the annexation. Shah Jahan hesitated for several days and then suddenly ordered Aurangzeb to return to Aurangabad. Aurangzeb was furious at being denied a great victory and seethed with anger against his eldest brother who he knew had been responsible for the emperor's abrupt decision.

Prince Shuja the subedar of Bengal was given the additional charge of the province of Orissa. He had first set up his capital at Dhaka near the sea but later, transferred it to the more pleasant environs of Rajmahal, the old capital of Gaur, where a branch of the great Ganga River turns southwards and flows towards the sea. He later conquered the kingdom of Kamrupa and Kooch Bihar, which were equal to a third province. He was a generous patron of numerous Persian poets and scholars. Like his father, Shuja was a great builder and many of the first great buildings in Bengal were built at his command.

Conscious of the importance of trade and commerce in the economic development of the land, he welcomed foreign traders and granted them privileges for carrying on their trade for a fee. He granted a royal patent to the Portuguese confirming their privilege of trade earlier granted to them by a firman of the emperor. He also granted privileges to the English East India Company and to the Dutch company.

Shah Jahan who had carefully observed the performance of all his sons in the campaigns in Balkh, Kandahar, Deccan and Bengal realized that they had all acquired considerable battlefield and administrative experience. He knew that they were all capable of usurping the Mughal throne and become increasingly anxious about how to keep their restless energies occupied.

Life is an island in an ocean of loneliness
where hopes are rocks, dreams are trees
and salty streams water the flowers of solitude.

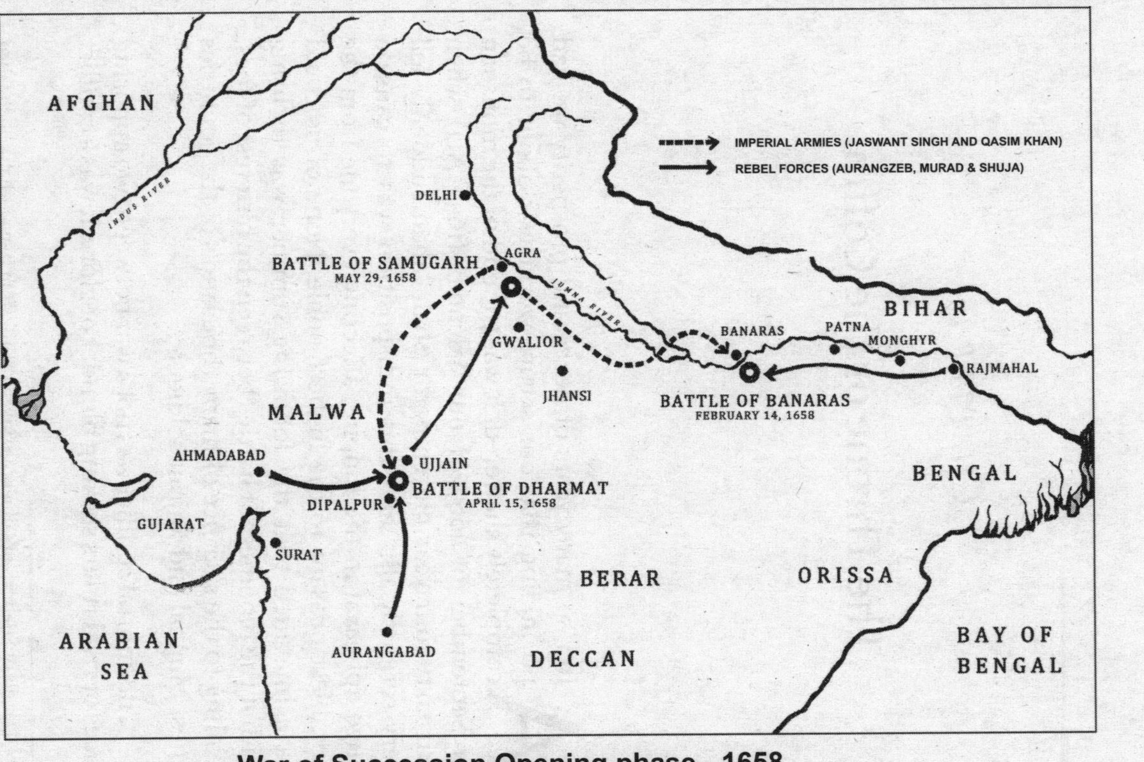

War of Succession Opening phase - 1658

(Map modified from original as per requirements of the narrative)
Source: The Peacock Throne by Waldeman Hansen (Holt, Rinehart & Winstone 1972)

CHAPTER 15

The Throne or the Coffin

After so many years of peace and prosperity we had no inkling that our secure world was about to be completely shattered. It was the end of the monsoon in September of 1067 of our calendar (1657 AD) when our sixty-four year old emperor Shah Jahan suddenly fell very seriously ill;[18] and this indisposition was to cause a huge upheaval in the Empire, affecting everyone from the humblest peasant to the highest noble. None of us could have imagined that the following summer was to bring with it the bloodiest of battles between the bitterest of foes, leading to the sacrifice of many thousand's of the countries finest Mughal and Rajput soldiers.

This mortal conflict was not a war between two opposing races or rival rulers seeking plunder or glory. It was a conflict

---

18 Details of Shah Jahan's illness are taken mainly from Inayat Khan's Shah Jahan nama (vol II, p 118)but there are far more detailed and exaggerated accounts by Bernard Tavernier and Nicalao Manucci.

between four competing brothers who knew that if they failed to win the Mughal throne, they stood to lose their lives, their wives, and everything that was valuable to them. No conflict could generate as much emotional intensity as antagonists who had been brought up in the bosom of the same family, where petty childhood jealousies could later trigger intense anger, pride and stupidity. It was these that drove all the princes to almost insane aggression leading to terrible consequences for the empire.

Even more surprising was the fact that the trigger to this conflagration was common lust. One of the new hakims seeking to take advantage of our emperor's need for stimulants to arouse his flagging virility, offered a new potion that he claimed would have miraculous effect. But he must have made the dose too potent with the result that the emperor became acutely constipated, was unable to pass urine for several days and lay completely prostrated with very severe pain. His condition did not improve even after strenuous efforts by the older hakims and he started running a very high temperature.

Dara, not wanting people to be alarmed, kept him confined and barred the entry of all visitors including the emperor's other children and family members. This proved to be a mistake as it only intensified the speculation. Rumours began to spread very fast and with many embellishments, especially when the emperor failed to appear at the jharoka for the daily morning darshan. Many feared that he was either dead or was slowly dying of poison.

One morning, as he was getting better, the emperor anxiously called out for Jahanara and, waving his outstretched hands plaintively cried out, "I cannot smell the apples! ... I cannot smell the apples! ... I can no longer smell the apples on my hands...... What has happened?... What will become of us?"

Jahanara, unable to understand what the emperor was saying, rushed inside to ask us but none could understand the emperor's strange outburst. It was then that I remembered a story told nearly thirty years earlier about the time when prince Khurram, who became the future emperor Shah Jahan, had been a fugitive in the Deccan and a pregnant Mumtaz had felt a sudden craving for apples. As if by a miracle he met a fakir who gave him two red apples and warned him to beware for when the scent of apples faded from his hands he would be in danger of betrayal by his third son.It was only now that we fully understood why the emperor had always been so cold and suspicious of Aurangzeb. As Shah Jahan began to slowly recover Jahanara tried to reassure him but a seed of deep doubt was planted in all our minds.

The spies of the princes inside the palace, including Aurangzeb's faithful informant Roshanara as well as Gauharara on behalf of Shuja, sent them messages about the emperor's condition. Many reports were probably exaggerated but when received more than a week later, they served to stir the princes to oppose what they all thought was a devious conspiracy by Dara to snatch the Mughal throne for himself. They trusted nobody and knew that only one of them was destined to sit on the Peacock Throne, the grave being the other alternative.

After my brief service with Aurangzeb I had continued to secretly correspond with a few members of his entourage. I learned from them that the usually reticent and controlled prince had uncharacteristically exploded in furious anger a few months earlier, when Shah Jahan had stopped him from annexing Bijapur and making it a province of the Mughal

Empire. He had angrily accused Dara of deliberately trying to thwart everything he was doing to enlarge and enrich the empire. He had often called Dara a pampered prince and a useless parasite who, under the cloak of religious exploration, was trying to gain the support of the powerful Rajput and Hindu nobles in the contest for succession to the Mughal throne. He also openly mocked his other brothers, he felt Shuja was a lazy debauch who could better command a band of dancing girls than an army. And Murad, under his sturdy military bearing, was a drunkard with a head as hollow as a drum. His courtiers laughed when he said Murad had the heart of a lion, the brains of a sparrow and the stubbornness of a mule.

Aurangzeb was most alarmed by the news of his father's illness. He felt it necessary to always be alert concerning all the risks and opportunities in his path and knew that he would only get the support of those who believed in him, feared him or those that he could wean from their support of his brothers. He had maintained a quite outward cordial relationship with Shuja and Murad but failed to understand the emperor's almost besotted love for Dara. This made him harbour a strong sense of injustice that rapidly developed into intense jealousy and hatred for everything about his eldest brother.

Reacting quickly to the developments in Agra, he sent out a number of emissaries and messages to unite the resolve of his brothers by saying that it was their sacred duty to thwart Dara who he said had become a heretic. He claimed that Dara was not just trying to snatch the crown from the emperor but that he wanted to encourage Hindu heresies to sully the purity of the Islamic Mughal Empire. His brothers were quick to respond as they feared that Dara was in the best position to exploit their ailing father's affections.

The forty - year old Shah Shuja was the first to declare his rebellion by crowning himself emperor, having his name called at the Friday *khutba* or noon prayers in all the mosques of his territory and had coins minted in his name. Quickly gathering an army, he began the long march from his capital Rajmahal towards Agra with part of the army advancing on foot and his artillery making its way up the Ganges in a large flotilla of river boats.

The impetuous Murad, aged thirty-two, was quick to follow. He had been living a languid existence in Ahmadabad with his affairs being managed by a very able minister, Ali Naqi, one of the few honest men in those treacherous times. Ali Naqi had been personally chosen by the emperor and was therefore disliked by Murad's hard drinking cohorts. They conspired to forge a letter, allegedly, written by him to Shah Jahan compromising his loyalty and then arranged for it to be intercepted. When the letter was shown to Murad he accosted the innocent minister and in a burst of anger personally killed him with his lance. He then raided the traders of Surat and collected a huge ransom along with forced loans from them. With these resources he too, quickly raised an army.

Murad's comfortable rule at Ahmedabad was greatly aided by the assistance of Shah Nawaz Khan, the father of his wife, Sakina Bano Begum. He was a very able and experienced officer who had been the governor at Ahmedabad for many years. His elder daughter Dilras Bano Begum was the senior wife of Aurangzeb but Sakina had been the apple of her father's eye.

Aurangzeb assured Murad that he had no interest in the throne but only wanted to ensure that the apostate Dara did not imprison the ailing emperor and take the throne. He declared that Dara was now following the religion of the Hindus while Shuja was following the faith of the apostate Shias. In his elegant Persian script he wrote that their joint mission was "to uproot the bramble of idolatry and infidelity from the realm of Islam and crush the idolatrous chief with his followers and strongholds, so that the dust of disturbance may be allayed in Hindustan."

Aurangzeb meticulously made his plans. He immediately sent a company of trusted troops to keep a close watch at the ferry over the river Tapti at Burhanpur to intercept all messages being sent between Dilli and the Deccan. This ensured that the emperor could no longer send orders to Mir Jamla whose armies had earlier been sent to assist Aurangzeb in the south. He then turned on the kingdoms of Golkonda and Bijapur to extract large indemnities from them to raise a fine army.

As Shah Jahan recovered he was mainly concerned about Aurangzeb, and sent orders to Mir Jamla, ordering him to immediately return to Agra with his army. As Mir Jamla's wife and family were in Delhi, he dared not openly defy the emperor but decided to connive with Aurangzeb and allow himself to be made a prisoner at the impregnable fortress of Daulatabad. Aurangzeb then took over his well equipped but now leaderless army.

Aurangzeb then wrote to the gullible prince Murad whom he flattered by saying, "You are the most worthy successor to the emperor. I would support you to the throne so that I may retire to live as a hermit." No one believed him as they knew that he was far too ambitious to allow any brother to ascend the throne. Everyone except Murad was aware that Aurangzeb's declaration about retiring as a hermit was only a ploy to deceive the others.

Aurangzeb also sent a flurry of secret messages to most of the leading noblemen in the capital in an attempt to undermine their loyalties to Shah Jahan and Dara. As soon as his plans were set, he marched north with an army of thirty thousand men including Mir Jamla's artillery commanded by European officers. His force included many battle hardened Marathas along with some disaffected Rajput clans. When he heard that Murad was bringing his *zenana* and a large entourage he wrote to him saying that they would hamper their swift movement and persuaded him to send them back to Aurangabad.

It was to be a hard month's march to join forces with Murad's army, who arrived first at their rendezvous north of the Narbada River and waited to hear from Aurangzeb. He, however, now got the disquieting news that a big imperial army, led by *rajah* Jaswant Singh and Qasim Khan, had already arrived in the area to oppose him.

Shah Jahan was now fully restored in health and demonstrated this by going on a hunt, appearing at the morning *darshan* and distributing alms. He also called together his generals and advisors to make plans to face his rebellious sons, appointing Dara as their commander. Several Rajput and Mughal officers were promoted to new commands including the Afghan commander Khaliullah Khan who was also made governor of Dilli. Although Khaliullah Khan was a very experienced commander I felt that his choice was unwise as I was informed by my friends that he still nursed a deep resentment against the Emperor who had once seduced his beautiful Turkish wife and made him an object of widespread mockery. I deeply regret that I did not tell Dara of my fears at this time.

The emperor then sent urgent messages to all his sons

saying that he was fully recovered and that they should all return to their *mansabs*. The rebel princes who had mustered large armies that were already on the march were however in no mood to meekly turn back. They claimed that the emperor's letters were forgeries as Dara could perfectly imitate his father's handwriting and had access to the royal seal. They said that they would only be satisfied when they saw the emperor with their own eyes.

In the capital there was no reliable news for some time about the movements of Aurangzeb and Murad. Then reports arrived confirming that Shuja was on the march so his rebellion had to be immediately opposed. An imperial army of thirty thousand of the empire's finest soldiers commanded by the veteran Mirza Rajah Jai Singh of Amer along with Dara's twenty-three year old elder son, Sulaiman Shikoh, marched east to do battle. Three weeks later, the opposing armies met near Benares on the north bank of the Ganges where Shuja, with the advantage of a large flotilla of river boats, seemed safe from danger. Sulaiman Shikoh, however, commanded his engineers to quickly make a bridge of boats across the great Ganges River, strong enough to transport the elephants and cannon.

Shuja's army and flotilla of boats seemed secure behind a loop of the river; and the imperial army could do little except fire the occasional cannon or rocket. But true to character, Shuja started relaxing in a haze of opium and wine and allowed his patrols to slacken their attention. Sulaiman quickly closed in upon Shuja's force and surprised them at Bahadurpur, a small town three *kos* upriver of Benares with an unexpected dawn attack on a cold and foggy February morning. The surprised Shuja was lucky to be able to escape on an elephant towards the river where he was protected by artillery from his boats. His scattered land army fled eastwards towards Patna in total panic to be looted by rapacious villagers all along the route.

The victory was mostly a result of the unremitting pressure by Sulaiman but he was not content just yet. He wanted to completely destroy his rebellious uncle. Shuja, though defeated, managed to retain his flotilla of boats and was able to conduct a fairly, orderly retreat towards his capital, even though it was over two hundred *Kos* away. But Sulaiman followed him relentlessly. Shuja reached Patna in just five days where he tried to rally his forces. Jai Singh, with his big baggage train, slowed down the speed of the pursuing imperial army that needed twenty days to reach Patna with Sulaiman rushing ahead and then having to stop to wait for him to catch up.

Shuja then made a stand near Monghyr, further east, where the hilly terrain made cavalry attack difficult. The long pursuit had however taken the imperial armies very far from Agra.

Soon rumours about a terrible defeat of the imperial forces by Aurangzeb and Murad at Dharmat began to trickle in. Jai Singh may have been happy to hear about the defeat of his Rajput rival Jaswant Singh but Sulaiman, immediately, understood the enormity of Aurangzeb's victory. He had to therefore make a hasty treaty with Shuja confining him in his former territories and then tried to rush back with his army to Agra to fight for his father.

Soon after the imperial armies left to oppose Shuja, word came to the capital that both Aurangzeb and Murad were also on the march. To counter these, two armies, with about fifteen thousand troopers each, were immediately sent southwards. One under the impetuous *Mirza* rajah Jaswant Singh was sent against Aurangzeb and the other under the veteran Qasim Khan was to oppose Murad.

Dara confided in me saying that it was very difficult to send out armies against the rebel princes because the *Amirs*, who would have readily given their lives to the emperor or a prince of the royal blood, were reluctant to go to war when led by one of their own fellow officers. The emperor did not seem to have fully realised the gravity of the situation and *rajah* Jaswant Singh,who had finally accepted the task, was hampered by an imperial command to only chastise the emperor's sons and not inflict any serious injury upon them.

The two new imperial armies marched side by side until it became clear that the enemy armies were likely to converge at a point somewhere north of the Narbada River and marched quickly in that direction. Jaswant was caught by surprise when his scouting parties came back very quickly with the alarming news that the rebel armies had crossed the Narmada, united and were much larger than expected. The two imperial armies had to unite but now faced a serious problem about who should take overall command. The Emperor decided to give the command to the more experienced Jaswant with the result that Qasim Khan was very upset that his Turki and Afghan army should be subordinated to a Hindu Rajput commander. We later learned that Aurangzeb had anticipated this possibility and had offered Qasim huge inducements to undermine Jaswant Singh's efforts. Jaswant was further weakened by his personal contempt for artillery and firearms that he considered to be 'unworthy of a heroic race like the Rajputs'.

The opposing armies finally met near the village of Dharmat close to Dipalpur on the steep banked Gambhira River, north of Ujjain on a hot day in mid April. When Jaswant finally assessed the odds facing him, he decided against a proposed surprise night attack claiming that it inconsistent with Rajput manliness to adopt such a devious stratagem. He may have also been reluctant as Hindu soldiers were hampered by their ancient traditions of getting up early for their morning rituals of ablutions and prayers, followed by their main meal of the day. So it took time before they were ready for battle, believing that they should only be fought in the hours of daylight.

Jaswant bravely took up a strong defensive position. Long trenches were dug that connected to a swamp behind him; to make the ground on three sides so marshy that the enemy cavalry could not outflank him. But as the Rajputs also relied mainly on cavalry, the soggy, uneven ground also hampered their own movements. Also being densely packed in a narrow space they could neither manoeuvre nor gather momentum for an effective charge. Serious fighting began after furious opening salvoes of guns and rockets. Jaswant's army was surprised that the new enemy cannon instead of aiming low to send balls rolling and bouncing to cut up the enemy ranks, were being aimed in the sky to fall directly on their targets.

Aurangzeb had not only marshalled a battery of excellent artillery but also had a very disciplined new command structure. The vanguard of eight thousand steel clad cavalry was commanded by his very capable eldest son Muhammad Sultan, supported by Murad Baksh who had his army on the right wing, while Aurangzeb personally commanded the centre with several loyal officers like Sheikh Mir, Saf Shikan and and Mulafat Khan.

The imperial armies with redoubtable warriors like

Mukand Singh Hada, Dayal Singh Jhala and Sujan Singh Sisodia, Qasim Khan and Iftikar Khan would not easily yield. A brave cavalry vanguard, quickly captured some of the new enemy guns and killed Aurangzeb's chief gunner before being forced back. But the French and English rebel gunners opened murderous fire on Jaswant's central column from higher ground and six of the Rajput chiefs fell gallantly in the intense combat. Qasim Khan, commanding almost half of the imperial contingent, did not seem to be making any great effort and it was the brave Rajput soldiers who did most of the fighting. As the day progressed it was became increasingly clear to Jaswant that he was facing very resolute enemies and that they were outnumbered, outgunned, out generaled and outfought. At the end of the furious eight hour battle, six thousand imperial soldiers lay dead on the field.

The valiant Jaswant Singh, who had personally sustained two wounds, was determined to either win or to die in the endeavour but his Rajput officers caught hold of the bridle of his horse and begged him to leave the field asking him, why he should sacrifice his life in a family quarrel between the rival Mughal princes. He reluctantly turned around and returned to his capital at Jodhpur where he faced another rude shock when his proud queen refused to let him enter the palace.[19]

Aurangzeb did not immediately pursue the defeated army. This was not only to rest his weary troops, but also to secure the huge treasure, war elephants, horses, artillery and other loot that were with the imperial armies. Aurangzeb kept two thirds of these while Murad was given the rest plus fifteen thousand gold pieces as

---

19 Jaswant Singh's ashes are buried in a cenotaph that was later built just outside the gate of the magnificent Mehrangarh Fort at Jodhpur.

surgeon's fees for his wounded followers. This critical battle was the first defeat suffered by the Mughal imperial armies in Hindustan.

Aurangzeb was to commemorate the victory over Jaswant Singh with a typically brief remark saying, "This is my first battle with the wicked infidels who had destroyed mosques and erected on their sites temples to their idols."

The tattered remains of the imperial army now streamed back from the debacle. The Rajputs fled towards their strongholds in Rajasthan while the Muslim soldiers set off in ragged columns towards Agra. The first messenger to arrive had been a fast courier from Jaswant Singh carrying a blue flag as a banner. This was in the old Mongol tradition to proclaim that the herald was the bearer of bad news. There was great consternation and the emperor realised that he would have to now marshal his depleted forces to meet the relentlessly oncoming threat. But Dara, despite the loss of Jaswant's army and the absence of hardened soldiers who were fighting with Sulaiman Shikoh, showed quick resolution to raise a new army with several experienced Muslim and Rajput commanders.

Shah Jahan in the meantime wrote to Aurangzeb, "The Emperor has recovered and is administering the state, trying to remove disorders that occurred during his illness. Your armed advance is therefore an act of war against your father. If you value your good name in this world and salvation in the next, you should obey your father and report your wishes without advancing any further."

To this Aurangzeb politely replied, "Shah Jahan has lost all real power and control. Dara is doing everything and is trying to ruin his younger brothers. Witness how he has crushed Shuja, foiled my invasion of Bijapur and poisoned the emperor's ears. Against such hostility I am bound to take up arms and advise that Dara should be sent away to his province in the Punjab to avoid mischief."

Even princess Jahanara added her earnest plea by writing to Aurangzeb, "The emperor has fully recovered and your armed advance is therefore an act of war against your father. Even if it is directed against Dara it is no less sinful, since the eldest brother both by common law and common usage stands in the position of your father. If you value your good name in this world and salvation in the next, you should obey your father."

Shah Jahan was also worried about reports that Aurangzeb had sent seductive inducements or threats to wean away many of the veteran officers to abandon Dara and join his cause. Dara knew that he could count on the loyalty of his Rajput officers and men but he was not so sure about his Muslim followers. He now knew that some considered him a heretic and had secretly decided to either stay neutral or join Aurangzeb.

I was standing behind Dara some days before the battle of Dharmat. The imperial spies had just intercepted traitorous letters between Aurangzeb and important Mughal nobles including the emperor's own brother-in law Shaista Khan. I believe that if Dara had promptly arrested these nobles and had them beheaded, as many at the court had expected, it might have discouraged further sedition but he hesitated to take this drastic measure.

Princess Roshanara had earnestly pleaded with the Emperor saying, "*Abbajan hazoor,* how do we know that these letters are not forgeries? You cannot condemn our own kinsmen because some mischievous people are trying to deceive us. " After some hesitation the emperor relented and ignored Dara's demand for salutary punishment but it was only after the fateful battle of Dharmat that Shah Jahan realized his mistake and then it was too late.

Responding to a small tug on my sleeve I looked down to see the princess Gauharara looking soulfully at me with her huge luminous eyes. She looked over the Jumna and softly said, "Look at the mist on the river. Sometimes, you can clearly see things on the far side and sometimes the mist sweeps in and blinds you to all that is there. Tell my brothers not to trust what they see or hear. I see thick clouds of mist and dust and great oceans of blood and tears. All the flowers will wither and die. There will be yellow and red tulips as far as the eyes can see. There will be betrayals after betrayals after betrayals. Aurangzeb alone trusts no one so he alone will not be betrayed. But who will listen to you or to me? Who? Who? Who? "

I nodded but again could not understand what she was trying to tell me but even if I had understood her as I do today, I would have been powerless to change the remorseless torrent of events. Who indeed would have heeded the words of a sheltered princess and an inconsequential court eunuch?

Dara wisely decided that with the advantage of numbers, fresh troops and horses, he must immediately move against the armies of Aurangzeb and Murad that must be exhausted after months of hard marching in the summer heat. They had undoubtedly suffered very greatly but heat or hardship were no longer a problem for those who had survived and become accustomed to the ordeal.

A fool cannot see his folly

... nor a madman his insanity

but they immediately see madmen and fools among others

Chapter 16

The Long Shadow of Samugarh

What a magnificent spectacle the imperial army was as it set out from the Red Fort at Agra on its way south to defend the throne. My heart swelled with pride on seeing prince Dara Shikoh dressed in a *jama* of white brocade, seated in his silver howdah on top of a huge Ceylon elephant called *Fateh Jang* (war victory). Its massive shoulders and long front legs were protected by an armour of overlapping shining steel plates and a quilted silver brocade apron to protect its legs. It also had two big horizontal swords attached to its long tusks that could cut down men and horses whenever he moved his head sideways.

Rank after rank of the ninety thousand horsemen, twenty thousand infantry soldiers and musketeers were spread out on both sides as far as the eye could see. Battalions of thousands of horsemen and squadrons of infantry *sipahis* marched in formation, dressed in the green colors of Farghana on the right and in the vivid yellow of Samarkand on the left with bright red, green, yellow and blue pom poms dancing on the headgears of their horses that nodded their heads in excitement. The dazzling sunshine reflecting off the shining steel helmets, breastplates, swords and lances was a sight to see.

The imperial guard flew the square Mughal standard dating from the time of Timur Lang. It had a crouching lion before a blazing yellow, rising sun set against a bright scarlet background. The imperial standard was twice the height of an elephant to give visibility along with the long venerated Mongol *'Tuman Tugh'* or yak tails swinging below it in the hot breeze. All the imperial guards wore crimson *jamas* in the tradition of Timur. Every battalion of a thousand soldiers had distinctive bright square pennants with their respective mascots and a *Sura*(verse) from the Quran painted on it for good luck. The artillery units and the bands with trumpets and brass kettle drums had their distinctive long banners. An elephant with two huge drums on either side followed Dara's mount so that his orders by drum beat could be heard above the sounds of battle.

The cavalry was the pride of the army, and whenever the horses moved, their jingling bridles made a thrilling sound. The rumbling thunder of thousands of hooves along with the snorting and whinnying of the horses as they tossed their heads, filled our ears. They were as full of excitement and anticipation as any horseman for the adventure that lay ahead. The Muslim soldiers wore armour with chain mail and steel plates to protect their necks, arms and legs. The Rajputs mostly wore tightly tied bright cloth turbans instead of helmets though some had helmets under their turbans as well. The *paidas,* or foot soldiers, wore thick padded waistcoats, turbans and jamas and ran bare legged on thick leather sandals.

All the soldiers carried small round shields with four metal knobs holding two leather loops inside for the left arm which allowed the left hand of the horsemen to also control the reins of their horses. Some soldiers carried lances, maces and battle axes and many horsemen also carried a leather holster holding the short Mongol bow belted to their left sides. Some of the infantry carried longer bows made of steel that were quicker and cheaper to make but they lacked the range and power of the famed Mongol bow.

There were two hundred elephants for the commanding officers. Bracelets of brass bells tied to their feet produced a dainty sound when they walked slowly but created a terrifying sound when they charged. Many elephants had swords or spikes attached to their tusks. Five hundred camels with long *zamburak* swivel guns that were like small cannons mounted on the saddles, could fire large charges from an elevation into the ranks of the enemy fighting below them. Pride of place was given to the hundred big cannons on huge four wheeled carriages hauled by two hundred and fifty female elephants and huge teams of big bullocks.

I doubt that such a pageant of pomp and might had ever been seen in Hindustan before. I pleaded with Dara to allow me to ride at his side but he told me to stay back with the emperor's entourage to be part of a group of messengers who would convey news between them and the commanders as the battle progressed. I was thus able to ride all over the battlefield and get news of every action as it developed without getting confused by the sounds and chaos of battle as it enfolded.

Dara got down from his elephant outside the great Agra Fort to receive a scarlet robe from the emperor who came down from Shahjahanabad in a small flotilla of river boats. He tied a silver amulet, containing verses from the holy Quran, around Dara's right arm before embracing him and kissing him warmly on both cheeks. The assembled army roared their approval as he turned in the direction of *Makkah* and raised his open hands upwards and recited some verses from the Quran. He then also recited a short prayer to the elephant headed Hindu deity Ganesh, whose blessings were invoked by all Hindus before any great enterprise. The army cheered lustily, *"Long live our emperor Shah Jahan... long live our prince Dara Shikoh... Allah ho Akbar... Allah ho Akbar... Allah ho Akbar... Allah ho Akbar."*

The infantry soldiers loudly banged their swords against their shields to make a sound like dull thunder. The ground reverberated with the sound of cheering from thousands of eager troops. Then a low murmur rippled through the ranks as the lips of every soldiers moved slowly in prayer. All the soldiers then dismounted and began the process of blessing their weapons, horses and elephants and seeking the blessings of God for the struggle that lay ahead. Many pressed small copies of the Quran, images of Hindu deities or other sacred talismans onto the heads of the soldiers. *Mullahs* dressed in green robes blessed the Muslim soldiers while saffron clad Hindu priests applied a crimson *tilak* to the foreheads of both Hindu and Muslim soldiers.

I was however troubled by very grave doubts. The emperor, who was now fully restored to health, should have entered the field to lead his armies himself. I knew that Aurangzeb, Murad and Shuja would have had no compunctions about meeting Dara's armies in battle but they would never have dared to oppose the emperor if he had come onto the field in person. Shah Jahan had once been a very bold and vigorous soldier and I could not understand why he stayed away from the most critical of all his battles. I tried to speak of this to princess Jahanara and to anyone else who would listen but who would heed the high pitched voice of a mere eunuch. It would have been useless speaking to Dara who was now completely obsessed by this opportunity to build his reputation as a soldier.

I was also deeply troubled by disquieting news concerning the loyalty of many of our *mansabdars* whose trustworthiness Aurangzeb's numerous messengers may have undermined. It was becoming increasingly clear that Dara could only rely on his Rajput commanders. There was ominous gossip going around that the eldest prince had never distinguished himself in war and lacked battle experience except for that ludicrous battle against the Persians at Kandahar. Many wondered if it would be wise to back the prince against a brother who had almost always been victorious.

Our imperial scouts now brought in information that the rebel armies had passed Gwalior despite the severe summer heat. The deep Chambal River with its steep banks would be a difficult barrier to cross. Dara's engineers had already set up well defended earthworks complete with cannons at Dholpur and all the other fords across the Chambal that the enemy might try to use.

We later learned from one of our spies that while Aurangzeb was mustering his forces to try to cross at Dholpur twenty *Kos* south of Agra, one of his Maratha officers asked for permission to speak to him. This Ganapati Shinde was shown in and after bowing before the rebel prince, told him that his Maratha soldiers had learned several tricks while fighting for and against the armies of the Deccan rulers as well as the imperial forces. He said that their small bands of soldiers had to fight far from any secure base. They had therefore adopted battle tactics that were very different from that of the grand Mughal armies. They believed in moving fast over long distances, striking quickly from an unexpected quarter and then moving rapidly to encircle and hit the enemy from the undefended rear. He said they called it a tactic of 'holding the enemy's nose and then kicking him on the backside'.

The informant had added that Aurangzeb's usually sombre grey face had broken into a rare smile and he called Shinde forward and said that he may need to use his tactics for the battle ahead. He told Shinde to wait for a suitable opportunity and then bring forward his contingent to fight beside the Mughal commander Badahur Khan.

This opportunity was to present itself much sooner than expected. A few Rajput *rajahs* with their small armies had switched loyalties to Aurangzeb out of some spite or in the hopes of gaining from the spoils of the great war. Among them was a Bundela prince, Champat Rai Bundela, who had fought with his contingent for Dara at Kandahar before falling out with him on some trivial matter. He had also long nursed a desire to avenge the disgrace of his uncle, Jhaujhar Singh of Orchha. He now came forward and told Aurangzeb about a little known ford at a small ferry station called Ater, at a considerable distance of some 20 *Kos* down the Chambal River. To reach it however, his army would have to swing about five *Kos* to the south east of Agra.

Following the Maratha's advice, Aurangzeb moved as fast as his army could be made to move, to quietly slip around Dara's lines before he became aware of their movements. Leaving most of his tents standing to mask their intentions, he mustered his troops at dusk when the surprise move would not be noticed. They reached Ater by exhausting, non-stop, double marches over two days. Marching such a long distance over the difficult ravine - rutted ground, in the intense heat was reported to have cost his armies thousands of casualties. On the following day, Dara's scouts were surprised to see very little movement in the camp despite some smoke from camp fires that had been lit to deceive them and it took a full day before they discovered that the bulk of Aurangzeb's army had vanished. It then took several more days to comprehend where they could have gone. Then there was consternation when their location was discovered and the significance of Aurangzeb's move was understood.

The ferry at Ater was a very difficult crossing. At a precarious bend in the Chambal River, the army had to first cross a wide field of large rocks and then the deep crocodile infested river. It was especially difficult for the heavy baggage wagons and artillery. Aurangzeb was fortunate that Dara was not able to move his forces quickly enough to oppose him, giving his engineers time to bring huge quantities of mud and smaller stones to quickly build a rough road over the rocks.

Some of his soldiers attempted to swim across the river until one of them was caught by a *Gharial,* a very big Indian crocodile with thin long jaws and a bulbous nose like a small pot. His companions watched in horror as several more of these vile reptiles joined it in a writhing mass of twisting scales and tore the poor screaming soldier to shreds. The single ferry pulled by ropes was insufficient to ferry such a big army, so Aurangzeb sent out foraging parties to bring in trees and drift wood to quickly make a number of makeshift rafts that plied night and day to get his army across the river.

Dara now realized to his horror that Aurangzeb's armies had come very close to Agra, so he was forced to abandon much of his heavy cannon at Dholpur and rush a long distance eastwards to try to intercept them before they could reach Agra. Being very alarmed about these developments I pushed my way into Dara's command tent. One of the Rajput princes, Ram Singh Rathor whispered to me that Dara, with a very much bigger army, should have immediately thrown his fresh troops into action and cut off the exhausted enemy army as soon as they had tried to struggle across the rock strewn river in a disorderly column.

The movements of Aurangzeb's' armies were now being reported by Dara's scouts every hour. With this intelligence he could have immediately taken measures to make Aurangzeb's passage much more difficult. How I wished that he could have been more decisive. Dara not only listened to his trusted military advisors like Khalilullah Khan and Daneshmand Khan but also to Dawani Das, his sly and devious court astrologer, who told him that the time was very inauspicious for an attack. He explained that the malefic influence of Saturn that lay in his twelfth house did not favour Dara but would favour Aurangzeb.

Though Dara should have attacked as soon as their armies had sighted each other, he wavered on the advice of the traitors around him, giving Aurangzeb's men and horses a few extra days to get some much needed rest. So while Dara hesitated for three valuable days, Aurangzeb and Murad succeeded in regrouping their forces in full battle formation on the western side of the river. This battle hardened army of about forty thousand soldiers was much smaller than Dara's ninety thousand. After their long marches the rebel armies lacked the colourful splendour of the imperial forces and although they looked quite tattered and dirty, they were also hard and resolute.

After three days of marching up and down in the horrible heat, Dara's army was very happy when he finally announced that the battle would be joined on the following day, filling the troops with excitement and anticipation. Lavish issues of food and refreshments were given to all while Hindu and Muslim priests went around the companies blessing and providing the soldiers with words of encouragement. Many soldiers began to sing and dance to the soft beats of the *dholak* drums invoking their gods to grant them victory and bards began to sing ballads about their legendary heroes to the sound of boisterous cheering from all the soldiers.

Our spies later reported that Aurangzeb too had addressed his officers that night and reminded them that small armies could triumph over bigger ones, if they were resolute and believed in the blessings of Allah. He motivated them with the story of Babur who had triumphed at the crucial battle of Panipat with just 12,000 hardy but determined soldiers, though Ibrahim Lodi had 100,000 soldiers and 100 elephants.

When the two armies finally met on a flat dusty plain east of a village called Samugarh, Aurangzeb's army had advanced to be only eight *kos* east of Agra. They finally engaged each other on an unbelievably hot day at the end of May, where the sun felt like a white hot furnace in a harsh cloudless sky. There was not enough water to drink so many soldiers and horses simply collapsed with heat and sun stroke. As I moved among them I saw that the Rajput soldiers suffered the most, refusing to drink water from leather water bottles as they considered leather to be unclean. The Muslim soldiers were more fortunate as they could drink from the leather bottles and eat strips of dried meat to give them strength as the horrible day progressed.

The featureless dusty plain had few trees, hills, rocks and gullies which suited Dara's larger army as it did not provide cover for any surprise manoeuvres. But Dara again hesitated, waiting for a signal from the astrologers. I also observed that many of his soft and inexperienced, newly recruited soldiers were now suffering their first exposure to the appalling heat and that some were quietly slipping away in the night.

Dara positioned his huge army in a wide formation two *Kos* across with his artillery carriages chained together to make a barrier to stop enemy cavalry charging through their lines. They were positioned in an extended line with gaps for our cavalry waiting behind the canons to be able to sally forth. Their banners and scarlet pennons fluttered furiously in the hot wind. Aurangzeb however, used a new Persian tactic that he learned from Mir Jamla. He deployed his cannons in smaller groups concealed within each of his fighting units so that they would fight side by side and move ahead with the soldiers and horsemen as the battle progressed. After a loud roll of kettle drums and trumpets, the imperial army began the attack with a cannonade but it was premature and most of the cannon balls fell short of their targets.

I was riding just behind the gunners and watching their technique as they first raised the barrels of the guns and pushed down measured amounts of gunpowder (already filled into coarse cloth bags) with a long rod. They would then push in the heavy cannon ball with a wad of cloth to hold it in place. When the command to fire was given, the gunners would first aim the guns at the selected targets and then drive a thin spike down the fire hole at the base of the gun to puncture the bag of gunpowder. More gunpowder would then be sprinkled around this fire hole and ignited with the glowing tip of a burning piece of waxed rope. In the few seconds that it took for the spluttering flame to reach the gunpowder, all the eight gunners would rush back to crouch behind a mud bank, close their eyes and put their hands over their ears.

When a cannon fired, the huge barrel along with its heavy wooden carriage would be lifted off the ground by the force of the explosion and would have to be repositioned for the next shot. The iron balls from the cannons could kill and maim dozens of soldiers and horses as they cut a swath through the defending lines.

The fighting had hardly begun when it was brought to an abrupt halt by a sudden summer thunderstorm with a violent hot wind that filled the field with clouds of blinding dust and tiny drops of rain. No one knew what this could portend but the dark swirling clouds gave me an ominous sense of foreboding.

After twenty minutes, the battle was resumed with pipes, kettle drums, trumpets and big brass drums to announce a general advance. Dara's mounted archers now rode forward in an extended line until they were about a hundred paces from the enemy and then filled the sky with a thick cloud of deadly arrows. The first barrage of arrows used long needle like points that could penetrate chain mail and chinks in the body armour. The enemy soldiers raised their small shields above their heads but the long hail of arrows caused many soldiers to fall to the ground in agony and many horses to rear up screaming or collapse in a writhing heap. As the archers came closer, they fired arrows with broader and heavier diamond shaped arrow heads that lacerated the flesh of both men and beasts.

The archers then rode backwards and were followed by a hail of arrows from the defending archers until Dara's reloaded cannons could resume the cannonade. The cavalry followed next, with our magnificent battalions of horsemen charging in with lowered lances and sabers as they smashed through the wall of infantry men facing them. What a sight the cavalry charge of many thousand horsemen was, with their colourful pennants fluttering and their armour and swords flashing in the sun. The charge over a distance of about a thousand paces would begin with the horses walking forward and then moving faster in a leisurely trot. They would then break into an undulating canter that accelerated into a fast gallop, when they were about two hundred paces from the enemy. As they approached, the rising thunder of their hooves went faster and faster as did the heartbeats of the terrified defenders.

The impact of charging cavalry on a well defended enemy position was very frightening and many in panic would try to run. Aurangzeb, however, massed a number of drummers whose furious kettledrums deafened the ears of his defenders and distracted their minds to stop them thinking of the impending impact. The first row of defenders, who crouched in a shallow trench, behind a low earth barrier carried lances with a short point at the lower end that would be firmly buried into the ground. At the last moment they would raise their lances to make a wall of spears to block the charging horses. Behind them were rows of musketeers and archers who would let loose deadly volleys of arrows. Though the attacking riders kept their heads bent down behind their shields, many were killed or wounded.

The first rows of the attacking heavy cavalry carried lances with which they would try to open a path for the lightly armed *awadis* riding behind them. The lances of the defenders would often make charging horses falter or slow down. When they lost speed, the attacking horsemen also lost their advantage. The defending infantry could then use the hooks on the lower ends of their lance heads to try to pull the horsemen off their saddles, while some used a halberd, a heavy axe on a long pole,that was swept in a wide circle to maim men and horses. There were many special weapons to penetrate the helmets and armour of the fallen horsemen like small battle axes with a big spike opposite the blade or spiked iron balls on a short staff.

The mounted attackers who penetrated the front ranks had to try to shake away the defending infantry soldiers who were harassing them. They would spur their horses to ride in tight circles with their reigns pulled hard to the left in order to make space for them to swing the swords in their right hands. As the cavalry had the advantage of height many defenders would also try to injure the horses to unhorse the cavaliers.

The muskets and bows of the infantrymen kept up a constant volley that effectively picked off the attackers. Some defending soldiers also threw small earthen pots filled with gunpowder, mixed with pieces of metal ignited by a lighted wick. They were devastating if they exploded but many misfired and were also difficult to ignite once the battle began. More effective were the rockets which if ignited near a cavalry unit could panic the horses and elephants that were terrified of fire. Though the muskets were very effective, it took time to reload them. As the fighting intensified it was very difficult to see through the choking cloud of smoke and dust where only the muzzle flashes of muskets or the explosion of rockets and cannons could be seen through the murky air.

The commanders of every company cantered around the scenes of action, urging their reserve units to fill any gaps through which the enemy could penetrate. They would also try to restore order to their fighting soldiers milling about by waving flags, blowing on trumpets and constantly shouting, "Keep in line... close the gaps... keep in line... quickly move to the right... close the gaps.... bring the yellow company forward. "

Whenever the enemy seemed to falter, the commanders would urge the cavalry units to charge in and rout the wavering defenders. There would be loud roars of triumph whenever an enemy commander was cut down, when a standard, banner or cannon was captured or when an enemy elephant was killed. Many crazed horses, having lost their riders, milled about covered in a lather of sweat with their rolling eyes wide with terror.

Dara's personal battalions were commanded by Sadat Khan who was riding just behind the central division. On his right wing rode Khalilullah Khan, with thirty thousand Uzbek clansmen and fifteen thousand Rajputs. Facing them on Aurangzeb's left wing was Prince Murad with his army of fifteen thousand. Dara's left wing was under the command of the redoubtable Rustam Khan with his famed Sayyid horsemen of Barah under the nominal command of

Dara's fifteen year old son, Sipihr Shikoh. This was opposed by Aurangzeb's eldest son prince Sultan Muhammad, who had developed into a fine soldier, with fifteen thousand horsemen under the command of seasoned generals like Bahadur Khan and Najabat Khan.

Dara deployed all his forces in a long line formation as he did not feel the need to keep a division in reserve behind them. There were also thirty thousand Rajputs led by Rajah Chattar Singh and Rajah Ram Singh Rautela.

The Rajputs fighting in both the armies were clad in saffron and their faces covered by a yellow turmeric powder that not only declared their fanatical commitment for victory or death but also protected their skin from the blisteringly hot sun. They had also eaten the intoxicating bhang and opium to render them almost immune to fear and the oppressive heat.

When the battle recommenced, Dara's left wing was initially disoriented by a few well placed artillery shots making it veer towards the centre but he continued the attack on the battalions commanded by Muhammad Sultan. Meanwhile, the headstrong prince Murad caused a similar crisis by recklessly advancing too soon in front of Aurangzeb's vanguard with his soldiers shouting, *"Allah ho Akbar"* or *"Din...Din...Din Muhammad."*

Dara's vanguard under Rao Chattrasal Hada with his proud Rathor and Sisodia clansmen responded heartily as they tried to vigorously break into the enemy ranks screaming, *"Ram...Ram...Ram"*, *"Gopal...Gopal... Gopal"* or "*Har...Har Mahadev*" as they charged in on their spirited horses wielding their swords and lances.

I began to see that the battle was fast developing into a

religious war with the Hindus valiantly supporting Dara and most of the Muslim *mansabdars* committed to or secretly supporting Aurangzeb. This feeling was confirmed when Khalilullah Khan's Uzbek horsemen on Dara's right wing rode forward quite leisurely and after firing a long volley of arrows, stayed back for most of the five hour battle.

Despite the hazards of battle, prince Murad had his eight year - old son with him in his howdah and was seen trying to protect him from the hail of arrows and bullets with a shield and his left leg wrapped around him. He was to suffer several wounds including one by an arrow through his cheek and he also lost many of his chief officers. The quilted armour of his elephant received so many arrows and lances that it looked like a porcupine. Some enemy soldiers tried to cut loose the ropes holding up his elephant's howdah and Ram Singh Rathore rushed forward and hurled his javelin at him shouting, "How dare you contest the throne with Dara Shikoh?" In response, prince Murad calmly pulled out a short Mongol bow from his side and taking careful aim killed Ram Singh at close range leaving his battalion leaderless.

Rajah Chattar Singh, with ten thousand imperial horsemen, led the first furious charge against Aurangzeb's centre on a front about three hundred paces wide. He allowed the left and right wings to hit the defenders on either side of the narrow fronts leaving the centre, where most of the enemy commanders were standing, badly shaken. To add to their confusion, a second block of horsemen now attacked the centre, closely followed by a smaller reserve force like the sting of the scorpion for a double blow to disrupt the position of the enemy commanders. Then the two wings, like the claws of a scorpion, would try to move inwards behind the enemy centre in a sweeping curve to get behind the shaken enemy commanders.

As all the horsemen knew of their disadvantage in a close melee, they would try to break away and regroup for another charge, leaving the infantry who had been following closely behind them to hold off the enemy. Now it was the turn of Aurangzeb's commander Bahadur Khan, under prince Sultan Mohammad, to let loose his cavalry in pursuit of the retreating Rajputs. Mounted on fresh horses, they easily struck down some of the horsemen whose mounts were tired or wounded until they were close to Dara's strong defensive line.

Dara's Afghan supporters now sensed that the tide was turning in their favor and rushed forward to strengthen the Rajputs who now furiously attacked Aurangzeb. By now Aurangzeb had lost most of his reserves and his close supporters were reduced to a mere two hundred. But Aurangzeb calmly ordered his soldiers to chain the legs of his elephant so that it could not retreat, thus signalling his determination to win or to die in the attempt. Opposing him was Rajah Chattrasal on horseback.

Then Dara, who should have advanced to finish the contest, moved his centre to his right where Khalilullah Khan had been advancing very slowly against prince Murad. This move inadvertently left his baggage train unguarded and some of his own recruits suddenly, abandoned the field and rushed back in the quest of easy loot causing considerable confusion in the imperial ranks.

I, now began to observe that it was the front ranks of the armies that actually fought most of the battles and that majority of the troops behind them would only press forward if the battle was going their way or if they were led by a very resolute commander. But when the front line wavered, the rows behind them would hesitate and many would retreat or try to run away. The ever suspicious Aurangzeb must have observed this during his earlier battles so he kept a line of horsemen riding behind his battalions with orders to deter and even kill any who attempted to desert. So even in his darkest moments his units kept together, remaining determined and disciplined.

Dara, followed by his personal bodyguard, now goaded his elephant forward to support the Rajputs but the momentum was beginning to slow down. Sensing that imperial victory was just a whisker away, the courageous Rajah Roop Singh Rathor jumped off his horse and single handedly cut his way to Aurangzeb's elephant, scattering the defenders and slashing at the padded legs of the elephant as well as cutting some of the ropes holding up Aurangzeb's howdah. Aurangzeb paused to admire his courage and called down to his followers to capture him but to spare the life of such a hero. However,in the chaos of battle, the gallant *rajah* was soon cut to the ground.

I had been riding for several hours between the positions of Dara, the head quarters of the emperor and the various commanders to convey numerous messages. Suddenly, one of the heralds galloped up to me with an urgent message for Dara. He whispered, "There is a terrible plot to betray prince Dara. One of his important officers is going to try to persuade him to dismount from his elephant and a group of traitors will loudly shout that he has been killed. You must immediately rush to him and warn him that he must not descend from his elephant under any circumstances."

Pushing my horse through the milling mass of soldiers

was not, however, an easy task. My horse suddenly reared up and fell after being hit by one of the many musket balls that were flying all around us. I managed to jump away and pull out my curved *talwar* just in time to save myself from a sword wielded by a big bearded Afghan on a black horse. As he turned to attack me I picked up a fallen lance and at the last moment, raised the sharp point to pierce the throat of the charging horse that collapsed as the point penetrated its armour. I managed to somehow roll away in time to avoid the horse falling on top of me.

The stocky unhorsed Afghan was on his feet in a flash and came at me shouting obscene curses as he wildly swung his sword. I, quickly, picked up a small battle axe lying at my feet and threw it at him with all my strength but the big Afghan only staggered slightly as he blocked it with his shield. He was on me again but I deflected his powerful sword strokes with my round shield. After exchanging a few sword strokes I quickly pushed his sword arm upwards as I pulled out a short *katar* (a heavy punching dagger that is gripped crosswise) from its sheath on the left of my cummerbund. I then moved in close to him to punch the short thick blade with all my strength so it could penetrate his steel breast plate before his sword arm could descend once again. Blood from his ruptured lungs spurted out of his mouth as he slowly sank to his knees.

There was no time to gloat as the enemy soldiers (dressed mostly in black) were attacking from all around. I stopped a panic stricken-horse that had slowed down before a pile of dead bodies and somehow managed to mount it and ride to where Dara was steadily advancing on his elephant as if oblivious to the chaos surging all around him. It was with great difficulty that I reached his side, but was unable to get his attention as my feeble voice was drowned by the deafening sounds of gunfire, clashing of swords and the screams of the wounded. I even snatched up a standard and tried to wave it in front of his great elephant to attract his attention, but Dara was oblivious to all except the prospect of his immanent victory.

Aurangzeb's elephant, however, came to symbolize his resolute courage just as Dara's elephant was to soon signal his doom[20]. I, now saw our commander Khalilullah Khan along with a squadron of troops rush up to him and insist that he must dismount and quickly finish the battle on a tall grey horse, conveniently brought up for him by one of his officers.

I had ridden up close enough to hear him urgently shout out, "Praise be to Allah, this victory is your own! But my God! Why are you still mounted on a lofty elephant? Have you not been sufficiently exposed to danger? If one of the numberless musket balls or arrows touch your royal person, who can imagine the dreadful situation to which we will all be reduced? In God's name descend quickly, mount this horse and pursue the miserable fugitives with all vigor."

Thoroughly frustrated, I had been trotting around the edge of the milling group and helplessly watched Dara's elephant go down on its knees to enable the prince to descend. Khaliullah's horsemen moved back to make room and a few officers dismounted to help Dara step down. Seeing a gap I violently spurred my horse and managed to get to Dara's side and again shouted, "*Hazoor, hazoor* this is a dastardly plot to betray you. Please get back onto your elephant so that your soldiers will always be able to see you."

---

20 The battle of Samugarh and this episode is widely reported by Jadunath Sarkar, Elliot and Dawson, Manucci and Bernier but most by Khafi Khan in 'Muntakhab- il-Lubab'.

I could not finish my message because Khalilullah angrily turned on me and struck me hard with his mailed hand, making me fall ignominiously to the ground. Dara looked at me clearly uncertain about what he should do and then mounted the horse. I desperately struggled to my feet and tried to raise my voice to protest but who would listen to the shrill voice of a poor slave who dared to challenge the authority of Dara's leading general.

Dara's battalion under Sadat Khan, however, continued the attack with Dara taking great personal risks as he urged his horse forward, swinging his sword courageously as an enemy horseman rushed at him with a lowered lance. Aurangzebs's soldiers began to falter until we suddenly sensed that something had suddenly changed in the tempo of the battle. The sound of gunfire no longer boomed in the air and many of our own troops were looking fearful and some were even riding away. Then there was a loud roar from the enemy camp that could be heard above the noise of battle, after which Aurangzeb's soldiers resumed their attack with fresh enthusiasm.

Very soon after Dara had descended, a huge shout had been sent up by Khalilullah Khan's squadron of supporters loudly proclaiming that prince Dara had been killed. When his bewildered soldiers saw through the thick swirling cloud of dust and smoke that the howdah of Dara's elephant was empty, they naturally feared the worst. Many of Dara's armies had been filled with recently recruited carpenters, masons, barbers and other common conscripts who, with no real taste for war, quickly abandoned the field and fled towards Agra.

An acquaintance in Aurangzeb's entourage was to later tell me that Khalilullah Khan had been offered huge inducements with promises of high rank and honour by Aurangzeb. It was also common knowledge that he had long been nursing a deep sense of shame, never forgiving Shah Jahan for seducing his beautiful red headed wife and making him an object of widespread mockery. I now understood why his experienced Uzbek soldiers had fought with such little enthusiasm in this great battle. By utterly tearing aside the veil of decency, he had betrayed Dara and given Aurangzeb his greatest victory.

The noise of battle quite quickly subsided and the dust and smoke began to slowly clear to reveal over fifteen thousand corpses lying on the dusty battlefield in hundreds of piles coated in vivid crimson blood. The Rajput corpses in their yellow jamas looked like untidy fields of saffron. A nobleman, Daneshmand Khan later said that the battlefield looked like a devastated field of red and yellow tulips. Nine top ranking Rajputs and nineteen Mughal nobles lay dead along with many thousand horses. For every dead body there were another three who had been wounded and were lying on the ground crying out piteously. But the intense heat quickly parched their throats so the deathly silence that followed the thunder of battle was eerie.

As I stood in that devastated battlefield, I recalled Princess Gauharara's sad but prophetic words, "I see thick clouds of mist and dust and great oceans of blood and tears. All the flowers will wither and die. There will be betrayals and betrayals and betrayals!"

A sharp, summer wind now suddenly blew from the south and all the fallen bodies were quickly covered by a huge shroud of choking yellow dust. A few swirls of spiralling dust, curling above the scene looked like ghosts rising up from the devastated plain until they too subsided and absolute silence pervaded the scene. The scorching heat, the swirling dust and the pitiful cries of the dying kept even the dogs, crows and vultures from approaching. But as it got dark, a crowd of robbers including many women and urchins scuttled forward from the surrounding areas to strip and loot the fallen bodies.

It was with great difficulty that I found, the imperial party retreating with a company of loyal soldiers, closely protecting the prince. I was stricken with a terrible sense of guilt for having failed in my duty to warn him of his betrayal; I felt as though the defeat had, in part, been my fault. Dara looked deeply dejected and exhausted as we rode in silence to his mansion. He called his few remaining followers and embraced them all, thanking them for their loyalty and for risking their lives. The *azaan* for the evening prayer now sounded and we all knelt down and murmured our prayers.

He then looked up and gently smiled and said to us, "It has been a very long and very sad day but it is just one battle. I did not fight this battle for wealth or glory that you know I have never coveted. As long as my esteemed father is alive I could not even think of usurping the Mughal throne. I wanted to defeat Aurangzeb because I despise the narrow hate - filled beliefs that he and many bigoted Muslims hold. These will never allow the Muslims and Hindus of our great nation to live together in harmony. This is the enemy that I am determined to defeat. We have the will and the means to fight again and we will never allow another wicked betrayal as we have just witnessed today. I know that I have the love of the people of Hindustan and with the will of Allah will be victorious the next time".

He then collected his family and valuables and left for Dilli shortly before dawn. While on the way back to his mansion he received a pathetic letter from Shah Jahan saying, "What has reduced you to such a state is only the decree of fate. It is better for you now to come and see me. After hearing what I have to say, you may go wherever fate leads you. Whatever is predestined for you will happen whatever you may do."

Dara sent a sad reply to his grieving father, "I don't have the face to appear before your majesty in my present plight... give up your desire to see my ashamed face. I only beg your majesty to pronounce the *fatiha*[21] (opening verses of the Quran that is recited at funerals) on this confused and half dead mortal in the long journey that he has before him."[22]

Shah Jahan then ordered a number of mules laden with gold coins to be sent to Dilli to help Dara to raise another army along with a letter saying, "Do not sorrow. You have many supporters who will rally to your side at the next battle where, with the blessings of Allah, we will be successful."

He did not know it then but the aging king was destined to never again set eyes on his beloved son. In fact he was never to see any of his sons ever again.

On the following day, the victorious Aurangzeb rewarded Champat Rai Bundela, who had shown him the way to the secret ford at Ater, by ordering his execution. He

21 Surat al-Fātihah is the first chapter of the Quran. Its seven verses are a prayer for God's guidance and stress His Lordship and Mercy. It acts as a preface of the Quran and implies that it is for the seeker of truth... to guide him to the straight path.

22 Mir Masum cited by Jadunath Sarkar and Qanungo

was a sick old man when the assassins approached him, as he was riding back to Orchha. His wife, Rani Lal Kanwar, rode forward to stop them but when she realized that it would be futile, she plunged her dagger into her stomach and ended her life. Champat Rai saw that his position was hopeless and followed her example by stabbing himself. Champat Rai's son Chhatrasal, who was just a boy at this time, believed that his father had been no traitor and was to henceforth become Aurangzeb's mortal enemy and was to severely plague him later as an ally of the Maratha leader Shivaji. Aurangzeb was to later make a memorial to his great victory at a place he named Fatehabad four *kos* east of Samugarh.

Strange indeed are the ways of destiny but what could be stranger than the manner in which an insignificant pair of Turkish slippers could cause the destruction of one of the world's greatest empires.

Man is like the foam on the sea

when the wind blows the froth vanishes

death too will blow away every trace of

Man and his dizzy dreams

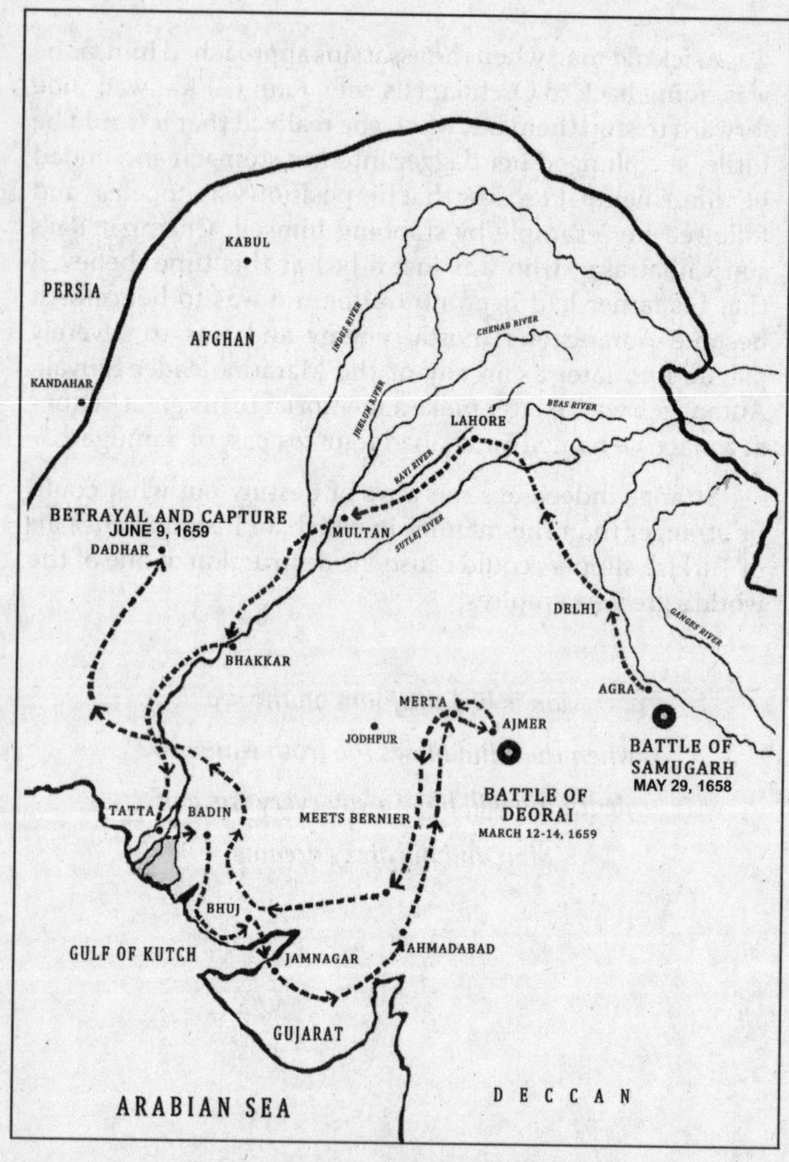

Dara Shikoh's Retreat (1658-59)

(Map modified from original as per requirements of the narrative)
Source: The Peacock Throne by Waldeman Hansen (Holt, Rinehart & Winstone 1972)

CHAPTER 17

A Moving Chessboard

A week after the battle of Samugarh, Aurangzeb ordered a public announcement of his victory. He then visited his injured brother prince Murad and congratulated him on his heroism. The two princes, with Aurangzeb clearly leading the way, now set up camp at the spacious garden of Nur Manzil outside Agra. Here they were joined by a long stream of grovelling nobles including traitors like Khalilullah Khan and Shaista Khan, who streamed out of Agra to eagerly demonstrate their willingness to serve him.

Despite his great triumph Aurangzeb realized that his position was very vulnerable. He could not be certain of the support of all the nobles and knew that many were still deeply loyal to his father and would rally to his cause if given the opportunity. He also knew that though Dara had suffered defeat, he still enjoyed great popularity and had enough treasure to quickly raise another army and resume the contest. An even more immediate danger came from his ally Murad who was expecting to be named emperor and had quite a large armed force supporting him in Agra itself. Then there was also Shuja, still far away in the east but Aurangzeb's spies had informed him that he too was on the march with a large army. The people were anxious and restless and he distrusted all the Rajput amirs. With all these threats all around him, he had no choice but to stay in Agra to consolidate his position rather than to pursue Dara and stop him before he reached the safe sanctuary of Dilli.

Aurangzeb continued to declare that he was nothing but a pious Muslim who only wanted to stop Dara's apostasy and had no ambition except to retire as a hermit after defeating the apostate Dara. As part of this charade he would address Murad as `Your Majesty' and the foolish Murad would in return address him as `Your Holiness."

Agra had been in an uproar since the arrival of Aurangzeb's victorious armies. There had been widespread looting and rioting despite Aurangzeb's strict orders to maintain discipline so, he sent his son Sultan Muhammad to replace Agra's *Kotwal* and restore order. Aurangzeb then wrote to the emperor apologizing for his actions saying that they had been forced on him by his enemies. He very formally wrote, "Obedience was my passion as long as power was vested in your venerable hands and I never went beyond my limit for which the all knowing God is my witness. But as a result of Your Majesty's illness, prince Dara, usurping all authority, has been bent on propagating the religion of Hindus and idolaters and brought chaos and anarchy to the entire empire. Consequently, I started from Burhanpur lest I should be held responsible in the next world for not providing a remedy for these disorders."[23]

Shah Jahan sent back a letter, written in his own hand,

---

23 Aurangzeb's letters cited by Jaffar. Vol VII p 252- 253.

cordially inviting him come and talk to him. He also gifted him his famous sword with a white jade hilt carved into the shape of an eagle that was reported to have been given to Babur on his coronation in Farghana. It was inscribed with the name *Alamgir,* meaning 'world encircler'. Aurangzeb liked this name so much that he chose it to be his own title at his coronation at Dilli a month later. After hesitating a few days, he politely declined the emperor's invitation to go and meet him. I believe that he did this at the behest of the devious Khalilullah Khan who fed his ever suspicious mind with the ridiculous claim that the emperor intended to get his personal bodyguards to strangle him as he sat unarmed in his father's presence.

After Sultan Muhammad occupied the city of Agra, the beleaguered emperor responded by shutting the huge spike studded gates of the redoubtable fort that was now virtually besieged. A few cannon and musket shots were exchanged but the fort was far too formidable to be taken by storm; capture would have also entailed a huge cost of time and lives. After a few days, the wily Aurangzeb sent a regiment in the early morning to capture the khirizi, or water gate that allowed water from the Jumna into the fort. The fort could not survive in the hot summer heat without water and it capitulated after three days.

Shah Jahan was to bitterly write, "Why should I complain about the unkindness of fortune, seeing that no leaf of a tree is shed without the will of Allah? Only yesterday I was master of nine hundred thousand troopers, while today I am in need of a pitcher of water. Praised be the Hindus who offer water to their dead while my devout son refuses water even to the living."

The great fort was quickly occupied and the emperor

with his immediate family were confined to the eastern part of the old *zenana* facing the river behind the Diwan-i-Am. Aurangzeb then casually turned to take possession of what must have been the greatest treasury of jewels, gold and precious books ever known to man.

He was to continue to justify his actions and sanctimoniously wrote to Shah Jahan, "So long as you held the reins of Government, I never did anything without your permission... May Allah be my witness! During your illness, Dara usurped all power, girt his loins to promote Hinduism and destroy Islam, setting you aside. I, was therefore compelled out of regard for the next world to undertake the heavy load and engage in looking after the interests of the populace and peasantry."

At the pleading of Jahanara, who he continued to respect despite her well known closeness to Shah Jahan and Dara, Aurangzeb agreed to visit the emperor and set out with an escort of kettledrums through cheering crowds. But his uncle Shaista Khan suddenly rode up and stopped him saying that it was another plot to assassinate him. As they were talking, a slave suddenly arrived with what must have been another forged letter, allegedly from the emperor to Dara reading, "Stay in Delhi... I will take care of matters here."[24] Everyone waited expectantly as Aurangzeb carefully read it. He then looked up and said that he was not one to be so easily fooled; the letter gave him the justification he needed for turning back. He was to never see his father again.

---

24 Taken from Aquil Khan and cited by Jadunath Sarkar, Bernier and Manucci

Aurangzeb's next task was to deal with his hollow-headed ally, Murad, whose jealousy was being inflamed by his band of followers who informed him that the energetic Aurangzeb was acting like a king and that the youngest prince was being left out of the rapidly changing scene. He also found that Aurangzeb's repeated delays in naming him emperor, as had been so solemnly promised, very irksome. As he recovered from his battle injuries, he tried to assert his authority and even attempted to seduce some of Aurangzeb's own officers with offers of higher rank and pay. But Aurangzeb knew his measure and of how to flatter him. In his presence, Murad was like a mouse hypnotized by a snake.

As always, Aurangzeb faced this threat with the stealth and speed of a serpent. He surprised the gullible prince at his camp with a sudden visit and generous presents of two hundred and thirty three fine horses and a huge sum of money in cash. He then invited him to a celebratory feast at the nearby city of Mathura where in Aurangzeb's tent Murad was persuaded to consume a feast of delicious foods and a few jars of an even more special pale wine that had been specially brought from Shiraz and Kabul.

They then decided to retire for a short afternoon rest in their own tents before planning their further strategies. Then while Murad slept, his faithful bodyguard Shahbaz Khan was induced to leave his side for a moment and was caught by four of Aurangzeb's guards and strangled. Aurangzeb then offered his own seven - year - old grandson Mohammad Azam, a beautiful jewel if could quietly sneak into Murad's tent and remove the sword and jewelled dagger lying beside the sleeping prince.

Murad was thus disarmed and was soon overpowered despite a brief struggle and was moved from his own tent with golden manacles on his hands and feet in deference to his royal blood. The entire operation had been meticulously planned. Four elephants with heavily screened ladies howdahs, each escorted by four thousand cavalry, set off in different directions to confuse Murad's followers. He was taken in one of them first to Salimgarh in Delhi and after a few months there, was imprisoned for the last three years of his life in the somber Gwalior fortress.

He once nearly escaped by using a long rope ladder smuggled in by some of his followers. The innocent prince, however, whispered his plan to his favourite concubine Sarsati Bai assuring her not to worry as he would return very quickly to rescue her. The hysterical woman, unfortunately, broke out with loud cries of lamentation that alerted the guards, and exposed the plot. Aurangzeb who was kept informed of all events in Gwalior now realized that he must put a quick end to the matter. So he sanctimoniously ordered a mock trail by the Qazis and Murad was executed, on a demand for restitution from relations of the Vezier that Murad had earlier speared in Ahmedabad. Aurangzeb had also declared that any prince who consumed intoxicants was unfit to rule as emperor of Hindustan.

The consolidation of affairs in Agra was accomplished in just one month. With Murad in prison Aurangzeb was now ready to oppose the approaching army of Shuja and pursue Dara, who were his last obstacles to the Mughal crown. Aurangzeb's generals did not face much resistance as they mopped up all the demoralized and leaderless garrisons near Agra one by one. He later occupied Dilli and had himself crowned as Alamgir Ghazi in late July and appointed the traitor Khalilullah Khan to be his governor of

Punjab with orders to hunt down Dara.

Seeking the spoils of the victory, Aurangzeb acquired all the things of value from Dara's mansion including Dara's Georgian wife Udaipuri Begum who was to become the love of his later life and the mother of his eleventh son Kam Baksh. He seemed determined to possess everything that Dara valued. Aurangzeb also asked for Dara's third wife, the former Punjabi dancing girl, Ranadil who surprisingly refused to go to him. When he persisted by praising her lustrous long hair, it is said that she cut it off and told him that he could have her beautiful hair but not her affections. But not one to take a refusal lightly, Aurangzeb sent word of praise for her beautiful face to which Ranadil responded by slashing it with her own jewelled dagger and sent a message to say that her beauty was now forever destroyed.

Exhasuted and dejected, prince Dara's small party set out from Agra. It took us six days to reach Dilli in forced marches of nearly twenty *kos* a day and Shahjahanabad warmly opened its doors and treasury to us. Despite Aurangzeb's attempts to block the roads, many belated followers eagerly rallied to Dara and his force quickly swelled to nearly five thousand. He was now encouraged to quickly raise a new army and was then able to relax a little when it became clear that Aurangzeb was not in close pursuit.

Dara was, however, counselled by his advisors to not make a stand at Dilli but to draw Aurangzeb towards Lahore where Dara had a strong following. They told him that Aurangzeb's position was very precarious in Agra with Murad and Shuja still his serious obstacles as well as the emperor himself who continued to enjoy wide support. Most of the Rajput Chiefs were opposed to Aurangzeb and many of the Mughal *umraos* who feared a vengeful leader were ready to support Dara. They maintained that the further Aurangzeb could be made to move from Agra, the weaker would become his position.

Just as we were preparing to leave Dilli for Lahore, I was summoned by Nadira Bano begum. She looked remarkably calm, despite the great tragedy that had overwhelmed the family. She was very worried about her beloved son Sulaiman as he was now very far away and would have great difficulty in getting back, once Aurangzeb's soldiers had command of Agra and all the roads to its east. She asked me to find and warn him not to take the imperial road but to seek lesser routes that Aurangzeb's soldiers may not be watching. Though she was confident that their many good friends would rally to fight another great battle, she was also afraid that Sulaiman's soldiers might desert or betray him. She gave me a bag of silver coins and told me to take some trusted soldiers and leave immediately.

Sulaiman, who had been unable to return in time to support his father at the great battle of Samugarh tried to come rushing back with *Rajah* Jai Singh by his side. His battle-hardened army had reached Allahabad when they heard the devastating news about the defeat at Samugarh. The previously loyal Jai Singh with his big Rajput contingent, then abruptly abandoned Sulaiman leaving him and his small personal army alone to face a large force sent by Aurangzeb to capture him.

I decided that it would be prudent to take a small inconspicuous section of just ten reliable soldiers on sturdy common horses and try to find him . A larger group would have attracted the attention of the many columns of soldiers who were streaming back from the east along with Jai Singh's army to join the victorious Aurangzeb. To look even less conspicuous we all wore rough tunics purchased in the market to cover our armour and weapons. When accosted by the patrols, we pretended that we too were a troop of soldiers returning to rejoin the service of a Bihar *Jagirdar*.

As a result of several delays and diversions, it took us twelve days to reach Allahabad and another two days to find Sulaiman. He had not been able to make much progress as his depleted force of nine thousand loyal soldiers were facing daily skirmishes with groups of enemy troops that had been hurriedly sent to arrest him. But when we finally met, I found him looking strong and confident and felt very proud to see that he had developed into such a fine soldier after his long campaign into Oudh and Bihar. He was delighted to see me and to get a full report about all the recent events. His sun bronzed face flushed in anger when I told him about Khaliullah's betrayal and he swore he would personally tear out his treacherous heart. We all laughed when he said that he would have his heart roasted on a bonfire made from all the ladies slippers of the empire.

Sulaiman understood that he must quickly bypass Agra and Dilli to reach Lahore as the usual route along the banks of the Jumna would be closely watched. So the royal route would have to be bypassed by a quick circle either south through Bundelkhand or north along the foothills of the Himalayas. After some discussion it was decided to split his army, sending three thousand troops on a diversion through Bundelkhand to mislead his pursuers, while he took the northern route through the forests just below the Himalayan Mountains with the rest.

We made very good progress for several days as there were no soldiers blocking our path. The main difficulty was in cutting through the thick forests and crossing the mountain streams swollen with the early monsoon rains. But by the time we reached the holy city of Hardwar on the River Ganges, we learned that Aurangzeb had got information about our plans and had sent a large army contingent under Khalilullah Khan to capture or kill the young prince. Sulaiman then split his force again and took his main force across the river near Rishikesh. He was however hemmed in again by another large force of Aurangzeb's soldiers approaching from the west.

He now had very little choice and was forced to keep going up the valley of the fast flowing Ganges until he and his remaining two hundred loyal soldiers were given shelter by Prithvi Singh, the *rajah* of Srinagar, at his small hill kingdom deep in the Garhwal Mountains. Here Sulaiman's dashing good looks so captivated the second daughter of the ruler that he agreed to give her to him in marriage with all the respect due to a royal prince. For a few months, Sulaiman lived happily with his small but very pretty moon-faced bride in a place situated above the turbulent Alakananda River. He would have been quite content at this heavenly abode had he not been so impatient to rejoin his father.

The little holy town of Devprayag just twenty *kos* down the river from Srinagar, on the confluence of the thundering Alakananda and Bhagiriti Rivers, was commanded by Kallilullah's army contingent that continued to pursue the young prince. This effectively sealed off Sulaiman's ability to escape down the river valley. The only alternate route was over the ranges to the south through very difficult trackless mountains with thick and dangerous forests. He kept looking for a way out towards the south, while ostensibly going out hunting but found that it would be very difficult to reach the plains through the trackless leopard infested jungles. After a long and frustrating month, Sulaiman ordered me to go back to his parents who should have reached Lahore, to give them news of his predicament. I reluctantly left, hoping that he would somehow be able to find a way to quickly break out of the ring of enemy soldiers that so closely surrounded him.

Sulaiman warmly embraced me as I bid him goodbye. I decided to travel as a poor religious mendicant with just a young Brahmin boy called Udai who had been serving in the young princesses's household. We set out before dawn and he walked ahead pretending to guide me, begging for alms through the towns and villages. We were clothed in coarse woollen blankets with me trying to look as if I was in a state of permanent spiritual trance muttering some mysterious sounds. We could not travel down the Ganges River as there were many enemy troops guarding the holy towns of Rishikesh and Haridwar. The thick tiger infested forests between the Ganges and Jumna Rivers were also too dangerous so we eventually walked westwards towards the Jumna, along the northern edge of the forest where it rose up to meet the mountains. One evening, while we were cooking a large bird that I had shot with my bow, we heard an ominous growl and saw a tiger approaching through the shrubs. We quickly scrambled up a tall tree and watched helplessly as the big cat pawed at the bird among the hot embers and then ate our sorely needed meal.

We went hungry the next day as most birds and animals were taking shelter from the monsoon rains. There were however, many mushrooms around and I was glad I could tell the edible from the poisonous ones. The Bhil tribals had taught me a trick many years earlier when I had been in the forests near the Tapti River. I told Udai to search the bushes to look for a colony of ants. When we put a few ants on poisonous mushrooms they would hurriedly try to run away but would be unperturbed on mushrooms that were safe to eat. We ate our fill and found a dry place to sleep under a big overhanging rock.

Next day, we followed the valley of the Jumna and walked south through the river's narrow defile to reach an open plain where instead of tigers we now needed to keep a wary eye for packs of hyenas and lions that preferred to hunt on the open plains. We were so frequently questioned by enemy soldiers that I sent Udai back to Srinagar to warn Sulaiman that with his height and striking good looks he would surely be recognized and it would be too dangerous for him to travel by this route.

Travelling mostly at night, I reached Lahore in a month. but it was a difficult journey. The last passage was the most difficult as I had to pass many patrols guarding the approaches to the city. I had earlier managed to get across the Sutlej River by climbing into the back of a well laden cart going over the boat bridge. After speaking to the people of Lahore, I discovered that Dara had moved his camp from Lahore city to a safer spot across the Ravi River that was in full flow with the monsoon rains. After waiting in frustration for a few days I decided that swimming would be the only way to get across the raging torrent. Holding onto a large dry log to prevent me from drowning I crossed the turbulent waters with great difficulty.

When I reached Dara's tents, the soldiers on guard saw a bedraggled, dirty and unshaven ruffian and refused to allow me to proceed further. They laughed when I recited the names of a few of Dara's commanders but fortunately one of the captains recognised me and after close questioning, led me to Dara's tent. Both Dara and Nadira Bano greeted me warmly, listening with rapt attention to my long account and asking many questions. Nadira was very happy to have the first real news about Sulaiman and to know that he was in good health and spirits. A *mullah* was summoned for a special prayer of thanksgiving. Dara was however, very troubled that Sulaiman was so closely trapped as he desperately needed him to be at his side for the campaign he was preparing to fight.

I later learned from young Udai,who I met in Dilli a few years later, that Rajah Jai Singh, who had been entrusted with Sulaiman's capture, tried to pressurize the hill *rajah* to give up the fugitive prince. He even tried to get the Brahmin prime minister to poison him with a tonic but Sulaiman became suspicious upon his insistence and gave it to a cat that, upon drinking it, died. Rajah Prithvi Singh became so furious when he learned about this incident that he had the minister beheaded. Later, Jai Singh was more successful with the *rajah's* elder son Medini Singh who helped get Sulaiman arrested while he was out on *shikar.* In deference to his royal blood, the handsome prince was chained with silver shackles and brought before Aurangzeb a month later.

Dara had never expected Aurangzeb to have so quickly imprisoned the emperor, eliminated Murad and consolidated his position. The only move left was to remove the danger of Shuja who was rapidly approaching with a big army from the east. Dara also wanted to gain time hoping that Sulaiman would be able to take command his armies as he had very few of his experienced generals in Lahore. Pacing up and down he would often say, "Oh how much I wish Jai Singh, Qasim

Khan, young Mahabat Khan or some of my other experienced generals were here with me." If the courageous Sulaiman had been at his side I believe he would have helped him muster a loyal army capable of achieving victory.

Dara's arrival had been greeted with great enthusiasm and soldiers from all over the north rushed to Lahore to offer their services. Thousands of wild and ferocious Afghans with their long Juzails, Baluchis from the distant west, Dogras from Jammu and even some of the rebellious Sikhs all flocked to Dara for a chance to fight and plunder. He had enough treasure to immediately raise a large army but had very few reliable officers to train and discipline them. Siphir however, collected the available officers and formed companies and battalions to train soldiers to execute battlefield commands.

Dara then began to correspond with all the officers in Agra and wrote a long letter to Shuja who had now reached Patna on the Ganges. "Dear brother", he wrote, "we are all of one resolve to defeat Aurangzeb and our best course is to unite to restore our dear father to his throne. We will then be able to bring together all our many supporters. If you agree, then we should also attack Aurangzeb simultaneously from the north and east and thus scatter his forces."

Communications were, however, slow and difficult as a fast rider would arouse suspicion and would be arrested. Four sets of messengers were therefore sent out hoping that some would get through but it still needed fifteen days for the message to reach Patna. Dara smiled and said to his courtiers, "When Aurangzeb intercepts one of these letters he will have to stay in Agra because he knows that two great armies are approaching him and that dividing his forces will weaken his position".

Dara now regrouped his forces and posted strong pickets supported by large contingents to guard all the fords across the Sutlej River that was in spate. But Aurangzeb, always the meticulous planner, had already sent a number of boats on big wagons to enable his troops to cross the river at any point. His troops were now able to force a crossing of the Sutlej and began advancing to threaten Lahore.

Dara was in Lahore for six weeks trying to regroup his army and while there, he gave an audience to the handsome Rajah Rajrup Singh, a Rajput prince from the hill state of Jammu. Nadira Begum personally received him in their private quarters, presented him a valuable string of pearls. She also performed a custom to bind his loyalty, as a foster son, with the old Mongol ritual of allowing him to drink the water with which she washed her breasts as symbolic of a mother's own milk. Rajrup drank the sacred water and faithfully swore to be true. Dara also gave him a huge sum of ten Lakh Rupees to raise an army.

Dara now called together all his generals and outlined plans to assemble a larger army of twenty thousand to oppose Aurangzeb's battalions. At this point, he also received a letter from Shahnawaz Khan, the Mughal governor of Ahemdabad, with a very tempting proposal offering him a huge army if the prince could come to Gujarat to lead them in attacking Aurangzeb from the south.

Getting increasingly confused by all this conflicting news and advice, Dara once again followed the counsel of the miserable astrologer, Diwani Das and disappointed his followers by deciding to go to Gujarat and abandoning Lahore instead of standing firm. Forgetting my station as a lowly eunuch I had the temerity to strongly remonstrate with my prince. Everyone looked astonished when I stood up and raised my voice to say, "Every great king can suffer the occasional defeat but few can survive the odium of fleeing, instead of boldly facing an enemy. How can the support of your followers be relied upon if they feel that their leader may let them down, leaving them to the vengeance of the new conquerors?"

I regretted that my voice lacked the masculine authority to give power to my words. Diwani Das rudely interrupted me, telling me to mind my station and told Dara to ignore the words of an ignorant slave, informing him that it would be another three moons before his stars were propitious. I was then surprised to hear the voice of Nadira Begum from behind the screen, urging Dara to heed my advice.

Diwani Das quickly responded and spread out a complicated map of the heavens on the carpet, tracing with his fingers the evil passage of Saturn through the stars of his house and explained how this had even affected the events at Samugarh. The crafty astrologer understood well that Dara craved to be remembered in the pages of history. It was not surprising that he succumbed when Diwani Das said that a glorious period of five golden years was destined to follow this darkness, assuring him of absolute success for even his smallest enterprise. He went on to trace out the beneficent influence of Jupiter and some other stars that would truly make him, Dara Shikoh... Dara the magnificent... the greatest emperor the world had ever known.

So, Lahore was abandoned along with my hopes. Dara had initially intended to go to Kabul commanded by his old ally, the redoubtable general Mahabat Khan, but Mahabat discouraged him saying that it would be unwise to completely move out of Hindustan. He, therefore, retreated south down the Indus. Dara's company, now plagued by numerous desertions, was reduced to a mere three thousand. He was forced to abandon strong defensive positions at Multan, Attock and the great island fort of Sakkar, where he sent over five hundred boats laden with treasure, munitions and food.[25]

Late one evening, just as we were about to leave Lahore, I heard a soft cough behind me and turned to see a young slave beckoning to me to follow him. We went into a tent and he handed me a small copper cylinder with seals at both ends. When I broke the seal with my dagger I saw that it contained a letter written by Aurangzeb in his own hand. The short note praised me for my loyalty and dutiful diligence to both Dara and Sulaiman but bluntly told me that I was following a lost cause. He said he truly appreciated my honesty and remembered my dutiful service to him many years earlier. He now ordered me to immediately leave Dara and travel to Dilli to join his service.

The letter left me in a state of utter confusion. On one hand, I felt flattered that Aurangzeb had been following my movements so closely and still valued my services but on the other, I knew I could not abandon Dara. Nadira Begum had also become very dependent on me and I knew she would find it very difficult to face any more betrayals. I told the slave that I would answer the letter very soon but was unable to ever muster the courage to pen a reply.

---

25 Most Mughal historians stop writing about Dara Shikoh after the battle at Samugarh, so Nicolo Manucci's 'Storia do Mogdol' remains the main source of information about Dara's retreat of 1658-59.

Shuja's large army marching up the Ganges towards Agra posed a serious threat to Aurangzeb who was also troubled about the fickle loyalties of many Mughal and Rajput chiefs. They had already revealed how easily they could be seduced by offers of power and wealth. There was also the possibility of the emperor himself escaping confinement and resuming control of the empire or even of Sulaiman Shikoh escaping from the hills to lead a new army to free the Emperor. He therefore, left the pursuit of Dara to Khalilullah Khan and turned back to Dilli at the end of September.

After Aurangzeb's victory at Samugarh, Mir Jamla had left the Deccan fort of Daulatabad and rushed up to Agra to renew his alliance with the new emperor. Aurangzeb had earlier offered Shuja the rule of both Bengal and Bihar, but Shuja did not trust him and marched to Agra to try to free Shah Jahan while Aurangzeb was away in Punjab pursuing Dara. But his army moved too slowly and it was near Allahabad that he found himself suddenly opposed by three large armies led by prince Sultan Muhammad, the wily Mir Jamla and Aurangzeb himself who had abruptly abandoned the pursuit of Dara and rushed back in double marches.

At the beginning of January, Shuja's forces were camped at a village called Khajua near Benares, close to a large lake surrounded by date palms (*khajur*) situated between the Ganges and Jumna rivers. Aurangzeb camped his ninety thousand troops on a nearby stream. Rajah Jaswant Singh, still smarting from his defeat at Dharmat, along with his fifteen thousand Rajputs now in the service of Aurangzeb, hatched a plot to sabotage Aurangzeb and help Shuja. In the middle of the night his soldiers suddenly fired three loud cannon shots and started galloping through Aurangzeb's camp stampeding the horses and elephants to cause utter confusion. It had been intended to be a signal for Shuja to begin a dawn attack. Shuja, unfortunately, suspected that it was another of Aurangzeb's wily tricks and missed a great opportunity to rout a confused enemy.

But the distraction did considerable damage to Aurangzeb's army who thought that it had been Shuja who had attacked during the night. Aurangzeb's treasure was completely looted by some of his own men and many army contingents quickly deserted and went straggling back towards Agra where people were told that Aurangzeb had been routed. The rumours spread very fast and encouraged many to hope for the rescue of Shah Jahan. Aurangzeb however remained calm and unperturbed, quickly restoring order.

Shuja then surprised everyone by showing that he was no longer the indolent prince he was reputed to be by fighting very valiantly on that cold January morning. His smaller force completely penetrated Aurangzeb's wide line in a compact column led by a bizarre new weapon of a number of huge elephants armed with heavy chains that they swung about with vicious sweeps of their trunks. These charging behemoths wrought havoc among the enemy ranks and allowed Shuja's horsemen and musketeers to cause great damage. Aurangzeb's larger army therefore had great difficulty in extracting a victory from such an unexpectedly determined adversary.

Aurangzeb's victory was, however, again owed to an act of treachery. One of Shuja's noblemen, Aliwardi Khan, rushed up to Shuja and begged him to get off his elephant and go for a quick victory on horseback. Shuja may not have heard about Dara's betrayal by a similar ruse at Samugarh and did not realize the significance of descending from his command elephant. When his soldiers looked up from the din of battle they were appalled to see his empty howdah and slowed their vigorous assault. The deception was to result in a complete victory for Aurangzeb. The unfortunate Shuja, who lost his artillery and huge treasure, was then relentlessly pursued by the wily Mir Jamla through Bihar and Bengal in a long series of engagements down the Ganges from Rajmahal to Dacca. He finally vanished after a pursuit of many months into the marshy jungles of Arakan never to be heard of again.

Many months later we were informed that Shuja's entire *zenana* of beautiful queens and princesses were in a large boat on the river near Dacca when they heard of Shuja's final defeat and faced the horror of capture by the ferocious Arakan pirates. Wailing in piteous despair they ordered their boatman to sink their vessel, preferring death by drowning to the horrors and humiliations of capture. Nothing was heard of Shuja ever again except for some fanciful stories that he had become a mendicant at Makkah or that he was living in Persia.

Why do you leave your wife and children
...and follow death for the sake of glory?
If it is an honor for a man to kill his brother
should we not erect a temple for
Cain who slew his brother Able?

CHAPTER 18

Defiance at Deorai

After we left Multan, Dara was relentlessly pursued by Khaliullah Khan, Saif Shikan Khan and Shaikh Mir along with fifteen thousand soldiers. The Indus River narrowed through rocky cliffs just before the island fort of Sakkar, making the strong currents of the great river very dangerous. We lost many of our precious boats to the surging waves and whirlpools. Also as a result of so many desertions, there were not enough trustworthy soldiers to protect Dara's treasure fleet which was so necessary to fund the raising of another great army.

From Sakkar the pursuers moved down both banks of the Indus to the island fort of Bhakkhar, further down the river and nearly caught up with Dara's depleted forces at Thatta, a port near the mouth of the great Indus. It was at Thatta that we met our friend the Italian gunner Niccolao Manucchi, who was among our last defenders.

Our long succession of failures and disappointments had made me increasingly frustrated and angry. With my military experience in Jhansi, the Deccan and at Samugarh,

I felt that I had more knowledge of war than any of the commanders who now remained loyal to Dara. Out of natural modesty I did not want to push myself forward but felt I had to do something to reverse our sagging fortunes and find a way for Dara to get the respect and loyalty of our motley collection of remaining soldiers.

As our depleted army was getting ready to leave Thatta, I sought a private audience with Dara and said to him that I had a plan to kill that betrayer Khalilullah Khan who commanded Aurangzeb's persuing force. If I could somehow kill him and cause a big disturbance in his camp it would completely disrupt their command. It would also be very good for our morale and gain several valuable days for our supporters to regroup. I politely declined to disclose my plan but asked him to assign me a small unit of ten absolutely trustworthy soldiers from his personal bodyguard.

I then assembled our small unit and moved to a large tent on the west of the camp where I made them replace their fine clothes with the coarse clothes of common soldiers and told them of my plan. They took off their breast plates but wore rough tunics over the chain mail covering their chests. They all carried *katars* or other daggers but hid most of their swords and muskets in our baggage. We also collected several pots of gunpowder and butter fat that we made into a number of cloth covered bundles. We packed these along with some food items onto twelve donkeys and mules. We then joined a number of other soldiers who were furtively deserting Dara and joining the pursuing armies in small groups.

It took us just one day to reach Khalilullah Khan's advance pickets where we were questioned and lightly searched but as we said we were soldiers about to join Aurangzeb's army they did not suspect anything. One of the soldiers, however, recognized me and knew of my closeness to Dara so our group was immediately taken to the old *amir*'s command tent. It was just getting dark as we waited for him to emerge from a meeting with his commanders. I quietly told my small band of followers to disperse and carry out our plan.

When the tall and thickset Khalilullah Khan, with his beard blackened to hide his advancing years, came out of his tent with a few officers, he roared with laughter and said, "This is my happiest day! Look who has come to visit us! It is none other than that coward Dara's closest companion... that miserable eunuch Mubarak Ali! Lord be praised! This is a sure sign that Dara is now finished and has no staunch officers left who can stand in our path."

Bowing respectfully before him I said that I had an important message from Dara that was for his ears alone. He again laughed and said, "Oh this is truly wonderful! You say that you have some secret message, do you? I will tell you what you want to say to me! You are carrying an offer from your heretic prince asking me to abandon Aurangzeb and join his hopeless cause. Do you take me for a fool? Dara can offer me all the gold, diamonds and high honors of the world but what use are such offers when he will soon be destroyed?"

Shaking my head I vehemently denied his allegation. He paused for a few moments, looked thoughtful and then beckoned me to follow him into his elaborately furnished tent where he leaned back on a wide divan with a thick *gaotakia* bolster behind him. He then clapped his hands to summon one of his servants and said, "Fetch us some *sherbet*. Our honoured guest has come a very long way and must be thirsty." Turning to me he said, "Now before we begin *firangi*, please tell me whatever you know about the officers who are loyal to Dara. Also tell me about his munitions and the deployment of his forces."

I was happy to be able to get a few minutes of time that would enable my small unit of followers to set about executing our plan. They had all quietly dispersed and had begun scattering small pots of gunpowder and streams of butter fat onto some of the tents surrounding Khaliullah's command tent.

After imbibing some excellent sherbet made from pomegranates,I began to dutifully answer the *amir*'s many questions. I mostly answered truthfully but did not tell him how wretched Dara's actual position was but made it appear that he had more troops, munitions and better morale than was really the case. After listening for some time he said, "*Accha!* That is good. Now tell me what is this great message that your cowardly prince Dara has sent for my ears alone."

I stood up and slowly lifted up my coarse tunic with my left hand, pulling out a fat red leather envelope from my belt. I opened it slowly and quickly extracting a katar punching dagger, leapt at the Amir saying,"This is what Dara has sent you! It is a passage to hell for a vile traitor!"

Khalilullah tried to rise up quickly from the divan on which he had been languidly lying. Despite his age and luxurious lifestyle, he was surprisingly strong. His left hand caught my descending right arm and held it firmly as he tried to wrest a jewelled dagger from his belt with his other hand. We both rolled furiously until we fell off the divan onto the floor. I managed to hit his nose hard with my clenched left fist and was then able to firmly push the katar into his left side just below his ribs. He let out a loud roar of pain that was certainly heard by his guards. I wanted to stay longer to ensure that he was dead but had to quickly leave before his guards could arrive.

I managed to slip out through a hole in the back of the tent that I cut with my dagger as the *amir*'s guards rushed into the tent shouting loud cries of alarm. This was the signal my followers had been waiting for and they all brought out their flints and began to ignite the streams of gunpowder and butter fat they had already poured around the surrounding tents. A sudden wall of flames with small explosions soon erupted all around the important tents at the centre of the camp. This was followed by louder explosions as some of our pots of gunpowder caught fire. By sheer luck one of the tents was a munitions magazine that went off with a huge explosion sending flaming objects and even a few rockets flying all over the camp. Some of my soldiers had cut the traces of the horses, camels and elephants in their paddocks and the panic stricken animals rushed about in the darkness adding to the chaos as they galloped furiously through the camp.

Soldiers began rushing out of their tents where they had been eating their evening meal and there were loud cries as they ran around in consternation. In all the noise and confusion most of our little group was able to slip out of the camp and return triumphantly to Thatta where Dara was delighted to learn of our exploits. The successful attack had been our first triumph in many months and the mood in our camp suddenly became quite cheerful and optimistic. Reports about our daring exploits soon spread and soldiers came out to cheer me and the seven surviving members of our heroic little group. I was soon very embarrassed when some of our soldiers began to shout, *"Firangi... Firangi... Firangi...* God bless you *firangi."*

Dara summoned me along with the members of our daring group later that day and had a small ceremony where he rewarded us all with beautiful jewelled daggers and gave me an exquisite *katar* embossed with gold to replace the ordinary one that I had used to stab the old Khan. He then called me aside and said that he wanted to raise me to the rank of a *mansabdar.* I humbly dissuaded him by saying that a eunuch as a nobleman could cause unnecessary ridicule and that we should only celebrate after our final victory.

I however added, "*Shahzadeh hazoor,* I will only make one request. We have no seasoned commander who can lead and inspire our dispirited troops. Please give me the authority to lead them until a more experienced commander can be found." Dara smiled with happiness, took off his own scarlet silk shawl and draping it around my shoulders, said, "Mubarak, you will no longer be called a slave but my brother. You are the only one who has remained unshakable in his loyalty to me. I will issue orders to all our units that they should now follow your commands". I also requested Dara to immediately dismiss the astrologer Diwani Das who had made him lose so many opportunities to stand and fight; my informant in Aurangzeb's camp had just told us that the astrologer had long been in Aurangzeb's pay.

I was very pleased that our remaining three thousand soldiers seemed to approve of Dara's orders. I realised that there was need to immediately reorganize our forces so I decided to try the old system of command begun by Genghis Khan who had devised a system based on the number ten, to ensure that his armies were closely controlled. I quickly called together my seven recent friends and added three to make up a new unit of ten officers. I asked them to each make a unit of ten reliable followers who they would train to respond to their commands, creating tight bonds of loyalty and discipline. When their ten had been trained for a few days, each of them were required to make further units of ten. With this we had over a thousand disciplined soldiers in a hundred small units ready for battle at all times.

We began a military drill where Dara enthusiastically participated and his cheerful authority greatly increased his popularity. The anxieties that had so burdened him seemed to lift and he rode out confidently leading a few cavalry patrols himself. One day we killed a number of antelopes and had a fine feast after many months of privation. I was very pleased to see that the mood of our small army seemed to have changed and that hope and determination had replaced the dejection and despair that could earlier be seen on every face.

Thatta, surrounded by flat plains with shallow branches of the great Indus River running through it was not a place where we could make a stand so we decided to turn westwards to Gujarat where we could raise a grand army. Dara now sent fast camel messengers to our *mansabdars* in Gujarat telling them glowing accounts about our victory over Aurangzeb's force and asking them to bring their soldiers, cannon and treasures into the field to help him fight to defeat his bigoted brother. Though our morale was now high we suffered a terrible passage through the treacherous quicksand-riddled salt desert of the Rann. It was an unending nightmare with the spectre of constant hunger and thirst that saw parched lips on every sun blackened face. Our pack animals were also collapsing one after another with thirst, hunger and fatigue.

We were, however, very relieved that the rulers of Bhuj, Nawanagar and Kathiawad warmly received us with generous hospitality. With their help our party was able to reach the safe sanctuary of Ahmadabad where the *subedar* Shah Nawaz Khan opened the treasury and enabled our royal prince to recover some of his dignity and raise a force of twenty two thousand soldiers. Some additional guns were also brought up from Surat. Although Shah Nawaz was the father of Aurangzeb's principal wife Dilras Bano, he was very angry with Aurangzeb for having so cruelly deposed of Murad who had been married to his favourite younger daughter, Sakina Banu Begum.

Dara, on hearing the belated reports that Aurangzeb had been routed in the east by Shuja and that his entire treasure had been looted by Jaswant Singh's soldiers, now felt very elated. With Aurangzeb's scattered armies still far away from Agra near Allahabad, Dara decided that he now had a god-sent opportunity to make a quick dash to free his father and restore him to the throne. He was further encouraged by a message received from Jaswant Singh who was fleeing to his fort at Jodhpur with his army after betraying Aurangzeb at Khajua. It seemed that Diwani Das's predictions were, at last, going to swing in our favour and we all rejoiced in the feeling that a terrible evil period was passing.

But our happiness did not last very long. Ominously more accurate reports began to trickle in that Shuja, instead of being victorious, had actually been severely defeated at Khajua and that Aurangzeb had somehow managed to cover the huge distance from Allahabad to Agra very quickly and was now moving rapidly southwards towards Ajmer.

Dara, in the meantime, had been able to muster an impressive and well equipped army and waited impatiently near Ajmer for Rajah Jaswant Singh, who had promised to join him with his battle hardened cavalry units.But our prince was to be deeply disappointed by this fickle Rajput chief. We learnt later that Rajah Jai Singh of Amer, who was now one of Aurangzeb's most trusted generals, had earnestly written to Jaswant saying that the normally vindictive Aurangzeb would, "bury all the past in oblivion" if he would abandon the cause of Dara and join him. After vainly waiting for several days for Jaswant to come on to the field with his troopers, Dara sent prince Sipihr with a small section of troops to Jodhpur to "hold up the mirror of Rajput honour". But it was of no avail. Dara even tried to enlist another old Rajput friend, the Maharana Raj Singh of Udaipur, who Dara had once saved from Shah Jahan's invasion. He was to, however, meet with another disappointment. None of the Rajput rulers were willing to sacrifice their future prospects by supporting Dara against Aurangzeb who seemed to have been able to overcome every obstacle that had came in his way.

Our scouts brought us continuous news about the movements of Aurangzeb's armies that were now rapidly approaching. We were camped south of Ajmer. The Sufi saint *Garib Nawaz*,who heeded the call of even the most insignificant being regardless of their religion or calling, was close to all Mughal hearts. While we waited for Siphir to return with Jaswant Singh, I decided to go to Ajmer to implore his blessings. I had intended to go to the *dargah* and quickly return. But when I got there I felt a strange pull that filled my senses with such sights, sounds, scents and sensations as I would never experience again. There were still some bright yellow mustard blossoms in the fields around the *dargah* that had not been harvested and the spring flowers had not yet wilted. A few leafy mango trees were laden with fragrant white blossom, and the bright red Polash trees in the full bloom of early summer were like a forest of flame. I walked through them until I reached the dargah.

The outline of the tall Taragarh Fort built on a hillside centuries ago, by the Chauhan Rajputs, was now visible after which could be seen the marble *masjid* of the *mazaar* (tomb) built by emperor Akbar. As I reached the sacred Sufi shrine, thirsty and breathless, I could hear the throbbing beat of the *tabla*, the whining notes of the *sarangi* and the lyrical voices of the *quawwals* who seemed to be pouring out their hearts in ecstatic frenzy.

I moved through the beggars at the entrance as if drawn by an invisible force and remembered nothing except that I was carried by a crowd surging forward. I offered some flowers at the *mazaar* and then prostrated myself before the grave of the revered saint. After a while, I felt overcome with a sense of tranquil calm; a feeling of being just a tiny leaf in the great wind of the power of Allah.

I was stirred from my reverie as the notes of the music grew louder with cries of *'Allah Hu... Allah Hu...Allah Hu'*, that blotted out all the other sounds. The *qawwals* were now singing loudly imploring the saintly spirit of the *Khwaja* to grant them their long cherished desires. They poured out their hearts to express their yearning for a *Daras* (a glimpse of the *Vali*, the divine companion of Allah) whom they sometimes described as the *Oroos* (a mythical bride who is unknown and mysterious) or the *Mashook* (a beloved with long flowing tresses, and dark hypnotic eyes). The *Khwaja* bound both Hindu and Muslim traditions together in an alliance based on love, compassion and peace.

Despite the deep disappointment with Jaswant Singh, a much more confident Dara now chose to engage his enemy at the hilly defile of Deorai,[26] just four *kos* south of Ajmer. Here, he thought he could not be outflanked by Aurangzeb's larger numbers who were fast approaching from the north led by his former allies Shaista Khan and Jai Singh.

Shah Nawaz Khan was a very experienced and energetic campaigner who had been mainly responsible for raising Dara's new army. Owing to a shortage of treasure, there was a larger infantry than the more expensive horse mercenaries. Shah Nawaz said that this would not matter because the hilly and forested terrain chosen by us was not very well suited to cavalry and that our well positioned infantry would win the day. Dara now took a very active interest in the disposition of our troops and rode to all the units to encourage them; his words were met with confident cries of approval from his soldiers.

As Aurangzeb's armies had needed considerable time to reach Deorai, Dara had several days to prepare his position and strategically locate his artillery and muskets on the higher elevations. Our camp was on the south side of a wide horse shoe shaped hilltop with a steep ridge to the east and another to the west with a grassy meadow of half a *kos* wide between them. The area behind our camp had steep cliffs that would keep us safe from any flanking attack.

We now observed that some advance units of our enemies were arriving and camping on an open plain on the north of this field and that their numbers kept growing for several days. On the late afternoon of the third day, we heard distant cheering in their camp and saw the tall crimson command flag of Aurangzeb approaching through

26 Dara's last battle at Deorai was fought over three hard fought days from 14th to 16th March 1659.

the dusty haze. His own small unit now came to nearly the distance of a cannon shot to survey our dispositions before returning to his command tent. Knowing that Aurangzeb never wasted time I anticipated that he would take a day to deploy his forces and attack us on the next.

I shared this opinion with Dara and our other commanders and requested permission to try to again disrupt his plans. As I was not completely sure of who could be trusted I did not reveal my exact plans but again asked for the service of the unit of the soldiers who had earlier helped me to surprise Khalilullah Khan. I gathered the eager group together with the aim of repeating our disruption of Aurangzeb's camp. Carrying small sacks of gunpowder, rockets and other weapons, ten groups of ten soldiers each left at dusk to ride past the enemy's picket lines with the intention of attacking simultaneously at three hours after sunset.

It was a dark moonless night and we waited expectantly, watching the small fires that dotted the enemy encampment go out one by one. After what seemed to be an interminable wait, we suddenly saw the flashes of rockets followed by the sound of exploding gunpowder and the loud shouting from terrified soldiers rushing from their tents. One of our teams had also penetrated the paddock and several thousand of panicked horses were let loose to gallop wildly through the camp that was in an uproar for several hours. Most of our troopers got back safely at dawn and were greeted with enthusiastic cheering from our camp that was very encouraged by their exploits. The loud beat of our drums celebrating our feat must have been demoralising to the enemy. It had been our first victory against an army led by Aurangzeb himself.

Aurangzeb's disrupted army could not attack the next day as had been planned but we knew that they would surely come on the following day. There was a nearly dry stream running through our valley that had cut through a small ridge of fallen stones about a *kos* north of our semi circular line. Taking a section of troops I descended into the valley and had them pick up bundles of straw from a fodder depot nearby. We placed these in a long line just below our side of the ridge where it would not be seen by the approaching horsemen. I then got some soldiers to lace the bundles with gunpowder and whatever inflammable materials they could find.

Shortly before dawn, we heard the sound of kettle drums heralding Aurangzeb's advance towards our positions. Their horsemen were soon seen cantering in our direction. We allowed some two thousand *sawars* (horsemen) to cross the ridge into our side of the valley before a few of our soldiers slipped out from behind the rocks and ignited the straw. The bundles immediately went up in a wall of flame and our artillery and muskets, that had remained silent till now, rained down death and destruction on the confused horsemen who circled about helplessly trapped below us. As horses were terrified of fire, many went almost mad with panic. The flames, however, died after a short time and the survivors, leaving several hundred dead on the field, were able to escape and gallop out of the trap, spreading havoc among the army units lined up to attack us. Our cavalry units hooted with derision as these terrified horsemen thoroughly disrupted their own columns. It was yet another very gratifying victory.

There were no further attacks that day as Aurangzeb had to reorganize his troops. Then one of our soldiers rushed up to inform us of some movement on the knoll, about a *kos* further down the ridge to the east of our barrier of fire. We sent scouts forward who soon reported that it was Aurangzeb himself who had climbed up the ridge to observe our dispositions. They later reported that he was also moving his command tent just out of our sight behind the knoll.

Emboldened by our success, I again went to Dara and said that Aurangzeb's forward position was very exposed and a surprise attack could be the end of him. Dara was very excited by this prospect but forbade me to lead the attack that was entrusted to one of his young commanders Fayaz Khan, a bold swaggering Afghan. With a hundred horsemen he rode out at dusk with the sky still filled with smoke and dust. The horsemen rode quietly out of sight along the side of the hill above the two armies and had nearly reached Aurangzeb's tent before the alarm was sounded. The surprised enemy, however, rallied very quickly and a few brave horsemen galloped up the hill to try to block our unexpected attack.

Aurangzeb with a few of his officers rushed out of his tent, mounted their horses and turned towards the attackers until one of his officers pulled his horse away by its reins shouting, "*Padishah hazoor,* your life is too valuable to risk in this petty skirmish. Please come away. We are quite capable of dealing with these scoundrels ourselves." Aurangzeb, clearly very reluctant to retreat from the scene realized the wisdom in the advice and hesitantly cantered away down the hill.

Aurangzeb's precipitate retreat was greeted with loud shouts from our soldiers who screamed... "Look how the coward runs... forward with all speed and rout the swines... kill the usurper." Then in unison they began to loudly chant, "DARA... DARA... DARA... DARA... DARA... DARA... DARA... DARA!"

The loud cries ringing through the valley must have been very disturbing to Aurangzeb.

Scattered groups of Aurangzeb's defenders now began to ride up the hill to try to block our band of attackers who, with the advantage of the slope, were quickly cutting their way towards Aurangzeb's retreating group. Just then a chance musket ball hit Fayaz Khan who fell from his horse and his company quickly lost heart and tamely cantered back to their lines. I so dearly wished that Dara had not forbidden me to participate as I felt certain that I would have been able to sustain the attack after Fayaz was killed. As if echoing my thoughts Dara, who was standing beside me watching the failed attack, softly said, "Mubarak *Mia*, if you had been out there I would have now been the emperor of Hindustan."

In the enemy camp soon after, our former ally, Rajah Rajrup Singh sought permission to meet Aurangzeb. He was the very same Rajput prince who had earlier so solemnly sworn loyalty to Dara by accepting Nadira begum's breast water at Lahore but had now switched his loyalties to Aurangzeb. He offered Aurangzeb a solution by which he said he could dislodge the enemy. He said that his Jammu clansmen, who were experts in climbing hills, had found a path on the far side of the steep and rocky ridge that would get them behind Dara's lines. They crept up in the gathering dusk close behind Dara's soldiers the next day and fired a small cannon that instantly killed Shah Nawaz Khan who was commanding Dara's left flank. He was completely blown away at close range, leaving his soldiers immediately demoralized.

Aurangzeb now threw in a vigorous assault led by

his veteran commanders that was met with an equally determined defence but Dara's valiant defenders were slowly pushed back wave after wave. Gradually Aurangzeb's bigger numbers were able to secure a very hard fought victory.

Despair clouds the senses;

eyes cannot see, ears cannot hear, nose cannot smell,

tongue cannot taste, we cannot

feel the things that we touch

... even our dreams become barren

CHAPTER 19

Blood and Tears

While Dara battled his younger brother for three furious days, Nadira, her family and the rest of our royal group waited anxiously near five arched marble pavilions built by Shah Jahan at the beautiful Anasagar lake of Ajmer. They were safe here with part of his harem and the remains of his once great treasure, though they kept hearing desultory gunfire in the distance. They also fervently prayed that their offerings at the shrine of the Chisti saints, who had blessed so many Mughal monarchs in the past, would now aid prince Dara in the epic battle, where the prospect of victory seemed to be steadily diminishing.

The sounds of gunfire continued until it was nearly nightfall. Then news of Aurangzeb's victory drifted in as groups of horsemen began to arrive. Fearing the worst, the family decided to immediately flee towards Ahmadabad and was only with the greatest of good fortune that they managed to join up with the remnants of Dara's force the next day, just as we they were beginning to despair. Nadira broke down in tears of happiness to be reunited with her beloved prince but he, with the shock of defeat, seemed to have become cold and remote. His face seemed frozen with disappointment and disbelief.

But our troubles continued as our few remaining loyal soldiers and slaves had to use all their guile and force to protect the remaining treasure and possessions from the numerous rogues who were trying to steal our precious remaining belongings. Many *bandis* who had once deserted us, suddenly returned with a ragged assortment of other soldiers and common thieves to try and rob what they thought would be a poorly guarded caravan.

Our depleted party was now down to just two hundred loyal defenders led by a young Asif Khan, who had to contend with numerous bands of scoundrels harrying our party like a pack of hungry dogs. We quickly made a ring of loyal soldiers around the ladies and our treasure and kept marching on. I, then led a sudden attack with six staunch soldiers and killed one of the bandit leaders. This kept them at a distance for some time. But they kept hovering around us though we moved as fast as we could towards the south.

It was just before dawn, when we were sagging with fatigue, that they made another determined attack and captured some of our camels carrying treasure, tents, clothes and other belongings.With two loyal soldiers I quickly chased them in the dark and caught hold of the camel that I knew carried most of our remaining silver coins hidden under a pile of tattered tents. There was a short muddled fight until one of the ruffians hit my head with his wooden stave and I fell down unconsciousness. I came to my senses quite quickly, spitting out a mouthful of mud and sand. My dazed mind thought of how wonderful it would if I could just lie quietly on the ground and be free from all my worries. Then I thought of Dara and Nadira who now had so few reliable supporters and had to force my aching body to get up and do its duty.

I staggered to my feet with some difficulty and was lucky to find that my sword had fallen under me in the sandy soil. I now heard the sounds of shouting and camel bells and guessed that our camel was still quite near and that the ruffians were fighting over it. Had I been in my full senses I would not have dared to attack the band of more than ten scoundrels but my head was still dizzy and I was in no mood to think, so I recklessly rushed into the group like a vengeful demon.

Some of the bandits closed in on me with swords and long sticks but I held them off till my sword suddenly broke on the shield of one of the thieves. With a cry of triumph, a tall bearded adversary rushed in to kill me but I fortunately remembered the trick about fighting with a balled fist that I had learned from the young white guard at Surat many years earlier. So, after pretending to cower in fear, I suddenly straightened up and hit him with my clenched fist so hard at the point of his jaw that he fell down unconscious. I then quickly picked up his sword and scattered his bewildered followers. I then rushed back with our recaptured camel.

With several armies fanned out to hunt us down, there was to be no rest for anyone. Our ragged group was utterly exhausted but needed to cover huge distances of at least twelve *kos* every day simply to keep ahead of the ravenous hyenas that were relentlessly pursuing us. Our journey through the salt marsh in the searing summer heat wore down our few remaining elephants, horses, mules, camels and cattle. Already weak from hunger and thirst, we struggled to move through the powdery saline soil that made our feet feel like lead. Then one day, our last elephant died followed by two horses and even our camels began to falter. We had very little fresh water and had to prevent our desperate animals from drinking at the murky pools of the salty water as that would have killed them very quickly.

Apart from water we also had to find some food to eat. There was very little that could be eaten in this barren land, except for the herds of wild asses that always kept too far away for us to shoot. We could not stop long enough at any place to trap birds or catch fish. I tried to recall some of the jungle lore I had learned years earlier from the Bhil *shikaris* near Burhanpur and walked away from our group looking for tracks. It was getting dark when I saw some tall brown birds near a pool and managed to shoot one with my bow. I also found ground nests of some other birds and ate a few of their eggs to keep up my own flagging strength. At one point while crossing a salty pool, I felt my legs sinking into the ground which I quickly learnt was treacherous quick sand. I threw myself flat on my back and very slowly pulled my legs out of the wet earth that seemed determined to suck me in.

As I walked the land in search of food, I saw the marks of a large reptile that had slithered over the damp sandy ground. I followed them and found a very large lizard resting near a stagnant pool. I approached it quietly till I was close and I had to shoot four arrows into its thick hide before it stopped moving. I then took out my knife and slit its throat before cutting off its head, and with great difficulty stripped off some of its thick skin. I cut the meat into smaller pieces so that no one would know what animal I had killed. It was quite dark now and I was lucky to remember what the *shikaris* had taught me about following the stars and was able to get near enough to our camp for them to hear my anxious calls.

Arranging fuel for our cooking was not too difficult for we found the dung of many animals drying out in the hot sun. The reptile's flesh tasted fishy but we desperately needed whatever food we could find and were too hungry to be particular. I made a little soup out of some of the bones and meat of the brown bird and gave it to begum Nadira and her little daughter Salima who were getting very weak.

The ordeal was too much for Nadira who had borne every hardship with such serene courage and kept all our hopes alive. She, for the first time was confined to bed with very painful sores on one leg making it difficult for her to move. It was our great fortune that we chanced upon a French doctor, Francoise Bernier, who happened to be in the area while he was travelling from Ahmadabad to Dilli. We eagerly led him to our ailing princess in the hopes that he might be able to treat her. But I sensed that something inside her was now broken. Though she continued to smile bravely and was as kind and hospitable as always, we could all see that she died a little more with every passing day.

We were all sagging with fatigue, suffering cramps of hunger and sinking into a state of deep despair. As I trudged through the powdery sand I could not help thinking about the utter futility of war. This struggle for the Mughal throne had cost more than a hundred thousand deaths in great battles at Dharmat, Bahadurpur, Samugarh, Khajua and Deorai, but an equal number of valiant soldiers had also died of fatigue, hunger, sickness and injuries while marching to or retreating from each battlefield. And for every corpse there was another that had been so grievously injured as to make him unfit for his duties as a man. Almost all the able young men of an entire generation had perished in these futile battles. It seemed to me that the death and suffering of these gallant men had been such an unnecessary folly, especially as every man boldly venturing into battle, inspired by visions of manly glory, must have known the terrible fate that awaited their wives, mothers and sisters who would all become homeless and be forced to surrender themselves to any man who had the means to offer them protection, food or shelter.

For the sake of their vulnerable children, the mothers would surrender not only their bodies but often their cherished traditions of caste and religion, although they would never lose their innate honour. This made them capable of huge sacrifices in having to submit to the demands of their new masters. So paradoxically, their children owed much more to the inheritance from their mothers than to the seeds of the men who they thought to be their fathers.

Even if the women secretly despised the men who had sired their children, they would soon forget the anguish of conception and the pain of delivery as they were secretly proud of producing children and proving their womanhood. Women knew how simple it was to flatter their new masters by saying that the lips, ears, noses or some other feature of their little babies resembled those of their supposed fathers. They knew that men were fools following dreams of glory while they remained behind to nurture the children. Women were driven by emotion that bound them to their families and to each other, while men were restless wanderers who wanted to possess new weapons, fast horses, beautiful women, fame and fortune. Men loved all these material things but women were mainly interested in the building of relationships that were necessary to hold their families together.

Though women never stopped thinking about their own customs and traditions, they would often appear to be the most passionate defenders of the new traditions they had adopted. While the men would sacrifice their lives in the name of honour, loyalty, race and chivalry, it were the suffering women who so valiantly fought to protect their children with honour and with devious cunning when cunning, was necessary, ensuring the survival of their traditions. I began to realize that men were romantic adventurers while women were the mothers of the human race.

We trudged on for endless hours on that flat hot plain where mirages shimmering in the distance, beguilingly offered us the tempting vision of cool lakes of fresh water. Our eyes had reddened with exposure as we plodded on,placing one reluctant foot before another under the pitiless white hot sun on what seemed to be a never-ending journey. We were very fortunate that one of the local Koli tribesmen, on seeing our pitiful state, agreed to guide us. The dirty brown, salty sand was very abrasive to the skin and our feet were soon covered with painful bleeding sores. All our finery were now sweat-stained filthy rags.

Even Dara, who had so far stood proud and resolute despite the hunger and thirst, began to show the first signs of weakness with a tremor in his hands. Throughout the march he had been shuffling back and forth helping not only Nadira, his two daughters and Sipihr, but even our few remaining slaves. He would pick up some of them himself and say encouraging words to others. What surprised me most was the endurance and resolution of the women who had been brought up in such pampered luxury. Unlike some men who showed off their bravery and strength, the women quietly plodded through the sand and even found the strength to assist others and carry small loads.

We tried to quicken our pace when news reached us that part of Rajah Jai Singh's army was on our trail with four thousand horsemen. I suspect that he did not push forward as fast as he could have out of a lingering respect for the royal prince. We did, however, rejoice when we got news from our tribal scout some days later that the *rajah* had in haste, tried to push forward too quickly and lost three thousand of his horses, reducing his proud cavaliers to the same pitiable state as ourselves.

Word of Dara's defeat, along with dire threats from Aurangzeb's agents had preceded us with the result that even our former friends and allies no longer dared to openly help or support us. The entourage of our great prince was now reduced to a pitiful party clad in worn and unwashed clothing with just one horse, one bullock cart and five camels for some of the ladies and just a hundred guards. But with enemies in relentless pursuit, we had no choice but to keep going on in the rising heat of April.

Surprisingly, it was the usually villainous, local tribals who offered unexpected assistance by giving us scraps of food and vital information. There was, however, one small occasion for laughter when we learned that while the treacherous cuckold Khalilullah Khan had been approaching the island fort at Bhakkar, he had been opposed by our brave defenders, led by a young eunuch called Basant. He had inflicted a very amusing moral blow on the mortally injured old general's self esteem by firing a salvo of ladies slippers from a cannon to mock him and remind his soldiers about the infidelity of their general's wife.

The main force of Rajah Jai Singh's horsemen was pursuing us from the east but he stopped as soon as we reached the boundary of our empire on the banks of the

Indus. Dara wanted to go on to Persia through Kandahar but Nadira Begum, who was now very sick and frail, begged him not to. The Persian monarch had a very bad reputation and the poor ladies could not bear the thought of being forced into his harem.

If the salt plain was a hardship, the rocky slopes of Baluchistan were even worse. Words cannot describe the desolation all around us. The landscape was harsh and dry, without trees to give shade or fodder to our starving animals. The dust coloured, rock strewn expanses were even more oppressive in the intense white heat of the midsummer sunshine. Our ankles were twisted by the broken rocks or burned, if they were not properly covered by our shoes that were now in tatters held together with ragged strips of cloth or leather.

Dara, suddenly, smiled as he saw a glimmer of hope for we now approached a small fort called Dadhar, where the *zamindar* Malik Jiwan was deeply beholden to him. Dara reminded us of a time many years earlier, when he had personally interceded with the emperor to save the life of this Afghan chief from execution under the foot of an elephant.

We were within sight of the fort on a rocky hill when one of Nadira's maids suddenly burst out in loud lamentations. We all stopped and saw that Nadira was lying slumped in a basket on the side of our best surviving camel. We gently lowered her frail body to the ground and Dara knelt down looking at her closely before tears welled up in his dark sunken eyes. We all discreetly looked away as he lowered his head between his knees, his back heaving as he surrendered to abject sorrow. The beautiful Nadira Bano had slipped out of life with as little complaint as when she had lived. She had been a truly serene and beautiful woman for every moment of her gracious life.

Malik Jiwan received us with respect, courtesy and every mark of gratitude. The mortal remains of Nadira Banu Begum were brought into the fort and I, along with the women of our group, bathed her frail body and wrapped it in a white cloth shroud to await her burial. In accordance to her last wishes, her mortal remains were entrusted to Dara's followers who were to take them to Lahore to be buried at the feet of the revered divine Mian Mir.

Even in that humble fort the pleasure of being able to bathe and again wear clean clothes was like a heavenly blessing. I, along with the fifteen year old Sipihr Shikoh, Dara's two daughters and just twenty servants and troopers were all that now remained of Dara's once proud entourage. Sipihr, taking after his mother, was not very tall but he had his father's proud Timurid eyes. He was mature for his years having participated in several battles and endured so many months of severe hardship. The two girls Jani and Salima were quite pretty but their eyes showed fear and fatigue from the unspeakable suffering, uncertainties and sorrows that they would never forget.

Late one evening Dara, who was lying on a cot near the battlement, called me to his side and looking up from a copy of the Quran held in his hands, asked me, even though I knew he was really speaking to himself, "Mubarak, my friend, you have been by my side for so many years. Tell me sincerely. Do you think that Aurangzeb was right when he said that all that a man needs to know can be found in this holy book and seeking beyond it will only cause him confusion and conflict? Is it right that I should only respect this holy book and not the books of others even if they contain words of love and wisdom? Also tell me, why must a king always have to be cruel and vindictive to be respected? Why cannot a kind and gentle king also get respect and obedience?"

He then took off a large ring on his left thumb and handed it to me. It was a piece of dark green jade encased in a simple gold band. On the top was inscribed the word *'Allah'* and on the inner side was inscribed the word *'Prabhu'*. He resumed speaking, "Why should we think that *Allah* is only a god of the *mussalmans*? The great cosmic creator can be known by any name or by no name at all, as long as the believer understands that He is the source of all life and all bounty. I am very confused... If I have never disobeyed the *suras* of the holy Quran nor injured any man or beast, why does this demon... this iblis... so vengefully pursue me and send me sorrow after sorrow?"

He paused and then went on, "How can I tell you of the depth of hole in my heart with my beloved Nadira no longer beside me! When I first saw her as a young girl selling roses, I knew in that instant that we would forever be part of each other's destinies. But where will my destiny lead me now? Are we to meet again in another world or perhaps in another lifetime as the Hindus believe? Have I been so evil that I am to be consigned to the fires of hell or will *Allah* have mercy on me and find me a little place in paradise? Dare I dream of a small place in God's great garden with my beloved Nadira by my side? Tell me. Has it been wrong for me to try to so diligently follow my beliefs even though it has caused so much suffering to all those who believed in me?"

I hesitated and then replied, "*Shahzadeh hazoor*, my noble prince, I have been by your side for over twenty years and I can boldly say that neither this humble slave nor any of the many thousands who have served you have ever doubted the love and sincerity with which you have tried to seek a better world for all humanity. We have always admired your noble spirit that could rise above the petty concerns of mortal men. In your recent hardships I have also greatly respected your indomitable courage that has enabled you to keep your head high despite the terrible misfortunes that have been cast in your path. Any lesser mortal would have been utterly broken."

"Then tell me my dear Mubarak, why has failure pursued me like an angry hornet and frustrated every project, every enterprise and every effort that I have made for those who have so generously given me their devotion and love? What will now become of all the great work we had so grandly begun? What will become of my beloved Hindustan when bigoted Muslims like my brother shame and injure not only good Hindus but also so many Shias and Sufis and others who do not follow his rigid beliefs. My heart sinks but I hold this holy book and pray for all those who have suffered as a result of my follies. May they forgive me and may the merciful *Allah* protect us all. May He be kind to me on the Day of Judgment."

I lowered my voice and slowly replied, "Noble *Shahzadeh*, all of us who believed in you have undoubtedly suffered. But none of us has ever blamed you, as you have never done anything for greed or your own personal benefit. We know that even your struggle for the rich Mughal throne was not for amassing wealth but to foster peace and harmony among the diverse people of the empire."

"You should not sorrow *hazoor,* or allow yourself to be angry because every one of your defeats has been caused by betrayals; the most despicable betrayals! If your trusted Qasim Khan had not left Rajah Jaswant Singh unsupported, our imperial armies would have surely won at Dharmat and stopped them marching on to Samugarh. If Rajah Champat Rai Bundela, who had been in your employ, had not shown Aurangzeb the secret ford across the Chambal, he would not have been able to get his army across the river so easily. Then if your trusted general Khalilullah Khan had not persuaded you to dismount from your elephant at Samugarh, victory would have surely been yours and you would have had your valiant son Sulaiman at your side today. *Hazoor*, it is I who should sorrow because I too have failed you. I had been entrusted with a task to warn you not to descend from your great elephant but failed to get your attention. This failure has been haunting me every day since Samugarh."

"Even that devious astrologer Diwani Das betrayed you as he was secretly in the pay of your brother. If he had not so consistently stopped you from attacking at the most opportune times, you would have immediately attacked at Samugarh, stood firm at Dilli, at Lahore, at Multan and so many other places and been victorious with the huge support from your many devoted allies. If the despicable Rajah Rajrup Singh of Jammu, who even accepted Nadira begum's breast water as a commitment to his everlasting loyalty, had not betrayed you, Aurangzeb could not have triumphed at Deorai." I went on, "Our scriptures warn us about the evils of greed, anger, lust and jealousy but I believe that betrayal should be considered a far greater sin. Betrayal is like a worm in the heart of a lion and can without warning, bring down the strongest and the bravest of God's creatures."

I went on to add something that I had often thought about, "*Shahzadeh hazoor,* it also seems a very strange paradox but I have often noticed that good people seem to be destined to suffer. As no one expects anything from those who are cruel, greedy or selfish, everyone applauds them if they should ever do something good. So much is expected from good people that there is always great disappointment if they ever fail to please others, regardless of how sincerely they may try."

I continued, "I have also noticed that people can forgive you when they feel anger, lust, greed or jealousy. What they cannot forgive is the envy and guilt that lurks secretly inside their own hearts. No one ever admits to harbouring envy or guilt but these sentiments are like venomous snakes that silently slither into the heart and poison it. The intensity of hatred that people within a family can feel for each other is not caused by simple emotions like greed or anger as much as from envy and guilt that silently poisons them. And then *Shahzadeh,* there is also the evil effect of *nazzar*. It is an evil eye that will always try to seek out all those who seem to be the most fortunate."

Dara lay inert looking at the distant sky without any expression on his face. He said nothing and it was only at night that I heard his quiet sobbing and entreaties to the almighty asking what sins he had committed to deserve such a fate. What had he done to be so utterly forsaken by all the gods and by all his friends?

But we had not yet reached the bottom of the well of our sorrows. It was a very hot morning at the end of the first week of June after we had left that wretched fort of Dadhar to resume our journey towards Persia. As we were moving towards the imposing cliffs just before the approach to Kandahar, the *malik* with a small section of horsemen slowly rode upto us and bowing low, asked Dara to prepare himself for his return to Dilli. We looked at him in astonishment but he refused meet the prince's eye and informed us that Bahadur Khan, with a battalion of soldiers sent by Aurangzeb had arrived to escort him back to the capital.

It seemed ironic that the *malik* had not surrendered my now, helpless prince to Aurangzeb's soldiers at the time when he was a guest in his own palace because such an act would have violated the time honoured the tribal code of hospitality to a guest. He, however, felt no promptings of honour to restrain him from arresting Dara as soon as he was outside his walls.

It was the ultimate betrayal. A man surrendering the life of a man to whom his own life was owed. But then, I had so often observed that while people always remember the injuries that they receive, they so easily forget the many things for which they should be grateful. Gratitude is usually demanding but betrayal always profitable.

Every soul needs a mirror to see itself.

A lake cannot see its own depth...

without the clouds and mountains that it reflects.

CHAPTER 20

A Sky Full of Ravens

It took us over two months on double marches to reach Dilli. Although we were treated with respect and courtesy, it was a hard and a very depressing journey. Bahadur Khan kept a hundred soldiers to guard us closely, two hundred followed a few hours behind us and the rest were ranged out ahead of us. It took us seven days to travel from Dadhar to the Indus where the water was low because the monsoons were late but it was still a huge river and crossing it on the ferry was a slow business. When we were across I saw that the guards had become very relaxed and careless and it gave me the idea that we could try to escape.

That night, after our evening meal of roasted deer, I quietly managed to get some of the cooking fat on to my hands and rubbed it over my bound wrists. Later that night I was, with a little effort, able to slip my hands out of the ropes. I then waited till the guards were in their deepest sleep at about two hours before dawn and quietly woke Dara and whispered my plan to him. We then woke up Sipihr, whose binding ropes I cut loose with a sharp dagger I had quietly slipped from the belt of one of the sleeping guards.

Dara whispered, "But what about Jani and Saleema?"

I whispered back, "It will be too risky so we cannot take them with us but fear not for Bahadur Khan is an honorable man and he will care for them properly. They are also princesses of the royal blood so no one would dare to touch them."

Dara quietly crawled over to the two sleeping girls and with a heavy heart, gently kissed them goodbye. We then crept out of the camp, walking silently over the sandy soil in the light of a pale moon. We walked west towards the river and swam across it holding onto a large piece of dry driftwood. On the far side we walked north in shallow water, leaving no footprints that our pursuers could follow. After an hour, we reached a small rivulet gushing down from the mountains from the west and followed it until we came to a small sandy bank nearly hidden under the roots of a big tree. It was a good place to hide until our pursuers gave up the chase. We did not have to wait very long. Two hours after sunrise we heard the excited sound of galloping horsemen followed some time later by the chatter of foot soldiers searching for us but we sat very quietly and escaped their notice.

At dusk, I ventured out and found a small pool a few hundred paces up the stream. We took off almost all our clothes and splashed about like little children in the clean and refreshingly cold water. After suffering the heat and dust of the past few weeks it was truly joyous to feel the cold fresh water of the stream gushing over us. Dara was smiling after many months and told us that it was the first time in his life that he was as naked as on the day on which he had been born. "This is truly heaven", he said,"where all *Allah*'s creations can be seen as they really are without the corruption of any human embellishments. Today I understand why our naked friend Sarmad always looked so full of joy."

Dara looked very happy lying on the cool sand. He and Sipihr spent hours holding hands, talking in low voices and smiling. The young prince listened as his father recited beautiful verses of poetry. Later that evening, Dara said to me, "Mubarak, my old friend, what more does a man need? I would so much prefer to live like a hermit in a small cave like this than face all the violence and intrigues of the court."

Fish and small birds were plentiful so we were able to eat quite well. One morning, I saw a large cobra slide out of a hole in the bank to the left of our cave. Sipihr quickly picked up my wooden stave and was about to kill it but I restrained him and said, "Do not fear! If you leave it alone it will do you no harm."

It left its burrow every morning and came back every evening after eating and basking in the sun. Early one morning, I woke with a start to hear Dara laughing for the first time in many months. We saw him looking at a small fox curled up in the far corner of our cave. Dara said, "We seem to be hiding in a veritable Garden of Eden watered by a running stream from paradise. All we now need is a friendly lion and a deer to join us in this little corner of *Allah*'s heaven."

We enjoyed our freedom for five days where I showed Sipihr how to catch fish. We made a small dam with river stones and would wait till some small fish had collected. Then we would beat the water with my wooden stave, which stunned the fish swimming below to enable us to quite easily pick up a few of them. One day, while we were engrossed in our little game I looked up and saw a small boy grazing his goats on the hill above us and immediately rushed back to hide in our cave. He ran away and we knew that he would have reported what he had seen to his family.

We left the cave and tried to deceive our pursuers by recrossing the Indus but had not got very far before we heard the sand muffled sound of galloping horses. We knew that it would have been futile to try to run and surrendered without protest. With deference to princes of the royal blood, Dara and Sipihr were led on a horse but I was roughly trussed up and made to stagger behind with my hands bound before me. We were brought before a furious Bahadur Khan who knew that he would have had to face certain execution if his royal charges had managed to escape.

He said nothing to Dara or Sipihr, knowing that I was the one responsible for the attempted escape. They quickly rigged up two long ropes from the branch of a big tree and tied my outstretched arms above my head. Then two *paidas* picked up long knotted camel whips and proceeded to whip my bare back. As I knew that it was going to be a very painful ordeal I held a small piece of wood between my teeth to stop myself from biting off my tongue. I swore to make no sound during the torment that seemed to last for hours.

After the whipping that left me unconscious, they cut me down and poured salt onto the bleeding lacerations on my back to produce such agonising pain that I very nearly cried out. Some of the Mina tribesmen working as guides for Bahadur Khan then approached and urinated on my back causing great laughter among the soldiers who were watching. As Muslims consider urine disgustingly dirty, the soldiers thought that the Minas were trying to add to my humiliation. But I knew that they were actually doing me a kindness by washing away some of the salt as many tribesmen regarded urine as a cure for severe wounds, having often seen injured animals try to cure themselves by lying in pools of their own urine.

The tall hawk-nosed Bahadur Khan came to see me the day after my whipping and examined the flesh that had been flayed from my back. He looked me straight in the eye and was gracious enough to say, "You have been very brave and loyal and would have made a good soldier". He then ordered his soldiers to apply a salve to cover the lacerations on my back and give me a shirt to protect my skin from the harsh summer sun. I was made to sit backwards and ride on a small mule until I was strong enough to walk again.

After a few days, he called his troops together and made them solemnly swear to observe absolute silence about our short lived escape. The fear of Aurangzeb's wrath was taken very seriously with the result that no one was to ever learn about our brief adventure.

As we neared Dilli, Aurangzeb sent a message that we should not enter the capital until ordered to do so. He wanted to be absolutely certain that he had full control of the city and there could be no uprising in support of Dara or Shah Jahan. We were, therefore, directed to a hidden valley south of Alwar. We entered a sheltered valley through a big gate and passed a number of abandoned temples with tall Jain statues until we reached a small fort called Kanakwadi and waited for further orders. We were imprisoned in the beautiful little fort on top of a steep rocky hill, overlooking a small lake surrounded by a grove of palm trees with thick forests stretching out beyond it.

After a week, two riders arrived with orders for us to proceed to Dilli. Dara and Sipihr were made to ride an elephant with a well-screened ladies howdah until we entered the city. I remember it to be a dull and overcast day in late August; the sky dark with heavy monsoon clouds. There was almost no wind and the entire city seemed shrouded by an ominous silence. Aurangzeb tried to keep people from knowing about Dara's return, but curiosity, like mercury, burns its way through the smallest hole. Somehow the people had learnt almost everything about Dara's flight, his determined battles, his pitiful retreat, his tragic bereavement and his final betrayal.

The next day was exceptionally hot and humid as Prince Dara and Sipihr were paraded through Chandni Chowk[27]and the most populous areas of Dilli. They were being shamed by sitting on a small mangy female elephant and were made to wear the coarse dirty clothes of common laborers. An ugly hunch backed eunuch, Nazir Beg stood behind them menacingly holding a huge naked sword above his head. Dara's head was bowed low. As the sorry procession reached the Red Fort, a beggar shouted out, "Great prince, you used to always throw a few coins our way. What can you give us today?"

Dara slowly lifted his head, took off his ragged turban and brusquely threw it towards the beggar only to hear furious abuse from Nazir Beg who rudely told him, "You are now a common prisoner and can no longer behave like a prince!"

Our French doctor Francoise Bernier, who was part of the crowd that day, was to later write in his record that the

---

27 An account of the incident is given in Mohammad Kazim's 'Alamgir-nama' quoted by Waldamar Hansen and also Francoise Bernier.

entire city wept. The pent up sorrow suddenly burst out into loud anger when someone saw Malik Jiwan, who had so treacherously betrayed Dara at Dadhar, riding behind the sorry procession. A huge roar went up and all the bystanders began to loudly abuse him and hurl stones, old shoes, rotten vegetables and other rubbish at him. The cries rose to a dangerous pitch and soldiers had to be summoned to quell a possible riot.

This spontaneous outcry of public sympathy throughout the city greatly alarmed Aurangzeb's courtiers who thought that there might be an open revolt and therefore decided that Dara had to be quickly executed. But ever the fox, Aurangzeb wanted no blood to stain his own pale white hands so he turned the prisoners over to the Imperial *Qazi* to be tried and punished according to Islamic law for the crime of heresy.

I had now recovered from my ordeal and managed to unobtrusively leave Dilli and regain entry into the much depleted *zenana* of Shah Jahan in the Red Fort at Agra, which was now under the guard by Aurangzeb's soldiers. I was delighted to see my princess Jahanara even though she looked a pale shadow of her former self. I fell at her feet and felt her hands tremble as she slowly raised my head. Tears welled up in both our eyes as we looked at each other in a long silence as no words could even begin to express all the sorrow that was so strongly surging through our hearts. She had aged a great deal in that single year, was much thinner and her drawn face betrayed deep lines of worry. There were dark circles under her eyes and streaks of white among the thick tresses of her long black hair.

She sat me down before her and asked me to relate all that I had been witness to since that glorious day when our prince had so proudly set out to battle against Aurangzeb and Murad. Some of the other women and eunuchs came in and quietly sat on the floor with us and listened intently as I related the many events of the tortuous past year. Tears welled up in my eyes and my feeble voice choked when I tried to tell them of my own failure to get past the traitor Khalilullah Khan and warn Dara of the plot to betray him at Samugarh. But I also felt quite proud when I related how I had led the daring attack into the camp of that traitor Khalilullah Khan and had mortally wounded him. My listeners nodded approvingly when I told them of how we had twice repulsed Aurangzeb's greater army at Dara's final battle at Deorai,which we may have won if not for another treacherous betrayal.

I noticed that little Gauharara was sitting next to me listening with rapt attention. She whispered in my ear but loudly enough for Jahanara to hear, "The rose blooms brightest before it withers and dies and the crows caw loudest when the heavens are disturbed. When the roses are dead, the crows will all gather. Thousands of crows... thousands of crows."

Jahanara and I looked at each other quite bewildered but I now knew that the little princess had premonitions of many things that were destined to occur. I had been speaking for nearly two hours until we were rudely interrupted by some of Roshanara's attendants who loudly entered and demanded that I should immediately be banished from the *zenana* as I was Dara's spy.

Houri Jan, the head of the *zenana*, now stood up and firmly said, "No! Mubarak has faithfully served all the princes and he is welcome to stay", gesturning for me to continue. When I finished my tale, she ordered me follow her to her chamber. Although she was a tough and vigilant mistress, she had always been kind to me. She told me how the bitter and vindictive Roshanara was now preening about like an overfed peahen and behaving as if she were now the *Padishah Begum* herself. I also learned that Roshanara had also become an almost unashamed voluptuary and used to have several young men covered in *burkhas,* or hidden in baskets, secreted into her chambers.

I now remembered my own vow of revenge and said, "Houri Jan, you are the mistress of the *zenana* but you know that the younger princess hates you and will surely have you disgraced and removed unless you can expose her first. Your strength lies in the fact that Aurangzeb is such an absolutely unforgiving puritan that if he gets to know about Roshanara's sinful ways he will surely punish her despite all that she has done for him. That serpent has a heart of stone and does not know the meaning of gratitude but he does know everything that Islam considers sinful. You must lose no time to expose her. Do not delay."

Houri Jan laid a trap and as if by accident, the *zenana* guards dropped a big basket of clothes being brought out of Roshanara's quarters and caught two nearly naked young men who were hiding inside it. She raised an alarm and the guards ran after the terrified boys who, in panic, jumped off the high balcony to fall to their deaths into the stone courtyard far below. Houri Jan made sure that a full report was sent to Aurangzeb who, though flooded with many urgent matters of state, was very troubled. Even though Roshanara's guilt in this incident had not been proven beyond doubt by a full confession, Houri Jan was now empowered to keep a much stricter watch. We had to, however, wait several months before she was able to lay another trap in which a poor offender tried to hide inside a big brass pot in the *hamam*. When boiling water was poured into it he screamed in agany and confessed to everything. Aurangzeb then withdrew many of Roshanara's privileges and never again gave her the respect he had earlier bestowed.

It was punishment but not punishment enough to satisfy me or many others that Roshanara had so viciously injured over the years. Except in this case, I had never allowed hatred to rankle in my heart or disturb the composure of my mind. In her case, however, I would have been overjoyed if *Allah* had granted me the opportunity to personally torture her just as she had terrified and tortured so many innocent people.

Much later that night I cautiously crept into Jahanara's chamber. She clutched me with surprising strength and said, "I was waiting for you. I thought you would never come. I thought someone would try to stop you." I gently lowered her on to her bed and we just lay together with our eyes swimming with tears. Our shared sorrow seemed to strangely unleash a storm of passion and we were soon devouring each other's trembling bodies with our mouths, tongues and exploring hands. After what seemed to be an endless age, we subsided into a state of nearly breathless exhaustion where our faintly trembling bodies seemed to continue radiating our intense emotions as if they were red hot furnaces slowly cooling down.

A long time had passed and I knew that I would soon have to leave for ever as Aurangzeb would never forgive me for disobeying his commands. Jahanara clung to me and said, "You must quickly go from here and hide as I fear that Aurangzeb will severely punish you for all that you have done for Dara. I wonder if we will ever meet again. Please come to me whenever you can as I just cannot bear to face this sorrow all alone. There is simply no one left."

I went to the home of a friend and sat looking at the river swirling past. The enormity of the epic events that I had been witness to now began to slowly dawn upon me. I began to reflect on the many emotions that had driven all the members of the royal family. I now understood that a bitter feeling of implacable envy of Dara had been the main force that had driven Aurangzeb and blinded him to all other thought and reason. There was, consequently, no guile he would not stoop to in order to reach his goal, disregarding all the pain or bloodshed that his actions were to cause.

It was however ironical that once Aurangzeb became emperor he seemed to lose all further ambition and purpose. He was to go through his long reign as if he were a spent force and it was strange that with his victory Aurangzeb seemed to have become completely emptied of purpose. He dutifully performed the motions of his royal and religious responsibilities but without any enthusiasm or joy. He was always very sensitive of any threat to his pride but wore the Mughal crown as if it were a terribly heavy burden.

Dara had been guilty of a consuming greed for fame and to be known as the greatest spiritual luminary of his age though he was, in the end, a victim of his own innocence. How wonderful it would have been if Aurangzeb could have had a few of Dara's qualities of compassion and intellect or if Dara could have had some of Aurangzeb's qualities of courage, guile, steadfastness and organization.

Shah Jahan had been intoxicated by the dreams of his glory and magnificence but had allowed himself to be seduced by sensuality and luxury, while Khalilullah had been driven by burning shame and a need to avenge his honour.

Roshanara had been driven by envy and avarice. All the brave Rajput *umraos* had been driven by their love of battle and chivalry, even though they too eventually succumbed to the inducements of power or position. Sulaiman Shikoh had stood out as a shining example of righteous courage as did Jahanara as the epitome of love, grace and compassion. All these remarkable people had reacted to each other and to their fast changing situations like the ivory pieces on some giant chessboard.

Dara's trial by the *Qazis* was to be such a mockery of justice; an absolute sham! But I was not surprised. The *Qazis* all knew that the patronage of the emperor was important for their own power. Four *mullahs*, all dressed in black robes, with a few nobles and family members in attendance assembled in the *Diwani-i-Khas*, or hall of private audience, at Dilli, to debate the matter and pronounce their judgment. To further humiliate him, the attendants made Dara stand before them stripped to the waist like a common slave.

After they were all assembled Aurangzeb entered the hall and first summoned the jackal Malik Jiwan who was ceremoniously raised to the rank of one thousand and given the grand title of *Bakhtiar Khan. Bakhtiar* meant fortunate but Malik Jiwan had little idea of what misfortune lay ahead of him. There is a Hindustani proverb which says... "*Khuda ki lathi mien awaz nahin.*" (The stave of God strikes without making a sound.) After the ceremony was over the *malik* was curtly dismissed with a few presents. We later learned that he had been waylaid and killed in a forest while returning to Dadhar. It was widely rumoured that the assassination had been carried out on the command of the emperor who despised treachery even though he unashamedly used treachery to serve his ambitions.

The trial then began. We all knew that the *mullahs* could be relied upon to give a verdict they thought would ensure the emperor's continued patronage. They were, in any case, hostile to Dara who had frequently reviled the narrow minded orthodoxy of priests to the amusement of others.

The first *Qazi* asked Dara to hand him the jade thumb ring that was still on his left hand. He turned it over and the *Qazi* examined it slowly and asked, "This green stone is inscribed with the words *'Allah'* on one side and *'Prabhu'* on the other side. Does this mean that you consider this Hindu God to be equal to our Muslim *Allah*?"

Dara raised his bowed head and answered, "Honorable clerics, the cosmic creator is known by many names. He is recognized and called God, *Allah, Prabhu, Jehova, Ahura Mazda* and many more names by devout people in many different lands. "

"So you are saying that the *Allah* worshipped by Muslims is no different than the Hindu *Prabhu*!"

"Yes, that is what I believe. I believe that *Allah* is the god of all people of the world who simply call him by different names. There is only one great cosmic creator even if people have different places of worship and revere God in many different ways."[28]

---

28 The Quran's Sura 35:24 says... "To every race, great teachers have been sent. God has not left any community without a prophet, warner and true guide." The Quran's Sura 23:24 further says... "To people after people have we sent Apostle after Apostle: mostly, though the people have rejected or even killed them."

A second *Qazi* asked, "Will you deny that it was under your personal orders that a group of Brahmin scholars translated Hindu holy books like the Upanishads and the Bhagavat Gita into Persian?"

Dara replied, "No, your honour. How can I deny what is so widely known. I did indeed commission these translations."

The *Qazi* continued, "Is it true that you had yourself said that these Hindu works are God's most perfect revelation and that there are references to them even in our holy Quran?"

"Yes, your honour. I do believe that these sacred texts clearly show that underneath the idolatrous outward forms of Hindu worship lies a monotheistic core that is older than those of Judaism, Christianity or Islam."

The Qazi angrily retorted, "So you are equating Hindu doctrines with the most holy words of Islam?"

"Only in essence, your honour. I have already said that the outward forms are very different. My studies have led me to most sincerely believe that the Upanishads and the Bhagavad Gita are none other than the '*Sirr i-Akbar*' or the great secret-which our holy Prophet suggested was none other than the '*Kitab-al-Muknum*' or the hidden book mentioned in the fifty-sixth chapter of the holy Quran itself."

The Qazi continued, "Is it true that you have written with your hand a book called *Majma-ul-Bahrain* - 'The Mingling of the Oceans' that dares to suggest that there is a common thread between the messages of our holy Quran and the *Brahma Shastras* of these idolatrous Hindus?'"

Dara replied, "Yes this is known to everyone. There are many great pearls of wisdom in the scriptures of every religion and I believe that mankind is richer when these are displayed before them. You will surely recall that it is written in our own scriptures that the merciful *Allah* had sent one hundred and twenty four thousand messengers to show all the people of the world the way of righteousness. I believe that the merciful *Allah*'s messengers carrying his messengers had been sent not only to Muslims but to all the people of the world in every age. I believe that all people have a pious duty to try to seek out these messages that have become obscured by the confusion of languages and ignorant interpretations of narrow minded priests of every faith."

A third *Qazi* now asked, "Is it correct that the Sikh faith has its roots both in Islam and Hinduism?"

Dara replied, "It would appear to be so, your honour, as the Sikhs have deep respect for both religions."

"Yet is it these very same Sikhs who are now such troublesome rebels to our governors in Punjab? Does this not prove that by allowing the pure stream of Islamic law to become contaminated by heretic pagan ideas we are only inviting trouble and confusion?"

Dara slowly replied, "Your honour you will recall that Punjab had once been my *mansab* and I know that some Sikhs are undoubtedly fighting a violent political war over land and taxes with the officers of our empire but I do not believe that there is anything of a religious nature in this purely political dispute."

The *Qazi* resumed, "Is it correct that a Guru Nanak, founder of this faith has equated the Hindu god Ram with Rahim?

Dara answered, "I am not fully conversant with the writings of the Sikh faith but I have heard it said that both Ram and Rahim convey the idea of mercy."

The *Qazi* quickly continued, "Has this Nanak not also said, "The *Qazis* sit in the courts to minister justice with a rosary in one hand and the name of God on their lips but commit injustice if the other hand does not receive a tribute of gold, and that if someone challenges them they seek refuge in the pages of their scriptures?"

Dara quietly said, "What you quote is quite possible but I cannot be certain. It is well known that the hypocrisy of many officials and clerics of every religion does not always go hand in hand with the pure spirituality of the faiths that they profess."

One of the *Qazis* now angrily added, "But you have yourself condemned and mocked the *Mullahs* and clerics of your own religion... not once but on numerous occasions."

Dara paused and then slowly replied, "Honoured clerics, may I respectfully ask where in our holy Quran does it say that the *Mullah*'s and *Qazis*' are to be honoured? Verily their names are not even mentioned in the holy book.You are aware that our holy prophet had never wanted Islam to have any order of priests but wanted any good person who was knowledgeable about the Quran, to lead the prayers of every congregation. You will recall that our own sacred book itself very clearly says... "many are the clerics and monks who defraud men of their possessions and debar them from the path of God."

Warming to the theme Dara now boldly asked, "Is it heretical to quote from the Holy Quran itself that clearly states, 'all prophets and saints had suffered torment because of narrow minded priests.' Yes, learned clerics, I have indeed spoken out strongly against the priests, but I have not spoken against the priests of Islam but of all religions, who claim that they are the only representatives of almighty God. Where in our scriptures is there any authority that gives *Mullahs, Maulvis* and *Imams* the right to represent *Allah*. I believe that neither *Allah* nor The Prophet have made any such appointments that so many priests so eagerly claim for themselves." Dara then added, "and learned cleric please instruct all of where in the Holy Quran is Blasphemy and Heresy described as a sin? Does not the Quran repeatedly say that the Prophet's neighbours had often mocked and abused him? Does not every 'sura' of the Quran begin with the words that Allah is beneficent and merciful?"

Some of the nobles in the gallery who had been listening began to shout in anger, while others looked at each other and then joined the discussions that quickly became loud and confused as they jostled with clever words to show themselves to be enemies of Dara until the shrill voice of Roshanara silenced them all from behind the red sand stone screen screaming, "Enough of all this nonsense! Why do we have to sit here listening to all this heresy? You have all heard this blasphemer condemn himself time after time. Why do you waste so much precious time on this empty nonsense? Do your duty as is enjoined upon you in our holy books. Punish the heretic as a warning to all."

The *Qazis* resumed asking their questions until the chief *Qazi* finally said, "Enough has been heard and it is now almost time for the evening *namaz*. We will now retire and consider what the accused has said and judge whether the words and the writings of the accused are blasphemous and whether or not his thoughts mean that he is an apostate who has abandoned the straight path of our religion to become a heretic. The four *imams* of the four schools of Islamic law - may Allah have mercy upon them - agree that the apostate who falls from Islam must be killed, and his head may be cut off and his blood may be spilled without reservation."[29]

Dara was led away and a few hours later Aurangzeb, who had kept studiously aloof from the deliberations, studied the judgment when it was presented to him by the *Qazis*. There was not the faintest flicker of expression on his face as he casually signed the order for execution, betraying no emotion. But we did not have to wait very long as he hurriedly put the orders for execution through, as he was concerned about the resentful mood of the citizens of Dilli.

Dara and Sipihr were led away and moved to the Khizirabad gardens near the Jumna where they were to await the judgment of the *Qazis* and I was allowed to go with them. It was just after dusk when we heard loud noises in the courtyard as we were trying to cook some lentils in a corner of the cell, not trusting the food that the captors had provided as it could have been poisoned. The misshapen hunchbacked thug, Nazar Beg then noisily entered the cell with six soldiers and told Sipihr and me to leave.

Sipihr clung to his father and the jailers tried to force them apart and a furious struggle took place in the small cell. Dara managed to stab one in the chest with a small knife with which he had been cutting the vegetables. He was still very strong despite the many months of privation. Then Dara suddenly, stopped struggling and to our surprise smiled gently and said to Nazar Beg, "Nazar *Mia*, you think that are going to kill me but do you not realize that you

29 The account has been described in Mohammad Kaim's 'Alamgir-nama' as well as by Khafi Khan and Jadunath Sarkar.

are only going release me from this world of sorrow and suffering? Souls do not die. They live forever! So I will bless you now before you kill me so that your soul should not be burdened by any guilt for doing the duty that has been entrusted to you. May *Allah* bless you all."

Nazar Beg fell silent for a moment looking perplexed and then shook his head angrily and urged his ruffians to resume their task. I too tried to intervene when they closed in on him but was soon rendered unconscious when one of the soldiers hit me on the head with a wooden stave. In the end it was only a matter of time. Sipihr was dragged weeping to the adjoining room and the rest turned angrily on Dara and stabbed him repeatedly before crudely hacking his head from his body.

I was told that later that night Dara's bloody head was placed in a basket and presented to Aurangzeb. It is said that he studied it closely for a few moments looking for distinguishing marks on his face and then lifted up an eyelid with the point of his sword to look for a mark in his eye. He then casually told Nazar Beg to wash away the blood from the face so everyone could see the end of Dara.

A few days after Dara's execution, Sarmad - with a robe covering his naked body- was summoned before Aurangzeb, who said to him "You had prophesized that Dara would succeed Shah Jahan." Sarmad calmly replied, "God has given Dara eternal sovereignty so my prophesy is not false." He too was tried and executed for being a heretic but when his executioner approached him with an unsheathed sword he calmly said, "My sweetheart (death) is here and his sword is bare; I know him in whatever disguise he may bear."[30]

---

30 Sarmad's body lies buried in a small tomb just outside the eastern steps of the Jama Masjid in Delhi and is visited by many devotees.

I was later told that Dara's head was also sent on to Shah Jahan who remained a captive at the Agra Fort but I very much doubt that this story is true as fevered minds invent many fanciful stories. I also heard that the head was strung up on an arch outside Kashmiri Gate but that it was removed when people refused to go to see it.

There were no crowds in the city the next day when the headless body of my noble prince was again paraded through the streets on the same mangy elephant. It was then taken to Humayun's tomb where the naked body was unceremoniously buried like a common criminal without even washing it, wrapping it in a shroud or reciting a prayer.[31]

Absolute silence seemed to envelop the city except for the raucous cawing of thousands of crows that suddenly filled the skies at dusk. All the shops and eateries closed their doors. And then it rained. The skies opened up as if to let loose an ocean of pent up tears. The streets were flooded and a very dark cloud hung over the city as if to portend dark times in the days to come. The glorious era of Shah Jahan had come to an end and a grim, gloomy and colourless epoch under Aurangzeb was about to begin.

I was plunged into a mood of deep gloom as I now had nowhere to go. I knew that Aurangzeb would never forgive me for ignoring his command to leave Dara and that my many former friends were either dead or under suspicion. I concluded that it would be prudent to leave Delhi and go to the now desolate city of Agra where I could live the rest of my days as inconspicuously as possible, away from the fast

---

31 A cenotaph for Dara was later built in a corner next to the main hall where there is the cenotaph of Humayun. All the corpses are interred in the ground some six meters below the platform.

declining royal household. Though memories of my time in Agra with the royal family- the princes, our numerous shikars, the days at court, my relationship wih the princess Jahanara would haunt me in the familiar streets of the city, I knew that it provided a better chance for me to start afresh away from the security of Aurangzeb.

But because I had been witness to such extraordinary events,I promised myself that all that I knew of the many remarkable people and momentuous circumstances I had witnessed should not go unrecorded.

Though there was little time to reflect on all that had happened, I thought of little Gauharara's cryptic words about the sky being filled with crows. I recalled a story from the holy Quran about the two sons of Adam[32] who had each made offerings to The Lord. God had accepted only the offering of the gentle Able but not that of his brother Cain who had furiously said,"I shall surely kill you." To which Able had replied, "God accepts offerings only from the righteous and if you add your sin against me to all your other sins, you will surely become an inmate of the Fire." After Able had been slain by his brother, God had sent down a raven to show Cain how to bury his brother's naked corpse.

I sat down, dumbstruck by the enormity of the thought.

Was it possible that the all-knowing Allah was showing us in his inscrutable way that it was the righteous Dara who

---

32 Quran, Sura 5: 31. Cain and Abel (Qabil and Habil) are believed to have been the first two sons of Adam and Eve although they are not mentioned by their names in the Quran. The story in the Quran is virtually the same as the Hebrew Bible where both the brothers were asked to offer up individual sacrifices to God. God accepted Abel's sacrifice because of Abel's righteousness and Cain, out of jealousy, slew Abel. This was the first ever sin committed upon Earth and Abel was the first martyr.

was destined to be accepted into the gardens of paradise, while the fires of hell awaited his sinful brother Aurangzeb?

Was it possible that the spirit of Dara was now basking in the radiance of Allah's grace, while the mortal body of Aurangzeb was destined to have many more years of suffering and anguish?

You sit upon your glorious throne

But I can now see an empty and lonely heart

Beseeching mercy and kindness from invisible ghosts

EPILOGUE

It is not known how Mubarak Ali's manuscript reached Delhi nor why it was hidden under the stairs of one of the buildings in the Red Fort complex. One of the damaged footnotes to the folios suggests that he may have sent it to Jahanara when she moved to Delhi after the death of Shah Jahan. Jahanara must have found Mubarak's account very precious even though she would have been embarrassed by the revelations concerning her intimacy with him. It can be conjectured that as she could neither part with it nor make it public, she might have had it hidden in a secret cavity of the building where she lived, and from where it was unearthed by the British troops many years later.

Aurangzeb had been Shah Jahan's least loved, least favored and least attractive son but by dint of his single minded determination he had managed to eliminate four powerful rivals including his father who was at the height of his power. The young prince had, by his wits and bold action, won one of the richest and largest empires of all time stretching from Kabul in the west to the Arakan in the east and from Kashmir to the Deccan in the deep south of India.

Yet despite Aurangzeb's best efforts he was unable to arrest his empire's relentless slide into ruin. This happened mainly because he squandered the support of all the main pillars that had earlier sustained the Mughal Empire. He was to die after a long rule of forty nine years as a broken old man of ninety-one who was helpless to arrest the steady decline of the empire into a shattered kingdom of warring and starving subjects. Although, the Mughal Empire was to stagger on for another hundred and fifty years, it had become completely broken in body and spirit at the end of his long reign.

What seems amazing is that this collapse should have been the achievement of an otherwise remarkable emperor who was highly intelligent, a meticulous planner and a very shrewd judge of men. He possessed unflagging energy and purpose and through his network of spies knew all that was happening in his vast empire. Such a failure was also surprising for a ruler who was completely free from vice, luxury, sloth or stupidity. His intelligence was proverbial and he took the business of administering his empire with justice very seriously. He was highly disciplined himself and demanded absolute discipline from all his subjects. He was willing to suffer the privations of a common soldier, knew no fear, was amazingly calm in crisis and never let pity deflect him from his purpose.

It was paradoxical that the richer and stronger the Mughal Empire grew, the weaker it became at its core. In its first generation Babur had built his small empire by constant war. This had been consolidated by his grandson Akbar, who built up the administrative foundations while he continuously battled to enlarge the boundaries. Under his son Jahangir, the empire devoted much of its energies to developing architecture, arts, music and culture that reached its zenith under Shah Jahan. The flowering of Mughal culture was arrested under Aurangzeb but became highly ornate and prolific during the years of decline after him.

War had been the foundation of the empire while culture, that survived its demise, was to be its tombstone with the Taj Mahal as its most outstanding icon. Aurangzeb was an emperor that his subjects could respect and admire but never one who could attract affection or love. Even his sons would tremble with fear when they were summoned before him. His subjects could understand the need for strong measures to defeat rivals for the throne but did not forgive unnecessary cruelties like the heartless treatment of Shah Jahan, Dara and Dara's popular eldest son, Sulaiman Shikoh.

When Sulaiman was brought before Aurangzeb he was received with courtesy and outward friendliness. Although, fettered with silver chains, Sulaiman stood proudly and said he only had one wish, "I am ready for death so let it strike me swiftly with all my senses alive. But do not poison me with *Poshta*."

In the open court Aurangzeb had firmly stated, "Be comforted, no harm shall befall thee. You shall be treated with tenderness. God is great and you should put your trust in him. Dara, your father was not permitted to live because he had become a *kaffir* (non-believer), a man devoid of religion." Sulaiman made a respectful *Tasleem* (bowing and turning one's face to the right saying "Peace be on you and the mercy of Allah" and turning one's face to the left and repeating the same words) and then withdrew. Some of the ladies peeking through the stone grille behind the durbar hall cried or swooned at the sight of the tall and handsome prince in such dire distress.

Poshta was a paste made of datura and poppy seeds that would reduce a victim to a brainless gibbering idiot in a few months. Although Aurangzeb had given his solemn word, Sulaiman was nevertheless poisoned with *poshta* in the state prison of the Gwalior fort. It was Sulaiman's robust determination that kept him alive for a year.

Shah Jahan lived in captivity for eight years until his death in 1666. His body was removed from his chamber head first through a hole cut in the wall that was immediately bricked up to prevent his soul from re-entering his chamber. It was then taken down river in a boat to the Taj Mahal to be interred next to the body of his beloved empress.

Jahanara became a poet of repute and on her death in 1681 at the age of sixty-seven, Aurangzeb gave her the posthumous title of *'Sahibat-uz-Zamani'* (Mistress of the Age). She is buried in a simple open tomb in the Nizamuddin complex, not far from Humayun's mausoleum in New Delhi. The inscription on her modest tomb reads:

"He is the Living, the Sustaining. Let no one cover my grave except with greenery, for this very grass suffices as a tomb cover for the poor. The annihilated fakir Lady Jahanara, Disciple of the lords of Chishti, daughter of Shah Jahan the warrior may God illuminate his proof."

Roshanara shamelessly exploited her position to gather great riches and her viciousness was to make many enemies. Aurangazeb frowned on Roshanara's libertine lifestyle and her greedy nature and was to later strip her of her powers, banish her from his court, and order her to remain in seclusion and live a pious life in her garden palace outside of Dilli that still exists north of the walls of the old city.

Little is known about princess Gauharara except that she never married and was to outlive her siblings and die in 1706.

Aurangzeb's greatest weakness was his inflexible religious bigotry that made him quickly lose the support of his earlier honored Shia subjects, as well as the more numerous Hindu and Rajputs followers. His bigotry was quite mild during the first twenty years of rule but hardened as as he grew increasingly frustrated by the endless rebellions.

Islam in the seventeenth century was the strongest religion in the world and considered itself duty bound to be just and merciful to all its subjects. Thus Hindus, who had been accustomed to subordinate positions for many centuries had felt no resentment towards Muslim rulers. It was only after Mughal rule became discriminatory that it created a strong backlash of Hindu resentment. When Aurangzeb ordered the re-imposition the *Jezia*[33] tax on non believers, there was such strong public protest to this small but discriminatory fee that it is doubtful if it was ever successfully collected. But taxes on Hindus at religious festivals and some restrictions on their clothes and customs were bitterly resented.

Though Aurangzeb did no more than Jahangir or Shah Jahan by permitting Hindu worship at old temples and in forbidding the construction of new ones and sometimes destroying new temples if they were built, Aurangzeb's reputation as a destroyer of temples became widespread. People remembered some conspicuous examples like the

---

33 All citizens of Muslim empires, except for women, children and the poor , had to pay a tax to the state. Muslims had to pay Zakat and Dhimmis (protected people like Christians and Jews who were 'people of the book') had to pay a slightly higher Jezia tax that was to enable them to get protection of the state through the Qazis appointed by the rulers who judged the Dhimmis according to their own laws.

destruction of a notorious temple dedicated to prostitutes in south India and the destruction of the famous Kashi Vishvanath temple at Benares[34].

Aurangzeb was very unforgiving and by a gradual policy of persecuting his Rajput followers, cut off his own arms and greatly weakened his military capabilities that had to soon face the rising power of Marathas. The great Maratha leader Shivaji initially had no anti Muslim sentiment and had been quite willing, even eager, to serve the emperor as a Mughal *Amir*. Aurangzeb's obstinate pride, however, alienated him and Aurangzeb's bigotry gave him a weapon to turn a purely political war against the Mughals into a religious war.

The Marathas, who had been a virtually nonexistent political entity at the time of Shah Jahan, were to become so powerful that they were to become the greatest cause for the demise of the Mughal Empire. They had earlier been hired mercenaries of the kingdoms of Golconda and Bijapur in their protracted wars against the Mughals but had gained valuable battle experience during the contest. It was only in Aurangzeb's time that they became strong enough for Shivaji to unite them into a formidable fighting nation. So Aurangzeb may have unwittingly created a monster that was to devour his empire. Roving bands of Marathas on fast horses, without baggage to slow them down would cover huge distances and surprise their slow moving enemies.

---

34 There are records to show that Aurangzeb endowed over 36 Hindu temples including the Someshwar temple at Benares as well as those at Mount Abu, Ujjain, Chitrakoot, Guwahati and Girnar. He did, however, order the destruction of the Kashi Vishwanath temple at Benares in 1669, that he felt was a necessary punishment for the ravishing of one of his guests, the Maharani of Kutch who had been in Aurangzeb's entourage by the temple priests. Aurangzeb ordered the temple to be destroyed but, ever the fox, first made the priests remove the idol of Shiva so that the building destroyed was no longer a temple but just a structure of brick and stone.

The successful rebellion of the Marathas not only encouraged the Sikhs to revolt but spawned many other Hindu rebels as well. First there were the Jats led by leaders called Gokla and his successor Raja Ram in 1685. They revolted against Mughal oppression with suicidal determination and even desecrated Akbar's tomb at Sikandra. Some twenty thousand Jats were later slaughtered in retaliation. Then there were the Satnamis who shaved off all their hair including their eyebrows and were led by a woman who claimed to possess the magical power to make her supporters invulnerable to enemy arrows and bullets. She soon gained thousands of devotees who were brutally suppressed.

Aurangzeb's puritanism even made life difficult for Muslims who had to wear dull clothes and were not allowed to wear beards that were longer than the four fingers of a hand. All fun and festivities were frowned upon. His disapproval of music caused the musicians of his capital to try to mock his edicts by taking out a large funeral procession of their instruments. But Aurangzeb was not moved when he was told about it. He had simply said, "Make sure that the grave is deep."

Aurangzeb not only alienated his Hindu and Muslim supporters but even his own children. His valiant eldest son Mohammad Sultan, who had fought so gallantly at Samugarh, impatient of Aurangzeb's severity, had even defected to Shuja when he saw an opportunity during the battle of succession. Although some said he might have also been infatuated by Shuja's ravishing daughter Gulrukh. But after Aurangzeb's general Mir Jamla had routed Shuja again,

Mohammad Sultan had to come crawling back to seek the forgiveness of his father who imprisoned him at Gwalior for the rest of his life.

His third son Prince Azam was married to Dara's elder daughter Jani, after Aurangzeb revoked Akbar's prohibition on the marriage by imperial princesses saying that the restriction was un-Islamic. His fourth son Mohammad Akbar, who had been married to Dara's younger daughter Salima, had been in an alliance with Rajah Jaswant Singh at Jodhpur and very nearly cornered Aurangzeb who was at Ajmer with a very small army. But the tricky Aurangzeb sent a letter to Akbar congratulating him for bringing Jaswant into the open where their combined armies could trap and destroy him. When this deliberately intercepted letter was shown to the Rajput chief he immediately left the field. Prince Akbar escaped to join the slothful Shambuji, son of Shivaji, and had to finally flee to spend the rest of his life in Persia. His modest second son Muazzam was to succeed Aurangzeb as the emperor Bahadur Shah I.

Akbar's daughter Zeb–un-nissa became a poetess of repute but had to suffer imprisonment at Salimgarh for having corresponded with her brother Mohammad Sultan. Only Kam Baksh, Aurangzeb's youngest son, stayed loyal but his name become synonymous with the word 'useless'. Although Aurangzeb sired eleven children he was quite insensitive to them. When his devoted Georgian wife Udaipuri begum died he callously remarked that he was glad to be finally free from the bonds of attachment.

In his long and eventful life there was just one brief moment of human frailty when he so utterly fell in love with a young girl named Hira Bai, later called Zainabadi begum, when he saw her as she was jumping up to pluck a mango at

Burhanpur. He nearly even sipped a cup of forbidden wine with which she wanted to test his love.

Strangely, while Aurangzeb had shown no mercy to Sulaiman Shikoh, he was quite kind to Dara's younger son Sipihr to whom he gave his daughter Zubdat-in-Nissa in marriage. After observing the implacable Aurangzeb, Sipihr lived a very quiet life in constant fear of his father-in-law who he was to outlive by a year.

As Aurangzeb began to lose control of the Deccan, he spent his last twenty-six years there trying to hold together the kingdoms of Golconda and Bijapur, and in fighting the maurading Marathas. It was therefore natural that Dilli and Agra languished due to lack of imperial patronage.

Aurangzeb was an energetic commander and a brilliant tactician who could deceive most of his enemies and quickly find bold or devious solutions, whenever in any difficult situation but he was no great strategist. He was as orthodox about the art of war as he was in religion and seemed to distrust innovations. He won almost every crucial battle but in the end lost the war for the Mughal Empire.

At the end of the titanic conflict with Dara Shikoh a big question comes to mind. What drove Aurangzeb to fight so hard, with such huge sacrifices and at such huge cost? As he disdained wealth, was his battle just a quest for power? Was it really a crusade to make orthodox Islam triumph in an idolatrous country? Was it ego gratification? Was it just jealousy for his elder brother or was it all of these combined?

Mubarak Ali may have been right when he said he had been driven by his passionate envy and hatred for everything that Dara stood for and had little to sustain his motivation after he had won the Mughal throne.

Aurangzeb died a feeble, broken and deeply disappointed old man and is buried in a plain grave at Khuldabad near Aurangabad. His sad last letter to his son Azam reads,

"I came alone and I go as a stranger. I do not know who I am or what I have been doing. The instant that has passed in power has left only sorrow. I have not been the guardian and protector of the empire. Life, so valuable, has been squandered in vain. God was in my heart, but I could not see him. Life is transient, the past is gone and there is no hope for the future... The whole Imperial army is like me bewildered, perturbed, separated from God and quaking like quick silver. I fear for my salvation. I fear my punishment. I believe in God's bounty and mercy, but I am afraid because of what I have done."

This letter clearly reveals his awareness that he had come to the end of his life as an utter failure. He was much too keen an observer not to have been aware that by the time of his death the Mughal Empire had become an empty shell, having almost completely lost its aura of glory and invincibility. He must have also realized that his inflexible character and rigid policies had been mainly responsible for the sorry state of affairs.

If Dara had won at Samugarh instead of Aurangzeb it is possible that his rule might have promoted harmony between India's many peoples. It is difficult to guess whether Dara would have been capable of abandoning his intellectual pursuits to be a ruler determined enough to command such a turbulent empire but if he had, a strong and united Mughal empire might have prevented India becoming so easily colonized by European powers.

Many Mughal customs, traditions, food, costumes and sychophantic flattery continue to influence India to this day but the victory of Aurangzeb over Dara Shikoh was to completely change its character. Aurangzeb's bigotry was to make the Indian continent the epicentre of Islamic fundamentalism but paradoxically it also helped to later shape a much more strident new Hindu identity. The conflict between Aurangzeb and and Dara Shikoh was a major turning point in the history of India.

Glossary of Hindustani and Persian words

Abbajan:	Beloved father.
Ammajan:	Beloved mother.
Amir:	Important Mughal nobleman.
Umrao:	Pleural of Amir.
Anais:	An Arab or Persian goddess of love.
Azraeal:	Islamic name for the messenger of death.
Bandi :	Servant
Burkah:	A veil covering the entire body.
Cammarband:	A wide coloured cloth belt over the tunic.
Chobdar:	Mace beater.
Crore:	A hundred Lakhs or ten million.
Dargah:	A Muslim tomb or shrine.
Darshan:	Glimpse of a great person or divinity.
Dholak:	A small two sided drum.
Diwan- i- Am:	Hall of public audience.
Diwan- I Khas :	Hall of private audience.
Fateha:	Last prayer recited before burial.
Firangi:	Frank or European.
Faqir:	A wandering Muslim holy man.
Iblis:	Another word for satan.
Firman:	An imperial order.
Jama:	A cloth tunic.
Pyjama:	Loose cotton pantaloons worn

	under jamas.
Hadis:	Islam's second holiest scripture.
Hakim:	A Muslim physician.
Hazari:	Commander of a thousand.
Haveli:	Mansion of a wealthy noble/ businessman.
Hazoor:	Honorific. Sir.
Hukah:	A hubble bubble pipe.
Jahanunam:	Hell.
Jannat:	Heaven.
Jharoka:	Balcony projecting from a wall or building.
Kafir:	Unbeliever. Heathen.
Kalam:	Reed pen.
Katar:	A thick triangular double edged punching dagger also called Jamdhar.
Karkhana:	Factory.
Kawwal:	Sufi spiritual singer who sings kawalis.
Kismet:	Fate or destiny.
Kos:	A Mughal measure of distance. 1.9 miles.
Kotwal:	Police post.
Lakh:	100,000
Malik:	Lord or master.
Mansabdar:	A nobleman. Territory commander.
Maulvi, Mullah:	Muslim priest.
Maund:	A measure of weight about 20 Kilo grams.
Mazar:	Tomb of a saint.
Mubarak:	Congratulations.
Namaz:	Islamic prayer.
Nauroz:	A Shia spring festival.

Nazar:	Sight of a great personage.
Nazzar:	A small tribute to a superior.
Nikkah:	Marriage contract ceremony.
Pardah:	Curtain. Often to shield women fom sight.
Pedas:	Native foot soldiers.
Padishah:	Badshah or emperor.
Peshwaz:	A muslin outer garment.
Raja/ maharaja:	A Hindu ruler
Sadhu:	A wandering Hindu holy man.
Sarai:	A fortified inn for travelers.
Shaitan:	Satan.
Shah:	Ruler.
Badshah:	Superior ruler. Emperor.
Shia:	The minority Muslim sect.
Shazadeh:	Prince.
Sharia:	Islamic law.
Shikar:	A hunt
Shikari:	a native hunter.
Subbah:	Mughal province.
Subedar.	Commander of a province.
Sunni:	The largest Muslim sect.
Tabla:	Drum used for musical events.
Takht:	A small bed or divan.
Talwar:	Curved sword or scimatar.
Tuladan:	Ceremony of weighing against valuables.
Padishah:	Mughal Emperor.
Qazi:	Judge in an Islamic court.
Zennana:	Harem or ladies enclosure in the palace.
Akbar:	Name of emperor, meaning 'Great'.
Aurangzeb:	Name of emperor, meaning

	'World encircle'.
Jahangir:	Name of emperor, meaning 'World surrounder'.
Shah Jahan:	Name of emperor, meaning 'King of the world'.
Dara Shikoh:	Darius the great. 'Wise and great'.
Jahanara:	Girl's name, meaning 'One who adorns the world'.
Roshanara:	Girl's name, meaning 'Light of the world'.

AUTHOR'S NOTE

I am well aware that a vaguely Mughal pedigree is no automatic qualification for writing a book on the Mughals. But, for what it is worth, my full name- Mirza Murad Ali Baig- has a little story to tell. I had stopped using the `Mirza', considering that, this rather decadent title, was incongruous in a modern world, until a Pakistani cousin informed me that there was nothing decadent about it. He told me that the word `Mirza' is derived from the words Mir Zada or descendent of the Mir. This Mir, I was told, had been the ferocious Timur Lang, or Tammerlane, so all Mirzas were supposed to be his descendants. Over the years the Mughal emperors had bestowed this title on many noble subjects, including several Rajput chiefs who clearly had no claim to Timur's DNA.

Murad is my given name. The surname Baig means that my ancestors were probably originally of Uzbek Mongol stock. These wild tribesmen of the steppes were not held in very high esteem by the Mughal nobility who traced their descent from the tribe of Chagatia, the second son of Genghis Khan. In Turkey, or countries under Ottoman rule like Egypt, Beg at the end of a name meant a nobleman. Ali means that I am supposed to be a follower of Ali the martyred imam of the Shia faith. My grandfather Sir Abbas Ali Baig was in the Kings Privy Council for India from 1910 to 1918 and was great grandson of the Kiladar, or fort commander, of Bijapur. His wife was half Arab (a sheik from Bahrain) and half English (daughter of Major General Boardman). My maternal great grandfather Sir K. G. Gupta was from an eminent Bengal family and my grandmother an American who could trace her family back to the Mayflower pilgrims. I suppose this makes me a mongrel of good pedigree. All this simply means is that Mughal history is close to my heart.

Like almost all Indian history students I had read about prince Dara Shikoh as a rather tragic footnote during my college studies while doing my BA and MA in history. Later, I had read almost all the books and novels about the colourful Mughal Empire and had often wondered why no author had written more about Dara, who I thought was the most interesting of all the Mughal princes, especially since the intrigues and battles of succession between Aurangzeb and his three brothers were perhaps the most emotive five battles in the magnificent history of the Mughals.

Few people today will know that India, in the time of Shah Jahan, was a Mughal and therefore a Muslim country. The Hindus may have been the much more numerous farmers, traders and artisans but the word Hindu had little religious connotation in Mughal times. Hindus and Muslims had lived together for centuries with very little conflict until alienated by Aurangzeb's unyielding orthodoxy. The widening antagonism in the succeeding years was to lead to the partition of India and make Pakistan and Afghanistan the global hub of Islamic extremism. Muslim and Hindu fundamentalists will find Dara's exploration of their core philosophies very hard to deny. I also saw that this narrative as a wonderful platform to explore the common spiritual base of India's many religious traditions.

During a career as a travel and motoring writer and an earlier career in the marketing of tractors and motorcycles,

I was fortunate to know the geography of India very intimately. During the years that I was writing this novel, I visited and studied most of the places where the extended drama took place including the battle fields of Samugarh and Deorai as well as Ajmer, Benares, Jhansi, Golconda, Aurangabad, Surat and Burhanpur and the forts and palaces of Agra and Dilli.

Having also been a keen student of military history, I found that very little was known about the Mughal armies and their command structures. The records of the Indian army mostly date from British times but they record very little of earlier times as they had the utmost contempt for the `native' armies. There are numerous trophies of Mughal swords and weapons in museums or army messes but very little is known about how the Mughal armies functioned and fought. Mughal armies were influenced by Persia who in turn was influenced by Turkey and Europe. I, therefore, visited the excellent military museum in Istanbul in 2011 to gain deeper insight into this as well as the evolving weapons technologies. Istanbul's Topkapi palace, that had so well preserved Ottoman opulence, also gave me the opportunity to see what the magnificence of the Mughal court, as it might have once been like, before it was looted turn by turn by Nadir Shah, Jats, Marathas, British and others. Most modern writers about the Mughals have been foreign and many do not have a real feel for India's customs and culture.

Although the many adventures of the energetic narrator Mubarak Ali are purely fictitious almost all the events and even the conversations he overhears are based on accurate historical records. Many incidents in the growing rivalry and jealousies between Dara and Aurangzeb are also well documented and I have had to only elaborate on them to make it the thread that runs right through the novel.

Select bibliography

Mubarak Ali and his many adventures are pure fiction but all the main personages and events in his narrative are historically correct. Many dialogues as related in the text are also a matter of historic record.

Some of the main books studied to evaluate these people and events described are:

Alam, Muzaffar	The Making of Indo-Persian Culture, Manohar. 2000
Armstrong, Karen	Islam A short History, Pheonix. 2006
	Muhammad – a biography,Phoenix 1998
Babur	Baburnama
Bernier, Franscoise	Travels in India
Dawood, N. J.	The Koran, Penguin. 1997
Elwin, Verrier	The Tribal World, Oxford UP 1992
Erady, Abraham	Emperors of the Peacock Throne, Penguin. 1997
Erady, Abraham	The Mughal World, Penguin. 2007
Gascoigne, Bamber	The Great Moghuls, Constable, 1998
Guillaume, Lyane	Jahanara, East West Books. 2004
Hansen, Waldemar	The Peacock Throne, Holt, Rinehart & Winston. 1972
Keay, John	A History of India, Harper Collins. 2000

M. Akhtar Ali	Mughal India, Oxford University Press 2009
Manucci, Noccolao	Storia do Mogor
Nicoll, Fergus	Shahjahan, Viking, Penguin 2009
Poole, Lane	Aurangzib, Low price publications. 1995
Preston, Michael	& Diana Teardrop on the cheek of time, Corgi books. 2007
Richards, John F	The Mughal Empire, Cambridge UP. 2000
Sarkar, Jadunath	Aurangzib part I & II
	A short history of Aurangzib
	Fall of The Mughal Empire Orient Longman 1997
	Military History of India Orient Longman 1960
Siddiqi, Mohd. Zubyr	The Hadith, Goodwood Books. 2004
Spear, Percival	A History of India, Penguin. 1970
Tod, Col James	W. Crooke Annals and antiquities of Rajasthan, Low Price Publications 1995
Younghusband	Francis Kashmir as it was, Rupa 2000
Zakaria, Rafiq	Mohammad and the Quran, Penguin. 1991

ACKNOWLEDGEMENTS

I was first introduced to Mughal history by Mr. Mohammad Amin my professor of mediaeval Indian history who had an eloquent way of infusing flesh and blood into the dry bones of his topics. All of us at St. Stephens College soon became fascinated by the subject. I subsequently read almost all that I could lay hands on the colorful Mughal characters but was puzzled about why so little had been written about the Battle of Succession between the four sons of Shah Jahan that, I thought, was the most dramatic event in the empire's history. I was also mystified about why so little had been written about the eldest prince Dara Shikoh who I thought was the most interesting of all the Mughal princes. As I delved deeper I discovered that his story was also one of high adventure, romance, war and great pathos. When I completed the first draft of a novel concerning his life I naturally took it Amin Sahib who read it carefully and gave me many very useful suggestions. I also took a draft to my old mentor the late Mr. Khushwant Singh who warmly endorsed my effort but wanted me to reduce most of the historic background and concentrate on the story of Dara himself.

A few friends who saw the evolving text were warmly encouraging and I am especially indebted to a few Rajput friends like Bhuvan Kumari from a Rajput lineage of Bundelkhand who knew a great deal about Mughal culture that is still such a big part of their own culture. Another dear friend Chanda Singh, who was a professor of history from another old Rajput family, was also very familiar with Muslim customs, especially marriage customs, of which I had little exposure. Dr. Karan Singh also saw an early draft and wrote... "It was, in fact, Dara's translations into Persian that first introduced the Upanishads to the West, for which we owe Dara a deep debt of gratitude. His broadminded approach to other religions, particularly Hinduism, took forward a process begun by his great ancestor Akbar around a century earlier".

In 2010 I was invited to speak at the Dara Shikoh Festival in Srinagar. Though the event was mostly concerned with Sufi music and writings I was very pleasantly surprised to learn that there were so many people who still remembered tales about this tragic prince with such respect and sorrow. Dara had spent four summers in Kashmir and set up an observatory at the picturesque Pari Mahal that had earlier been a Buddhist monastery. The large audience were fascinated by my account about the life and works of Dara and seemed very anxious to know more.

To add drama to Dara's tumultuous life I chose to write it as a novel with a purely fictional eunuch in the Imperial Zenana known to all the princes and princesses to be the narrator of an otherwise accurately researched history of the period. I had been a fairly prolific writer of straight narratives and naively thought that writing a novel would be easy but I soon learned that I needed a lot of help to become a novelist. In the end I must have had to rewrite it at least fifty times before it became the text that it now is.

Apart from my wife Tannie who prodded but also unstintingly encouraged me, my greatest debt is to my publisher Anuj Malhotra (Redink and Bahrisons) who had

published my earlier book `80 Questions to Understand India... history mythology and religion' that went into four reprints. His editorial team headed by Sharvani Pandit really put me through the wringer but I greatly appreciated her professional objectivity. Rima Zaheer made me take the text apart chapter by chapter and rewrite it and finally Aanchal Malhotra helped me put it together in a form that I hope you will enjoy. The `Ocean of Cobras' is a great story about a wonderful period on a cusp of India's cultural history
(Map sources acknowledged at individual map placements).